"Uh-oh. Looks like you're falling in love."

Kaitlyn shifted her gaze from the moonlit water to Mitch, and her heart caught in her throat at another wonderful sight, this one of a beautifully rugged man whom she was starting to like entirely too much. "Excuse me?"

"With Sweetwater Springs," he clarified.

"Oh." Her gaze swept to her feet and back out to Silver Lake. "Maybe I am. There's a lot to love about this place." She looked up at him again. Big mistake. Either she'd taken a step closer or he had. She held her breath.

Then he reached up and swept a lock of her hair from her cheek. The tip of his finger caressed her skin as it slid past, sending shivers through her body. And for a moment, she thought he was going to kiss her.

Do I want him to kiss me?

Did he want to kiss her too?

CHRISTMAS
ON MISTLETOE LANE

ANNIE RAINS

FOREVER

NEW YORK BOSTON

Copyright © 2018 by Annie Rains
Preview of *Springtime at Hope Cottage* © 2018 by Annie Rains

Cover design and illustration by Elizabeth Turner Stokes
Cover copyright © 2018 by Hachette Book Group, Inc.

"A Midnight Clear" by Hope Ramsay copyright © 2015 by Robin Lanier

Forever
Hachette Book Group
1290 Avenue of the Americas, New York, NY 10104
forever-romance.com
twitter.com/foreverromance

First Edition: September 2018

Forever is an imprint of Grand Central Publishing. The Forever name and logo are trademarks of Hachette Book Group, Inc.

The publisher is not responsible for websites (or their content) that are not owned by the publisher.

The Hachette Speakers Bureau provides a wide range of authors for speaking events. To find out more, go to www.hachettespeakersbureau.com or call (866) 376-6591.

ISBN: 978-1-5387-1395-2 (mass market), 978-1-5387-1394-5 (ebook)

Printed in the United States of America

OPM

10 9 8 7 6 5 4 3 2 1

For Ralphie, Doc, and Lydia. May your dreams in life be as big as your hearts.

Acknowledgments

No book is ever written alone. There are so many people who come together to make a book come alive. First, I want to thank my family for making sure I have the time I need to put my stories on paper. Sonny, you win the "Best Husband Award" for spending an entire day touring bed and breakfasts with me as research for this book. And to my mother-in-law, Annette, for watching the kids during said research. Thank you to my parents for always encouraging my love of writing. Your support means everything to me, and I love you all to pieces!

Thank you to my editor, Alex Logan, for believing in this project and pulling me aboard the Grand Central / Forever team. Working on this book together has been a dream come true for me. I'm still pinching myself! A huge thanks to the entire Forever team for everything that goes on behind the scenes! I would also like to thank my agent, Sarah Younger, for your tireless work in finding this book its perfect home. I am so honored to be a part of your team and NYLA!

Thanks to my wonderful critique partner, Rachel Lacey. Your advice is worth its weight in gold, as is your friendship. Also to the #TeamSarah ladies and my #GirlsWriteNight gals. You all inspire me so much! Thank you for everything (to include ideas, support, and friendship).

A huge thank-you goes out to my readers group for offering up ALL the Christmas ideas to incorporate into this book. Thank you to all my readers for spending time in my stories and falling in love with my characters. Every review, message, and line of encouragement means so much! Xoxoxo.

CHAPTER ONE

Kaitlyn Russo twisted the key in her hand but the front door to the Sweetwater B&B didn't budge.

"Great. Just great," she muttered under her breath, which floated away in a little white puff of air. Shivering and wishing she'd worn a heavier coat, she turned the key again, pressing her full weight into the door as she did. This time it flung open and promptly dumped her on the pinewood floor inside. Dust flumed under her nostrils. With a cough, she looked up and inspected her grandparents' old bed and breakfast.

Scratch that. *Her* bed and breakfast.

She climbed to her feet, grabbed her luggage, and then closed the front door to bar the wintry cold. Turning on the light in the front room, she surveyed the homey design with high wood-beamed ceilings, a detail that, as an interior designer, she'd always loved. The furniture was a tasteful blend of antique and contemporary. This place was exactly how she remembered it from her infrequent childhood visits, minus the dust mites.

Nothing a little hard work couldn't fix.

But first she had plans to meet with the lawyer handling her grandmother's estate. He'd be arriving sometime in the next half hour. When she'd spoken to Mr. Garrison by phone earlier, he'd mentioned something about another person in Mable's will. Kaitlyn couldn't imagine who that would be. Other than her parents, who'd inherited various other family heirlooms, her grandmother didn't have any living family. The Russos were a dwindling clan—all the more reason to keep their legacy alive.

From the corner of her eye, Kaitlyn saw movement in the window. Then a dark figure filled the space behind the curtain. Something told her this wasn't Mr. Garrison. Lawyers tended to be civilized people who knocked on doors. Maybe a squatter had been camping out here since her Grandma Mable's passing last month.

The shadow slipped out of sight. A moment later, she heard a shuffling sound behind the front door.

Terror sliced straight down her middle, and her heart kicked into a choppy staccato. She dashed to the fireplace and lifted one of the long metal pokers used to move hot coals. It could second as a lethal weapon if necessary.

Like it had for her, the front door didn't release immediately. *Why, oh why, didn't I lock it after myself?* If she were still in New York, she would have.

The intruder gave the door a firm push, and it swung open, crashing against the wall behind it and making Kaitlyn scream.

Standing before her was a broad-shouldered man with dark eyes, wavy, overgrown hair, and a close-trimmed beard. He was dressed in a nice pair of jeans and a weathered leather jacket. Her gaze fell to his brown mountain boots. Definitely not homeless, she decided.

She held the fire poker up like a sword. "Don't come any closer," she warned with a shaky voice.

"Are you planning to use that on me?" His voice, in contrast to hers, was deep and gruff. And if she wasn't mistaken, there was a little humor threading through it.

Was he teasing her? Because while, yes, he was larger than her, *she* was the one holding a pointy metal death stick. "I might," she said, wishing there wasn't a warm, tingly awareness settling low in her belly, competing with the fear still coursing through her veins. Rugged good looks had never been a more accurate description. This guy had it down to an art form.

He held up his hands in surrender. "So, you're little Katie Russo?"

She cocked her head to one side. "How do you know that?"

"Mable spoke of you often."

Kaitlyn lowered the metal poker just a notch. "She did?" she asked, keeping her eyes pinned on him.

"Your grandfather too—when he was alive."

Grandpa Henry had died several years earlier, leaving Grandma Mable to run the Sweetwater Bed and Breakfast alone. They'd been the only two people in the world to call her Katie, and her mom had always been vocal about her objections, preferring the formal name Kaitlyn instead.

"My name's not Katie. It's Kaitlyn. And you could've read that on my luggage there by your feet." She'd met her fair share of con men living in the city. Guys who could conjure a name with only a pair of initials. "A simple inquiry into this place could've told you who my grandparents were."

The man stepped forward and offered his hand. Kaitlyn didn't move to shake it.

"I'm Mitch Hargrove. I grew up around the corner. Mable and Henry used to take care of me after school while my mom worked. They kept me supplied with milk and cookies and helped with my homework."

That sounded exactly like something her grandparents would do.

"In exchange, I did odd jobs for them here at the inn during the school year. During the summers, my mom and I RV'd with my aunt, much to Mable's disappointment. She always said she wanted to introduce us."

He continued to hold his hand out to Kaitlyn. "Guess Mable finally got her wish. She always was a stubborn one."

Reluctantly, Kaitlyn returned the rod to its place on the hearth and slipped her hand in his. Rough, calloused skin dragged across her palm as they shook. "I think I remember my grandmother speaking of you. She had a photo of you on her nightstand." Kaitlyn was only able to come for a brief visit once each summer, the trip sandwiched between various camps her parents had enrolled her in. Each year, the photo on her grandmother's nightstand was updated with a more recent version of the boy with the magic eyes. That's how Kaitlyn had thought of him back then. Dark, magic eyes that seemed to jump out of the frame. In all honesty, the boy in that picture was her first crush.

And now he was standing in front of her.

Pinning her gaze to his, she recognized those eyes, changed only by a shimmer of something that resembled sadness. "I'm so sorry for your loss," she said quietly.

"You're family. I'm just"—he shrugged—"the neighbor boy. I'm supposed to be offering my condolences to you," he said.

Kaitlyn swallowed thickly. Mitch was almost a foot taller than her, which required her to look up at him. "Thank you.

So, did you break into the B and B to introduce yourself?" she asked.

"Jacob asked me to meet him tonight. Since I already have a key, he told me to come inside and wait where it's warm."

"Jacob Garrison, the estate lawyer? Why would he want to meet you here?"

"Seems Mable left half this place to me." Mitch's gaze roamed around the front room as he said it.

Kaitlyn shook her head, feeling breathless with panic. "No. You must be mistaken. *I* inherited this B and B."

His gaze dropped to hers. Mistaken, but *holy moly hot*. Her cheeks flushed, and she looked away, reminding herself of her resolution on the drive down Interstate 95. This was a fresh start for her, an opportunity, and she wasn't going to blow it.

"All I know is what I was told," Mitch said.

As if on cue, someone knocked on the front door.

Mitch held up a hand, signaling her to stay where she was. "Wouldn't want you to threaten Mr. Garrison with that fire poker," he teased.

Kaitlyn watched as he opened the door to an older man with salt-and-pepper hair and a dark-gray suit buried under a heavy coat.

Despite the cold, the man smiled warmly from the porch. "Hey, Mitch. Good to see you."

"You too, Jacob."

They shook hands, and then Mitch gestured the man inside, closing the door behind them.

"Mr. Garrison, I presume," Kaitlyn said, stepping forward and shaking the older man's hand.

"That I am. Nice to finally meet you, Ms. Russo. Your grandparents spoke of you often over the years."

"Please, call me Kaitlyn. Thank you so much for coming. I know it's late." She'd offered to meet Mr. Garrison tomorrow at his office but he'd insisted on seeing her as soon as she arrived in town. He'd apparently asked Mitch to come as well. And that little tidbit wasn't sitting well with Kaitlyn at the moment.

"No problem at all. I'm on my way home, actually," Mr. Garrison said.

"Well, let's sit and get to business, shall we?" She moved toward the room's high-backed Victorian couch and sat down. "I would offer you a warm drink but I just arrived myself. I'm not sure what's in the cupboards."

"Oh, I'm fine." Mr. Garrison sat next to her and laid a briefcase on the coffee table in front of them. She watched as he pulled out a file. Hopefully, it would set things straight. *She* was the owner of the Sweetwater B&B, and only her.

Mitch sat in a matching antique chair off to the side and leaned forward, propping his elbows on his knees. His chest was thick and broad like a linebacker's, although his appearance made her think of a man who'd emerged from a mountain cabin rather than a football field.

Kaitlyn pulled her gaze back to Mr. Garrison. What if she'd misunderstood on the phone? What if this place wasn't hers after all? She'd purchased a used car and had moved out of her pint-sized apartment in New York City, taking everything she owned with her. She had no home or job to return to because she didn't plan on going back. It'd been a rash decision, yes, but she hadn't really had another viable option. This was it, her only lifeline, and she'd latched on with all the grit and determination that had once made her an up-and-coming interior designer.

"So." Mr. Garrison clapped his hands together. "Congratulations, you two. Looks like you'll be business partners."

Kaitlyn straightened. "I'm sorry. What?"

"Mable left you half of the Sweetwater B and B," he told her and then looked at Mitch. "And you the other half. I'm sure you know the Russos thought of you as a grandson, Mitch. They were very proud of your service as a military police officer."

Kaitlyn's eyes darted between the two men. "Excuse me, Mr. Garrison, but I was under the impression that *I* was the new owner."

"You are. Along with Mr. Hargrove." Mr. Garrison pointed at the papers in front of him. "Says so right here. Under one condition that your grandmother spelled out in no uncertain terms."

Kaitlyn's head was spinning. "Condition?" she asked.

Mr. Garrison nodded. "That's right. The condition is that you and Mr. Hargrove must run this place together for the first two months after signing these documents." Mr. Garrison settled his glasses up on his long, narrow nose as he read. "Both parties must stay in Sweetwater Springs and run the Sweetwater Bed and Breakfast on Mistletoe Lane as a fully functioning inn for exactly two months from the date of signature. If either party declines, the bed and breakfast is forfeited for both parties and turned over to charity."

"What?" Kaitlyn sat up straight, panic gripping her as it had when she'd thought Mitch was an intruder. And he was. She did not want him here, claiming half of what she'd thought was solely hers.

"No way I'm staying in Sweetwater Springs for two months," Mitch said flatly. "I love Mable but charity can have this place."

Kaitlyn shot him a scornful look. "This was my grandparents' business. We can't just let it go."

"I hate to break it to you but this place has been declining for years," Mitch said. "Mable rarely had a full inn. Any charity we offered it to likely wouldn't even take it. A bed and breakfast requires time and money. I say we save ourselves the trouble and forfeit now."

"We are *not* forfeiting," Kaitlyn snapped between gritted teeth. She didn't care how big or attractive Mitch Hargrove was—and he *was* big and attractive—she'd lost too many fights lately. She was fighting for this B&B with every ounce of strength she had. "Is there any way to get around the legal terms?" she asked. "So I can run the B and B and Mr. Hargrove can go on his merry way?" Which would be best for everyone. The sooner, the better.

Mr. Garrison frowned. "I'm afraid not. The will is detailed. Mable was insistent that you two work here together. Leaving the inn to the both of you was her final attempt to revive this old place."

Mr. Garrison angled himself to look at Kaitlyn. "Mable was proud of how creative you are. She said you could turn menial things into magic." He turned back to Mitch. "And she said you could fix just about anything. Between the two of you, she was adamant that the Sweetwater Bed and Breakfast could be transformed back into the jewel it once was. Her words, not mine. Two months. That was Mable's terms, and she asked me to make sure that's what happened."

Mr. Garrison's gaze flitted between them. "She knew it would take the talents of both of you combined."

Kaitlyn stared at Mitch. She'd liked him a whole lot better when she'd thought he might be trying to kill her.

"So," Mr. Garrison said on an inhale, "do you accept or not?"

"No," Mitch barked at the same time that she said, "Yes."

Kaitlyn folded her arms across her chest. How dare he

even consider refusing her grandmother's final wish. "We're not giving up on this B and B."

"Do you have money for repairs? Money to keep the lights and heat on for guests? This inn is a money pit. We'd be fools to go into business together." Mitch shook his head. "And I don't know about you but I have a life to get back to. Two months of trying to avoid the inevitable isn't in my plans."

"I have a life," Kaitlyn shot back. Albeit one that seemed to be in shambles lately. Apparently, Grandma Mable had been struggling too. How had Kaitlyn not known her grandmother was under so much financial strain? Not that Kaitlyn could've helped. All she'd really had of value when she'd driven down from New York to the North Carolina mountains was hope, and even that was dwindling fast.

* * *

Mitch was having a hard time listening to Mr. Garrison. Partly because he was too distracted by little Katie Russo all grown up. She was gorgeous, yeah, but also feisty enough to threaten a six-foot-one former marine with a poker stick. He could've disarmed her faster than she could bat those long eyelashes of hers, if he'd wanted to. He'd enjoyed watching her think she had the upper hand though. He'd enjoyed watching her, period.

"The B and B doesn't make a profit?" Kaitlyn asked as Mr. Garrison laid out the paperwork.

"Not in recent years, no," Mr. Garrison said apologetically.

Mitch already knew this. He'd always visited Mable whenever he'd come off a deployment and returned to Sweetwater to see his mom. Since Henry's death, Mable had been struggling financially. She'd never seemed undone by it though. She was a strong woman, didn't give up easily, and was as stubborn as the valley here is deep. Mable was always expecting a surge of new business. Always hoping the Sweetwater Bed and Breakfast would return to its glory days.

"This business belonged to my grandparents. It means something. At least to me."

Mitch swallowed, remembering how he'd sat in this very room after school. As a teen, he'd worked behind the scenes at the bed and breakfast on weekends too. Mable had taught him to cook fancy breakfasts and fold napkins just so. Henry had taught him to care for the landscaping. There weren't a lot of good memories locked up in this town for Mitch but the Russos and the Sweetwater B&B were some of them.

He turned to Mr. Garrison. "So, you're telling me that in order for Katie to keep this place, I have to stay in Sweetwater Springs?"

"Kaitlyn," the woman in question snapped.

"That's correct," Mr. Garrison said.

"And if I leave?"

"Then she loses the business as well."

Mitch rubbed a hand over his forehead. *Thanks a lot, Mable.* He couldn't stay in Sweetwater Springs—wouldn't—and she'd known that. The last few times he'd come to visit, he'd mentioned that he wasn't reenlisting in the corps. Mable had known he would have time available. But she'd also known he was planning on taking a contract job running security in Northern Virginia. He knew quite a few ex-military who'd done the same kind of work after getting out. The job offered good money. Too good to pass up. *This* would complicate things.

"Two months?" he clarified.

"Two months. And what a perfect time. You'll be home for the holidays, Mitch," Mr. Garrison said, as if that was a selling point.

Mitch hadn't been home for the holidays since he'd joined the military when he was eighteen years old. There was a reason for that. One that made the stipulations of Mable's will feel more like a death sentence than a vacation.

"How you go about running things isn't specified," Mr. Garrison continued. "After the two months are up, we'll complete the paperwork and the bed and breakfast is yours to sell or do with as you choose."

"Please," Kaitlyn said, turning to Mitch, her brown eyes wide and hopeful.

He didn't know this woman from a stranger off the street. He didn't owe her anything. But he did owe Mable and Henry. They'd practically raised him while his mom worked two jobs. Mable and Henry had stood by him after the accident too. He'd never forget their loyalty. "I'm not making any decisions tonight," Mitch finally said. Especially not a decision that would cost him the next two months of his life.

"Of course. The clock doesn't start until you sign the preliminary paperwork though," Mr. Garrison advised.

Mitch nodded, catching the look of disappointment in Kaitlyn's eyes. He couldn't help that. This deal was a lot to ask.

The lawyer closed his briefcase and stood. "Just give me a call when you two make your decision."

"We will." Kaitlyn followed him to the door. "Thank you for coming."

"Of course. Anything for Mable."

That should've been Mitch's immediate answer too. Anything for sweet, caring, kind Mable Russo.

Anything but this.

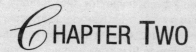

CHAPTER TWO

"Look, it's been a long day," Mitch said, turning to face Kaitlyn, who stood only a few feet away. "Neither of us were expecting this...*complication*. Let's get some rest and revisit how we'll handle things in the morning."

She hugged her arms around herself, lifting tired, beautiful eyes to meet his. "Yeah, you're right. The drive from New York was exhausting. We can meet back here first thing and look over the papers Mr. Garrison left us."

"Meet back here?" Mitch didn't like the sound of that. Since he was 50 percent owner, he thought he would at least get a room at the B&B.

"Well, you're not staying here. This is where I'll be sleeping."

"It's a bed and breakfast. It's meant to house more than one person," he said.

"Yes, when it's open, but we're not open. *Yet.*"

An argument rose in his throat and settled on the tip of his tongue. Then his gaze caught on the poker stick resting against the wall behind her. He'd unintentionally scared her when he'd gotten here. Understandable, considering he was a stranger who appeared to be breaking and entering. As much as Mable had told him about her, she obviously hadn't told Kaitlyn much about him. A young, single, beautiful woman had every reason to be wary of a strange man staying under the same roof.

"Fine," he said, wishing he wasn't such a nice guy, because he didn't want to impose on his mom. He hadn't even told her he was coming to town. His mom, being the workaholic she was, would've insisted on cleaning and cooking and driving him absolutely nuts with all her doting. She had enough to do without taking care of him. "I'll sleep somewhere else tonight and be back at seven a.m. tomorrow."

Kaitlyn's jaw went lax. "Seven? Isn't that a little early?"

He smiled. "Get used to it. If you're set on running this place, Mable was up at four thirty every morning cooking breakfast for her guests." He got a little satisfaction as the realization dawned on his would-be business partner's face. He guessed she hadn't thought that far ahead. It didn't seem like she'd thought about this at all.

Gesturing behind him at the door, he said, "I'll see you tomorrow. *Bright and early.*"

* * *

Kaitlyn dragged her tired body and suitcase past the wooden staircase and headed down the long hallway to her left. She remembered that her grandmother had always stayed in the downstairs bedroom near the kitchen and laundry area. The three rooms were blocked by a swinging door and made separate living quarters, which, even on their own, were much larger than her city apartment had been.

What Kaitlyn didn't remember is her grandmother waking so early to cook breakfast. Then again, like a good hostess, her grandmother had the first meal of the day ready when she'd stayed over. Kaitlyn was none the wiser about when or how it'd been prepared.

Four thirty? Well, if that's what she had to do, so be it. This was a new life for her. A godsend. At least that's what she'd thought on the drive down. Now doubt niggled in the dusty recesses of her mind, not unlike the inn's unkempt corners. This place was run-down, and she'd already spent a good portion of her savings on a used Ford Taurus to get here.

With a sigh, she dropped her luggage on the bedroom floor. The room was spacious with a king-size bed on one side fitted with a handmade quilt that Grandma Mable had likely made herself. An antique dresser sat along the wall and a rocking chair invited Kaitlyn to sit and possibly cry her eyes out later. Right now, she bent to unzip her suitcase and search for her favorite pair of flannel pajamas. As she sifted through her belongings, her cell phone rang against her hip. She pulled it from her pocket to her ear.

"Well?" her best friend Josie said in lieu of a hello. Josie still lived and worked in New York. "How is it?"

Kaitlyn climbed into the wooden rocker and clutched the phone to her ear. "It's awful. I mean, the inn itself is gorgeous but it needs work. And according to my new co-owner, this place can't even cover its own power and heating bills."

"I'm sorry—what?" Josie asked on the other end of the line.

Kaitlyn sighed. "Apparently, I'm not even the full owner. Grandma Mable left this place to me and the guy who grew up down the street." The image of the large, sexy man that

Kaitlyn had spent the last hour with came to mind. "According to the will, Mitch and I have to run the bed and breakfast together for two months or we both forfeit to charity."

"Whoa. That's an unusual scenario," Josie said.

Indeed it was. "After the time is up, we can do as we like with the B and B, and since Mitch doesn't seem to care about staying, I plan to take out a loan and buy him out."

"There you go. That's perfect."

Kaitlyn pressed her head back against the rocker and closed her eyes, grateful to shut out at least one of her senses. "Except he hasn't said yes to the agreement. Also, since the business isn't turning a profit, there's no way the bank will give me a loan to buy him out. I thought this place would be my fresh start." Those tears threatened behind her eyes. She swallowed hard, refusing to let them through.

"Well, if this is really what you want, you can't give up," Josie said in the determined spirit that was her hallmark. "You have to make it a success."

Kaitlyn opened her eyes. "As much as I want to, I'm not sure that's even possible."

Josie hummed thoughtfully into the receiver for a long moment. "Maybe it is. I think I have an idea."

Kaitlyn resisted the hope springing up in her chest. Josie was the queen of good ideas. That's how she'd become such a successful magazine editor, managing the lifestyle section of *Loving Life* magazine. Josie had interned with the magazine fresh out of college and had immediately started impressing those around her, moving up the ranks.

"*Loving Life* is doing a December cover story on the most romantic holiday getaways in America. I wrote the article myself so I can add in one more spot, if I want. In fact, I gamble to say that Sweetwater Springs, North Carolina, might be *the* most romantic holiday retreat in America. And the Sweetwater Bed and Breakfast is the perfect place for couples, new and old, to stay while they discover the magic there."

"That would be a lie, Josie. Didn't you take some kind of journalistic oath or something? This place is hardly the most romantic, and it's nowhere near ready for business. The holidays are just around the corner."

"You just said you only have two months to make this happen. You don't have time to think like that. Besides, I owe you. Whether you think so or not, I'm the reason you ever got a gig with Bradley Foster. That makes me partly responsible for—"

"I don't want to talk about that," Kaitlyn said quickly, cutting her friend off. In fact, Kaitlyn would be happy to never hear celebrity extraordinaire Bradley Foster's name again. "That wasn't your fault. You couldn't have known."

A slight pause hung between them.

"Even so," Josie finally continued, "if running that B and B is really what you have your heart set on, you can turn that place into whatever you want. It really can be the most romantic holiday retreat in America. And as my best friend, you better not make me a liar, because I'm adding Sweetwater Springs to my article tonight. The magazine goes into circulation a couple of weeks before each new month, so you better get your partner to agree and then get busy."

* * *

Mitch cut his headlights before he pulled into his mom's driveway. She was early to rise and super early to bed so he guessed she'd already be asleep. He'd considered calling one of his buddies in town for a place to stay but his mom lived around the corner from Mistletoe Lane, where the Sweetwater Bed and Breakfast was located, so this seemed most practical.

He grabbed his overnight bag—leaving the rest of his belongings in the cab of his truck—and headed up the front porch steps. There was a spare key in the flowerpot off to the side. It wasn't a wise hiding location but he couldn't convince Gina Hargrove of that. His mom was as stubborn as Mable had been. That was maybe one reason they'd been such great friends.

He quietly let himself in and headed straight to the guest room down the hall. Shutting the bedroom door behind him, he stripped off his shirt and lay back on the twin-size bed of his youth, staring up at the ceiling. He couldn't stay here. That was a fact. The money from the contract security job was double what he'd made as a police officer in the corps. Not only that, he had a past in Sweetwater Springs. One he'd rather not relive.

The choice was clear. When he met back with Kaitlyn Russo in the morning, he'd just tell her there was no way he could make this arrangement work. It would break her heart since she was obviously determined to reopen Mable and Henry's B&B but one day she'd thank him. The inn was a lost cause. There was no resuscitating it. Turning the deal down would be doing her a favor.

* * *

The aroma of freshly brewed coffee stirred Mitch to life early the next morning. He followed the scent down the hall and into the kitchen.

"Hey, Mom."

His mother nearly dropped her mug of coffee as she whirled to look at him. "Where did you come from?"

"Sorry. Didn't mean to scare you," he said, immediately thinking of Kaitlyn and her poker stick from last night. "I got to town late."

"I didn't even know you were coming." She set her mug down and pulled him in for a tight hug. "It's so good to lay eyes on you. I was beginning to worry. You got out of the military a month ago. Where have you been?"

"Around," he said. He had tried to get back for Mable's funeral but he'd still had one week left to serve, and his request was denied. "I'm fine. You know that."

"I don't know it unless you pick up the phone to tell me so," she said in a voice reminiscent of the one she'd regularly used on him growing up. He'd had a few rebellious years that were no doubt the cause of her initial few gray hairs. Now, at fifty years old, Gina Hargrove had a head full of solid gray hair that she wore past her shoulders. She could probably attribute all of it to him, he thought.

He walked over, grabbed a mug from the cabinet, and poured himself a cup of coffee. "Busy day ahead?" he asked.

She took a seat at the small table off to the side of the kitchen. "No more than usual. I need to clean the Mallorys' house today and then the Lances' after that."

Mitch's hand tightened around the mug. "I wish you wouldn't work so hard." She didn't need to. He made sure of that, sending money home from every paycheck he got.

"Hard work never killed anyone." She continued to sip. "Soon as I pay this house off, I might slow down. You know, after Laura Brown retired, she found out she didn't have enough money to live off. She lost her home and had to move in with her son and daughter-in-law. If that happened to me, where would I go? You don't even have a place to live right now."

"That won't happen to you," he said. With his looming

contract job in the works, he'd be even better able to ensure that her needs were met. His gaze dropped from his mother's bloodshot eyes to her shaking hands. "What's that about?" He gestured as he stepped toward her.

She settled her hands down on the table. "Just tired. These old things are resisting any kind of work after cleaning up the debris and leaves around the Dennys' rosebushes yesterday. That stuff will harbor pests if you don't."

"Yard work? I thought you stuck to cleaning houses."

"Well, they asked me to help. What am I supposed to say? No?"

"Yeah. That's exactly what you say."

"It's fine." She waved a hand.

It wasn't fine with him though. Looking at her closer, he noticed she looked pale and tired.

"So, tell me why you're here," she said, changing the subject.

"Can't a guy visit his mother?"

She narrowed her eyes.

"Fine. I need to handle a few things at the Sweetwater Bed and Breakfast."

"Really? It's been closed since Mable passed away last month."

"I know, but her granddaughter is in town working on the place."

"To reopen it?" his mother asked, pulling her coffee mug toward her again.

"Doubtful." Because he wasn't going to fulfill his end of the will's stipulations. He guessed Kaitlyn might be able to take out a loan and buy it from whatever charity it was left to when all was said and done. That was an option if she was as headstrong as she appeared to be.

He took one more long sip of coffee and set his mug

down. "Actually, I've got to get over there pretty soon. Mind if I use the shower?"

"Of course not. This is your home and always will be," his mom said warmly.

He kissed her temple and looked down at her shaky hands once more. Something in his gut tightened.

"And when you get home tonight, I'll cook you something tasty for dinner," she said. "We'll talk some more. It'll be nice."

He pointed a finger. "You're not going to cook me dinner after working all day. I'll cook for you."

"I'm not one of your marines. Put that finger away." She rolled her blue-gray eyes.

He was tempted to laugh at her stubbornness. Instead, he shook his head and headed down the hall to the shower.

After a quick rinse, he dressed and drove his truck to the century-old inn at the end of Mistletoe Lane. It was a large two-story Victorian home with navy blue shutters. The wraparound porch featured several wooden swings for guests to sit and enjoy the mountain air and scenery. In Mitch's mind, the view was the best part. From this location, the mountains dipped and rose over his cozy hometown nestled deep in the valley. He'd always thought they seemed to encase and protect Sweetwater Springs. But that was before the car accident. He'd been an inexperienced driver on the icy mountain roads that night and more than *his* life had veered off course.

All in a blink of an eye. In a single heartbeat. Life had swerved left and had never made itself right again.

His cell phone rang beside him as he parked in the B&B's driveway. It was still early in the civilian world but not in the military.

"Yeah?" he said, cutting the engine.

"Mitch. Hey, man. This is Jim Smalley."

Relief flooded Mitch at the sound of the man's voice on the other end of the line. It was his contact with the security firm in Virginia. Jim was supposed to call when everything was lined up. The sooner, the better. "Jim," Mitch said, feeling a smile lift through his cheeks. This was the perfect excuse to give Kaitlyn for why he couldn't stay.

"Bad news," Jim said, cutting to the chase. "There's a hang-up with the funding for the job."

Mitch's smile fell like a stack of heavy bricks. "How long?"

"Probably not until right after the new year."

"I see." Today was October twenty-ninth. What was Mitch supposed to do until January?

"I'll give you a call when I know more but I wanted to give you a heads-up. That's how these contracts go sometimes. The job is yours when it opens, but I understand if you need to find something else."

"No. I'll wait," Mitch said. "Thanks for calling, Jim."

"Sure thing. I'll be in touch."

Mitch disconnected the call and sighed. If he didn't know better, he'd guess the infamous Meddling Mable was sabotaging his plans from heaven. Well, she must know that he was just as stubborn as she was.

"Still not staying, Mable," he said under his breath in case she was listening. Then he glanced at his watch. It was earlier than the time he'd agreed upon with Kaitlyn. Well, maybe having someone knock on her door at this early hour would serve as a wake-up call. Once Kaitlyn realized the reality of the situation, she could go back to wherever she'd been holed up all these years. New York, he thought he remembered Mable telling him. The delay in his contract job didn't change his mind about staying in this town one

Annie Rains

bit. He'd been wise with his money over the years, not just sending some to his mom but also putting a portion away in savings. Two months without a paycheck—if it came to that—wouldn't break him. Two months of staying in his hometown, however, just might.

Climbing the porch steps, he felt a wave of sentimentality about the fact that Mable would never again greet him at the door with a plate of freshly baked chocolate chip cookies. Even as a grown man, she'd met him with a batch—and he'd never resisted. For one, Mable Russo was a hard woman to say no to. Two, he'd always believed her cookies had some secret ingredient that made a person feel better just by taking a bite. He could use some of Mable's cookies right about now.

He rang the doorbell and waited. It took several minutes, which he assumed meant Kaitlyn was still asleep. Then the door opened, and she surprised him, dressed in a peach-colored sweater and fitted jeans with her dark hair pulled neatly into a ponytail. She definitely hadn't just dragged herself out of bed.

"Hi," she said, holding a plate of chocolate chip cookies. "Sorry it took me a minute. Had to get these out of the oven." A smile bloomed on her fresh face. No sign of pillow creases in sight.

He looked between her and the plate, the scent of chocolate and butter circulating under his nose, mixed with something acutely female.

"Grandma Mable didn't have much in the cupboards. She did have the ingredients for cookies though. Except for the milk and eggs, but I stopped on the way into town for those staples last night."

Mitch's mouth watered.

"I thought this could be our breakfast. I have coffee too, if you want some."

It was hard to be anything but agreeable when she was offering him caffeine and sugar. He gave a quick nod and stepped inside after her. The front room seemed less dusty than it had the night before. The floors shined beneath his boots too. "Looks like you've been hard at work."

She glanced over her shoulder as she led him toward the kitchen. "It was a late night for me. I couldn't sleep. Too excited."

"Yeah? About what?" Certainly not about this place. She'd cleaned, sure, but there was still a laundry list of things to be done. The inside of the house was livable, albeit dusty and in need of minor repairs. The outside had lost its curb appeal though. And most importantly, the place hadn't drawn in real guests for a while. With the ski resorts that had popped up in the neighboring town of Wild Blossom Bluffs, Sweetwater Springs wasn't as appealing to tourists. There was nothing here to grab their attention.

"About being here, of course." She set the plate down on the granite countertop—one of the few updates to the bed and breakfast in recent years—and gestured toward a stool. "Sit and I'll get you a cup of coffee."

"What's so special about here?" Mitch asked, watching as she poured him a cup.

She shrugged a shoulder, sliding his mug in front of him. "It's gorgeous, for one. I remember thinking Sweetwater Springs was a magical place as a kid."

"Mable thought so too." Mitch chuckled as he pulled the black coffee to his mouth. Bitter and smooth, just like he liked it. "And when I was a kid, I believed her."

"Not anymore?" She sat on the stool across from him.

He met her eyes and hesitated. "Nah. Same as Santa Claus. The beard has been snatched, so to speak."

She frowned. When she did, he noticed the plumpness

of her pink lips. He pulled his gaze away and stared down into the black abyss of his coffee instead. He wasn't here for attraction. He was here to put an end to whatever well-intended but naive thoughts the Russos' granddaughter had running through her mind. They could struggle for two months and then admit defeat—because this place was hopeless—or they could walk away now.

And he was voting for the latter.

CHAPTER THREE

*K*aitlyn's heart had been racing ever since her conversation with Josie last night. If *Loving Life* magazine promoted the town and her B&B, then surely people would come. Maybe a lot of people. She'd almost argued with Josie when she'd made the suggestion. She couldn't let Josie put her and the magazine's reputation on the line.

But if I can pull this off...

Kaitlyn looked at Mitch, who was sampling one of her cookies. She hadn't been thrilled about him being here last night but if she was going to do this, she was glad there was somebody here to help her. Josie said the magazine would be going into distribution sometime in the next two weeks. After that, the Sweetwater B&B needed to be ready for business. The thought of hosting happy couples was terrifying. And electrifying.

The town itself was already living up to the claim. It was cozy and had so much to offer. There was a charming downtown area with quaint shops and good restaurants, and she couldn't wait to try them. The town was enclosed in a mountain valley, and there was a park with hiking trails that passed natural hot springs and led to some of the best lookouts in the area. The stage was already set. Sweetwater Springs just needed a hook to draw people in, and this was it.

"So," Kaitlyn said, leaning over the counter. Mitch met her gaze, and her mouth immediately went dry. She'd never noticed it in his childhood photographs but his eyes were brown and green with a hint of blue too. They were like the stained-glass windows of the Trinity Church in New York. She'd made a point of walking by it every day, even though she knew a shortcut that would get her to the subway faster. Part of her had wanted to live in those stained-glass windows. And now Mitch's eyes held the same appeal.

She swallowed and dropped her gaze for just a second. "So," she said again, clearing her throat. If he was going to be her business partner, and she fully intended to convince him to be, she needed neutral feelings toward him. "I have a plan to make this work."

Mitch chewed on a bite of cookie as he watched her. "You mean you haven't come to your senses yet?"

A frown tugged at the corners of her mouth. "Meaning do I want to walk away? No. And you're not walking away either. If my plan works, we can have this place booked solid with a waiting list running into the new year."

He chuckled softly. *Was he laughing at her?*

"I'm serious. My best friend, Josie, is the executive editor for the lifestyle section in *Loving Life* magazine." If he recognized the name of the periodical, it didn't show. "It's one of the biggest, most widely read magazines in the country. Josie is about to run a feature on the most romantic holiday getaways in the country. Some couples like to have a little private time before they're bombarded with family events."

He nodded. "Okay. What does this have to do with anything?"

Kaitlyn ignored the irritation in his voice. "Well, I was talking to her last night and she offered to put Sweetwater Springs on the list. Not just on the list, she offered to put it at the top of the list." A swell of excitement ballooned in her chest. The idea was genius. It would work. She knew it would.

Mitch's face held no expression. "Has she been here before?"

"No, but she hasn't gone to all the other places on the list either. That's what Google is for. You can research pretty much everything about a place, to the point you almost feel like you've been there. Even this old B and B is online."

"Yeah, but the website showcases how it was ten years ago." He glanced around the kitchen to make his point.

Yes, the cabinets were old, and the color of the walls was tired but she could fix that. And although her parents had never been big on celebrating the holidays, decorating was her specialty. She held out her hands and realized they were shaking. Mitch's laser-sharp eyes noticed too. *So what?* This meant a lot to her. She didn't care if he knew she was nervous. "If this B and B is promoted in *Loving Life*, it'll bring customers. Customers bring in money. Then the bank will approve me for a loan to buy you out at the end of the two months."

He narrowed his stained-glass eyes. She needed him to buy into the plan. There was no backing out once they got started. Turning the B&B on its head and transforming it into a romantic holiday haven wouldn't be easy. But it was doable.

"It's a lie," he finally said.

"It's not a lie. Sweetwater Springs *is* romantic. I've always thought so. And there aren't that many repairs to be done here. Not really. I'm sure my grandmother has a tree and other festive décor. I'll find it."

His mouth was set in a grim line.

It was hard to take him seriously with a cookie crumb lodged in the corner of his mouth though. She focused on that as she pressed on. "Look, my grandparents must've meant something to you if Grandma Mable put you in the will."

"Mable and Henry meant a lot to me. But running a bed and breakfast isn't my dream. I'm not cut out for greeting strangers and making them feel welcome. And I'm certainly not jolly old Saint Nick."

Obviously. "Great. Then you'll get a payday and leave at the end of the agreement, which if we signed today, would fall on Christmas Eve." She pointed to a calendar she'd conveniently laid on the counter. "See, that makes eight full weeks, which according to the fine print of the contract, defines two months. Then it's a merry Christmas for both of us." She watched him run a hand through his overgrown dark locks as he seemed to consider what she was telling him. Her fingers suddenly itched to run through his hair too. She'd never been attracted to a man with a beard before. Not until now.

His jaw ticked on one side as he studied her. Then he lifted a finger and wiped his mouth, removing the crumb. "*If* I agree, I don't want to be front and center. I'll handle repairs, anything you need while I'm here, but this place is yours. You can buy me out at the end of the agreement. Even though I don't think you'll be anywhere near ready to do that by Christmas Eve."

"We'll see." She reached for a list she'd been working on last night. "I started writing down the things that need to be done. These are the jobs I think are better suited for you."

Most of the items she'd written down were small. The chimney needed to be swept. Lightbulbs and air filters needed to be changed. A fuse had blown for one of the rooms upstairs and there was no electricity running to it. One of the biggest repairs she'd listed was that there was no hot water in the house. She'd discovered that this morning after enduring an ice-cold shower, which she still hadn't managed to warm up from.

Mitch took a long moment scrutinizing the to-do list. "Fine. I'll get started on this today," he finally said.

"Does that mean you'll stay?"

He hesitated, and it almost looked painful for him to nod even though physically she suspected he was in tip-top condition. "I'll call Mr. Garrison and tell him it's a go."

She squealed in excitement and, unable to help herself, ran around the kitchen island and threw her arms around his neck. "Thank you, thank you, thank you!"

After her brain caught up with her body, she realized her chest was pressed up against the hard mass of his muscled body. And *oh, heavens*. He smelled divine, like pine trees and honey and alpha man. Her body buzzed with awareness.

Squelching it, she pulled away.

Mitch was staring at her, and if she wasn't mistaken, his kaleidoscope eyes had gotten darker.

She swallowed, wondering if he could also hear the boom of her heart in her chest. Just from that brief physical touch—which she would be sure to avoid from now on.

Taking the list, he stood.

"Sorry. I just got excited." She offered her hand for him to shake. "Partners?"

He slipped his warm, calloused hand in hers. More physical touch. *Crap.* "For the two months. Then I'm leaving," he clarified.

"Understood."

* * *

Three hours later, Kaitlyn collapsed on the sofa in the main room. She'd cleaned until she was breathless and sore, and she'd barely made a dent in the long list of to-dos she'd assigned herself. Pressing her head back into the couch cushion, she closed her eyes for a moment. Perhaps she could hire someone else to help her. Except she didn't have money for that.

Maybe she could ask her parents for help. But they hadn't even approved of her coming here in the first place. Running a B&B was career suicide, her mother had told her on the phone as she'd packed. And then again on the drive down Interstate 95.

Kaitlyn had gone to the New York School of Interior Design. She'd worked her butt off for the last couple of years building a solid reputation in her field. Little did her mom know that Kaitlyn's career was already dead in the water though, thanks to Hollywood's favorite action hero, Bradley Foster.

Kaitlyn scanned the long list of things that still needed to be done before the article released in two weeks, resisting the sudden fear climbing through her like unwanted vines. This was just the cleaning. To make good on Josie's promise, the inn needed to be merry and romantic too. That was the fun part. Maybe she could browse Pinterest for ideas.

As she considered her options, her cell phone rang on the coffee table.

Kaitlyn gave a quick glance at the caller ID and answered on the second ring. "Hey, lady."

"All right, the December magazine has gone to press. Your neck and mine are on the line so I hope you're prepared to make this happen."

Kaitlyn's mouth dropped open. "We just talked last night. It's not even been twenty-four hours."

"Maybe in your world, but in mine, time moves fast. No rest for the weary, blah, blah, blah. Please tell me your partner is in."

Kaitlyn warmed just at Mitch's mention. It was an unconscious, physical reaction. *What is wrong with me?* "He said yes."

"Perfect!"

"Yes, it is." Kaitlyn stood and walked to the mantel above the fireplace where several framed pictures were displayed. Her gaze paused on a photo of her grandparents standing in front of the B&B, the pride on their faces clear. A grand-opening sign hung behind them. Kaitlyn had always favored her father, who'd obviously gotten his looks from Mable. All three had the same dark hair and large, brown eyes. The same straight nose.

Kaitlyn regretted that she hadn't spent enough time with her grandparents to really know who they were. Not that she'd had any say in the matter as a child. Her parents preferred to spend their vacation time at fancy resorts and on cruises. Once Kaitlyn was in college, she'd always stayed in the city and spent her Christmases with friends who didn't have anywhere to go, or she'd gone home with Josie. Because Kaitlyn had spent so little time here, coming to see her grandparents for the holidays just didn't feel natural. Even so, she wished she'd come anyway.

Josie cleared her throat on the other end of the line.

"Listen to this. The Sweetwater Bed and Breakfast in Sweetwater Springs just might be *the* most romantic holiday retreat in America. How could an inn with an address on Mistletoe Lane be anything less? Each of the large, airy rooms, named after a few of America's favorite romantic couples, features a breathtaking view of the North Carolina mountains. Stay in, snuggle, and read by the fire. Or take a walk under a blanket of twinkling stars. Make a wish on one and watch it come true as you live out your most romantic fantasies this Christmas season."

The breath caught in Kaitlyn's chest. "Is that what you wrote?"

"Something like that. I pulled a late night on your behalf. I described the town and then I pitched the bed and breakfast hard. I was praying the website was up to date."

Kaitlyn cringed. As Mitch had already pointed out, the website was slightly behind the times. "The rooms aren't named after romantic couples but that's a genius idea."

"I thought so too, especially since you're such a romantic-movie buff."

"You're a closet buff," Kaitlyn accused.

"I only watch them with you, and only for the popcorn and soda you provide."

Kaitlyn laughed, suddenly sad that she and Josie wouldn't be having any of those girls' nights in, watching movies and stuffing themselves silly, anytime soon.

"Now go make it happen. I, on the flip side, need to get started on articles for the January issue of *Loving Life*."

"Or you could try sleep for a change," Kaitlyn suggested.

"In broad daylight? You must be crazy."

After they hung up, Kaitlyn went to retrieve her list from the coffee table. She grabbed a pen and added, "Update website." She'd loved what Josie had written about the B&B. It made her want to come and visit this place herself. And she couldn't wait to name the rooms. The interior designer in her already had the wheels spinning. The first room could be named after *Anne of Green Gables*. Anne Shirley and Gilbert Blythe were the first fictional characters to ever make her heart skip a beat. The room could be done in a multitude of pasture greens with antique furniture from the early 1900s.

Yes. A smile molded her lips. This was exactly the kind of work that had thrilled her in interior design school. This was going to be amazing. She was going to transform this inn into everything the feature article Josie wrote had promised. In two very long, sleepless weeks.

* * *

Mitch had been plugging away at the list that Kaitlyn had given him over the last few days. There were just a couple of items left to do but those would wait until tomorrow. Right now, he needed to check on his mom, who'd looked exhausted when he'd left her early this morning.

He packed up his toolbox that he kept in the cab of his truck and gave Kaitlyn a wave on the way out, forgoing talking to her because, one, he was tired, and two, he'd been keeping his head down, focusing on his work—or trying to—instead of allowing himself to get distracted by her. She was definitely distracting. The way she walked. The way she twirled her hair around her index finger when she was lost in thought. Her every little mannerism was driving him insane. How the heck was he supposed to work with her for two months?

Climbing in his truck, he drove to the stop sign at the end of Mistletoe Lane, turned the corner, and pulled into his mom's driveway, letting out a deep sigh of relief when he cut the engine. His mother drove him crazy too but in a completely different way. No doubt she was inside preparing dinner just like she'd done every night since he'd arrived, even though he'd insisted she didn't need to.

He climbed out of his truck and headed up the porch steps. "Mom?" he called as he stepped inside.

The TV was blaring as he entered. He was doubly accosted by a thin veil of smoke in the air. "Mom?" he said, adrenaline firing through his veins. Like a hound dog on a scent, he followed the smoke to the kitchen just as the alarm started shrieking on the wall overhead. There were two items on the stove top, one of which was bubbling over and spilling onto the hot surface with a sharp sizzle. He grabbed the handle to remove it and then jerked back as the heated metal stung his palm. "Mom?"

The smoke detector continued to wail in his ear. *Where the hell is she?* He grabbed a dishtowel and pushed the overrunning pot to the back of the stove. Then he turned the stove's dials off on the back panel. Finally, the alarm silenced.

As he walked briskly back through the empty living room, he scanned the surroundings for his mom. He followed the hallway down to her room and paused at the sight of her lying across the bed. "Mom!"

She wasn't moving. Not at first. She began to stir as he grabbed one of her shoulders and gave an urgent shake. The smoke detector must have been loud enough to alert the neighbors. How had she napped through it?

Her eyes fluttered open. "Oh, Mitch, you're home," she said groggily.

"What's wrong?" he asked, giving her an assessing once-over.

She grimaced and scratched the side of her cheek. "Nothing. I guess I dozed off. I was just—" Her eyes widened. "The stove! I have food cooking on the st—"

"Already turned it off," he said, concern tightening his chest. "Mom, the smoke detector was going off, and you didn't wake up."

Her brows pinched above red, tired eyes. "Really?" She sat up, moving slowly for a woman who never slowed down.

"Are you feeling okay?"

"Oh, I'm fine." She laughed softly as if to think otherwise was silly. "It was just a long day between the two houses I cleaned. I only intended to rest for a minute."

Mitch didn't like what he was hearing. He remembered being so tired when he was in boot camp that he would practically pass out as soon as his head hit the pillow. A grenade could've gone off and he wouldn't have woken, as tired as he was. He didn't like to think that this was how his mom was living these days. He knew she was serious when she cleaned houses. She scrubbed the floors and cabinets by hand, vacuumed, dusted. It was the reason everyone in Sweetwater Springs wanted to hire her. "The house could've caught fire," he said.

"Oh, I would've woken up eventually." She patted his knee as he sat beside her on the bed. "Don't worry about me. Are you hungry?" she asked, flipping the subject.

"Do you ever stop?"

She shook her head. "It's not often that my only son comes home to visit. I love cooking for you."

"Not tonight." He got up, walked over to the headboard of her bed, and propped up several pillows. Then he pointed. "You're sitting right here and having dinner in bed tonight."

Her mouth fell open to protest.

"No arguing. I'm serving you here, and I'll eat beside you."

She chuckled softly. "Okay. That sounds nice."

"Good." He watched her climb under the covers and sit up against the pillows. Then he went back to the kitchen and got to work finishing their meal. But he wasn't hungry anymore. Instead, worry sat heavily in his stomach. His mom was one of the strongest people he knew. She was always caring for others and evidently neglecting herself in the process. While he was here, he'd change all that, he promised himself. At least that was one good thing to come out of this situation with the bed and breakfast. If he and Kaitlyn really could revive the place and she did buy out his half, then perhaps he could pay off his mom's mortgage. He'd continue to send her money too, of course, and her days of working to the point of exhaustion would be over.

"Here we go," Mitch said, carrying their dinner plates into the bedroom a few minutes later.

"You really are the best son a mom could have." She secured her plate of baked chicken, brown rice, and green beans on her lap.

He took the spot next to her.

"It's burnt," she commented as she stabbed her fork into the dry chicken breast. "My fault."

"I like it burnt."

She snorted. "Liar. But I love you for it. You've been here a few days already. How long are you staying this time?"

He swallowed the bite of chicken he was chewing. It tasted more like cardboard than actual food. It struggled to go down almost as much as his next words struggled to come up. "I'll be staying longer than expected."

"How long?" she probed.

"Two months."

His mom whipped her head to the side. "You'll be home for Thanksgiving and Christmas!"

Not by choice. "I have some things to take care of."

Her smile engulfed her face. "Well, this is reason to celebrate. Maybe we should open the bottle of champagne I keep in the refrigerator."

Mitch laughed unexpectedly. It felt good in comparison to the stress he'd been shouldering just being in Sweetwater Springs. "No. After dinner, you're going to sleep while I clean up the kitchen." He popped another bite of extra-crispy chicken into his mouth and chewed.

She was quiet for a moment. "Well, if you're staying for any amount of time, you should know that Brian Everson is—"

Mitch held up a hand, every muscle in his body suddenly tense. "Stop right there." He had a rule. He didn't talk about the Everson family. He kept his distance out of respect and a promise he'd made when he was eighteen years old. Shutting the door on any information about the Everson family was for his own sanity. He was a fixer but no matter how hard he tried, he'd never be able to fix what had happened to Brian in the accident.

CHAPTER FOUR

Kaitlyn lay across the couch and yawned. She wasn't ready to head to bed just yet. Not when there was so much to do. She pulled her sketchbook toward her and stared down at the basic layout of the house. It was two stories with the main entrance opening into a formal living room. To the right was the sitting room, where she was now, and to the left was a dining area. The B&B had five guest rooms upstairs and living quarters for the host on the first floor.

Most curious was the first-floor ballroom. What had her grandparents done with a ballroom? She never remembered seeing it when she'd come to visit as a child but those were very brief trips hallmarked by smiley face pancakes, piggy-back rides, and Grandpa Henry reading her books by the fireplace.

Kaitlyn drew a question mark in the box on the inn's layout that represented the ballroom. She'd keep that room closed off for now. Any guests that came to visit didn't need to go there. All they needed were their own rooms, which she'd already started preparing. The rooms didn't feel quite as romantic as she wanted them to yet. Grandma Mable had made them cozy enough but Kaitlyn wanted to make each one unique and unforgettable. She envisioned guests wanting to come again to experience a different room.

With another yawn, she traded her sketchbook for her laptop and settled it over her thighs. Then she opened a browser and searched for romantic interior designs on Pinterest. She'd always gained inspiration from what others had done before her. "Why reinvent the wheel?" one of her professors had liked to ask in college. "Just redecorate it." Kaitlyn liked that philosophy. She'd loved everything about interior design school. Being there had only solidified her desire to create beauty in her environment.

Scrolling down the Pinterest search page, she looked for something that would catch her eye and then froze when she came across a design she'd done for Bradley Foster. With her design firm, she'd worked for lots of important people in New York—mayors, athletes, newscasters, business executives. But Bradley was her first celebrity job. Designing a room for him had been a dream come true. A step in the right direction for her career, or so she'd thought.

A sick feeling slithered through her stomach as she stared at his image. Being an action movie hero, he didn't lack for muscles. He had dark hair and eyes that could intimidate any bad guy on-screen and make any female with one good eye swoon. Heck, his good looks aside, the man's voice had enough appeal to attract the opposite sex from one end of the world to the other.

Below his photograph was a picture of a majestic-looking living room that Kaitlyn had helped design. Most clients didn't get involved with the details of the work but Bradley had. He was always there, and at first, it was exciting. Then there was a moment when she'd thought Bradley might try to kiss her while working on that front room pictured on the computer screen, but she'd diverted his attention. She wasn't romantically interested in Bradley Foster, world-famous movie star or not. For one, he was married with kids. He was just getting carried away from being in such close quarters, she'd reasoned, making excuses for him and putting it out of her mind. But his advances had only escalated after that. He'd hired her for another job, and she'd agreed because it was the opportunity of a lifetime. How could she possibly say no to Bradley Foster?

Kaitlyn closed her laptop with a huff. She was done with this walk down memory lane. She needed every bit of her energy—physical, mental, and emotional—to get the Sweetwater Bed and Breakfast up to par on a nickel-and-dime budget. And that meant not letting herself get sidetracked by thinking about her ex-client.

Or by drooling over Mitch.

* * *

Christmas music floated through the overhead speakers at the local hardware store as Mitch headed inside. Really? It was barely November. Plus, there was no need to put shoppers in a gift-buying frame of mind here. All he needed was a chimney brush and some pipe extensions to check off yet another item on Kaitlyn's to-do list.

On his way through the aisles, he also grabbed a couple of large tarps to cover the living room, a pair of goggles, and a face mask to keep him from inhaling any smut or ash.

As he was heading to the checkout, he heard someone call his name.

"Last-Ditch Mitch!"

A groan settled deep in his throat. He hated that nickname. Turning, he saw Tucker Locklear grinning at him. Looking at his longtime friend, Mitch wouldn't know that the last couple of years had been rough on him, losing his wife Renee. The only clue was the dark telltale shadows under Tuck's eyes that even his Cherokee Indian complexion couldn't hide.

"Hey, man. I thought the lighting in here was playing tricks on me," Tuck said as he approached.

Mitch shook his head and then Tuck's hand. "No, I'm home for a while."

"Yeah? How long?" Tuck was a physical therapist now, which was fitting because, as an adrenaline junkie, Tuck knew injuries and how to treat them. He'd likely strained or broken every muscle and bone in his body over the years.

"I'm helping the Russos' granddaughter fix up the B and B for business."

Tuck's brow lowered. "Really? I thought that place was closed now that Mable has passed. I'm sorry about that, by the way. I know you thought a lot of her."

"Thanks." Mitch folded his arms at his chest, applying pressure to the ache there. He did miss Mable, more than he wanted to let on. Henry too. That old couple had been as good as family to him. "I actually inherited half the business," Mitch confided. He hadn't even told his own mother yet. If he wasn't careful, she'd find out from someone in town before he got to tell her himself. That wouldn't be ideal for either of them.

"Wow. That's great, man. So you're going to run a bed and breakfast now that you're out of the corps? Is that the plan?"

"Not a chance," Mitch said without hesitation. "Can you see me baking cookies and playing nice with difficult guests?"

"I don't know." Tuck shrugged a shoulder. "Your muscles are a tad oversized and maybe a little intimidating but you're nothing but a big bear, in my opinion. I think you'd be good at it."

Mitch narrowed his eyes. "Not happening."

Tuck grinned wide. "So, at least a couple weeks, huh?"

"Something like that."

"Great. I'll call Alex and set up a night for us all to catch up. Maybe a case of beer over at the bluffs for old times' sake."

"That's still illegal," Mitch pointed out.

"True. And since you and Alex are both law enforcement now, I guess we'll just knock a few back at the Tipsy Tavern."

Mitch nodded. He and Alex had always wanted to be police officers growing up. They'd both been junior cadets in high school and had planned to attend police academy together. After the accident though, Mitch had needed the quick ticket out of Sweetwater Springs that the military recruiter had offered him. He'd achieved his dream of working in law enforcement by becoming a military police officer while Alex had stayed local.

"Did you hear that Skip runs the tavern these days? His Uncle Jake retired and handed over the reins," Tuck continued, oblivious to Mitch's mental sidetrack.

"Skip Mazer runs a bar?" Mitch asked, blinking his old friend back into focus. One Christmas tune in the background switched out for another as Tuck slapped a hand on his back.

"See what happens when you stay away too long? Everything changes."

Not everything.

"I'll bring you up to speed when we go out." Tuck started

to walk away and then jabbed a finger in Mitch's direction. "I have your number, and you better answer. I can get Alex to put out an APB on you if you don't."

"Hanging out sounds good. I'll answer," Mitch promised, offering a wave and continuing toward the checkout again. A night of drinks with his old friends would be fun, he told himself. Catching up on the goings-on in Sweetwater Springs would also be good. There was never a risk of running into one of the Eversons at the tavern. Most of them were too good to hang out with the locals. At least that was Mitch's perception. Except for his former classmate Brian Everson, who'd always been a nice guy.

Mitch got in line and shifted back and forth on his feet, trying not to let the guilt settle in around him like it usually did when he thought about Brian. The sweet holiday music compounded his agitation and chipped away at his patience as he waited in line. *Bah humbug.*

After finally purchasing his items, he climbed into his truck and drove to the B&B, where Kaitlyn was on a ladder leaning against the large wraparound front porch. She was at least ten feet off the ground.

Cursing under his breath, he pushed open the driver's side door and headed over. "What do you think you're doing?" he barked.

She whipped her head around to face him and squeaked as she momentarily lost her balance. Her body swayed in the air.

Mitch's reflexes were primed. He took off running toward her and anchored the ladder as it shifted.

"You scared me to death!" she accused, white-knuckling the ladder's rungs.

"Well, you shouldn't be up there. Especially when there's no one here to help if you get in trouble."

"I was doing just fine until you shouted at me, thank you very much."

He closed his eyes and took a steadying breath. One hard-headed female wasn't enough in his life, apparently. Now he had both his mom *and* Kaitlyn Russo to deal with. "Please come down," he said, tempering his frustration.

"I'm not done yet."

"Done doing what?"

"There are a bunch of branches on the roof of the veranda."

He followed her gaze and noticed that the second-story windows were open too. Wreaths now hung on each one. He imagined her dangling out the windows to hang them. A low growl emitted from his throat. "There are a dozen things to take care of and you decide to hang Christmas wreaths? It's still two months away."

"I found the box of wreaths when I was in the storage building getting the ladder," she explained. "And it's only seven weeks away. Christmas will be here before you know it."

He could only pray that was true as his hands anchored the ladder. Because the sooner the holiday got here, the sooner he could leave.

He looked back up where he had the perfect view of her perfect backside. A surge of unruly, unwanted attraction curled through him.

"You can let go. I'm not going to fall, you know. Unless you start yelling at me again." She glared down at him.

He hesitated before stepping away. "I didn't yell. I was concerned. Now, please come down. I'll get the branches myself." His shoulders relaxed as she started to do as he asked. She traveled down two rungs and then missed the third and her body went into free fall—straight into his ready arms.

He gripped her against him. "I got you," he said, noticing how wide her brown eyes had become. And how delicious she smelled, like a rose garden in bloom. "If I hadn't been here, you'd be laid up on the couch for the rest of the week."

"I don't have time for that." She didn't move to get out of his hold on her though. Not immediately. Resting against his chest, her face was dangerously close to his. They spoke in quiet voices because they were only inches apart. Close enough to lean in and kiss her, if he wanted to. And yeah, there was some foolish part of him that thought that was an excellent idea.

"How do the wreaths look?" she asked.

His gaze shifted momentarily. "Like you could've broken your neck putting them up."

She smiled, and that spoke to the foolish part of him that desperately wanted to taste those lips. Therefore, the only reasonable thing to do was put her down and take a step back, which he did, quickly and efficiently.

"The front of the house is the first thing people see when they pass by," she explained. "First impressions are everything."

"How about this? From here on out, you take care of the inside of the house, and I'll manage things out here," he said.

"Okay. There are plenty more things to do in the guest rooms. But I might need your help with a few of them."

"You got it. And next time you decide to climb up on the roof, don't." Not unless he was here to catch her, because he wouldn't mind holding her in his arms again. What the hell was wrong with him?

He watched her stubborn chin tip up and fully expected those plump lips of hers to spout off something smart.

Instead, she whirled on her heel, turning her back to him. "Don't fall," she called back to him. But her tone of voice made him wonder if she wouldn't mind seeing him bust his butt.

Mitch worked steadily until dark and then stepped inside to say good night. He purposefully walked with heavy feet on the hardwood floors to make his presence known. Kaitlyn had proved to be a little jumpy since he'd met her. Granted, her first impression of him had been to think he was an intruder. But every time he'd rounded a corner over the last week, she'd seemed to stiffen.

She turned to acknowledge him. "Hey."

She had soft music streaming in from an old-time radio off to the side of the room. Thankfully, not Christmas tunes. A few of the tarps he'd gotten earlier were scattered on the floor along with a couple cans of paint.

"I found the paint and brushes in the laundry room closet. What do you think of the color?"

His gaze settled on the soft yellow of the walls. "It looks great. You did all this while I was outside?" he asked, winning a smile from her.

"It still needs a second coat but it's amazing what a difference a little paint can make."

"Seems so."

"I also named a few of the guest rooms while I worked."

He lifted a brow. "Have you been sniffing the paint too?"

She laughed. "All the guest rooms are going to be named after a famous couple in books or the movies. The whole room will have a theme to match."

"I think that's a great idea. Who do you have so far?"

She set her paintbrush in the roller tray and wiped her hands on the apron she was wearing. Then she ticked off her responses on her fingers. "I'm starting with my favorites. Anne of Green Gables and Gilbert Blythe. Scarlett and Rhett."

"Good ones," he said.

"Those are both books that were made into movies, so two birds with one stone. I was thinking Scarlett and Rhett's room could have a Deep South décor. There is actually some Civil War–era furniture here that I can relocate to that room."

"I'll help you with moving furniture," he said, enjoying how her whole face lit up as she talked about her ideas. Her passion was evident. "Any other couples?" he asked.

"Just one more right now." She pulled her lower lip between her teeth. "Baby and Johnny."

He shook his head, trying to figure out who she was talking about.

She gave him a look of total disbelief. "Oh, come on. From *Dirty Dancing*."

"Oh, right." He nodded. "Let me guess. That room will have a sixties vibe."

She grinned. "Wouldn't that be fun?"

"It would."

"Any other suggestions for me?"

He scratched his chin beneath his beard. "I prefer action movies," he said, noting how her smile wilted just slightly. He guessed she stuck strictly to romance. "Also nonfiction books. The books I read don't really talk about well-known couples. How about I handle the repairs and you do all the decorating, including naming the guest rooms?"

She nodded, smiling easily again. "Seems like we make a good team."

He was usually more of a solo kind of guy. As an MP, he'd never had a partner, unless one counted his police dog, which he did. Scout was retired a few months before Mitch got out of the corps. The lucky canine now lived with a nice civilian family, hopefully spending his days chewing bones and barking at birds.

"Yeah," Mitch said, knowing he should say his goodbye and walk out the front door. Instead, he stared at Kaitlyn for a moment longer. She was marked with paint and beaming with creative energy. Seeing her in her element unhinged something inside him. There was nothing more attractive than a woman having fun. It made him want to stay and have fun with her.

Bad idea.

He cleared his throat. "Okay, well, I'll see you in the morning. Don't climb any tall ladders while I'm gone," he teased, and then grinned as her mouth dipped into a playful frown.

"I won't. And come hungry. I'll have breakfast and coffee waiting for you."

"You don't have to do that."

"I figure I better get used to serving others. I'll practice on you."

When she put it that way, it was hard for him to say no.

* * *

Kaitlyn had been up since five thirty. She'd grabbed a few groceries the day before, hoping they'd last a week, but she'd already burned the toast, twice, and was on her second batch of scrambled eggs because the first batch had been a disgusting mush.

She glanced at the clock above the stove. Mitch would be here any minute. She pulled a cast-iron frying pan to one of the vacant burners and began placing sliced bacon inside.

"You're supposed to wait until it's hot first," a voice said, coming up behind her.

She jumped and whirled in one simultaneous motion

while also pulling a hand to her chest. "You snuck up on me!" she snapped, suddenly buzzing with adrenaline.

Mitch stopped for a moment, giving her an unreadable expression, and then stepped beside her. "You should lock the doors."

"I did last night but I guess I left it unlocked when I went out to get the newspaper this morning."

He surveyed her breakfast display. "You didn't cook the eggs long enough. It helps to add a little milk if you want them fluffy. Maybe put in some shredded cheese for flavor too. Did you add salt?"

She pressed her lips together. "I grew up with two working parents. They were always in a rush so breakfast was usually a Pop-Tart on the way to school."

The corner of his mouth twitched. "I would've given my right arm for a Pop-Tart. They were too expensive. Our neighbors had chickens and gave us eggs in exchange for my mom doing odd jobs for them. So that's what we had every morning."

He took a commanding step closer, causing her to move aside. Then he began lifting the bacon off the pan and placing it on a napkin. He adjusted the dial from high to medium heat.

She watched him work, taking mental notes and trying not to let her emotions get in the way. So she wasn't a fantastic cook—yet. She'd learn. She'd do whatever it took. How hard could cooking for a house full of guests be?

"Eggs, bacon, what else?" he asked, grabbing a mixing bowl from one of the cabinets. He expertly cracked several eggs with one hand.

"What do you mean *what else*?"

"Well, if I were a guest, this wouldn't be enough. You usually want a starch as well. Mable was famous for her made-from-scratch biscuits but I don't expect you to tackle that."

Kaitlyn shoved her hands on her hips. "Why not?"

"No offense. Mable used to say it took her the better part of a decade to get them right. It's not fancy but you could serve grits."

Kaitlyn wrinkled her nose, which made him chuckle. It was a reserved, quiet sound that reverberated through her. She liked it and suddenly longed to hear it again.

"You are definitely not from the South, are you?" He splashed some milk with the egg yolks and beat them with a wire whisk that he'd located in a drawer beside the stove.

She was amazed at his cooking skills. A man who knew his way around a kitchen was a definite turn-on. And a woman who didn't... probably not so much.

"Did my grandmother teach you how to cook?" she asked.

He looked almost apologetic as he nodded. "Yep. She ran the gamut with her meals. Sometimes she offered up a simple country sampler breakfast like this one. Other times, she treated guests to gourmet omelets and pastries. She was a talented chef."

"And you know how to make her famous made-from-scratch biscuits?"

"I'll teach you," he said. "Mable tended to exaggerate. It only took me a couple years to master her biscuits." He winked in Kaitlyn's direction.

Her insides turned mushier than her eggs. "Hopefully it won't take me that long to master them." She needed to learn fast, before the guests started making reservations and Mitch left. "I'm expecting customers to start booking after next week. Josie told me that the magazine hits stands and mailboxes a couple weeks before each new month."

She stepped aside and watched as Mitch took over preparing the bacon and eggs. Then he set a saucepan of water to boil and retrieved a cream-colored bag from the pantry. "You can't move south and not love grits. I'll make them, and you'll wonder where you've been all your life."

She folded her arms across her chest, watching him work. "I've been in New York having my food delivered. I have all my favorite places on speed dial."

"Well, today is the day you'll learn the art of making breakfast, the most important meal of the day," he said, measuring out the contents of the bag of grits.

Twenty minutes later, they sat down together at one of the dining room tables with full plates. The aroma wafted under her nose and made her mouth water. So did the man in front of her. She'd been snuffing out little fires in her belly ever since he'd entered her kitchen this morning. Ever since he'd walked into the B&B a week ago.

She picked up her fork and stabbed at a fluffy lump of perfectly golden eggs. "Long jog this morning?" she asked, making small talk. There was something about that strong, silent alpha vibe Mitch had going that made her uncharacteristically nervous. She could usually talk to anyone. But the man sitting across the table had her stomach fluttering and her tongue leaden.

"Only about seven miles."

She choked on the lump of eggs that she'd just forked into her mouth.

Everything in Mitch seemed to stiffen as he watched her. She held up a hand to ward him off, guessing he was about two seconds away from hopping over the table and performing the Heimlich. And while the thought of his arms wrapped around her again was appealing, having her breakfast fly across the room in front of him was not.

"I'm fine," she choked out. She took a drink from her glass of orange juice. "Just surprised that you jogged so far."

"You wouldn't believe how good it feels when you're done. Better than sex."

She started to choke again. "You . . . did not just say that," she said on a laugh.

A smile crept through his angled features. "Sorry. I'm used to being around a bunch of marines, I guess."

"Well, if you're going to be helping me with the B and B, you can't talk to the guests like they're marines."

"I'll just try not to talk to them at all. I'm good at flying under the radar."

She raised both brows. "I've noticed. You've been sneaking up on me ever since we met." She bit into a piece of salty bacon, chewed, and swallowed. "You said your mom still lives in town?"

He nodded while continuing to eat. "Yep."

"What about your dad?"

His fork paused momentarily. "He died when I was nine."

Her heart broke a little for him. "I'm sorry. That must've been hard for you."

"It was. And watching my mom work two jobs to make sure we had what we needed was hard too."

"Is that why you're so set on leaving again?" She regretted asking as soon as the question had come out of her mouth. It was none of her business why he wanted to leave. He'd agreed to the stipulations of the will, and that's all she needed to know.

"It's more complicated than that," he said after a long moment. "Sweetwater Springs represents my past. Not my future."

"I see."

"My turn to ask questions," he said, locking her gaze and holding it captive.

"Okay."

"Who hurt you?"

She nearly choked again. "Excuse me?"

"Every time I walk into the room, you stiffen. Why?"

Her heart was beating fast now. Thanks to Bradley Foster, she was jumpy. He hadn't gotten what he'd wanted but he'd still taken something from her. Her trust. "No one. I'm fine," she lied, pulling her gaze to her plate. But she had every intention of making that lie a truth. Her nerves would eventually settle. Her memories of Bradley's hands on her would soon fade—hopefully.

Mitch didn't speak again until she looked back up at him. "You don't have to worry about me," he said in a quiet voice, his eyes steady and sincere.

She nodded. "I know."

"A friend of mine says I'm just a big bear." The hard angles of his face softened as he smiled.

Her insides turned to mushy eggs again. "Well, I'll try not to poke you."

One of his eyebrows shot up, and heat flooded her cheeks. That comment had unintentionally sounded sexual. The entire vibe between her and Mitch was unintentionally sexual, and that's what she had to worry most about with him. He was temporary, and she wasn't looking for a relationship. It wasn't the right time in her life to get romantically involved. She had a life to reconstruct, one room at a time.

CHAPTER FIVE

$\mathcal{O}$n a late Friday afternoon, three weeks into the contract, Kaitlyn checked off yet another to-do item on her dwindling list of things to be done. Mitch had been taking care of the outside of the house all day. She'd barely laid eyes on him since breakfast when he'd given her another cooking lesson. This one on Grandma Mable's famous made-from-scratch biscuits.

She glanced around the large, open front room of the B&B. In less than a month's time, it had transformed from dusty and shabby to a warm and welcoming home. She'd left a lot of things the same but she'd added her own flair to the place. Her bachelor's degree in interior design had to be good for something now that she'd lost her dream job.

Gah, she'd been such an idiot to think Bradley Foster had seen something in her that the other newbie designers didn't have. Yeah, he'd seen something, all right, but it hadn't been talent. That should have been clear as his excuses to have her come over had increased. His advances had become more blatant every time she went. Why had she been a fool to keep going to his place alone? Why hadn't she listened to her gut before things had gotten so out of hand?

A chill ran up her spine. Bradley had been harder to push off that last night. There'd been an arrogance about the way he'd leaned over her, touching her even after she'd told him she wasn't comfortable.

Sexual harassment, for sure. Would it have turned into more? She didn't know.

"Who do you think you are? You're nobody," he'd gritted out as he'd pawed her like a cat on its scratching post. "You don't deserve to be here. The only reason you're here is because I wanted it. Working for someone like me will look good on your résumé. You owe me for pulling you ahead."

"Stop." She'd tried to yank her wrist out of his grasp as his other hand crept higher on her thigh. "Bradley, stop!" she said a little more forcefully.

Did I say it forcefully enough?

Then she'd heard the downstairs door slam. He'd pulled back just for a moment, and she'd swung away from him. But not before shoving a knee between his legs—hard.

His shriek had been loud and high-pitched—unworthy of his action hero persona on-screen.

"You're right. I don't deserve this job. I deserve better." She'd marched past the cleaning crew, trembling and praying to God he didn't chase after her. Then she'd taken a cab straight to the police station to file a report. She doubted it'd done any good though. There were no witnesses, and a hand up her skirt was as far as Bradley had gotten. When she'd gone to work the next day, her boss had summoned her to his office. Bradley had called to complain. He'd said that Kaitlyn had made an inappropriate and unwanted advance toward him. She'd also assaulted him with her knee to his groin, and he was threatening to press charges.

Kaitlyn had tried to explain what had happened. *She* was the victim, not Bradley Foster. But her longtime boss had fired her anyway. Her career with one of the leading design firms in New York was over.

Kaitlyn blinked, realizing her eyes were stinging. A tear slipped down her cheek. *Crap*.

Then the front door opened, and Mitch stepped inside.

She could feel his gaze assessing her as she quickly wiped the tear away. "Hey. I was just, um, cleaning. All the dust in here seems to be stirring up my allergies." She kept her gaze hidden, hoping he'd buy her excuse even though the house was spotless these days.

He nodded. "I thought I'd get to work fixing the front door. It's still catching a little bit."

"Um-hmm." She pulled her sketchbook to her and pretended to make herself busy, though the page was blank and her pencil lead broken. She'd never been good at lying, and even if she were, she doubted she could pull anything over on Mitch.

He graciously pulled his gaze from her and looked around the room. "Looks like you found more of Mable's Christmas decorations."

Kaitlyn looked up and watched him assess what she'd done. "Hopefully there's not a rule about waiting until after Thanksgiving here."

"Not according to Mable. She was as bad as the stores, playing 'Jingle Bells' before Halloween."

Kaitlyn smiled at this. Thanksgiving was next Thursday so she wasn't quite that bad. And she'd never had a house and several boxes' worth of decorations to put out. This was new, and it challenged the interior designer in her.

"You've been busy."

"So have you. We've barely stopped working over the last few weeks, and it's paid off, I'd say. The magazine will be floating around the country anytime now. Then I expect the phone to start ringing off the hook." She looked over at the old-fashioned phone on the table by the wall. It was silent just as it had been all day. No matter if the December issue of *Loving Life* wasn't out yet, the B&B was in the phone listings. People could happen upon it and book reservations anytime.

Mitch was watching her again. She probably looked a mess. "You know what? This place is ready," he said.

She shook her head. "No. There are still a few things left to do."

"Maybe, but everyone deserves a break." He stepped closer. "You haven't explored the town since you've been here. When the guests arrive, how are you supposed to direct them where to shop or eat?"

"I've been to Sweetwater Springs before," she said.

"Not recently. Go get dressed. I'm taking you out."

"You don't have to. I'm sure that's not how you want to spend your afternoon."

"And you'd be right about that. I hate sightseeing almost as much as I hate shopping."

She cocked her head to one side. "Then why are you offering to take me out to do just that?"

"Because I know you'll love it."

* * *

What am I doing? All Mitch knew was he'd walked into the B&B and Kaitlyn had been in tears. She'd been working too hard. Blue circles underscored her brown eyes, telling him she wasn't sleeping. How could she when she'd spent the last couple of weeks cleaning and decorating so that she could revive this old inn in such a short time? He could suffer through a couple hours of exploring downtown if it'd help her relax.

She didn't move an inch.

"Might want to wear a heavy coat," he advised. "Once the sun goes down, it's freezing in the valley this time of year. I have spare clothes in the truck. I'll clean up and change in one of the guest bathrooms." He wasn't taking no for an answer.

"Mitch, really, I'm fine. You agreed to help me fix up this place, nothing else."

He walked over and sat down on the edge of the couch. He'd been working outdoors all day and didn't want to dirty anything up. "Okay. Have it your way. It was a bad idea. I was kind of looking forward to the homemade fudge though."

She turned to look at him.

This was going to be easy. He almost felt guilty about manipulating her. "Triple chocolate. Dawanda makes it better than anyone I know. I used to crave it on deployments, where the most you could hope for was a MoonPie from someone's care package."

"That's a shame."

"Dawanda's Fudge Shop is one of my favorite stores downtown. It's right next to a little gift shop my mom enjoys going into. You know, the kind where you're afraid to move because you might break something?" He looked at Kaitlyn, whose big brown eyes were narrowed.

"Do you really think I'm that easy?" she asked.

He shifted his gaze. "I'm not sure what you're talking about."

"You *do* think I'm that easy," she said, surprise lifting her voice. She let out a small laugh. "You actually think the mention of chocolate and knickknacks is going to make me race down the hall to get dressed and go out with you." She chuckled harder.

Well, this was one way to make her feel better. Apparently, he'd made a fool of himself, and she thought it was hilarious. Watching her catch her breath, he decided he'd be a fool for her any day of the week.

She looked at him seriously. "Thank you," she finally said. "I needed that. You know, you're pretty adorable when you try to do something sweet."

The *s* word made him twitch a little bit. "I'm not sweet."

"It's okay. I won't tell anyone." She grinned and punched a soft fist into his shoulder. "It'll only take me a few minutes to get changed. You can put on fresh clothes in the Elizabeth Bennet and Darcy room."

"Thought you just called me out on my BS."

She nodded. "I did. And to pay you back, I'm going to enjoy watching you suffer as we go into every single store downtown."

* * *

After getting cleaned up, Mitch drove Kaitlyn to the town square. They parked and strolled along a strip of shops that hugged Silver Lake. He'd been right about the weather. The windchill was already in the upper twenties, even with the sun at their backs. Since she hadn't heeded his warning about a heavy coat, he leaned in and wrapped his arm around her as they made their way along the boardwalk.

"For warmth," he said, hoping to convince himself as well.

"I never would have guessed you were so sweet."

"Not sweet, just trying to help."

She laughed. "Does the word *funny* offend you too? Because I also find you pretty funny. Why do you hide it under a serious, macho shell?"

"I'm a marine," he told her as if that were any justification.

"Were a marine," she corrected. "Or is it 'once a marine, always a marine'?"

He considered his answer. He'd enjoyed being a military police officer, but he'd always known he wasn't a lifer. He'd only joined because he'd needed to leave town and wanted to help his mom financially. Now that he had job experience and highly sought-after skills, he could continue to help her as a civilian. "I guess I'll always have a little marine in me. And a little cop." He tugged her over to keep her from stepping on a broken piece of sidewalk.

She looked up and started to say something.

"Don't call me any of those cutesy words," he warned, only half joking, "or no fudge for you."

"Grouch," she teased.

"That's better."

* * *

The air was a mixture of the surrounding evergreens and Mitch. Two of Kaitlyn's new favorite scents.

"Fudge first, right?" he asked, his arm still draped around her.

"I'm curious about the best fudge I've never tasted. You know New York boasts just about the best of everything. You can't walk a full block without seeing a sign promoting something that's either the best in the world or at least world famous."

"I've never been to New York," he confessed.

She was surprised. "Everyone's been to the Big Apple."

"I've pretty much been everywhere else in the world though. And I can say with all confidence that Dawanda's fudge puts everyone else's to shame." He stopped walking in front of a glass storefront. "Forewarning," he said before pulling the door open, "Dawanda also likes to do complimentary cappuccino readings."

Kaitlyn lifted her face so she could get a good look at him. Was he kidding? "I've never heard of cappuccino readings before."

He laughed—a full-on, sincere chuckle. "Well, there's one thing Sweetwater Springs has over New York. Maybe you can send some of your guests in Dawanda's direction once they start arriving."

The way he said *your guests*, referring to the B&B's customers, didn't go unnoticed. She and Mitch were just having a good time this evening and nothing more.

They walked into the fudge shop and were greeted by a woman in her mid to late fifties with short red hair that formed tousled waves atop her head. She had lipstick color to match. Bright-blue eyes complemented her fair skin and vibrant hair and lips.

"Mitch!" the woman squealed, clapping her hands in front of her. "You're home!" She came running around the counter, a tiny fireball shooting toward them.

"Just for a little while," he said.

The sprite of a woman gave him a huge hug. "That's what you say, but I told you"—she pulled back and pointed a finger at him—"one of these days you'll come home, and some young thing will steal your heart and make you stay. The cappuccino never lies." The woman, who Kaitlyn guessed was Dawanda, turned and looked at her. "Or maybe you've already found her. Who is this?" Dawanda pulled her hands away from Mitch and offered a hand to Kaitlyn to shake. "I'm Dawanda. You're new in town."

"Yes. Just arrived three weeks ago. I'm Kaitlyn Russo."

Acknowledgment registered in Dawanda's expression. "You're Mable and Henry's granddaughter." The store owner's eyes colored with sadness. "I'm so sorry about your grandmother. Mable spoke of you often. She was so proud of her granddaughter working in the big city. She used to tell me about some of your clients. Big names too!"

Kaitlyn lowered her gaze for just a second, thinking of the biggest name she'd worked with. The one who'd sunk her career.

"Kaitlyn inherited the Russos' bed and breakfast," Mitch told Dawanda.

"Oh, how wonderful. So you'll be fixing it up?" the shop owner asked.

Kaitlyn gestured between herself and Mitch. "Mitch and I both inherited it, actually. We're fixing it up together."

"But I'll be selling my half and heading out as soon as possible," he clarified. "I have a security job lined up in Northern Virginia."

Dawanda's red lips tugged into a frown. "There are security jobs here. I know for a fact that the police department is shorthanded. What's Virginia have that Sweetwater Springs doesn't?"

"Certainly not the best fudge I've ever tasted," he said.

"They certainly don't. *I* have the best fudge." Dawanda winked at Kaitlyn. "Would you like to try some, sweetie?"

"I'd love to."

Kaitlyn and Mitch followed Dawanda to a table along the side of the wall and sat down.

"How about a sampler?" Mitch said.

"A sampler plate coming right up." Dawanda disappeared, leaving them alone.

"Dawanda did one of these cappuccino readings on you?" Kaitlyn asked.

He shook his head and looked down at his clasped hands on the table. If she wasn't mistaken, he looked a little embarrassed. "She did. But I'm not giving you any of the details."

"Oh, come on. Something about a girl stealing your heart away?"

He met her gaze and stole her breath. "I don't believe in fortunes, especially ones that come out of a coffee mug." The corner of his mouth quirked softly.

She giggled in response. "Does she believe in them?"

"Who? Dawanda? Oh, definitely. Don't try to convince her it's just foam. I love Dawanda though. I've been coming to this place since I was a kid. Dad used to bring me here. My mom couldn't much afford to take me out after he died. Dawanda always insisted on giving me a free treat when we came to town though. It meant a lot."

"I'm sure."

"Here you go!" Dawanda set a plate of fudge squares in front of them. "No fighting over them, you two," she said. "And when you're done, you'll have a complimentary cappuccino."

Mitch gave Kaitlyn a look that told her she was in for something she'd never forget, and she couldn't wait. She was enjoying every second of this unexpected outing with Mitch, maybe a little more than she should.

CHAPTER SIX

$\mathcal{M}$itch didn't have that much of a sweet tooth but he was enjoying the hell out of his visit to Dawanda's Fudge Shop, thanks in large part to Kaitlyn.

"I think I have a sugar high," she said, laughing at something he'd said.

"One might think you've been drinking Dawanda's equally famous eggnog."

"Eggnog too? I can't wait to try it."

It was good to see Kaitlyn having a good time. That was the whole point of tonight.

She shook her head as her laughter died down. Then her gaze fell on the last piece of fudge on the plate.

"Dawanda said no fighting, remember?" he reminded her.

"I won't have to fight you." She grinned, and a little spark of mischief lit up her brown eyes. "We'll decide who gets the final piece like two civilized adults."

Honestly, he didn't want that last piece but he was intrigued by whatever plan she had up her sleeve. "Okay." He leaned forward on the table, resting his elbows there. "What do you have in mind?"

"A game of chance." Her gaze flicked to the door, where only a handful of people had come and gone since they'd arrived half an hour earlier. "I say the next customer to walk in will be a woman."

"How old?" he asked.

She tapped her chin thoughtfully. "Late twenties. Your turn. Whoever is closest to the actual truth wins the last piece of fudge."

"Okay. I'll guess that the next customer is a man in his fifties. Graying hair."

She rubbed her hands together in front of her. "No way. The man would probably need to be watching his blood sugar."

"Dawanda makes sugar-free fudge." He liked how playful Kaitlyn had become now that she was away from her long to-do list. She seemed relaxed and carefree. And for a moment, he forgot that he was neither of those things as long as he was in Sweetwater Springs.

They both turned to look at the door but no customers walked through. Kaitlyn drummed her fingers on the table and looked at the plate of fudge again. Mitch was just about to surrender it to her when Dawanda buzzed over.

"Okay, you two. Cappuccino time!" She placed a tray with two cups of coffee and a metal pitcher of steaming milk in front of them and then grabbed a chair from a neighboring table and pulled it up to sit beside Kaitlyn. "All right, sweetheart. I'm sure Mitch here has told you about my special skill."

Kaitlyn met Mitch's gaze. "A little bit."

"So you're going to let me read your drink, yes?"

"Umm..." Kaitlyn hedged.

"Ah, come on. Don't be a chicken." Mitch gestured to the mug. "It's all in fun."

Dawanda jerked her head up. "No, it's not. It's serious. I know you don't believe me but you will. One day." She moved her gaze back to Kaitlyn. "So, is the answer yes?"

Lifting a shoulder, Kaitlyn nodded. "Okay, I guess."

"Good." Dawanda set one cup of coffee in front of Kaitlyn and turned the handle until it pointed in Kaitlyn's direction. "We need to make sure the cup knows who it's reading." Then she reached for the pitcher of shiny, white milk and ceremoniously held it up to the mug. "The cappuccino never lies," she said solemnly as she poured directly into the middle of the beverage, making a creamy froth at the top.

Dawanda didn't blink. She kept her blue eyes pinned to the design that formed inside the drink.

When Dawanda had read his cappuccino a couple of years back, she'd predicted he'd fall for someone here in Sweetwater Springs. If that happened, he'd be tempted to stay, and no part of him wanted to do that. But it was all in fun.

"Hmm," Dawanda hummed, leaning over Kaitlyn's mug. Her face was only a few inches from the drink. Not very appetizing.

"What is it?" Kaitlyn asked, looking worried. If Mitch didn't know better, he'd think she actually believed in this unheard-of form of fortune-telling.

"Well, this is very interesting." Dawanda looked up. "It appears that you will be entering into a long-lasting partnership that will change your life. See the door?"

Kaitlyn squinted at the frothy topping in her drink and shook her head. "Not really."

"Right there." Dawanda pointed. "The door is fully open.

That represents a partnership or relationship." Dawanda frowned into the mug. "Well, this is very unusual."

"What?" Kaitlyn leaned forward.

Dawanda lifted her gaze to meet Kaitlyn's. "I can usually read what type of relationship a person is entering into but yours is unclear. I'm not sure if it's a friendship, business arrangement, or maybe something romantic. Could be you'll fall in love in Sweetwater Springs too. Whatever the relationship, it's a good thing for you. I don't see any bad signs here. Embrace the relationship when it comes." A wide lipstick grin spread through Dawanda's high cheekbones.

A timer beeped in the kitchen. Dawanda pushed back from the table and stood. "That's my cue. I have fudge cooking." She lifted a second cup of coffee off the tray, added the milk, and then pushed it in front of Mitch. "Enjoy your drinks and holler if you need anything!" she called as she scuttled away carrying the tray and pitcher of milk with her.

Kaitlyn furrowed her brow as she stared down into her cup of cappuccino. "How in the world did she read anything from this? All I see is coffee and foam."

Mitch chuckled. "Who knows?"

The door to the store dinged behind him.

"Customers," Kaitlyn said, her eyes lighting up.

Mitch hoped for her sake that the description matched what she had guessed. He'd hand over the final piece of fudge to her regardless. Turning, he inspected a blond woman in her late twenties holding the door open as a tan-skinned man entered the shop. Mitch's stomach turned, twisted, and then flopped like a dead fish in his belly. Brian Everson was the last person he wanted to meet here tonight. And the last person he wanted to see him.

Mitch ducked his head, feeling caged in the store suddenly.

"Looks like I win!" Kaitlyn cheered.

He pushed the plate toward her. "All yours. Now let's get out of here."

* * *

The sun had crept down below the mountains, and in turn, the temperature had dropped even further while Kaitlyn was in the knickknack store with Mitch. They'd stepped into the pottery shop after that, and Kaitlyn had found a beautiful piece as a Christmas present for her mom. Not that her parents were likely to be around for the holidays.

Kaitlyn hugged her arms around her body as they retraced their path back to Mitch's truck. He hadn't offered to put his arm around her for warmth this time. He'd been noticeably distant ever since they'd left Dawanda's Fudge Shop, making her wonder if it had anything to do with the cappuccino reading. It wasn't as if Dawanda had said Kaitlyn would enter into a long-lasting relationship of any type with him.

"Thanks for tonight. You were right. This was just what I needed," she said, trying to get Mitch to snap out of his sudden funk.

"I'm glad you had a good time."

"I did." She looked over at Silver Lake and stopped in her tracks. The moon was full tonight and reflected perfectly in the pool of water. "It's so beautiful," she said, her words making white puffs in front of her. Then she looked up at the sky and the twinkling blanket of stars just like Josie had described in her article. This was a different world from her life in the city, where looking up she only saw lights from the neighboring apartment buildings.

"Uh-oh. Looks like you're falling in love."

She shifted her gaze to him, and her heart caught in her throat at another wonderful sight, this one of a beautifully rugged man whom she was starting to like entirely too much. "Excuse me?"

"With Sweetwater Springs," he clarified.

"Oh." Her gaze swept to her feet and back out to Silver Lake. "Maybe I am. There's a lot to love about this place." She looked up at him again. Big mistake. Either she'd taken a step closer or he had. They were standing only a foot apart now. She held her breath. Then he reached up and swept a lock of her hair from her cheek. The tip of his finger caressed her skin as it slid past, sending shivers through her body. And for a moment, she thought he was going to kiss her.

Do I want him to kiss me?

She wasn't looking for anything romantic but if ever there was the perfect moment to share a kiss, it was this one, with the starry sky and illuminating moon, standing by a lake and staring into Mitch's dusky eyes. *Oh, goodness*, she wanted to feel his lips on hers. Needed it almost as much as her next shallow breath.

Did he want to kiss her too?

Without thinking, she flicked her gaze to his mouth. Nothing subtle about that. She might as well have whispered, "*Kiss me. Kiss me now.*"

Hearing her loud and clear, he dipped his head toward her and pressed his mouth to hers. She braced a hand over his muscled chest as she went up on tiptoes and parted her lips, allowing his tongue to sweep inside her mouth. Just like with everything else, he was good at kissing. Very good.

What am I doing? The question was short-circuited by the pure pleasure firing through her. Didn't matter. She'd worry about the repercussions of kissing Mitch later. It'd been a long time since she'd been kissed. And she'd never been kissed quite like this. The feel of his beard tickled her cheek and aroused her from head to toe.

His hand curled behind her neck, a welcome anchor because otherwise she might have just floated up and away into the starry night sky. Maybe she was already floating. That's how she felt. Light and free.

After a long moment, he pulled back. "I'll, uh, take you home."

She looked into his eyes, hoping to read what that kiss had meant. It was so good that it had to mean something. In answer, she saw a coolness in his gaze. Then he turned and started walking again as if nothing special had happened at all.

* * *

Mitch was well practiced in self-control. Or so he thought but Kaitlyn's lips had offered an escape he couldn't resist. After seeing Brian in the fudge shop, he'd needed an escape more than he needed air to breathe. Taking Kaitlyn into his arms had felt as natural as anything he'd ever done.

But kissing her was wrong. He had too many regrets in this town and didn't want to add her to the list. Parking in front of the B&B, he glanced over. There was a look in her eyes. Hope that he might kiss her again? Worry that he would do just that?

He cleared his throat and looked away because the temptation to lean in and taste her once more was too strong. She'd tasted like cappuccino and chocolate. Like heaven in his mind. "I'll, uh, see you in the morning."

"Yeah. Okay." She reached for the door handle.

"Hold on. Let me get that for you." He wasn't necessarily a Southern gentleman but he wasn't a brute either. If you kissed a woman, the least you could do was open the truck door for her.

He ran around and pulled the passenger door open.

"Thanks," she said, stepping down onto the driveway's pavement.

The movement brought her close to him—too close. He could smell her, could practically taste the sweetness of her lips again. His mouth watered in response.

Get it together, Mitch.

He took a step back, feeling awkward and restless and completely out of his element. Kaitlyn's eyes still offered that same escape. Tempting as it was, he needed to bolt. Right about now he was counting his lucky stars she hadn't allowed him a room at the B&B while he stayed in town. Because going inside with her would break his steel willpower. He had no doubt about that. There were limits to the kind of temptations a man could resist, and he was walking the edge of that limit.

"Good night," he said, turning away before his body betrayed him. He climbed into his truck and scolded himself all the way to his mom's house.

"Hey," his mom said, looking up from her recliner when he let himself in.

"What are you doing awake?" She was normally early to bed and started working as soon as her feet hit the floor, usually before the sun came up.

"Can't sleep."

"Not tired?" he asked, unable to imagine how she wouldn't be. He set his keys on the coffee table and took a seat on the couch across from her. There was a book in her lap, he noted. The woman couldn't be idle for a second.

"Oh, I'm tired, all right, but my body doesn't seem to have gotten the message."

Mitch frowned. "When was the last time you had a checkup?"

She shook her head. "I've already told you: I'm not sick. Maybe I should get some vitamins or something."

Mitch leaned forward and propped his elbows on his knees. "What's the worst that could happen if you see a doctor? Huh?"

She looked at him and swallowed. "Oh, I don't know. He could tell me I'm dying." She laughed weakly but neither of them really found it funny. That's what had happened to Mitch's dad. He'd had a lingering cough. Just a cold that wouldn't go away. Everything had been fine until his dad had gone to the doctor and was told otherwise. Then nothing was ever fine again. His dad was diagnosed with stage-four lung cancer and had died six months later.

"That won't happen," Mitch said, reaching out a hand to place on her knee. He squeezed gently. "You need to make sure everything is okay, Mom. Please. For me."

She blew out a breath, patted his hand, and then finally nodded, much to his relief. "Fine, fine. I'll call and make an appointment tomorrow if it'll make you happy."

"It will." He leaned back. "And seeing you get to bed will make me happy too. Just lie in bed and close your eyes. Isn't that what you used to tell me? Fake it until you make it? It always worked when I couldn't sleep."

They both stood.

"What did I do to deserve a son like you?" she asked. She meant it in a good way, he knew, but he'd often asked himself the same question. His mom had endured so much heartache in her life, and some of it had been his doing.

* * *

"You did what?" Josie gasped on the other end of the line.

Since Mitch had dropped her off, Kaitlyn had turned on one of her favorite romantic movies and was halfway through a tall glass of white wine. She was now feeling the buzz tangled with a bunch of unruly hormones and a large dose of confusion. "I kissed him. It was a mistake." Saying so didn't seem right though. Kissing Mitch had felt amazing.

"*Okayyyyy,*" Josie said.

Kaitlyn could imagine her friend sitting behind her desk working, even though it was past ten p.m. Josie was always working on her next article or interview or big idea.

"Are you going to kiss him again?" Josie asked.

Kaitlyn sipped more of her wine. "Of course not. We work together, and then he's leaving after Christmas."

"Well, I don't recommend kissing people you work with but kissing men who are leaving is perfect. It takes the pressure off."

"Perfect for you maybe," Kaitlyn said, swirling her wine around the glass in little circles. "I kind of like the idea of getting attached to a man one day."

"Someday, but not right now. Right now, you're building your business. There's no time for anything else. But, just for kicks and giggles, was he a good kisser?" Josie asked.

Kaitlyn rested her head back against the couch cushion, staring at the muted television screen. "The best. He has a beard that's soft and rough. I've never kissed a man with a beard before."

Josie sighed. "Bearded kisses are the best. Did his hands roam while you were kissing? Or did they stay put?"

Kaitlyn thought back. "One of his hands started at the

back of my neck and slid around to my cheek." A shiver ran through her at the memory, and she could almost feel that calloused finger brushing over her skin again.

"I wrote an article on kissing once. When I interned at *Teen Vibe* magazine in college. I think we labeled that the sweet kiss."

Yeah, it was definitely sweet. And sexy too.

"The sweet kiss is a prelude to the let's-get-it-on kiss. Make sure you're wearing your best lingerie next time you plan on kissing him."

Kaitlyn choked on her sip of wine. She didn't plan on kissing Mitch again but the thought of experiencing a let's-get-it-on kiss did things to her.

"So, back to business," Josie said. "Has the phone started ringing yet?"

"Not yet. But the December issue just went out, right?"

"Right. Like I mentioned before, we start circulating a couple weeks ahead of each new month so it should hit mailboxes in the next couple of days. Let me know when people start booking."

"I will. Thank you again. I wouldn't be doing this without your help."

"That's what friends are for. But listen, I need to go. If I don't get this article for the January issue drafted, I might not see my bed tonight."

"You're a machine," Kaitlyn said with a yawn. Bed sounded nice, if she could convince her legs to walk her there. "Good night." She disconnected the call and placed her cell phone on the couch at her side. Then she grabbed the remote and turned the TV off. Standing, she felt her head go fuzzy. Perhaps she'd had a tad too much wine.

She headed toward the hallway and then stopped short when the doorbell rang. She froze for a long moment. Who visited this late? And she didn't know anyone in town except for Mitch, who usually just snuck up on her.

It rang again.

Well, this was a functioning bed and breakfast. She'd updated the website just this morning. Maybe someone had found it online and needed a room. She set her glass of wine down and walked to the door. On an inhale, she pulled it open and offered up a smile.

To a tall, dark-haired man in a leather jacket, tight jeans, and biker boots.

Her heart may have stopped in that moment. He looked like he belonged on a Harley driving down an open highway. And if she had to guess, there was probably a motorcycle in the driveway that wrapped behind the house. She hadn't heard it rumble in but she'd been distracted by her phone call with Josie. "Hi. Um, can I help you?"

"Yeah. I know it's late but I need a room." His voice was deep and smooth. He had pale blue eyes that seemed to pop against his all-black clothing.

A little fear and excitement sliced through her, which was silly. Bikers weren't dangerous or aggressive. But famous movie stars like Bradley Foster weren't supposed to be aggressive either.

"This is a B and B, right?" he asked, when she didn't respond immediately.

"R-right. Yes. Come in." She gestured for him to step through the front door, despite the sudden anxiety prickling inside her.

"So, do you have a room available for me?"

He stepped over the threshold, and she willed herself not to take a step backward. This would be fine. Everything would be fine.

"Of course we do. Like you said, we're a B and B after

all." Only there was no *we*. Mitch was gone for the night. It was just her. "You can stay in the, um, *Dirty Dancing* room."

The biker lifted a pierced brow.

Heat scorched her skin. "That came out wrong." She laughed nervously. "All of the rooms are named after a romantic couple. The *Dirty Dancing* room is named after Baby and Johnny."

And this man oozed Johnny. He was gorgeous and had "bad boy" written all over him but he didn't stir the same kind of rumblings in her belly that Mitch did.

"Cool," he said, and then offered his hand. "My name is Paris." Before she could respond, he nodded. "I know. Not a name fitting for a guy who rides a bike. My folks were romantics. They honeymooned in Paris, and then I came along nine months later."

She smiled, relaxing just a notch. "I love that. I'm Kaitlyn Russo." She offered her hand. "Welcome to the Sweetwater Bed and Breakfast. If you don't mind, can I wait to give you a full tour of the place until morning? It's a little late." And the thought of roaming through the house alone with a sexy biker was a little intimidating after what she'd been through.

"That's fine." Paris pulled a wallet out of his back pocket.

She'd played around with the credit card swipe machine the other day to make sure she was ready. She took his card, walked it over to the machine, and swiped it. After a moment, the information went through without a problem.

Handing it back to him, she said, "Okay, Paris. Let me show you to your room."

She walked with him upstairs to the room at the end of the long hall. She adored the *Dirty Dancing* room. It was simple and reminded her of a hot summer day. The curtains were sheer like Baby's dress in the final scene of the movie. Every time Kaitlyn stepped inside, she heard the beat of that final song play in her head and thought of Baby running across the dance floor and Johnny catching her as she dove like a bird in the air.

Paris set his lone bag down on the floor. "This is great. Thanks."

She nodded and stepped back. No matter how nice he seemed to be, he was a stranger, and she was still unnerved by her recent past. "Um, what time would you like breakfast?"

He shrugged. "Seven or eight, I guess."

"Either of those times will be fine. The dining room is downstairs. It'll be a home-style breakfast, where you serve yourself."

"Sounds good."

She exited the room and headed downstairs. The buzz of the wine was gone now, replaced with a bubbling *uh-oh-what-do-I-do* nervousness coursing through her. When she got to the landing of the stairs, she cast a glance back up to where she'd just left Paris. She'd imagined couples coming to the B&B, two people absorbed in their own love for the other. She was fully prepared for that. She'd never considered that single, gorgeous biker dudes would show up or that she'd be in a house all alone with them. Which would've been completely fine a few months ago. But after her last episode with Bradley . . .

Not fine. Not fine at all.

She retrieved her cell phone from the couch, sucked in a breath, and dialed. She didn't know what else to do or who else to call.

"Hey." Mitch's deep voice calmed her as soon as she heard it. "Something wrong?" he asked.

"No. Yes. I was wondering if you could do me a favor."

"Sure. What is it?"

Gah. This was more than a little embarrassing to ask. "Can you stay with me tonight?"

CHAPTER SEVEN

After the kiss, Mitch had decided to steer clear of Kaitlyn. They'd gotten too close for comfort tonight, and that wasn't part of the deal. He'd heard the shaky quality of her voice when she'd called just now though. She hadn't sounded like a woman inviting him back for a nightcap. Instead, she'd sounded upset.

He pulled his truck around the back of the house and parked beside an unfamiliar motorcycle. A guest? As he climbed the porch steps, Kaitlyn opened the door.

"Thanks for coming," she said, looking sheepish. "Come on in."

He stepped past her with his overnight bag and watched her lock the door behind him. "Whose bike is that outside?" he asked.

"That's why I called. We have our first guest," she said, offering a wobbly smile.

"Is that the reason you asked me to spend the night with you?"

Her cheeks flushed. "Well, spend the night at the inn. Not...with me." She looked away. "I guess having someone arrive tonight took me off guard. I might need your help cooking breakfast in the morning."

"I usually get here early enough to cook breakfast with you," he said.

"I know." She pulled her lower lip between her teeth. "I'm sorry to pull you away from your mom."

"Don't worry about that. She can take care of herself." Or so she kept telling him. At least she'd agreed to call and make a doctor's appointment tomorrow. "I don't mind staying tonight if it'll make you feel more comfortable. It's not a problem."

Kaitlyn nodded quietly. "Thanks. I was just having a glass of wine before our guest arrived. Want one? Or a beer."

"A beer would be great." He followed her to the kitchen and sat on one of the barstools at the center island, watching as she bent into the refrigerator to retrieve the beer. His eyes unintentionally fixated on her curves from behind. Soft and inviting.

That kiss they'd shared earlier tonight kept playing on a continuous loop in his mind. He'd been nowhere near sleep when she'd called.

Kaitlyn closed the refrigerator, retrieved a glass from the cabinet, and carried the items back.

"You were drinking alone before the new guest arrived?" he asked. "Nightcap or is something bothering you?"

She pushed his can across the counter and poured herself a deep glass of wine. "A little of both, I guess." Her gaze hung on his. Something dark passed across it. He'd gotten good at recognizing the darkness. "If it had been a couple or a single woman, would you have asked me to come over tonight?" he asked.

Averting her gaze, she shook her head. "Probably not."

"There's nothing wrong with a woman not wanting to stay alone in a house with a man she doesn't know. Except now you're sleeping under a roof with two men you don't know."

She looked back up at him. "I know you."

He liked that he'd won her trust. "There's another reason you wanted me to come tonight. You don't have to tell me what it is if you don't want to. I just wanted you to know I understand what it's like to run from things." He reached for his beer and took a drink. "Sometimes it helps to talk to someone." Not that he'd ever talked about the accident that had paralyzed Brian Everson.

"There's not some big secret in my past, if that's what you're thinking."

"But there is something eating away at you. I get that you're excited about inheriting the bed and breakfast but a person doesn't just drop their entire life and move if they're happy where they are. I assume you had a home, friends, a job."

He could almost see her considering whether she was going to open up to him. Fidgeting with her hands around her wineglass, she lifted a shoulder. "Growing up, I used to redecorate my bedroom every couple of months. I've always loved making places feel happy. Or energetic. Sad. It's always kind of fascinated me that you can walk into a room and have your entire mood change." The corner of her mouth twitched in not quite a smile. "So, when I went to college, I knew exactly what I wanted to study. And I always knew exactly which design firm I wanted to work for. Beautiful Designs is the most well-known interior design firm in New York City. They work with some of the richest and most famous in the area. My friend Josie had done an article on the firm's owner. She pulled some strings and got me an interview with him. That's how I found myself working with Bradley Foster."

Mitch blinked. "Bradley Foster, the movie star?"

"That's the one." She looked away as she continued. "I thought Bradley saw something special in me after he looked at my portfolio. Talent. He said he loved my designs. It was a dream come true. Then he started needing me to stay late at his vacation house. I was flattered, I guess, because he turned down the other more experienced designers. He said he only wanted me."

Mitch was already jumping ahead of her story, putting the pieces together, and feeling an angry blaze erupt in his belly on her behalf. "Did he hurt you?" he asked, the muscles tightening uncomfortably in his jaw.

She lifted her gaze to meet his. "No. He was more aggressive the last time I worked with him though. He wouldn't take no for an answer. If not for the interruption of his cleaning crew, I'm not sure he would've stopped. I tried to tell my boss at the design firm the next day but Bradley had already called to complain about my inappropriate behavior. He also threatened to press charges against me for assault."

Mitch lifted a brow questioningly.

"My knee might have bumped him in a sensitive area before I ran out." Her cheeks flushed a deep rose color. "My boss didn't want to believe me, probably because Bradley Foster is one of the business's biggest clients. I was fired, and now my reputation is ruined. Once you've worked for the best, there's only one way to go in New York, and that's down." She reached for her glass and took a sip. "My firm also won't give me glowing references for any other jobs. I'm sunk."

"That's despicable," Mitch ground out.

She released a sincere laugh. "Yeah. I can drink to that."

"Want me to beat Bradley Foster up?"

Kaitlyn eyed him curiously. "Something tells me that's not an empty offer."

"I don't make empty offers." And part of him wanted to get in his truck and drive to New York regardless of what she wanted from him. A guy like Bradley Foster needed to be taught a lesson before he found himself alone with another woman who wouldn't be as lucky as Kaitlyn.

"No. And I wasn't running when I came here. I could've stayed in New York and searched for another job. Or got in the unemployment line. Truthfully, I haven't felt inspired by my work in a long time. For Bradley, I designed a living room and a kitchen. I'd picked the colors and the theme based on his personality, which I got to know a little too well. Before that," she said, frowning, "I'd worked on restrooms and boring boardrooms, where I had zero creative liberty. When I found out that I had inherited this place, it felt like fate. Like at the exact right time, my grandmother had opened an amazing opportunity that I couldn't say no to." She shrugged. "I guess I'll have to get comfortable with having attractive single men staying here with me."

He thought she was talking about him until she gestured upstairs.

"I mean, he's probably a nice guy," she added.

Mitch blinked. She was talking about the new houseguest. Mitch hadn't laid eyes on the guy yet, but apparently he was alone, attractive, and probably a nice guy. That sounded like bad news to Mitch. "I'll stay as long as you need me to," he said, feeling equal parts protective and suddenly jealous.

"Thank you. That means a lot. And you're right. It does help to talk to someone. If you ever need me to return the favor..."

He swallowed and looked down at the beer in his hands. Not a chance. Some burdens weren't meant to be shared.

* * *

Kaitlyn stared at the ceiling in her bedroom. Mitch had the *Beauty and the Beast* room right above her—fitting because he had that beastly, untamed quality about him, and she was itching to run her fingers through his mane.

She squirmed under the heavy quilt on her bed. Her room was the only one in the house that had yet to be named. She guessed that was all right since it wasn't for guests. She didn't need a themed room.

Blinking, she tried to make sense of the shadows along the wall. She'd spent so little time in here that she didn't have the floor plan memorized yet. When she'd been a child, she'd been terrified of the shadows. Now the main thing that scared her was failing.

Okay, the thought of coming face-to-face with Bradley Foster again was a little scary too. She didn't care if she ever saw another of his movies again.

Sitting up in bed, she decided to get a glass of water to quench her post-wine thirst. She slid her feet into a pair of slippers. *Gah.* She was going to town tomorrow to buy something a little more attractive and less old lady–like than flannel pajamas and slippers. And it had absolutely nothing to do with either of the men currently sleeping upstairs.

Doing her best to be quiet, she shuffled across the kitchen floor and swung open a cabinet. Then she grabbed a glass and carried it to the sink.

A soft knock on the wall behind her made her whirl around.

"Hey." Paris was standing at the edge of the kitchen in a black T-shirt and holey pair of jeans. "I didn't mean to scare you."

She appreciated the knock. Mitch usually just appeared out of nowhere, like Casper the sexy ghost. "You didn't. Do you need something?" she asked.

"I thought I'd see if I could get something to drink."

She pulled a hand to her chest. "I'm so sorry. I should've left a glass in your room with bottled water and complimentary beverages. I'm a little new to this B and B host role."

"It's no problem." His smile was slow and easy.

"Have a seat. I'll get you a drink." She grabbed a second glass from the cabinet and then turned to look over her shoulder at her guest. Muscles popped from his fitted undershirt. "Water okay?"

"That's fine. Anything to wet my palate...That sounded strangely inappropriate, didn't it?"

Kaitlyn laughed nervously as she filled the glasses. "Well, *now* it does." She slid his in front of him.

"Thanks." He took the water and drank.

She did too, keeping one cautious eye on him. "So, Paris, what do you do for a living?" she asked, taking the stool across from him.

"Graphic design. I'm self-employed," he said.

Her eyes widened. "Really? That's awesome."

"Yeah, I'm not really one for rules and dress codes. Plus, I can pretty much work from anywhere."

"Will you be working while you're staying here?" she asked.

He nodded. "I have a few projects that need finishing."

"Well, we offer free Wi-Fi. The code is in your welcome

packet upstairs. I'll try to place any other guests who arrive at the other end of the hall so they don't disturb you. If you're planning on staying, that is."

He set his glass on the counter in front of him. "Thought I'd stay through next week if that's all right."

"Of course."

They talked for a few minutes more, and then Paris waved good night and headed back to his room.

That wasn't so bad, Kaitlyn thought. She'd enjoyed talking with Paris and he seemed like a nice enough guy. Tomorrow, she'd tell Mitch he didn't need to stay another night on her account. Not unless he wanted to, which of course, he wouldn't.

* * *

The room Kaitlyn had given him was fitting because Mitch felt like a beast right now. He didn't like this wild, crazy feeling consuming him. First, he hadn't been able to sleep after what Kaitlyn told him about her former client. Mitch wanted to meet that creep in a dark alley, give him an old-fashioned shakedown, and leave him in one of the dumpsters where he belonged. Second, he'd walked up on Kaitlyn and the new guest in the kitchen. They hadn't noticed him, of course, because they were too busy laughing like old friends. And maybe they'd been flirting a little bit too, which left Mitch unnerved. Not that he had any claim to Kaitlyn. One kiss didn't mark her as his. One kiss that never should've happened in the first place. Except now it kept repeating itself in his mind. That was the third reason for his insomnia.

He lay back on the king-size bed in his room. He wouldn't be able to go to sleep until he heard the stairs

creak and knew that Mr. Muscle Head was back in his room.
Alone.

Mitch blew out a heavy breath. If Kaitlyn wanted to join
Muscle Head in his room, she could. She was a grown
woman. She'd asked for Mitch's protection tonight though,
and he didn't like the idea of another strange man's hands on
her body. Or his mouth on her sweet-tasting lips.

The top landing creaked.

Mitch's ears pricked. There was just one set of footsteps
heading down to the opposite end of the hall. Muscle Head
was alone, and Kaitlyn was still safe and sound, and presum-
ably tucked into her bed alone downstairs.

Mitch massaged a hand over his face because now he
was thinking of her alone in her bed. Thinking of all the
things he wouldn't mind doing to her in that bed. Stripping
off those flannel pajamas that were unreasonably sexy.
Touching her soft skin. Giving her another kiss, or two or
three.

He cursed under his breath. This just might be one of the
longest nights of his life.

* * *

Mitch awoke with a start and looked at the clock on his
nightstand. Eight a.m. He'd slept in for the first time in ages.
He lay in bed and let last night come streaming back. He was
at the Sweetwater B&B. Kaitlyn was downstairs, and there
was a guest here that she found hot.

That got him out of bed. He flung his legs over the side
and started reaching for his clothes. They didn't know anything about this new guest, and the whole point of Kaitlyn
calling him here last night was so she wouldn't have to be
alone with the guy.

There was the sound of kitchen clatter downstairs. Mitch pulled on a shirt and some pants and then jammed his feet into a pair of shoes and headed in that direction.

"Hi." She turned and offered him a bright smile as she cleaned up the dining room table. "Paris has already had breakfast," she said. "And I didn't do so bad with those made-from-scratch biscuits on my own."

"Paris?" Mitch asked.

"That's our guest's name. He went back to his room. I have leftovers if you want some."

"I don't have much of an appetite right now." Not after learning that Kaitlyn and Paris had shared a nice breakfast alone. Probably flirting. Mitch hadn't even met this guy yet, and he hated his guts already.

"Okay." She grabbed several items from the table. "Do you mind helping me get those plates to the dishwasher?"

"Sure." He grabbed the dishes and followed her. He'd never been a jealous man, and he didn't like the feeling. She dipped and placed the dirty dishes in the washer and then reached back and retrieved what he was carrying. "Thanks." She straightened. "Guess the room I put you in was satisfactory?"

"Yeah."

"Good to know. Well, don't feel like you have to stay again tonight. It was silly of me to be afraid yesterday." She looked away. "I don't know what I was thinking."

He did. She was thinking of her would-be attacker. A guy unworthy of his fame and fortune.

"I don't mind," Mitch said. "And I think I will stay another night."

"You don't have to—"

"I said I don't mind." He wanted to make sure Paris (and

what the hell kind of name was that?) kept his hands to himself.

"Great. Then you can help make our new guest feel at home. He said he'll be staying through next week."

"Love to," Mitch lied. Making people feel at home wasn't exactly his forte. He was only doing this because he wanted to protect the woman in front of him, he told himself. But that was partially a lie too.

CHAPTER EIGHT

*K*aitlyn pulled the magazine out of the mailbox on Monday and hugged it against her chest. This was it! Josie had only come up with the idea a short while ago and already it had become real. She pulled the magazine away and started reading the cover as she hurried back toward the B&B.

"Walking and reading is a dangerous sport, you know?" Mitch said, sneaking up on her as always. She only jumped a little this time. She guessed that meant she was getting used to his presence. But her breath froze in her lungs when she looked up. She'd never get used to those hot chocolate eyes or that barely there grin buried under a short, sexy beard.

"It's here," she said, unable to contain her enthusiasm. "The article about Sweetwater Springs."

"Oh yeah?" He stepped closer to read over her shoulder.

"America's Most Romantic Holiday Retreats," he read, his breath tickling her ear.

She swallowed and stepped away from the large, beautiful man who was making her heart beat in triple time.

"I'm going to go inside and have a hot apple cider. Want some?"

He gave her a strange, amused look. "Mable was always forcing that stuff on me during the fall and winter months. Not my cup of tea, you might say."

Kaitlyn climbed the steps, aware that each one put her butt at his eye level. She climbed more quickly. "I found my grandmother's secret recipe tucked away in one of her cooking books the other day. It's actually very simple to make. And once I have a cup in hand, I plan to read this article until I have it memorized. Then we're going to finish fulfilling its promise."

"Oh, we are, are we?"

She glanced over her shoulder. His teasing tone matched the look in his eyes. She was glad he wasn't fighting her on this anymore. He'd done everything she'd asked and more, and they already had one satisfied guest. Paris had ventured out this morning to work at Dawanda's Fudge Shop, per her recommendation. "Yes, we are."

A few minutes later, with her cup of hot apple cider and a notepad in hand, she leaned over the article on the kitchen counter. It was mostly a fluff piece, painting a picturesque town, which wasn't an exaggeration by any measure. Sweetwater Springs did have beautiful rolling mountains and natural hot springs that could be found by a simple hike through the pine-filled woods. She hadn't seen the springs yet but they were in the brochures on display at the B&B's front entrance.

Her gaze moved from the article to Mitch's lower half. The rest of him was currently hidden behind the refrigerator. He was fixing a slow leak from a loose water line to the ice maker. She'd checked out his backside before but now she stared unapologetically.

Her cell phone rang beside her, and she jerked upright. She placed it to her ear. "Hello?"

"Well, what do you think? Can Sweetwater Springs and your little B and B live up to the promise?" Josie asked.

"Oh, definitely. The town was never a concern. And Mitch and I have already fixed a mile-long list of things here at the inn. Actually, he fixed most of them and I've done all the decorating." There were only a few little tweaks left to make and the place would be perfect.

Kaitlyn dragged her gaze back to the article. "The only thing I'm missing is the Christmas tree."

"No tree? The perfect holiday getaway demands a tree, Kaye," Josie said. "And not one of those artificial ones."

"Of course it does. I'm sure there's a farm or something around here." But how would she get it back to the B&B in her small car?

Mitch straightened from behind the fridge. "Merry Mountain Farms sells the best trees," he said. "Sorry. Couldn't help overhearing you."

"It's okay. I'm talking to the friend who wrote the article," she told him.

"Oh, he sounds sexy," Josie purred into the receiver. "No wonder you have such a crush on him."

For a moment, heat crawled through Kaitlyn's skin. Until she remembered that Mitch could only hear her half of the conversation and not Josie's. *Thank goodness.* "Merry Mountain Farms. Good to know. I'll try to check it out later this week."

Josie cleared her throat. "Okay. I just wanted an update. The tension between you two can be felt all the way in New York. So please don't let me interrupt you jumping his bones."

Kaitlyn choked. "That's not...I'm not."

"Just keep me updated. I'm expecting a windfall for the B and B."

"I hope so. You can come visit it for yourself anytime, you know."

"Tempting," Josie said. "Maybe I will if I can ever get out from under these deadlines."

After a minute more, they said their goodbyes and disconnected.

Mitch stood and stared at her. Josie was right. The sexual tension could be sliced with a nail file.

"I, uh, need to take off early this afternoon. I'm taking my mom to an appointment in town."

"Oh." Kaitlyn nodded, surprised at the disappointment settling over her. She'd gotten used to having him around all day, and now during the nighttime too. She liked having him here.

"Will you be back tonight?" she asked, trying to keep the hope out of her voice. She grabbed her cup of cider and took a sip.

He nodded. "Yeah. I'll take you to get that Christmas tree if you want."

"Really?"

"Sure. I'm afraid if I don't, I'll find you out in the woods with an axe."

She placed her hands on her hips and feigned insult. "I'm perfectly capable of using one, you know."

"Of course you are. But humor me and let me take you to get a tree anyway."

Kaitlyn had to admit spending time with Mitch was even more exciting than picking out a real live tree. All she'd ever had were the small artificial kind that sat in a corner of her room.

"Who will watch the inn though? I can't just leave this place. We have a guest now."

"My mom used to come by for Mable and Henry all the time," Mitch told her. "She won't mind at all."

Kaitlyn blinked, unable to think of any excuse to say no. Not that she wanted to refuse the invitation. "Wow. Problem solved. I'd love to go tree hunting with you, then."

"Good. It'll be fun." He turned back to the refrigerator and began shimmying it back into its place against the wall.

It wasn't a date, she told herself as she watched, ignoring the flurry of anticipation falling over her like the first winter snow. Definitely not.

* * *

Mitch was glad he'd told his mom he was taking her to her doctor appointment this afternoon. Because the more time he spent with Kaitlyn, the harder it was to keep his hands to himself. And now he'd promised to take her Christmas tree hunting tonight. It was like he lost his mind whenever she was around.

He pulled into his mom's driveway and honked the horn. Her appointment was at 3:30 p.m., and there was no time to meander. She better not have changed her mind, he thought. He'd go inside and carry her to the appointment kicking and screaming like a toddler if he had to.

He relaxed when he saw her open the front door and head out, dressed in a heavy coat and pale-blue knit hat.

"You didn't have to do this, you know?" was the first thing she said upon opening the passenger side door of his truck.

"I know that's what you think but you're wrong. I'm your son, and I do have to do this." He watched her buckle herself in and then reversed back onto the street. "Especially since you're not taking care of yourself." The night she'd passed out on the bed hadn't been a fluke. He'd witnessed her dizzy spells several times since then. There were other symptoms too. She was pale and had a few bruises.

"Who are you to talk? What about that time you sprained your ankle a couple years back and wouldn't go have it checked out?"

"It was a sprain, Mom. I know how to treat a sprain. And a sprain is no big deal." He glanced over and pinned her with a stare. He hoped to God his mom's condition wasn't a big deal either, he thought as he returned his attention to the road.

"So, how's the B and B coming along?" his mother asked, changing the subject.

Mitch blew out a breath. "Good. Kaitlyn got her food-handling license, and the inn passed inspection last week. It already has its first guest too. Speaking of which, I have a favor to ask you." He saw his mom perk up in the seat beside him. She lived to help others.

"Oh?"

"I need to take Kaitlyn to get a tree tonight. Do you think you could watch the inn?" Mitch doubted any medicine the doctor offered today would be as good for her as this request.

"Well, of course I can. I've always loved working at the B and B—you know that." His mom's tone of voice was suddenly upbeat and cheerful.

"Not work," he clarified. "Watch. Feet up. TV on."

His mom didn't argue but she didn't agree either. "Your dad used to take me to get our Christmas trees. Do you like Mable's granddaughter? Is she pretty?"

Mitch groaned as he pulled into the physician's parking lot and cut the engine. "Don't make me regret asking you."

She turned in her seat and pointed a finger at him. "Only

if you promise not to try to go in the examining room with me. I'm a grown woman, Mitch, and there are some things a mother doesn't want her son hearing about her body."

He frowned. "How am I supposed to know what's going on with you if I'm stuck in the waiting room?"

She shrugged. "I guess you'll just have to trust that I'll tell you."

A growl emitted from deep in his throat. He trusted his mom but he didn't put it past her to keep things from him. Judging from the stubborn lift of her chin, he could see he wasn't winning this argument though. "Fine."

He opened his door and got out, meeting her around the back of the truck and walking toward the small doctor's office, which was in a string of other businesses. "But you'll tell me everything." He wasn't asking.

His stern tone of voice and demeanor seemed to be lost on his mother as he held the office door open for her and she walked in ahead of him. "Of course, dear."

* * *

Later that afternoon, Kaitlyn set out a dish of sugar cookies and accommodations for hot tea in the dining room.

"Did you get a lot of work done?" she asked Paris, as he walked in the room to peruse the selection.

"Mostly. Dawanda kept interrupting though."

Kaitlyn giggled to herself. "She didn't serve you a cup of cappuccino, did she?"

"She did. Apparently, my fortune couldn't be read. She said it was the first time that ever happened."

"That's strange."

He shrugged. "I'm not sure I buy into cappuccino readings anyway."

Kaitlyn was surprised that part of her did believe. There was something about how seriously Dawanda took the reading that chased away Kaitlyn's doubts. "Well, I can promise a distraction-free evening for your work if that's what you want."

"Thanks. Mind if I take a couple of cookies up to my room?"

"Of course." She turned as the phone rang on the wall. "Excuse me." The landline phone was the one that guests would use to make reservations. She crossed her fingers at her side in hopes that it was a potential customer and not a telemarketer as she went to answer. "Hello. Sweetwater Bed and Breakfast. How can I assist you?"

"Yes. Hi there. I'm Marvin Krespo," a man's voice drawled. "I was hoping to make a reservation for me and my wife. You got any rooms open?" he asked.

"Yes, of course. When will you be coming?"

"Tomorrow if you have vacancies. My wife doesn't think I'm romantic anymore. She said I need to step up my game or else."

Kaitlyn's mouth fell open. "Um, well."

"I doubt that means she'll leave me, but she likes to withhold my favorite foods and sex when she's in a tiff."

"I see." Kaitlyn cleared her throat. "Well, tomorrow will be fine. We'll have a room prepared for you."

"Great, darling. See you soon."

Kaitlyn hung up and went to retrieve her appointment book nearby. She scribbled in Mr. and Mrs. Krespo's names.

"Will you be needing anything else tonight? Dinner?" Kaitlyn asked as Paris headed toward the stairs with a handful of cookies. She wasn't planning on cooking full meals every night for her guests but since there was just one, she didn't mind.

"No. I thought I'd head out later and explore more of the area."

"Okay. Well, I'm actually heading out myself. Mitch and I are going to pick out a Christmas tree for the inn. His mom will be watching over the place if you need anything."

"I should be fine. Don't worry about me. Enjoy your date," he called before disappearing up the stairs and into his room. Before she had the opportunity to correct him. Getting a tree together was simply part of her arrangement with Mitch. The inn needed one, and she couldn't do this on her own.

Even if it wasn't a romantic arrangement, she still needed to look nice before heading over to Merry Mountain Farms, she decided. She checked her watch. Mitch would be coming back soon. Her heart did a little dance. Stealing a cookie from the tray, she hurried to her room to change.

An hour later, Mitch walked into the inn. Beside him was a slender woman with long, gray hair and a huge smile.

"You must be Kaitlyn Russo. I'd recognize you even if Mitch hadn't told me you'd taken this place over." Mitch's mom wrapped Kaitlyn in a warm hug. "Mable was always showing off the pictures your parents sent her way." The woman pulled away and looked at Kaitlyn. "My, you've grown into such a beautiful young woman."

"Thank you. It's nice to meet you, Ms. Hargrove," Kaitlyn said, almost at a loss for words at the heartfelt greeting. "And thank you so much for agreeing to watch the inn tonight."

"Please, call me Gina. And I'm happy that you gave me something to do."

"As if you sit around twiddling your thumbs all day," Mitch said sarcastically behind her.

Gina rolled her eyes. "If you listen to him, I work myself

nearly into a grave." Her smile fell. "Oh, I'm sorry. That's so insensitive of me, considering your grandmother just died."

Kaitlyn shook her head. "It's fine. Please make yourself at home. We won't be gone long."

"And no cleaning," Mitch bellowed as he ushered Kaitlyn out the front door and into the driveway where his truck was still running. He opened the passenger side door for her and then reappeared in the driver's seat.

"Your mom seems really nice."

He nodded. "Oh, she is. Nice and stubborn, if you ask me."

"Did everything check out at her appointment earlier?" Kaitlyn asked, even more concerned now that she'd met Gina.

Mitch cranked the engine. "Dr. Jacobs ran some labs. We should get results sometime next week. Until then, Dr. Jacobs said for her to rest and take a good multivitamin."

"That's always good advice," Kaitlyn said.

"Assuming Mom actually listens to it." He glanced across the seat as he came to the stop sign at the end of Mistletoe Lane. "Now, what do you say we go pick out a Christmas tree?"

Kaitlyn grinned. "If I didn't know better, I'd say you sound a little excited yourself."

"What can I say? I'm a man. We like to hunt and gather."

Something about that made Kaitlyn's blood heat. He was a man, for sure. Big and strong, doing exactly what he was made to do. And she absolutely was not going to kiss him again tonight. Their kiss at Silver Lake had been a mistake. One that shouldn't happen again.

CHAPTER NINE

"I've never been to a Christmas tree farm before," Kaitlyn said, glancing across the seat at Mitch.

He kept his eyes on the road, following the curves and bends precisely. "I used to go with your grandfather to pick one out," he told her. "Henry always liked to get the biggest one on the lot."

Kaitlyn laughed beside him. The sound was completely angelic. "I regret that I didn't get to spend a lot of time with them but I do remember Grandpa Henry having a fancy for doing things large."

Mitch nodded. "The larger the better. Your grandfather was a very good man."

They talked a little more about Mable and Henry, the inn, and Kaitlyn's continuing plans for improvement as they drove to Merry Mountain Farms on the edge of town. Mitch hadn't been here in years. Not since before his senior year of high school.

He pulled into the lot, which was already crowded and

buzzing with couples and families in search of their own perfect tree this holiday. Christmas music jingled in the air along with the laughter of children as he stepped out. Although it was frigid outside, Mitch's chest grew warm. Once upon a time, he'd loved Christmas more than anything.

"Do you think your truck will hold the biggest Christmas tree in this lot?" Kaitlyn turned to look at him as he walked around the truck to meet her. "Because that's the one I plan to get."

"No Charlie Brown tree?" he asked.

She shook her head. "If that's all I were planning to get, I wouldn't need you, would I?"

He walked beside her up the dirt path that led to the expanse of fir trees ahead. Kaitlyn walked down every path, inspecting each tree. Then, true to her word, she did pick out just about the biggest of the bunch forty-five minutes later.

"That one!" She rubbed her gloved hands together and beamed at him, her soft brown hair flowing underneath her bright-green knit hat.

"You sure?" he asked.

"One hundred percent. That's the one."

Her enthusiasm was contagious. "Okay."

"Last-Ditch Mitch!" He heard a familiar voice call from a few feet away.

Mitch spun to see Tuck and his sister, Halona, with her son, Theo. It seemed Mitch couldn't really go anywhere without running into people in this town. "Hey, looks like you guys had the same idea," Mitch said, inspecting the tree they were carrying. "Did you pick that one out?" he asked Theo, who merely stared at him.

"He's not much of a talker these days," Halona said, a hint of worry wrinkling her brow. "Good to see you, Mitch."

"You too. This is Kaitlyn Russo," he said, introducing Kaitlyn.

"Russo? You're Mable and Henry's granddaughter," Halona said. "They were wonderful people. I'm so sorry about Mable's passing."

"Thank you. How do you know Mitch?" Kaitlyn asked.

"We all went to school together," Tuck informed her.

"And why do you call him Last-Ditch Mitch?"

Mitch cupped a hand to the back of his neck and answered Kaitlyn's question himself. "Because if all else failed, I was always the sucker to call in high school. For a ride or homework. I even got asked to help someone break up with his girlfriend once. I said no to that request."

"Mitch is steadfast and responsible," Tuck explained. "You can ask him for anything, and he'd do it."

"Within reason," Mitch said.

"Well, it was nice to meet you, Kaitlyn," Tuck said. "I'm afraid this tree is heavy, and Theo over here has a bedtime soon." He tipped his head at Mitch. "We still need to get together, buddy."

"Yeah." Mitch shoved his hands in the pockets of his leather jacket. "Sounds good."

Tuck grinned. "See you later, guys! Have fun on your date."

"It's not a date," Mitch corrected, perhaps a tad too surly.

Tuck looked between him and Kaitlyn and then to his nephew, who was still watching them. "Theo, give Mr. Mitch a piece of what's in your pocket to help him out."

The mischievous sparkle in Tuck's eyes made Mitch wonder if he should hold out his hand for what the boy was now offering up. Halona's son was so cute though, that Mitch dutifully opened his palm. Then he blinked at the sprig of mistletoe the child had dispensed.

"Good night, you two!" Tuck called as he and Halona continued forward with their tree and little Theo chased behind them.

Kaitlyn's cheeks were red when he looked up at her. "Mistletoe," she said.

"It grows rampant around these parts this time of year."

She nodded, and he suspected they were both thinking about that kiss at Silver Lake. The kiss that had been way out of line.

He shoved the sprig in his coat pocket and set about cutting down the perfect tree for the inn. It was time to be on their merry way before they ran into someone else. Or before he decided to pull out that mistletoe and make good use of it.

* * *

The doorbell rang at two p.m. the next afternoon. Kaitlyn used her hands to iron out the wrinkles in her shirt and locked her stray hair behind her ears. With a smile, she pulled open the door, expecting to meet the Krespos, who had reservations for today.

Instead of an older couple, however, a very young couple stared back at her.

"Yes?" she asked.

The young man slapped a wiry arm around the girl and pulled her close. "Yeah. We're hoping to get a room here."

Is that a pimple on his cheek? How old are these kids? Do their parents know they're here?

Kaitlyn blinked, speechless for a moment. "Umm. Okay. Well, let me check and see if we have availabilities. Please come in," she said, leading the young couple to the couch.

"I'll be right back." She took off walking down the hall toward the kitchen to find Mitch.

Could she in good conscience rent a room to those two kids? Knowing they were likely to have sex?

"What's wrong?" Mitch asked, standing with a toolbox just outside her bedroom.

"We have more guests," she told him.

"The Krespos?"

"No. They're not here yet. This is a young couple. They look like they might be twenty or possibly younger. They want a room. I can't give them a room, can I?" Her gaze dropped to his toolbox. "What are you doing outside my bedroom?"

"Installing a lock. You shouldn't sleep in a room that doesn't have one. Any one of the guests could stroll in anytime they want."

Including him, she thought, hoping he'd had a hard time going to sleep last night too. After they'd gotten the tree, they'd brought it back here and relieved Mitch's mom from her post. Then Mitch had returned and had a nightcap with her, keeping a safe six feet of distance between them at all times. As if he were scared that coming any closer might lead to something more.

"I'm still not so sure about this Paris character," he continued, as if that explained the lock. "He's overstaying his welcome. This will be the fifth night."

"He's our guest, and he's welcome here as long as he wants. So, what do I do?" She intertwined her fingers in front of her, trying to contain her nervous energy.

"What do you mean?" Mitch asked.

"I can't rent them a room, can I? Isn't there a minimum booking age here? What would Mable have done?"

He tipped his head and looked at her through long, black

eyelashes. It wasn't fair that a man could have such beautiful lashes.

"Are you serious? If the kids are legal age and have money, they can do whatever they want."

"They want to have…*sex*," she said, lowering her voice to a whisper.

The hallway was dimly lit, and Mitch's eyes narrowed, pinning her to where she stood. "Everyone who comes here is probably going to want to have sex, Kaitlyn."

"Not Paris," she said, folding her arms in front of her.

Mitch's jaw ticked. "He might want sex too. Which is why I'm putting a lock on your door."

"Paris and I are *not* having sex," she said, keeping her voice low. She hoped he couldn't see the burn moving up her chest and past her neck.

"A single man who shows up at a bed and breakfast alone is suspect. Your picture is up on the website now. Maybe he saw it and thought he'd come see if he had a shot with you."

"Now *you're* being ridiculous." *And completely adorable.*

"I know guys. There are two main things we think about." He ticked off those things on his fingers. "Food and sex."

She swallowed, knowing she shouldn't ask. "You're a guy. Is that what you're thinking about right now?"

He looked at her long and hard with those dark coffee-stained eyes of his. The ones that made heat swirl in her belly like hot fudge on an ice cream sundae. She melted in the look, and part of her wanted to take his hand, pull him into her bedroom, and test that new lock he was installing. That was the part of her that was a glutton for punishment. The part she was suppressing.

"Mable would've gotten their credit card information and then rented the room to them," he said, avoiding the question. He gestured down the hall to the living room where the young couple was still waiting. "It's not your job to judge or condone other people's sex lives."

"That's not what I'm doing."

He lifted a brow. "They're adults. Give them a room."

She pressed her lips together. Then she sucked in a breath and blew it out. "Fine. But I don't have to like it." She headed down the hall. "Good news. You're in luck," she told the couple and then waited for them to stop French kissing on the couch. The boy with the pimple had roaming hands— one on the girl's butt and one creeping up her miniskirt. Didn't she realize it was twenty degrees outside?

Kaitlyn cleared her throat. "Good news," she said again, a little louder and more cheerful this time.

Finally, the couple came up for air.

"I have availabilities. You'll be staying in the *Pride and Prejudice* room. It's inspired by Elizabeth and Mr. Darcy."

"Who are they?" the girl asked, twisting her expression.

"You know—Jane Austen?" Kaitlyn waited for recognition to cross the couple's features. From the corner of her eye, she noticed Mitch standing off to the side.

"All the rooms here are named after famous couples," Kaitlyn explained. "Scarlett and Rhett, Baby and Johnny, Anne and Gilbert Blythe—my personal favorite."

The couple looked at her as if she were speaking an alien tongue.

"Do you have a Bella and Edward room?" the girl asked.

Now Kaitlyn stared at them as if *they* were the ones from another planet.

"You know, from *Twilight*."

Mitch coughed but Kaitlyn suspected it was really a laugh. She wasn't amused.

"No. I'm afraid we don't have a room named after vampires."

The boy shrugged. "We won't be paying much attention to the decorating anyhow, babe," he told his girlfriend.

Kaitlyn glanced over at Mitch. He was right. It wasn't her job to judge but who came to a bed and breakfast and didn't pay attention to the décor? "Okay. So, how will you be paying for your stay here?"

"Plastic," the overeager boyfriend said, handing her his credit card.

Kaitlyn ran it, secretly hoping it would be declined. When it wasn't, she handed the card back and forced a smile. "Well, let me lead you to your room."

The couple followed her up the stairs.

"I can't wait to get you behind closed doors," the boy said.

The girlfriend moaned. "Me either."

Do they realize I can hear them?

"*Okayyyyyyy.*" Kaitlyn swung open their door. The Elizabeth and Mr. Darcy room deserved so much more than this for its initiation. "Enjoy and let me know if you need anything."

"Yeah, we need a DO NOT DISTURB sign." The boyfriend grinned.

"Trust me. You won't be bothered." Kaitlyn couldn't leave fast enough. Mitch was waiting for her downstairs. When she saw him, she submitted to a total-body shudder.

He laughed again, not bothering to hide it this time.

"I seriously want to call their parents and tell them what's going on."

"They're probably on fall break from the local college. Mable used to get quite a few couples from there."

"And she didn't mind?"

"Oh, your grandmother was old-fashioned and romantic. She minded. She didn't discriminate though."

Kaitlyn folded her arms over her chest. "I'm glad you're here."

"Me too," he said, and the crazy thing was that he sounded like he meant it for once.

"Hey," he said, looking a little shy. He scratched his chin and averted his gaze. "Mom wanted me to ask you if you have plans for Thursday."

Kaitlyn frowned, forgetting momentarily that this was the week of Thanksgiving. "Oh. No. My parents usually go to an expensive restaurant. Mom doesn't really like to cook. I'm not even sure she knows how to turn the oven on." She smiled weakly. "Dad usually wore the apron when I was growing up but he didn't inherit Grandma Mable's talent in the kitchen."

Mitch shifted on his feet. "Mom wanted me to ask you to have Thanksgiving with us. Nothing big. It'll just be me and her." He shrugged. "Feel free to say no. I told her you probably couldn't because of the B and B."

"Right." Kaitlyn nodded. "One of us needs to stay when there's a guest." Disappointment flooded through her. Going to Gina Hargrove's home for Thanksgiving would be wonderful. "Hey, I have an idea. Why don't you invite your mom here? I can't leave unless you or someone else I trust is watching the place. But she can come here." Kaitlyn drew her hands to her chest. "And I'm pretty sure Paris doesn't have any plans. It'd be a shame for him to be all alone."

"Maybe he wants to be alone," Mitch said gruffly. If she didn't know better, she might think he was jealous of their leather-clad guest.

"No one wants to be alone, even if they say they do. Do you think your mom will come?"

Mitch nodded. "I think she'd be thrilled. And she'll insist on taking over your kitchen to do the cooking. She might allow you to help if you ask nicely."

Kaitlyn burst into laughter. "Wow. I was just going to let

the day come and go but now I'm actually excited. This is going to be great. Then maybe after dinner, you and I can decorate that Christmas tree of ours." And yeah, without intending it, there was a flirtatious tone to her voice.

"Thought you were the decorator in this arrangement," he said.

"I am. But you told me, in no uncertain terms, not to get on a ladder without having you around. So you can catch me when I fall."

Her heart melted as he smiled back at her. And then it stuttered to a halting stop. She seriously doubted she'd be falling from a ladder. But falling for the man in front of her wasn't so far-fetched.

* * *

On Thanksgiving morning, while the women had been cooking, Mitch made himself useful getting the outdoor holiday decorations out of the storage building. Kaitlyn had already hung the wreaths in the windows a few weeks ago, but Mable had also been putting out a nativity scene alongside a blowup Santa Claus for as far back as he could remember. After spending an hour or so setting them on display just like he and Henry Russo used to, Mitch headed back inside the house.

The air was thick with spice, butter, and fried things. Mitch had to admit that his mom was an excellent cook. Kaitlyn had been in the kitchen for the last few hours, helping and hopefully doing most of the work. Who was he kidding though? His mom was no doubt bustling around like a darn turkey with its head cut off. Dr. Jacobs's office still hadn't called with results but his mom kept insisting she was fine. Mitch wouldn't believe that until he had proof.

"Hey, Mitch," Paris said, coming out of the sitting room.

"Hey." Mitch's mouth wobbled in not quite a smile. He still didn't trust the guy but his gut was telling him it was for no other reason than Kaitlyn had called Paris attractive that first night. "You able to work down here?" he asked.

Paris glanced back to the sitting room, where he'd likely left his computer. "Hard to concentrate with the smell of delicious food looming."

At this, Mitch gave a sincere laugh.

"I offered to help but the women shooed me away."

"Sounds about right," Mitch said with a nod. Mitch stood there for another awkward second. Paris was a guest here, and as part owner, Mitch was technically a host. He didn't know a thing about hosting though. "Want to watch some football while we wait?"

Paris furrowed his brow. "Nah, man. I don't watch the games."

Mitch felt his whole body relax. "Me neither. That's just what guys do on Thanksgiving, I guess." Mitch couldn't really remember. He'd stayed far from home for the last few Thanksgivings. And Thanksgiving while on shift as an MP meant take-out food at the station and maybe a delicious piece of dessert from one of the wives if he got lucky.

Paris sat down on the front room's couch while Mitch took the high-back chair across from it.

"So, you're a graphic designer?"

"That's right," Paris said. "I do freelance work."

"And you're just traveling up the coast alone?" he asked, not intending the suspicion that coated his words.

"I guess you could say that. I lived in Florida when I was married. Divorced now."

"Sorry to hear that."

"It happens," Paris said. "It's not a whole lot of fun when it does. You ever been married?" he asked Mitch.

Mitch shook his head. He'd never had time to even consider the idea. He'd leaped from high school to the military, from one deployment to another. "No."

"Well, it's a great idea if you find the right one. Otherwise, it's a really *bad* idea." Paris chuckled.

"All right, you two." Mitch's mom came breezing down the hall wearing a food-splattered apron and a huge smile. Kaitlyn followed behind her, looking fresh and beautiful. Mitch breathed a little easier just seeing her face. "Men are allowed to help set the table, so come on." His mom waved a hand, signaling them back.

Fifteen minutes later, they all sat around the table for Thanksgiving dinner and began passing dishes of stuffing, lima beans, rolls, cranberry sauce—you name it. This wasn't so bad. Especially watching how much Kaitlyn seemed to be enjoying herself. That was something to be thankful for.

As expected, his mom quickly zeroed in on the newest person at the table and started peeling off his layers, which Mitch found a welcome distraction. He'd learned a little bit about their guest but it wouldn't hurt to learn more.

"So, what brings you to town, Mr. Montgomery?"

Paris appeared to flush a little at that title, which Mitch found humorous. "You can call me Paris. I'm here to meet up with the Bikers for Santa group at this weekend's Lights on the Lake event."

Kaitlyn straightened. "I've never heard of that. It sounds like fun."

"Oh, it is," Mitch's mom agreed. "The event always kicks off the holiday season with the lighting of the town's Christmas tree. It can't be missed. All the downtown stores stay open late, and they show off their holiday decorations for the first time. There are carolers and fake snow for the kids. The real snow won't come until later in December or early January, of course."

"And there's an Angel Tree in the town square," Paris continued. "That's why the Bikers for Santa are meeting. We'll all pick an angel off. A kid's wish list is on the back of each one, and it's our job to make it come true."

"I think that's a wonderful cause," Kaitlyn said.

Mitch had to agree. Of all the reasons he'd expected to hear for why Paris had chosen to come to Sweetwater Springs, this was not one of them.

Paris shrugged. "I grew up in foster care and had a lot of miserable Christmases. There was only one that was ever worth remembering, and it was here. Seems fitting to be back. I've actually been considering moving here."

"Really?" Kaitlyn asked, stabbing at several lima beans on her plate.

He nodded. "Can't stay at a bed and breakfast forever. I do well with my business but not *that* well." He winked across the table, which put Mitch back on guard.

"Well, there's a sign posted in Alice Hamilton's yard. She has a garage apartment for rent," his mom said.

"Mom, Ms. Hamilton might be looking for someone a little more...conservative." Mitch turned to Paris. "No offense."

"None taken."

"Nonsense. I'll put in a good word," his mom promised. "And I'll bring you over there to introduce you two myself."

Paris nodded. "Thanks. That might work out well."

"It would put you close to the inn," Kaitlyn said. "And I was thinking of hiring a good graphic designer soon to help me with some promotional items."

"I'll help any way I can."

"That's perfect." Mitch's mom shoveled some sweet potato casserole into her mouth and shook her head as she chewed and swallowed. "Things just seem to work out exactly how they should. Just like your grandmother leaving this inn to you, Kaitlyn. I know you're going to love it here."

"I wish I could thank her." Kaitlyn turned to look at Mitch. "Leaving the inn to us was an unexpected gift."

Mitch stiffened. To think he'd naively thought the conversation wouldn't turn to him.

His mom set her fork down and narrowed her gaze. "Us?" she asked. "Is there something you failed to mention to me, Mitchell Douglas Hargrove? *You* and Kaitlyn inherited the B and B?"

He closed his eyes and counted to five before facing her. "Yeah. I've, uh, been meaning to mention that. That's why I came back to Sweetwater Springs."

She clapped her hands together. "To run the Sweetwater B and B?" she said, breathless with excitement. "This is fantastic Thanksgiving news!"

"No, Mom. To sell it."

She blinked.

"The will says that Kaitlyn and I have to run the inn together for two months. Then Kaitlyn can buy me out and run it on her own," he explained. "That puts me here through the holidays, so stop frowning and be happy."

His mom clamped her mouth shut, lifted her fork, and stabbed at a stalk of asparagus. "I am happy you're home. Especially this time of year." She looked up with her smile pinned back in place.

Mitch wasn't fooled though. He knew she wished he'd make Sweetwater Springs home again. He would do just about anything for his mom but that wasn't really in the cards. She must've known it too because she didn't bring the subject back up. Instead, she turned the conversation back to the Lights on the Lake event. "You have to go, dear. Mitch can take you, and I'll watch the B and B. I won't take no for an answer." Her eyes shifted to Mitch's, daring him to break her heart again. "Right, son?"

Kaitlyn was watching him too.

The entire town would be at the lighting of the Christmas tree. Not his idea of a good time. He chewed on his food and his excuses—none of which he thought his mom would accept.

Then the doorbell rang. *Saved by the bell.*

"Maybe that's the Krespos," Kaitlyn said, scooting back from the table.

"Great," Mitch said, following behind her. Instead of an older couple though, she opened the door to two young men wearing ugly Christmas sweaters. One had his arm draped around the other.

"Hi," Kaitlyn said. "Can I help you?"

"Yes. I'm Nate Trapp and this is Chris Trapp. We were hoping to get a room for a couple of nights," the taller one said. "Sorry for the late notice but my mom won't allow us to sleep in the same room even though we're married now."

"Don't worry," Chris told him, "she'll come around. I can tell she likes me."

"Of course she does." Nate shared a look with his husband. "What's not to love?"

Kaitlyn smiled at the couple. "Well, you're in luck. We do have a room for you. And dinner if you're hungry."

Nate held his stomach. "Mom may not want us sharing a bed but she had no issues feeding us."

Kaitlyn laughed. "I'm Kaitlyn Russo." She gestured to Mitch, who was standing behind her. "This is Mitch Hargrove."

"Hey," Mitch said.

"We're the owners here. Come inside. We'll get you settled for your stay."

Mitch took Chris's credit card and scanned it while Kaitlyn showed the couple around downstairs. Then she took them upstairs to their room. A moment later, she came down the steps and met Mitch in the front room.

"What's wrong?" she asked, no doubt seeing the lines of distress on his face.

"I would just prefer if people would make reservations. This could quickly get out of hand."

"Well, like you just told your mom, you want us to make enough money for me to buy you out. A full house is how we're going to make that happen. We'll just have to deal with the chaos." She grabbed his hand and tugged him back toward the dining room. "Now, let's return to our feast before your mom and Paris eat all the food."

Hopefully, they had, which would mean the meal was over. He really didn't want to take the hot seat again and tell his mom he absolutely would not be taking Kaitlyn to the Lights on the Lake event.

CHAPTER TEN

I don't think I'll be able to eat again until Christmas," Kaitlyn sighed as she loaded the last of the plates into the dishwasher.

"Me neither," Mitch said.

Kaitlyn had insisted that Gina not help with the cleanup, and surprisingly she'd listened and gone home. As Kaitlyn was hugging Gina goodbye and thanking her for all her help with dinner, a newlywed couple, the Jamiesons, walked up the steps. The Trapps hadn't seen the article about the B&B but the Jamiesons told her they had. They'd visited their family in nearby Shadow Ridge earlier and had made the short trip into the valley in hopes of getting a room here.

The inn only had five rooms, which were now occupied by Mitch, Paris, the Trapps, the Jamiesons, and Missy and Joe, aka the horny college couple, who'd gone off to spend their Thanksgiving afternoon in a nontraditional way at the local movie theater.

"Did my mom look okay to you?" Mitch asked as he wrapped tinfoil over the leftovers.

"She seemed just fine. Full of energy and excitement. She's probably in bed resting already, so stop worrying." Kaitlyn laughed softly under her breath. "Your mom is amazing, by the way. I've only known her a few days, and it feels like I've known her forever. She had so many stories about my grandparents to tell." Kaitlyn cleared her throat. "And *other* stories."

She saw him straighten from the corner of her eye.

"Okay. Let's have it. How many embarrassing stories of mine did she tell you while you two were in the kitchen?"

"Only a few," Kaitlyn teased as she closed the dishwasher. "There. All done." As she was wiping her hands on a dishcloth, her cell phone dinged from the counter. She walked over and checked the screen to see a message from Josie waiting for her.

> Missing you today. Hoping you've advanced from the sweet kiss to the naughty one. That would give you something to be thankful for.

Kaitlyn tapped the screen quickly in case Mitch decided to look over her shoulder. She usually went to Josie's home for Thanksgiving Day. Her own parents—who hadn't called or left a message, by the way—didn't typically do much. Josie's mom wasn't the most domestic but at least she tried. She usually had a turkey that was as tough as jerky and a series of fancy bowls filled with vegetables that she'd warmed from the can.

Kaitlyn put her phone back down and made a mental note to text Josie back later. Maybe she'd call her parents too. She could tell them about the inn's first holiday event. Not that they'd likely be impressed.

"Okay. Are you ready?" Kaitlyn asked, pushing away her regret and disappointment and turning back to Mitch. It was a day to focus on the good. She didn't need a naughty kiss from Mitch to be thankful. She had this inn, and she'd just enjoyed a five-star meal with her newfound friends. In addition to that, all five guest rooms were occupied.

"Ready for what?" Mitch asked skeptically.

"Well, now that the inn is booking, we definitely need to get that Christmas tree decorated." She led the way to the sitting room where they'd set up the evergreen tree on Monday night. Then she turned on the old-fashioned radio inside an antique cabinet against the wall. She'd already loaded a holiday CD, and all she had to do was push Play to fill the room with soft carols.

With that done, she stepped over to a box of ornaments she'd found a few weeks ago and lifted off the lid. "This is a ton of ornaments. It might take us all night." And despite his frequent surliness, she didn't mind that prospect at all. Kaitlyn had seen a totally different side of him this afternoon. For a short time, he'd been relaxed and doting. The very image of a tad overly protective son. And he'd made sure his mom and Paris had felt welcome here. He'd done the same for the Trapps and Jamiesons when they'd arrived. He could protest that he wasn't cut out for hosting all he wanted but he'd been wonderful today.

Kaitlyn reached for the strings of lights and stood. "First, we have to add these." She plugged one set into a drop cord and retrieved the small ladder that Mitch had placed here earlier in the day.

"I got it." Mitch immediately took it from her and set it up.

He wasn't just overprotective of his mom, it seemed, and that sent gooey warmness trickling through her.

* * *

This was a form of torture somewhere, Mitch thought, watching Kaitlyn climb up the ladder for the millionth time in the last hour to hang another ornament. It wasn't the fact that she wanted to discuss each one in detail. No, it was the curves of her body positioned right in front of him. But he had no choice. What if she fell off the ladder like she had outside the other week? It was his duty to make sure she was safe. So why the hell did he keep secretly wishing she'd misstep and land back into his arms?

"You're awfully quiet," Kaitlyn commented, whirling to face him on the ladder. She was only on the second step, so doing so put her eye to eye with him. "What are you thinking about?"

Things I shouldn't.

"Nothing."

The corner of her mouth quirked as if she knew that was a lie. She turned back to the tree with her ornament and climbed a few steps higher.

He braced the ladder, just in case, as she reached for the spot she'd deemed worthy of the little heart-shaped decoration in her hand. As she reached, one of her legs came out to balance her weight and plowed right between his legs.

Mitch let out an unexpected cry of pain. Which, in turn, sent Kaitlyn spinning on the ladder again.

"I'm so sorry. Did I just..." Her gaze dropped to his hands cupped over his groin as the music sang about chestnuts roasting over an open fire. His nuts weren't in such good shape right now either.

Both of Kaitlyn's hands flew over her mouth. "I didn't mean to do that. I'm so, so sorry. That's twice in a month. First with Bradley, now you. Although Bradley was intentional. Yours was an accident. I'm going to get a reputation if I don't stop."

"Hold on to the rungs," he bit out, forcing his hands up to brace the ladder again.

She shook lightly as she suppressed a giggle. "I wouldn't want to put a crimp in your sex life," she finally said.

"You let me worry about my sex life."

She gave him a curious look and then turned back to the ladder and descended to retrieve another ornament from the box. "I'll tell you if you tell me."

"Tell you what?" he asked.

"About your sex life." She grabbed a candy-cane-shaped ornament and climbed the ladder once more while tossing a mischievous look over her shoulder. "I'll start. I haven't had sex in nine months, and that was with an old boyfriend who came to town. We'd been together before, and we were going through a dry spell. So we decided to be adults about it."

The distraction of the conversation alleviated the pain in his nether region. "Adults about having sex? So you were just satisfying needs?"

She shrugged. "Trying to. He was satisfied, but... Well, let's just say I'd forgotten that he had never been great at satisfying me. It's one of the reasons I wasn't that sorry we broke up in the first place."

She traveled down and then climbed back up as she talked. As if this were just a casual conversation between two people who weren't supposed to be attracted to one another.

"Your turn," she prompted.

He hesitated but fair was fair. She'd just told him her

story so he went ahead with his. "Three months ago. I wasn't out of the marine corps yet. It was just a small break. I came home, drank too much at the Tipsy Tavern, and hooked up with a waitress there."

"A one-night stand." Kaitlyn twisted on the ladder again. "I've never had one of those."

"I wouldn't recommend it. You probably wouldn't find satisfaction in that either."

Her brows drew up. "So you didn't even know her?"

Mitch had a feeling he was going to regret spilling so many details about his last sexual encounter. "I knew her from growing up here. She was younger than me. We were just casual acquaintances, and that's all I'm dishing on that subject. A gentleman doesn't kiss and tell."

Kaitlyn clamped her mouth shut. Then she continued to quietly go about her task for several minutes.

"What's wrong?" Mitch finally asked.

"Just lost in thought. Maybe I should have a one-night stand," she pondered, more to herself than him.

He swallowed. "I don't think a woman like you would enjoy that kind of thing."

"What does that mean, 'a woman like me'?"

"Well, from what I see, you're passionate. You don't do things halfway. If you wanted to find a good man to satisfy all your needs, not just the sexual, I'm sure you could find one without any problem."

She stared at him for a long moment, and for some reason, he had a longing to be that kind of guy.

She took one step down, still facing him, leveling her eyes to his, her mouth to his. Daring him to kiss her again.

Her gaze flicked to his lips. His arms, bracing the ladder still, pinned her body almost to his.

"Not a good idea," he whispered.

"Why not?" Her bottom lip pulled down just slightly.

"Like I said, you deserve more than just some guy who can satisfy the now."

"Do you protect everyone in your life?" she asked.

Heat pulsed in the space between them. "I guess so. I was a marine corps cop after all."

"Since when is kissing a crime?"

He swallowed, wanting more than anything to taste her again. She brought one hand up and curled it behind his neck, tugging softly. It didn't take much to break him. Then his mouth was on hers.

Her hot, wet tongue slid up against his.

Mitch's hands moved to Kaitlyn's waist. His quickly waning willpower kept them from sinking any lower.

"That was the last ornament," she said, when they finally pulled away. "I guess we're done for tonight." Something twinkled in her eye, and it didn't take a cup of Dawanda's cappuccino to read what she was thinking right now. He'd meant what he said though. She deserved a better man.

"Great. I'm pretty tired," he said. Which was a lie. After that kiss, he might not get a wink of sleep tonight.

Disappointment shone in her eyes now. "Yeah. Me too," she said after a long pause. "Thanks for helping."

"That's my job, isn't it?"

"You went above and beyond though. As always. I'm not sure what I'll do after you leave."

"You'll be fine. I have faith in you." And he did. Kaitlyn had proved herself to be steadfast and strong. She was a fighter, and she'd make this bed and breakfast work no matter what obstacles came her way. He admired the heck out of her.

And if conditions were different, maybe...

They cleaned up and headed out of the sitting room.

"Good night, Kaitlyn," Mitch said, forcing his feet to move toward the stairs that led to his room and not to follow her down the hall to hers.

"Mitch?"

"Yeah?"

She pulled her lower lip between her teeth.

Anticipation hung in the air. His willpower was already near its breaking point. If she put into words what she wanted, if she made him make that choice, he wouldn't be able to say no. She could ask him to strip naked and climb Mount Pleasant right now. Or jump into Silver Lake in the dead of winter. His answer would be yes.

"Do you think—"

The doorbell rang behind them.

"Who's that?" he asked as they both turned.

She shrugged. "We really should invest in a CLOSED sign. I don't like people showing up after dark."

He took the lead in answering. Pulling the front door open, he stared back at a short, older couple. The man had a white comb-over. The woman had fluffy bluish-colored hair and sloppy lipstick.

"Good evening. We're the Krespos." The old man smiled. "We meant to come earlier in the week but we're here now. Ready to claim that romantic room you promised us."

Mitch looked at Kaitlyn, who was now standing beside him in the doorway. They'd been resigned to the fact that the Krespos weren't coming.

Her eyes were wide and her skin, which had been flushed and pink when they'd been beside the tree together, was now pale as new-fallen snow.

"The Beauty and the Beast room is available," he said, offering up his own room. "I just need a quick minute to prepare it for you. Please come in. There is water and fruit at the table along the wall if you need refreshment," he told the couple, gesturing them inside. The old man was frail in comparison to his robust wife.

Mitch offered a reassuring glance to Kaitlyn before heading upstairs to pack his things and change the bedsheets. Ten minutes later, he returned downstairs. "All set. The Beauty and the Beast room is yours."

"I'm Beauty, and she's the Beast," Mr. Krespo joked as he stood from the couch.

Mrs. Krespo jabbed an elbow into his ribs with enough force to crack a few. In return, Mr. Krespo moaned in pain.

Kaitlyn turned to Mitch, a slight crease in her brow.

"I'll see them up," he told her.

She nodded. "Thank you."

"No problem." He didn't mind giving up his room but that meant either he had to head to his mom's house tonight—and he didn't like the idea of leaving Kaitlyn alone with so many guests to cater to—or he had to sleep on the couch, which he guessed wasn't exactly good B&B host etiquette. Not that he'd ever been one for etiquette.

He showed Mr. and Mrs. Krespo upstairs to their room and then headed back down the staircase, where Kaitlyn was waiting for him.

"You can sleep in my room," she said, giving him a third option for where to sleep tonight.

"I'm not sure that's the best idea."

"Why not? We're two adults, and I trust you."

He stepped off the bottom stair and walked toward her. "I'm not sure I trust myself," he said quietly, in case other guests were in listening range. "Especially after that kiss."

Her eyes widened, her lips parted, and he wanted nothing more than to keep kissing her.

She took hold of his hand and tugged. "Don't be silly.

You're staying in my room tonight, and I'm not taking no for an answer."

* * *

Kaitlyn sat on the edge of her bed and watched as Mitch pulled out the old air mattress from her grandparents' closet and attempted to blow it up. This was not what she had in mind when she'd dragged him to her room.

She was already in her flannel pajamas featuring multi-colored snowflakes. She wished she had something sexier to wear right about now. Not that she wanted to be sexy and lure Mitch to her bed.

Okay, that was totally what she wanted. When her hormones were in charge, she didn't care if he was forever material or not. She wanted him on top of her, underneath her, all over her. Mitch didn't think she was the type of girl to have a one-night stand but maybe she was.

As if hearing her blaring thoughts, he turned back to look at her. "The pump isn't blowing this thing up. There must be a leak in the mattress somewhere." He continued to try for several more minutes and then shook his head.

"This is a king-size bed. It's big enough for the two of us," Kaitlyn offered. Even if it were a twin-size bed, it'd be big enough for them. In fact, a twin-size would be far better.

"I'll just go to my mom's tonight and return early in the morning to help out."

"Not necessary. I mean, she's probably sleeping, and you'll wake her. She needs her rest, remember?"

Mitch stood just a few feet away. "I can sleep on the floor, then. It's fine."

"Will you just stop?" She pulled back the covers on the

opposite side of the bed. "You're sleeping in my bed with me, and that's final."

"Not a good idea." Those were the same words he'd used at the Christmas tree, right before kissing her. And he'd been wrong. That had been an excellent idea.

"Why?" she asked, feeling the tension between them dial up to crackling.

"You know why, Kaitlyn. Kissing is one thing. Anything more is irresponsible."

"For who? Me or you?"

"Me. Mable didn't leave this place to us for me to take advantage of you."

"Is it taking advantage if it's what we both want?" Sucking in a breath, she reached for the hem of her shirt and pulled it over her head.

"Kaitlyn," he said on a deep groan. She watched his gaze flick down to her white lace bra.

It was a bold move, unlike her for sure, but she was tired of waiting for Mitch, who seemed to have the patience of Job. Her desire bordered on need. She could barely breathe as she waited for him to make his move.

"You're going to have to invite me over there," he finally said in a gruff voice.

"I kind of thought taking my shirt off was an obvious invitation. Being together doesn't have to change things between us, Mitch. It can just be two adults having consensual sex."

Sex had always meant something to her in the past though. Maybe it would now too, but she didn't want to think about that at the moment. Her body needed him. She hadn't been satisfied sexually by a man in a very long time, and she had a feeling Mitch would raise the bar for any man who followed him.

He took the smallest step toward her, his gaze unwavering. Then, detouring, he flipped off the lights and climbed onto the opposite side of the bed with his back turned to her. "It's been a long day," he said. "We're both tired. We should get some sleep."

She blinked, feeling hot tears descend. Snatching up her top, she put it back on and stared once more at the shadow of a man. *Gah. How embarrassing.* She'd offered Mitch sex with no strings attached, and he'd rejected her.

Burrowing under the covers, she hoped sleep would find her fast. By the sound of the heavy breathing beside her, it'd already found her bedmate.

CHAPTER ELEVEN

*M*itch flopped restlessly onto his side as he slept. He was in one of those dream states where he was right on the edge of waking but he couldn't get his eyes to open. And he needed them to open.

He was at a party where he probably shouldn't have been. But when you're seventeen, the things you shouldn't do usually sound like the best ideas. He had a beer in his hand but he didn't intend to drink it. It was all for show. He also had his eyes on the head cheerleader across the room. The night was promising to be one of the best of his life.

Not the worst.

"Last-Ditch Mitch," his buddy Tuck called, grabbing his elbow and pulling his attention away from the blond. "Something's wrong with Tim."

Mitch turned to Tuck, whose black hair was overgrown, making waves that turned in varying directions on his head. "What's wrong?"

"He's sick."

Tim Sampson was always sick. He was one of those kids, chronically pale, thin, catching every virus in the air. If survival of the fittest were in play, Tim would be the first one to die in their group of friends.

"He'll be fine," Mitch said, curling his fingers around his bottle. It'd taken some convincing from his friends to even come tonight but he was glad he did. All the worry that came with being a teenager in a single-parent home had melted away with the crowd, music, and girls.

Tuck gestured at Mitch's drink. "You've barely taken a sip from your beer. I've had a whole one. We all have. You should be the one to drive him home."

Mitch looked at Tuck as if maybe his friend had lost his mind.

"Don't you remember how Tim almost died last year? After eating the bad burgers?" Tuck pressed. "My parents don't know about this party. If we call an ambulance, they'll definitely find out, and I'll be grounded until college."

Mitch started to argue but Tuck raised a good point. Tuck came from a strict home, and having the party here tonight while his parents were away would get Tuck grounded for life. He'd probably never see his friend again.

"He only lives a few minutes away. Drop him home and then you can come back and flirt with Tanya."

Mitch sighed. "Fine. Where's Tim?" He went in the direction that Tuck pointed and nearly had to carry their scrawny classmate to the door. The air was chilly as they stepped outside. Ice had been forming every night lately, and Mitch had to watch his step on the pavement to make sure he and Tim didn't bust their asses as they walked.

With Tim secured in the passenger seat, he got behind the wheel and jabbed the keys in the ignition of his mom's car. She worked for the prestigious Everson family in the daytime and usually let him have the car in the afternoons and evenings to go to his job at the local diner. That's where she thought he was tonight. He felt mildly guilty for lying to her but he deserved to be a normal kid like his friends sometimes too. Right?

He turned on his headlights and took to the winding mountain roads, trying to remember which turn led to Tim's house. "Hey, Tim." He nudged his friend, trying to get his attention. "Tim?"

Tim stirred in the seat beside him.

"Which road do you live on, man?" Mitch reached over and gave his friend's shoulder a harder shake.

"I don't feel so great," Tim moaned. "I think I'm going to barf."

"No, no, no." Mitch glanced across the seat. "Please don't vomit in my mom's car. She'll kill me, dude." And he'd be busted on his lie. He hated disappointing his mom. She was always working so hard.

Tim lurched forward, making a gurgling sound as he did.

No, no, no!

Mitch grabbed an empty fast-food bag from the floor and started to shove it into Tim's lap. Then a sharp squeal shot terror into his lungs. Mitch whipped his head up to look at the road and saw only lights, so blinding that he yanked the steering wheel right, but not before something hit the front of his car, throwing his mom's old Cavalier into a tailspin on a patch of black ice.

The moment seemed suspended in time. One split second seemed to float like one of the snowflakes starting to fall from the sky. A million thoughts raced through his mind.

What is happening?
What did I hit?
Is this the end?

His mom would be so disappointed. So lost without his dad and now him too. How could he do this to her?

The moment broke, and Mitch's head slammed forward into the steering wheel, bouncing off like a rubber ball. Pain, like a lightning bolt, seared his brain. Then Tim's body fell into his lap like a rag doll.

Is he dead?

The car finally came to a slamming halt against the guardrail. Or maybe they'd gone over, had fallen down the mountain, and this was death.

Mitch's eyes cracked open, a splinter of light jabbing into his pupils.

Tim stirred on his lap. Still alive. Still in one piece—hopefully.

Turning, Mitch saw the SUV he'd hit rolled over on the other side of the road. He knew deep in his gut that the accident had been his fault. He had dipped to get a paper bag for Tim, taken one hand off the steering wheel as fate had tossed black ice in his path. Instead of turning into the spin, he'd jerked the wheel. His driver's education teacher had taught him better but that training had gone out the window in his terror.

Mitch focused on the SUV, thinking it looked familiar in the beam of his broken headlights. He knew the person who drove it but in his groggy state he couldn't remember who it was.

Sirens sang in the distance. *Please get here. Please help us.* A passerby had pulled over on the roadside now and was running toward the scene of the accident.

Accident. It was all a terrible, horrible accident. He hadn't intended for any of this to happen. Hopefully everyone would be okay, and he'd just be grounded from now until he went to the police academy next year with Alex.

Watching the SUV, with no sign of life inside, he had a sinking feeling that wouldn't be the case.

* * *

Mitch's eyes flung open. A thin layer of sweat covered his skin. He blinked in the darkness, making sense of his surroundings. He glanced over at the dark figure lying next to him in bed. Kaitlyn. That hadn't been a dream. She was real.

They hadn't had sex but he'd wanted to. All those years of practicing self-control in the marine corps had paid off. Kaitlyn wouldn't be waking up with any regrets related to him this morning. He didn't want her to wake up next to him sweating and shivering like this either.

Careful not to wake her, he got out of bed and pulled some jogging clothes and sneakers out of his bag on the floor. He needed to go work off his pent-up sexual energy and frustration before showering.

After dressing, he slipped out of the bedroom and then the front door. He hopped into his truck and drove to his favorite jogging spot at Evergreen Park. It was still dark out, but he didn't mind. He locked up his truck and started down the path.

Between his interaction with Kaitlyn last night and his nightmare about the accident, he was ready to implode: physically, mentally, and emotionally. He upped his speed, running from the weight of it all, but it stayed steady on his shoulders.

Up ahead he could hear the natural hot springs. The sound called to him as each foot pounded the earth.

Then the image of Kaitlyn's lace lingerie popped into his mind. What was he going to do about her? He didn't have a clue. He hoped it would come to him by the time he got back to the B&B. He had a feeling she still might use that fireplace poker on him if provoked.

Which he might've done last night.

* * *

Kaitlyn rolled over and stared at the empty space beside her in bed. Before nodding off last night, Mitch had turned on his side, away from her, and he went to sleep without a second thought. Then apparently, after she'd finally drifted off, he'd slipped away. He'd rejected her and then decided he didn't even want to stay in the same bed as her.

Jerk.

Blowing out a breath, she sat up on the edge of the bed. The clock read five a.m. She supposed she needed to get up and start preparing to be the happy host for her house full of guests. She headed into the bathroom, showered and dressed, and then dragged herself down the hall to the kitchen. Mitch was nowhere to be seen. A quick glance out the window revealed that his truck was missing too. Maybe he'd gone back to his mom's place. *Gah*—she shouldn't have thrown herself at him last night. What was she thinking?

"Need a hand?"

She jumped and whirled to face Paris. He was dressed in his usual jeans and black T-shirt. She wondered if he owned anything else. "You know how to cook?" she asked.

"I didn't survive this long on cold cereal." He went to the sink, washed his hands, and then started collecting ingredients from the fridge. She had been doing this routine for a couple weeks now, and she was getting good at it. It was nice to have help though.

"You are a godsend, you know," she said as she beat eggs in a bowl.

"I could say the same. I got on my bike and headed down here without planning for a place to stay. I'm glad your inn had a room for me."

"Me too."

She and Paris prepared enough food to feed a dozen people and set the tables just as the first guests started to arrive downstairs. More guests spilled into the dining room a few minutes later and took their seats. Kaitlyn had decorated the tables yesterday, setting floral bouquets inside mason jars at each one, creating a cheerful environment.

Mr. Krespo pulled out a chair for Mrs. Krespo. The old woman eyed him suspiciously. "You're going to pull that out from under me when I go to sit," Mrs. Krespo accused, talking loudly enough for the other guests to hear.

"I would never do that, sweetheart. That's your paranoia and dementia talking."

"I don't have those two things. Are you trying to lock me away so you can find some other hot, young thing to live out the rest of your days with?"

"No, I'm trying to be more romantic. That's what you said you wanted, remember?"

Mrs. Krespo shook her head. "By trying to kill me?"

Mr. Krespo's hands flew up at his sides in surrender. "I give up."

"Want me to do damage control?" Paris offered.

Kaitlyn shook her head. "No, I've got this." She walked over and grabbed the back of the chair that Mr. Krespo had already pulled out. "Why don't you have a seat, Mrs. Krespo, and I'll bring your breakfast?"

Mrs. Krespo gave her a suspicious look too but Kaitlyn had no reason to do the older woman harm. On the contrary, if Kaitlyn harmed Mrs. Krespo, she had a feeling the older woman would go after her for all this place was worth, which still wasn't much.

The older lady sat and frowned at her husband, who took a seat next to her.

"There you go. Why don't you two talk while I get breakfast for you?" Kaitlyn gave a slight nod at Mr. Krespo when he looked up at her. "Maybe talk about what you'd like to do today," she suggested, and then grabbed a nearby brochure. She laid it on the table in front of Mrs. Krespo. "This might give you some ideas. I recommend going downtown and walking along Silver Lake. Dawanda's Fudge Shop sells hot chocolate nearby. You might stop there after your walk."

Before Mrs. Krespo could argue with the suggestion, Kaitlyn walked away to get the serving dishes passed around. Then she sat down with Paris, Chris, and Nate.

"How was your stay last night?" she asked them as she filled her own plate.

"Wonderful. Much better than it would have been at your mom and dad's anyway," Chris said, looking at his partner.

Kaitlyn looked between them. "If you don't mind me asking, why won't your mom let you two share a room, Nate?"

He shrugged. "She's still getting used to the idea that we're not just friends, I guess. We're married now, and there won't be any grandchildren for her."

"Not in the traditional way, at least," Chris said, smearing strawberry jam on his biscuit. "We can adopt," he told Nate. "I love kids."

"Me too." Nate turned back to Kaitlyn. "My mom sometimes takes a while to come around but she usually does. This just means that Chris and I might be booking more nights at your inn over the next couple of years."

"Well, you're always welcome," Kaitlyn told them. "And

if you have any suggestions to make the stay better, please feel free to tell me. I'm still learning the ropes of running a bed and breakfast. This is all very new to me."

Chris shook his head. "I can't think of any recommendations. It's absolutely perfect here."

They continued to make small talk, and then Nate leaned over to Chris and whispered loudly. "Chris, why don't you ask her?"

"Ask me what?" Kaitlyn looked between them.

"Well"—Nate grimaced slightly—"Chris and I can't figure out which one of the guys who work here is your partner."

"Business partner?" she asked.

"No, *partner* partner," Chris said.

The room suddenly went very quiet.

"I mean, you were with the big guy with the beard last night," Nate said.

"That's Mitch," Chris offered and then nodded at Paris. "But you're eating breakfast with him."

Paris started choking on a bite of his biscuit. "I'm just a guest here," he said when he finally swallowed. "Kaitlyn and I are just friends." He looked at her. "Once you've shared a Thanksgiving dinner together, you're officially friends, right?"

Kaitlyn nodded, a little stunned by the Trapps' question. "Yes. We're definitely friends. *Just* friends," she told the group.

"So, the other guy, Mitch, is your boyfriend? I say boyfriend because there's no ring on your finger." Nate nodded at her left hand.

She pulled her hand back from the table. When she'd decided to be the host here, she'd had no idea she would be the object of such speculation. "I'm single, actually. Mitch is also just a, um…um…" She had no clue what Mitch was to her. Maybe they weren't even friends anymore.

"Sex toy?" Mrs. Krespo asked from across the room. "That's how me and Marvin started out too. Sex buddies, and then he knocked me up."

The room filled with gasps. Then Missy and Joe started giggling uncontrollably.

"You laugh," she said, pointing a finger at Joe, "but I sure hope you used protection with her last night, young man, or your good times are over. Once the baby comes along, all the fun is sucked right out of life. No more staying at fancy bed and breakfasts like this one. Not until you're old like me, at least. And by then you're no longer attracted to one another." Mrs. Krespo gave a pointed look at Mr. Krespo, who was busy keeping his head down and nibbling on his bacon.

Awkward.

Kaitlyn made a mental note to offer Mr. Krespo some more tips that might put him back in favor with Mrs. Krespo. He'd told Kaitlyn over the phone that his wife wanted romance. Kaitlyn could certainly help with that.

The front door to the house opened, and Kaitlyn heard heavy footsteps in the living room. Her breath stuttered in her chest.

"You go check on who it is," Paris said. "I can help out here if anyone needs something. That's what friends are for." He winked.

"Thanks." Relieved to distance herself from the conversation, she headed to the front, even though she already knew who was here. The only person who would enter without ringing the doorbell.

"Sounds like everyone is already having breakfast," Mitch said when she rounded the corner and stopped to look at him. He was sweaty and dressed in jogging clothes, and something about that turned her on.

Which also infuriated her. After last night, she didn't want to be attracted to him.

"The guests started coming down early. Paris helped. In fact, I think I can handle things on my own from here on out. You can just come by during the day for the next month to satisfy the conditions of the will."

His gaze was steadfast. "Kaitlyn, I'm trying to be a good guy here."

She folded her arms. "I don't know what you're talking about."

"Good guys don't make plays for a woman when they know they aren't staying."

She shook her head. "If you're so eager to leave, then why did you agree to stay in the first place, Mitch? Why didn't you just go?"

"I couldn't do that to Mable. Or to you."

"I was a stranger. You didn't owe me anything." Tears burned in her eyes. She wasn't going to cry in front of him though. No way, no how.

"Kaitlyn." He took a step closer. "You're upset about last night. I get it."

"Last night was poor judgment on my part. I'm glad you wanted nothing to do with me. I couldn't be happier that you saw me with my shirt off, then rolled over and started snoring."

"That's not what happened, and you know it," he said. "I did want you. I think that was pretty obvious."

The image of his heated gaze on her flicked across her mind. He hadn't turned away immediately when she'd stripped off her top. "What's obvious is that you and I could never work together. I don't know what my grandma was thinking when she set up this arrangement."

"Kaitlyn," he said, reaching for her hand, "it's not that I didn't *want* to have sex with you. Because believe me, I did."

Her body temperature dialed up.

"Ahem."

Both Kaitlyn and Mitch snapped their attention to the corner where a few of the guests stood watching them. Kaitlyn pulled her hand away from Mitch's.

"Hi, guys," Paris said. "Um, sorry for interrupting this, um…"

"Lovers' quarrel," Mrs. Krespo called behind him. "That's what you call this." She seemed to be an expert on everything this morning.

"No." Kaitlyn shook her head but she couldn't explain away what the guests had just witnessed. Mitch had just mentioned her and sex in the same sentence. "We're not lovers," she said before turning and walking toward the kitchen to clean up.

And not being lovers was the problem.

* * *

Mitch ran his forearm across the layer of perspiration on his forehead. He'd worked himself into a sweat setting up spotlights to shine on Mable and Henry's wooden cutouts that he'd put out on Thanksgiving morning. People loved to drive around and look at decorations this time of year. In addition to spotlights, Mable had always insisted the house be strung with lights from top to bottom. Mitch had always helped Henry with the lot while Henry fussed and complained under his breath.

Damn, he missed Henry just as much as he did Mable. Those two made Christmas nice. And they'd always taken

Mitch to the Lights on the Lake event while his mom watched the inn when he was growing up.

After last night, he guessed he didn't have to worry about taking Kaitlyn to the event anymore. As angry as she was, she may never talk to him again.

Done, he carried his ladder back to the shed and retreated to his truck. He needed a shower but he wasn't about to go in the room he and Kaitlyn had shared last night to grab clean clothes or rinse off. He wasn't crazy. He had clothes at his mom's house. She would let him shower there, and he guessed maybe he'd stay the night with his mom too. He supposed he'd be staying the next month with her.

Mitch rounded the corner of Mistletoe Lane and pulled into the driveway of the second house on the right. He got out of the truck and walked up the porch steps of his childhood home, remembering how he used to race out the front door when his dad drove up from work every evening. He'd idolized the man. His dad was the exact kind of guy he'd hoped to be. The kind he'd never live up to, no matter how hard he tried.

"Mom?" he called, as he stepped inside the house.

"Mitch. What a surprise. I thought you'd be busy with the duties of hosting a bed and breakfast." She walked through the living room in her bathrobe.

"Why aren't you dressed?" he asked. The mother he knew was always dressed before sunup. "Is something wrong?" he asked.

She waved a hand. "Stop treating me like that."

"Like what?"

"Like you're my parent and not the other way around. It's the day after Thanksgiving. I worked hard and ate too much. I'm taking the day off if that's okay with you."

He kissed her temple and sat on the couch, waiting for

her to sit across from him in the recliner. He couldn't help scrutinizing her every movement. "You sure you're okay?"

"Never better." She wiggled back into the chair and looked up at him. "I'm taking the vitamins like Dr. Jacobs told me to, and I'm already feeling much better. I have the energy of a twenty-year-old, in fact."

He pointed a finger. "I know you. Just because you have renewed energy doesn't give you a license to double your workload. Have you gotten your lab results back yet? Maybe we should call and see what the holdup is."

"I'm fine, Mitch. I promise. You, on the other hand, are not," she said. "I can see it on your face. What's going on?"

He leaned forward over his knees and blew out a breath. "I got in a fight with Kaitlyn. I wish I didn't have to stay and fulfill Mable's final wishes. It's time for me to get out of Sweetwater Springs."

His mom was quiet for a long moment. "For such a brave man, which you are, you always seem to be running."

"I'm not running. I just don't belong here. You know that. I'm just idling while I wait for the security job to open up in January."

"You could find temporary employment here until then."

"In Sweetwater Springs?" He grunted. "There's no money to be made here."

"Money? Is that what this is about, Mitchell Douglas?" she said with a scoff. "I don't care about money. And I didn't raise you to care about it either."

"I need to make sure you're provided for."

"You've spent the last ten years making sure I was well taken care of, sending me money that I never asked for." She lifted her chin stubbornly. "How many times do I have to tell you I'm the parent? I support you, not vice versa."

"You lost the job with the Eversons because of me. For

the past decade you've worked twice as hard for half as much, and that's my fault. So sue me if I just want to make sure you're taken care of." And judging by how run-down she looked, he wasn't doing a very good job. "I shouldn't have let you prepare Thanksgiving dinner yesterday."

"Nonsense. I don't need taken care of. All I need is for my son to be happy. And you're not happy."

Happy. Mitch had experienced bouts of that since coming back here, which surprised him. Most of that had to do with Kaitlyn but he'd messed that up just like he had every good thing in his life.

He ran a hand over his head, missing the way his crew cut used to bristle at the touch. Now his marine corps crop was grown out. He'd liked it last night when Kaitlyn's fingers had sifted through his longer hair while they'd kissed beside the tree though. Right before she'd invited him to her bed and taken off her shirt.

He cleared his throat, shaking that thought away. "I'm not staying at the B and B tonight."

"Well, where are you staying, then?" his mom asked.

He thought it was a joke at first but her expression was deadpan. "Here."

She grimaced. "Sorry, honey. I gave the guest room to your aunt Nettie tonight. She's arriving in about an hour. Better late than never for Thanksgiving, right? Which I guess means I need to get up and get dressed."

Mitch furrowed his brow. "Okay, well, I can sleep on the couch."

"I don't think so, dear. You know how Aunt Nettie and I are once we get together. We stay up all hours, watching movies and laughing." His mom shook her head. "I could really use a girls' night with her. You're the one always telling me I need to relax and have fun. This'll do that for me."

Aunt Nettie was his father's sister but she and his mom were as close as if they were blood related. "So I can't stay here?" he clarified. "In the home that you said would always be open to me?"

"It is. Just not while your aunt Nettie is here. I suggest you make up with Kaitlyn before sunset." She shifted and stood back up.

"Seriously? You don't want my help and then refuse to give me a place to stay?" He said it teasingly but his world was being turned upside down right now. Where was he going to stay tonight? Even if he made up with Kaitlyn, the only room available at the inn was her room, in her bed—and that had been a disaster last night. He didn't want to repeat it. And he didn't think he had enough self-control to last another night without giving in to his desire and ravaging Kaitlyn's body.

He got up and headed toward the door.

"Where are you going?" his mom asked.

"To find a place to stay. Not at the B and B. I'll check with Tuck or Alex." And if they couldn't help, he'd get a room at a hotel up the mountain—although they might be full because of the Thanksgiving holiday.

"Just don't run from that beautiful woman too long. She's a jewel. Some other man is liable to snap her up."

Mitch didn't bother acknowledging that comment. First off, he wasn't running. Secondly, Kaitlyn finding another man was exactly what he was afraid of. He wasn't supposed to be interested in or attracted to her. Wasn't supposed to care about her in a way that went beyond a business relationship.

Stepping outside, he took a moment to breathe in the fresh mountain air. There was no place on earth that cleared his lungs so easily. And no place where he felt more claustrophobic either. Fishing his cell phone out of his pocket, he tapped on Alex's contact in his list and thumbed the phone number. Alex had an extra guest room that Mitch had stayed in during past visits to Sweetwater Springs.

"What's up, man?" Alex asked in lieu of a hello.

"Hey, buddy. I need a place to stay tonight," Mitch said.

"Thought you were staying with Mable's granddaughter now," Alex teased.

Word in a small town traveled about as quickly as an echo from Wild Blossom Bluffs. "Not anymore," he said.

"Tuck and I are actually meeting up at the Tipsy Tavern tonight for our own little post–turkey day celebration. Why don't you join us?"

"A drink sounds great, actually," Mitch said, sucking in some more of the cool mountain air. If he could bottle up this stuff and take it with him when he left, he'd be good to go.

"Great," Alex said. "I'll head over there around seven."

"See you then." Mitch hung up and headed back inside. No matter if his mom didn't have a bed for him tonight, he still needed a shower. He'd needed an ice-cold one since last night. Between that and a few drinks with the guys tonight, he planned to get his head on straight before facing Kaitlyn again.

$\mathscr{C}$HAPTER TWELVE

$\mathscr{H}$e'll come back," Paris said, taking a seat beside Kaitlyn on the couch later that evening. She had a design sketchbook in her lap. Even though she would probably never work in New York again, she still liked designing big, beautiful rooms that felt magical when you stepped inside them.

"Who?" she asked.

"Mitch is the reason you're moping, right?"

She leaned back into the couch cushion with a heavy sigh. "Well, you and several other guests heard our argument this morning. You know what happened." She shook her head, still embarrassed over it all. "Rule number one of hosting a bed and breakfast: Don't throw yourself at any of the guests or your business partner. Why didn't my grandmother leave me a rule book for this job?"

Paris chuckled. He was holding a glass of red wine in his hand. Shouldn't a biker drink beer? He was a walking contradiction in her mind. "Life doesn't have rule books, unfortunately."

"Have you found anyone who sparks your interest since your divorce?" she asked, suddenly curious to know more about him.

Paris shrugged. "Not really."

She frowned. "Well, I was happy to hear you might be making Sweetwater Springs your home. I'm new here too so that would be one more friend I'd have in town."

"Who needs romance when you have friends, right?" He bumped his shoulder against hers. "You know what? The best medicine for a broken heart is a night out on the town. That's my experience at least."

"A night out?" she asked.

"Yeah. We should go have drinks," he said, and she was beyond certain he wasn't flirting with her. She had nothing to worry about with Paris.

"I would but I can't leave the inn. A host's job is never done. No more barhopping for me," she said on a laugh.

"Did someone say bar?" Joe asked, bounding off the bottom stair with Missy following close behind him in a short skirt and skintight leggings. "Because I am so in."

Kaitlyn had learned that their prolonged stay was because of their fall break from college. Both of their families lived too far to drive back for the week. And while Kaitlyn had been put off by their behavior at first, she'd grown fond of the young, overly affectionate couple.

She turned to look at them. "The Tipsy Tavern downtown is supposed to be good. Why don't you two go with Paris and check it out?" She narrowed her gaze at the couple. "Wait. Are you at least twenty-one?"

Missy giggled. "I love getting asked that question. I just became legal last month."

"I love being asked too," Kaitlyn said. "Even if it isn't happening as often as I'd like anymore," she whispered to Paris.

He laughed and then nudged her with his elbow. "The Jamiesons told me earlier they were going out for drinks tonight. They asked me to come along. Why don't we all go?"

Kaitlyn hedged. "I'm not sure the Krespos would enjoy that. But I can stay here while the rest of you go have fun. Really, I'm fine."

They all turned toward a sudden commotion that erupted at the top of the stairs as Mrs. Krespo chased her husband with her cane down the open hallway.

The Trapps peeked their heads out of their room to see what the disturbance was.

"Uh-oh," Kaitlyn said, prepared to run interference.

Instead, Paris stood to address the group. "A few of us are going out to a bar tonight. Do you all want to come along?"

"It's okay if you don't," Kaitlyn assured them, knowing the older couple would likely refuse.

"Oh, I'd love to!" Mrs. Krespo said, surprising her.

"Us too," Chris and Nate agreed, heading out of their room.

Paris turned back to Kaitlyn with a mischievous grin. "Looks like a group event. I'll call a taxi van. No need for a DD. Just a good time."

A good time. Right. Going to a bar with two horny college kids, a mysterious biker, a gay couple, newlyweds, and an old lady with a cane and a husband who loved her as much as he seemed to fear her. What was the worst that could happen?

* * *

An hour later, Kaitlyn walked into the Tipsy Tavern with Paris, Mr. and Mrs. Krespo (canes and attitude included), the

Jamiesons, Chris and Nate Trapp, and the young college love-birds. Maybe this would be a regular activity at the B&B, she considered. Friday nights at the tavern. *Yeah.* She liked the idea.

Paris pointed at a long table with a booth lining the wall toward the back of the tavern. "We'll all fit over there. Not that we'll be sitting. That dance floor looks tempting."

"I'm not much of a dancer," she called over her shoulder, unsure if Paris could even hear her over the cacophony of music, laughter, and glasses clinking on the scarred wooden tables. She looked back to make sure the Krespos were okay. Mrs. Krespo whacked her cane back and forth, scooting people to the side in a not-so-subtle way.

Kaitlyn choked on a laugh. It was hilarious and a bit concerning. She reached the back table and plopped down in a seat.

"Oh, no you don't." Chris shook his head. "Dance first, drink later."

"I think it goes the other way around. I need drinks to make me dance. And maybe not even then." She signaled the waitress who was walking by.

"Need a drink?" the twentysomething blond asked. She was tall, thin, and beautiful in an obvious kind of way.

Kaitlyn remembered Mitch saying he'd had a one-night stand with a waitress here a few months back. She sized the waitress up with a smile, wondering if this was the one. "Yes, anything strong that you have on tap, please."

"Coming right up." The waitress headed off.

"Are you checking her out?" Nate plopped down in the space next to Kaitlyn.

"Yes. Actually, I was. But not for the reason you're thinking. Someone I know had a fling with a waitress here. Just wondering if it was her."

"You are as see-through as that woman's dress over there." He gestured to the dance floor and a woman who looked naked at first glance. "Would that someone happen to be Mitch?" he asked. "And are you jealous?"

Chris snuggled in beside Nate, leaning over to listen. "She has good reason to be jealous. I hate everyone in your past," he told Nate. "Even the ones I like I still hate."

Nate grinned. "Must be love," he told his husband.

"Oh, no." Kaitlyn shook her head. "Mitch and I aren't...We don't have that kind of relationship. We just, well, we might have kissed. But only twice."

"You're not telling us anything we don't know. The whole house is buzzing about that fight this morning and what happened last night." Chris bounced his eyebrows.

Kaitlyn sighed and looked around. The Jamiesons were seated at the bar. The Krespos had moved to the dance floor along with the college kids. By the looks of it, Mr. Krespo still had quite a few moves. Mrs. Krespo was actually smiling as she tried to keep up with him.

Kaitlyn turned back to Chris, Nate, and Paris. "Unfortunately, nothing happened last night, and that's the problem." She covered her face with both hands. There was nothing like complete honesty with friends—kind of—to humble you.

A drink was set in front of her. She lifted her head, thanked the waitress—whom they were all watching with interest now—and took a healthy sip.

"So you made a move on him?" Nate asked.

She bit her lower lip, weighing how much detail to disclose. "He's been giving me mixed signals since we became business partners. He looks at me with those eyes and talks to me in that voice. I thought he was feeling the vibe between us too."

"You sure you weren't imagining it?" Paris asked.

She swallowed, remembering the night she'd gone downtown with Mitch. She hadn't imagined the heat between them. "Mitch kissed me. But maybe"—she shook her head—"maybe he didn't want to take it any further. Maybe that part was just me." She shook her head again. "This is so embarrassing. I'll never be able to look at him again."

"Hate to break it to you, sweetheart," Paris said.

She looked at him curiously. "What?"

Gesturing, Paris pointed across the room.

Kaitlyn's heart sunk and did a little somersault at the same time. Her heart was evidently just as confused as she was at the sight of Mitch Hargrove.

* * *

Mitch was halfway through his first beer and having a decent time with the guys. He'd laughed more than a few times, and it'd felt good. *He* had felt good until he'd overheard a commotion going on behind him. He turned around to see a little old lady with a walking cane parting the crowd like Moses with the Red Sea.

What is Mrs. Krespo doing here?

Scanning the room, he noticed the entire gang of B&B guests weaving through the bar. Then he spotted Kaitlyn and his heart stalled for a second. What was it about that woman that made her so damn hard to resist? Why did he want her so badly? And why did the sight of her alongside Paris make him want to go punch a hole in the wall?

He wasn't eighteen anymore. He might've done that over a girl back then but now he was marine strong with an iron cast will.

"Earth to Mitch."

Mitch turned toward Alex's and Tuck's raised brows. "Sorry. Mr. and Mrs. Krespo are here."

Tuck and Alex followed where his gaze had just been.

"Who?" Alex scrunched his face. "I know everyone in this town, and I've never seen them before."

"They're staying at the Sweetwater B and B."

"Right. That article in *Loving Life* magazine is drawing a small crowd to the area. That's good for commerce but it'll make the department busier. I'll have to hire more officers if the tourists keep coming in. I'm shorthanded as it is."

"Looks like the host is here too," Tuck said. "Kaitlyn seems awfully friendly with that Harley Davidson model."

Mitch frowned. "That's Paris. He's in town for some kind of Santa thing."

"Bikers for Santa," Alex said with a nod. "They're meeting up at the Lights on the Lake event this weekend."

"Yeah," Mitch said with a nod.

"Since I'm short-staffed, I'll be working the event myself," Alex said.

"You expecting trouble with the carolers?"

Alex frowned. "Janice Murphy spiked the eggnog last year."

Tuck laughed out loud. "That was the best. I'll be there with my nephew, Theo. Halona is keeping her flower shop open late for customers that night."

"You going?" Alex asked.

Mitch gave his head a shake. "As much as I'd hate to miss the drunk caroling, I don't think so."

"You have to. It's the town's biggest event," Tuck pressed.

"Exactly," Mitch answered. Attending Sweetwater's biggest event was akin to skinny-dipping in a lake full of piranhas. At least in Mitch's mind.

"Hey, guys." A waitress stepped up to the table.

Mitch inwardly groaned, recognizing the voice before he even looked up. "Hi, Nadine."

"Long time since you've been at one of my tables, Mitch," she said. "I've missed you."

Mitch briefly looked at his friends, which was a mistake. He hadn't told them about his one-night stand with Nadine the last time he was home but these guys missed nothing.

"Sounds like your lucky night," Alex told Nadine. "Maybe you can take a break and Mitch here can sweep you across the dance floor."

"I don't dance," Mitch said through gritted teeth. If he put his hands on Nadine, she'd expect another night together. Despite what everyone said, one-night stands came with strings attached, which was why he'd turned away from Kaitlyn last night.

The image of Kaitlyn's bare skin against white lace flashed in his mind for the millionth time today. Given a second chance, he wasn't sure he'd be able to resist her again.

"Well, if you change your mind . . ." Nadine winked. "I've got customers to attend to. See you, guys."

"She's pretty," Tuck said, pulling from his beer and watching Nadine sashay off.

"Well, you take her home then," Mitch grumbled.

Tuck shook his head. "Not my type."

"You've barely dated since Renee. Maybe taking Nadine for a spin on the dance floor or out to dinner sometime would help get you back out there," Alex suggested.

Tuck frowned grimly, and his eyes dulled. "Maybe I don't want to get back out there. I'm good."

Just like with Mable's passing, Mitch had been unable to get leave from the corps when Renee had died from cancer two summers ago. Neither of them had been blood relatives. He'd thought a lot of Renee though. She and Tuck had started dating in high school. Mitch hated to think about his friends not getting the happy ending they deserved. He couldn't imagine what Tuck had gone through or how he was even functional enough to be here tonight. Life went on, Mitch guessed. People did the best they could with the cards they were dealt.

"If you don't go break in on that dance, there's a chance that Kaitlyn and Paris might go home together tonight," Alex said, pulling Mitch from his thoughts.

Mitch turned to look back at the dance floor. The music was fast paced, and Kaitlyn was swaying back and forth in front of Paris. There wasn't a good chance that they'd go home together tonight; it was definite. They were both staying at the Sweetwater B&B. Whether they returned to the same bed, though, was over Mitch's dead body.

He set his beer down and pushed back from the table.

"Yeah, buddy!" Alex shook a fist in the air. "Go get her."

Kaitlyn wasn't his to get. He just didn't want her to get hurt—all the more reason he should skip breaking up the happy couple and head to the men's restroom instead.

He continued forward until he was standing somewhat awkwardly in front of a dancing Kaitlyn and Paris. Everyone was moving to the beat except him.

"Oh," Kaitlyn said, finally noticing his presence. Her smile quickly fell. He guessed she was recalling that she was still ticked off at him about last night.

"Hey, Mitch," Paris said, freezing to a halt. "What's going on, man?"

The muscles of Mitch's jaw bunched. "I'm cutting in. That's what."

* * *

Kaitlyn wrapped her arms around Paris's neck and pulled him to her. "I don't think so," she said.

Is he serious right now?

Mitch had rejected her last night but he didn't want her dancing with Paris?

Paris grabbed hold of Kaitlyn's arms and gently loosened them. "Actually, I have to visit the men's room. She's all yours, buddy." He winked at Kaitlyn, which she took as an apology, but he'd be hearing from her about this later. They'd only known each other a week but they were supposed to have each other's backs. Friends didn't let friends dance with burly, sexy, off-limits men.

"Kaitlyn?" Mitch said. As he did, the music transitioned from a fast, upbeat tune to something slow and romantic. The lights dimmed, reminding her of a middle school dance. She'd never liked those. They were awkward, and she'd spent most of her time holding up the wall and avoiding eye contact because she was too nervous to approach any of the boys. And the cute guys never asked her to dance. Instead it was always the sweaty ones with an overeager smile.

Mitch was the cute guy tonight. The cute guy was asking her to dance, and she couldn't say no. Not to him, no matter how much she wanted to.

"Fine. But just so you know, this doesn't mean I like you." In fact, she was doing her damnedest to hate him. But he was right when he'd told her earlier that he was one of the good guys. He'd proven that time and time again.

Mitch anchored his big hands on her waist and pulled her body toward him.

Her arms dutifully went to his shoulders but she didn't make eye contact. She clamped her mouth shut and didn't say a word. If they were going to talk, he was going to have to be the one to start the conversation.

"Kaitlyn?"

Reflexively, her gaze went to his. *Traitorous gaze.* "What do you want from me, Mitch?" she asked on a sigh. "Last night you acted like you wanted nothing to do with me. Fine. You got it. But now you're here asking me to dance and looking at me with those puppy dog eyes, and it's just confusing. Make up your mind. You either want me or you don't."

"I don't want to want you, but . . . "

She swallowed thickly. "But?"

"But I do, and I'm not sure what to do about that."

"You probably didn't hesitate with that waitress when you took her home a few months back."

"No," he admitted, his expression unreadable. "And I regret that. I had too much to drink that night, and I'd just gotten off my last deployment. I had a lot going on in my head. Nadine was just a Band-Aid for the crap I didn't want to deal with. The same way you wanted me to be your Band-Aid last night."

Her eyes widened. She considered arguing that point but wondered if maybe it was true. Was she just trying to use him last night? "Well, what's wrong with Band-Aids? If I want you and you want me, then what's wrong with just going with it? It doesn't have to *mean* anything."

His mouth was set in a flat line. Not a frown, but not a smile either. She studied the growth of hair that surrounded his lips, remembering how soft it'd felt when they'd kissed. Full-force tingles rushed over her. She was still mad. Still wanted to hate him. Still wanted to take him back to her bedroom and use him as the fuel to her sexual fantasies for the next year. Screw the consequences—she wanted to live in the moment. She wanted to be whisked away from all the crap of the recent months.

Her arms tightened around him. Even as the song ended and transitioned to something more upbeat, she didn't pull away.

And neither did he. Their bodies were stuck to each other like magnets.

"Why did you ask me to dance if you don't want me?"

His gaze lowered, and their mouths were dangerously close to one another. Close enough to kiss a third time.

"Aren't you listening? I never said I didn't want you."

Those tingles combusted into flames.

"My turn," a high-pitched voice said as the waitress who served Kaitlyn earlier stepped up beside them. "Thought you weren't up for dancing, Mitch, but it looks like you changed your mind." Her gaze slid to Kaitlyn for a millisecond and then back to him. "The beer on tap here will do that to you, I guess."

Kaitlyn debated whether she was going to allow this to happen. Before she had a chance to decide, Mitch shook his head.

"I'm sorry, Nadine, but not tonight. I'm actually on my way out."

Nadine's gaze slid from him and back to Kaitlyn. "I see. Some other time, then," she said, looking disappointed.

He nodded. "Would you mind calling a cab for the group over there when they're ready to go?"

She shrugged. "Sure. I never let anyone leave this bar if they've had too much to drink anyway."

"Thanks. Have a great night, Nadine." Mitch grabbed Kaitlyn's hand and then started leading her toward the door.

"I can't leave," Kaitlyn said, even though her body was begging to differ. Going anywhere alone with Mitch right now was a terribly fantastic idea.

"The guests will be fine. Paris will make sure they all get back in one piece. I trust him that much."

"You just don't trust him to be alone with me?"

Mitch stared at her with heated brown eyes. "I don't want any other man to be alone with you. You can text Paris from my truck."

"Where are we going?" she asked—not that she cared.

There was a sudden urgency in his movements as he pulled her toward the exit. "To settle this thing between us once and for all."

CHAPTER THIRTEEN

$\mathscr{M}$itch was quiet as he steered the truck along the curvy road, revisiting the memories that flashed through his mind only briefly. Kaitlyn was beside him, no doubt wondering where he was taking her. Her silence told him she was nervous. Or still mad, although the anger had definitely melted away by the end of their dance. This attraction between them was building every time they were together. It was too strong to resist, and he was tired of trying.

The road turned again, and pain seared through his heart the way it always did at this spot. "This is where I crashed my truck when I was seventeen." He kept his gaze forward. Instead of speeding up as he sometimes did, he lifted his foot off the gas and slowed the truck, taking in the natural beauty of what was an awful place for him.

Kaitlyn gasped softly. "Were you hurt?"

"It depends on what you mean by hurt. I'm still alive but the accident hurt someone else." He hated being responsible for Brian Everson's disability. "It paralyzed a guy I went to high school with."

Her hands flew to her mouth. Mitch couldn't bear to look at her though. He hated himself for that one mistake. How could he ever expect anyone else to feel differently?

He pulled the truck to a stop at Majestic Point, a favorite lookout for sightseers. Putting the truck in park, he gripped the steering wheel as if his life depended on it. "I never should have been on the roads that night. I was young and stupid, and the domino effect of my poor choices ruined lives. Mine. My mom's. Brian Everson's."

She placed a hand on his forearm. "You didn't mean to."

"Intent doesn't matter." He finally looked at her. "Brian was training for the Olympics. My actions took that away from him. He'll never walk because I decided to go to a party. If he and his family never want to see my face in this town again"—which was what they'd told him in no uncertain terms in the accident's aftermath—"then that's the least I can do for them."

"I'm not sure what to say. Mitch, I'm so sorry."

"I walked away from that accident with barely a scratch," he said.

Kaitlyn's eyes were glistening as she listened. In the dark, they sparkled like Silver Lake under a star-filled sky.

"It wasn't your fault. Bad things happen sometimes. You can't blame yourself."

Even though that's exactly what he'd been doing ever since that fateful night. He didn't know how *not* to carry this blame. And the Everson family certainly blamed him.

"This is why you don't like Sweetwater Springs." She turned her face to look out the front windshield. From this spot, they had a perfect view of Mount Pleasant, cast in the light of a waxing moon.

"I joined the marines so I could escape and provide for my mom. She'd worked for the Eversons at the time. They fired her. She lost her benefits and had to work several jobs just to make enough to pay the bills." His mom had been working herself to exhaustion ever since.

He soaked in Kaitlyn's face and the softness there. "If things were different, kissing you would be easy, Kaitlyn."

Kissing her was already way too easy.

She leaned across the seat.

"What are you doing?" he asked in a gruff voice.

"Kissing me doesn't have to mean anything. Sometimes people just need a Band-Aid," she said, reminding him of his own words. "Kiss me, Mitch."

"Haven't you heard anything I just told you?"

"Every word," she whispered. "And it only matters to me because it's part of who you are. I'm not worried about yesterday or tomorrow. All I care about is tonight, and tonight I want to be with you."

Who is this woman? She was beautiful, strong, amazing, and yeah, he wanted to kiss her more than he wanted his life right now. Crossing the rest of the distance, he gave in, fully this time, shutting off his mind, which would no doubt object. Their lips met and opened to each other, and with her kiss, he swore she reached into his very soul.

Her arms wrapped around him, holding him, pulling him in. "Let's get a room," she whispered, pulling back as his hands continued to roam lower on her waist. Now that he'd started, he couldn't stop touching her this time.

"I know a place. Recently under new ownership, actually. I hear it's supposed to be one of the most romantic places to spend the holidays."

She grinned and then kissed his lips again. "Sounds perfect. Take me there."

* * *

The B&B was quiet as they entered. Either the guests were still at the Tipsy Tavern or all were in bed sleeping. Mitch didn't really care as long as they didn't stop what was about to happen between Kaitlyn and him. He was tired of fighting their attraction. All he wanted to do was rip Kaitlyn's clothes off and explore every inch of her.

Taking her hand, he tugged her down the hall into the room they'd shared last night and locked the door behind them. Then he kissed her, grabbing hold of the hem of her shirt at the same time. He lifted it over her head and tossed it across the room. Assisting him with the mission, she reached behind herself and unclasped her bra.

His gaze fell on her breasts, soft and round in the dim cast of moonlight streaming through the window. His hand followed, squeezing one softly, and then harder as she moaned, driving him insane.

"Please tell me you have a condom," she half whispered, half moaned.

He did. In his wallet. It crossed his mind that he could stop what was about to happen by telling her he didn't. That's what he needed to do. It was a ready excuse that would leave no hard feelings between them. But he'd been taken to the edge of his willpower, and it was now shattered. "I have protection," he said.

Then, kissing her all the way, he led her to the bed, shedding clothes in their wake and letting the moment take them wherever it wanted. Fear prickled in the back of his mind as he let himself go. Some lines couldn't be uncrossed. Just like crossing lanes and hitting a classmate. Or signing on the dotted line that committed your next four years to the marines. Somehow having sex with Kaitlyn felt like one of those lines that couldn't be uncrossed, and yet he wouldn't, *couldn't*, stop himself this time.

* * *

Kaitlyn eased into wakefulness, not letting go of sleep too quickly. She'd just been having the best dream. A sleepy smile crossed her face as her eyes fluttered open to see Mitch sleeping beside her.

Not a dream. Last night had been real, and it had surpassed all her past experiences with a man—not that she'd been with many. She watched him for a moment as he slept. He was a tough alpha male, and he was sleeping like a baby.

"Stop staring at me," he growled quietly and then cracked open an eye to look at her. The corner of his mouth turned up.

"I didn't know you were awake." Or that he could see through his eyelids. This was a man of many talents.

His hand reached under the covers and caressed her arm, the touch sending her body into full need.

She could spend a million nights like the one she'd just had.

"Oh no!" She sat up in bed and turned to the clock on her nightstand. "I have to make breakfast. The guests." Those ooey-gooey feelings that had been flooding her were now a flurry of panic.

"I'll go get takeout." Mitch tugged on her arm, attempting to pull her in for a kiss.

She stopped just short of his lips. "Takeout? Don't the guests expect something…more? I mean, it's called a bed and breakfast. I'm supposed to supply both of those things."

He leaned in and finally kissed her. Then he pulled away and started to dress. "I suspect the guests are all experiencing a bit of a hangover from last night. All they'll need is hot coffee and lots of it."

She watched him yank on a pair of jeans. He was still bare chested, and her fingers itched to slide over the smooth contours of his muscled abs. "No takeout." Tearing her gaze from him, which was no easy feat, she got up and hurried to her dresser. She chose a pair of jeans and a long-sleeved I LOVE NEW YORK T-shirt. "You make the bacon, and I'll make the eggs and grits. I have frozen biscuits in the freezer. Not Grandma Mable's recipe but those'll have to do."

"Your choice."

She went to the bathroom and then hurried down the hall and into the kitchen where she began bustling around on autopilot.

"You've really gotten this routine down," Mitch observed a few minutes later. "Mable would've been proud."

Kaitlyn grinned up at him. "I'm kind of proud of myself. I wasn't sure I'd be able to pull this off. But I am. I wish..." She shook her head. What was the point of wishing for something that wasn't going to happen?

"What?"

"It's just...my parents thought I was crazy to leave New York and come here. I wish they could see this place now and how I've got it all handled."

"So show them," he said. "Invite them here to be your guests."

She considered the idea. "We just reopened. I'm not sure it's ready yet."

He flipped the slices of bacon to their other sides. "You just said you weren't sure you'd pull this off but you are. You have guests and they're plenty satisfied with their stay here. You're ready."

You're. This was still her endeavor, not his. Last night had meant a lot but it hadn't changed the end game.

"I'll think about it. Thank you."

"What for?"

"Listening. It's one of the many things you're good at." She winked at him.

"You too." There was a serious note in his voice despite her air of flirtation. He'd shared things with her last night that she suspected he didn't talk about very often. Somehow that felt even more intimate than what they'd done in bed afterward. This had been more than a one-night stand—even if it had only been for the one night.

She fetched the bag of corn grits from the pantry and laid it on the counter. The water was already boiling. All she needed to do was add some substance and stir.

"Ho, ho, hoooooooo!"

Kaitlyn exchanged a glance with Mitch and then hurried toward the dining room to find Santa Claus standing among the other guests. Except Santa was tall, thin, and had pale-blue eyes like Paris. He was also wearing all black except for his bright-red Santa hat and white fluffy beard.

"I guess today is the big day?" Kaitlyn asked.

"Tonight actually. I'm heading down to the Sweetwater Café to meet some fellow bikers this morning though."

"So you're not staying for breakfast?"

He shook his head, his beard scraping low on his chest. "The café is offering us free breakfasts if we dress up."

"That's nice of them," Kaitlyn said.

"You're a crappy excuse for a Santa," Mrs. Krespo bellowed from one of the tables. "Though I can see why Mommy was caught kissing Santa under the mistletoe if he looked like you."

Kaitlyn pressed her lips together to keep from laughing.

"Afterward, I'm checking out the garage apartment for rent down the road. Do you think it'll help if I wear my hat and beard?" Paris asked.

Kaitlyn tilted her head. "Maybe. Although I'll be sad to see one of my favorite guests leave if you do rent that place."

"Your nightly rate is reasonable to a point," he said. "After two weeks, it'd be unreasonable for me to stay. I'll see you all later." He headed out the door, and a few minutes later, she heard the sound of his motorcycle roaring out of the driveway.

Kaitlyn walked over to the Krespos' table. "Sleep well?" she asked.

Mr. Krespo gave her a sheepish smile. "Very well," he said.

"No kissing and telling, Marvin," Mrs. Krespo muttered, reaching for her coffee cup. "Kaitlyn doesn't need to know you got lucky last night."

Mr. Krespo's face turned beet red. "I didn't tell her that, Evie."

"Well, you might as well have." Mrs. Krespo gave her husband an assessing look. "I haven't danced in years. I forgot how good of a dancer you were. It did things to me."

Kaitlyn nearly fell over in her shock that the older woman was being civil, even flirting with her husband.

"Maybe I should take you dancing more often," Mr. Krespo said with a small grin.

"Maybe you should," Mrs. Krespo agreed, her stiff demeanor softening as she smiled at him.

Well, wonders never ceased. The bed and breakfast was already bringing couples closer.

"All right, everyone. Who's hungry?" Mitch asked, coming into the dining area with his hands full of food.

Kaitlyn whirled, finding herself surprised a second time

this morning. The Mitch Hargrove she'd come to know was standoffish with guests. He didn't make grand entrances. Instead, he usually snuck up on people.

She watched as he set the dishes at the center of one of the tables and began serving the guests with a smile on his face. He also made easy chitchat, which Kaitlyn had never seen him do here. After a moment, he looked up at her.

Right. She was just standing there, equal parts stunned and charmed by this new side of Mitch.

* * *

Christmas was exactly one month from today. Mitch was halfway home with his commitment and suddenly trying to throw a wrench in things by sleeping with Kaitlyn.

Not that he could bring himself to regret even one moment.

The prospect of one more month with her didn't sound so bad if it went like last night. The prospect of another month in Sweetwater Springs going stir-crazy in this inn, however...

He'd already checked off everything on Kaitlyn's to-do list. He'd power washed the outdoor Jacuzzi this afternoon and then showered the grime off and spent time online perusing places to rent in Northern Virginia. That was it. Now what was he supposed to do for another month?

Kaitlyn came breezing into the room where he'd been sitting and staring at the blinking lights of the tree. "What do you think?" she asked, doing a little twirl in front of him.

He hesitated. "Is this some kind of trick question?" She was wearing a bright-red turtleneck with a pair of fitted blue jeans. A crystal snowflake necklace added just a little cheer to what she was wearing.

"Your mom and aunt Nettie are here," she said as if that explained her question. It only raised more in his mind.

"Why?" he asked.

"To watch the inn for us."

He furrowed his brow. "Again, why?"

Kaitlyn placed her hands on her hips. "So you and I can go to the Lights on the Lake event, remember?"

Mitch tensed. "I don't remember agreeing to that."

"Mitchell Douglas Hargrove," his mom said, walking into the sitting room. She paused from lecturing him to admire the tree. "Oh, how lovely!" she said. "Isn't that pretty, Nettie?" she asked his aunt, who'd stepped into the room as well.

"It really is," Nettie said. "So bright and colorful! You two must have worked so hard." She turned to look at him. "Hello, my favorite nephew."

"Your only nephew," Mitch said, suddenly feeling like a hostage in this room of women.

"Kaitlyn is new in town," his mom continued, "and she deserves to go. I raised you to be a gentleman, which means you're taking her."

That didn't sound like a request.

Mitch massaged his temple where a headache was forming. The entire town would be there. Including the Eversons. "Mom, you're supposed to be taking it easy," he reminded her. "Not minding the inn for us."

"I'll have you know that Dr. Jacobs's office called this afternoon."

Mitch swallowed. "And?"

"And aside from being a little low on my iron level, I'm as healthy as a horse. Those were Dr. Jacobs's exact words."

"Low on iron?" Mitch asked, scrutinizing his mom's appearance. A rosiness had replaced the pallor of her skin over the last week. She was almost glowing, part of which he knew was because she was happy to have him home.

"Dr. Jacobs said I have anemia," his mom said, "which can cause a whole host of problems. It accounts for me being so tired and weak all of a sudden. Dr. Jacobs said to take an extra iron supplement along with my multivitamin and to come back to see her next month."

"Well, that's wonderful news!" Kaitlyn said.

"It certainly is," Nettie agreed.

Mitch narrowed his eyes. "Is Dr. Jacobs sure?"

"Very. She also told me to tell you to stop worrying and to have a little fun. Doctor's orders. Now get moving. You're taking Kaitlyn out tonight, and we're watching the inn."

There was no arguing with his mom once she'd made up her mind on something.

Mitch turned to Kaitlyn. "Wouldn't you prefer if I took you to a nice restaurant?" Because it wasn't Kaitlyn he had a problem with.

Kaitlyn opened her mouth to speak but his mom held up a hand. "She would prefer to go to the one town event that everyone will be talking about until next year's Lights on the Lake. Mable would've insisted on it."

How could Mitch argue with a dead woman? "Fine," he finally said.

"Are you sure?" Kaitlyn's forehead wrinkled. "If you don't want to, I'm sure I can get a ride over with Paris."

"On the back of his bike?" Mitch ground out, hating that idea even more. "I said I'd take you."

"It'd be his pleasure," his mom said, narrowing her eyes at him.

Pleasure was taking Kaitlyn back to the bedroom. Not walking into what felt most certainly like enemy lines.

* * *

The moon was on a slow rise in the nearly December sky. Music floated above the crowd.

"I know why you were hesitant to come," Kaitlyn said, reaching for his hand.

Surprising himself, he took her hand as if it were as natural as holing up and hiding himself from the world. He was also surprised that being out and about didn't bother him as much as he'd expected. He had a large dog-eared hat covering his head and a full beard on his face. In such a thick crowd, no one would likely even recognize him. He'd been worried for nothing. "I'm glad I came."

Engines roared from somewhere in the distance.

"Sounds like the Bikers for Santa." Kaitlyn squeezed his hand excitedly. "I'm going to pull an angel off the tree too. It's for a good cause."

Mitch nodded. "Mable and Henry always did. They were my Santa as well, although I didn't know that for a long time. Mom couldn't afford to buy me a lot."

Kaitlyn's hand squeezed tighter as they continued down the row of stores, all lit up and decorated, enticing shoppers to come inside and let the holiday shopping begin. Now that Mable was gone, there were only two people on Mitch's list to buy for this year. Make that three. He wanted to get Kaitlyn a little something too.

"Hey, aren't those the Trapps?" Kaitlyn asked, pointing across the busy street.

Mitch followed her gaze to the two young men standing with an older couple. "Yeah. Those must be Nate's parents."

"Hmm. Well, being the good hosts we are, we should go say hello," Kaitlyn suggested.

He wasn't in the mood for socializing but he didn't want to argue. "Sure."

Kaitlyn stepped slightly ahead of him as they approached. "Fancy seeing you guys here," she called out, gaining their attention. "I didn't know you two were coming tonight."

"Kaitlyn." Nate went in for a hug, and then Chris did as well. After that, they shook Mitch's hand. "Paris convinced us to come. Then we roped Mom and Dad into coming along too." Nate turned back to his parents. "Mom, Dad, this is Kaitlyn and Mitch. They run the Sweetwater Bed and Breakfast. Kaitlyn and Mitch, this is Tina and Jim, my doting parents."

Mitch shook their hands, very aware of Tina's disapproving look.

"Thank you for giving the boys a place to stay but I really wish they would have spent the holidays at our home. That's where they belong, not with strangers," the woman said.

"Mom," Nate warned, "you know why we didn't stay with you. We aren't discussing that here." Nate's tone and demeanor were relaxed. "We're together tonight, and we're going to have fun."

Tina shook her head. "It's just that Christmas is coming, and I don't want you staying at some cold inn when you have a perfectly good home."

"With all due respect, Mrs. Trapp," Chris said, putting an arm around Nate's shoulders, "Kaitlyn and Mitch's bed and breakfast is anything but cold. It's warm and cozy. They've taken very good care of us."

"Thank you," Kaitlyn said.

Mitch looked over at her and could tell she was working hard not to say whatever was on her mind. He also knew she'd eventually say it.

"Nate and Chris have been such a delightful couple to

have," Kaitlyn said after a moment. "We gave them one of my favorite rooms at the inn."

"Together, I gather?" Tina asked, making no attempt to hide her disapproval.

"Of course. I agree that family belongs at home for the holidays but a married couple belongs in the same room."

Mitch noticed the worried glance between Nate and Chris.

"You are so lucky that your son found someone to love," Kaitlyn continued, keeping her smile steady even though her tone was pointed. "Not everyone does. It's something to celebrate. Don't make Nate choose between you and his husband. It's not fair. And if you do, it'll likely work in my favor," Kaitlyn said, "and I'll see Nate and Chris at the Sweetwater B and B more often over the coming years."

Tina frowned and then looked at her husband, who kept his head low. Mitch guessed Jim didn't mind the couple sharing a room. Kaitlyn was right. Tina's behavior would eventually put a wedge between her and her son if she didn't change her rules.

"It was so nice to meet you," Kaitlyn said, offering her hand to Jim first and then Tina. Tina hesitated before taking it. Mitch shook the couple's hands as well. Then they said their goodbyes, and Kaitlyn promised Nate and Chris a delicious breakfast in the morning.

"Kaitlyn Russo is not someone to mess with," Mitch teased as they continued down the sidewalk.

She gave a sidelong glance at him. "Or she never learned when to keep her mouth shut."

"Nah. Nate's mom needed to hear that. You did a good thing. I'm impressed." Mitch reached for her hand again as they walked. It felt natural. Family belonged at home. Married people belonged in the same room. And he belonged here, with Kaitlyn.

Where did that come from?

Before he could analyze his thoughts, Kaitlyn pointed.

"Oh wow, look! Carolers!" She tugged him toward a group of festively dressed singers. Kaitlyn and Mitch blended in with the crowd and watched for several songs. He'd spent many a Christmas at this very event when he was growing up. Somehow, he'd never appreciated it until now when he'd stayed away for so long and missed so many years.

A strong hand slapped his back, sending Mitch into a cough that he quickly suppressed to avoid drawing attention from the onlookers.

"Hey, man," Alex said with a laugh. He was dressed in his full police uniform tonight. "You must be Kaitlyn," he said, offering his hand to her.

Kaitlyn dropped Mitch's hand to shake with Alex.

Alex looked at Mitch and lifted his brows. "No wonder you didn't need a place to stay last night," he said just loud enough for Mitch to hear.

Mitch shook his head. "You'll always be a jerk. Some things never change," he said in the most affectionate of ways.

"Having fun tonight, Kaitlyn?" Alex asked, ignoring him.

"Oh, definitely. This is amazing. I can't wait to see the Angel Tree. I've heard so much about it."

"It's my favorite part of this shindig. The Sweetwater Springs Police Department adopts quite a few kids each year. Make sure you check out the cake walk too. The ladies in town make dozens to give away. I'm sure your guests would love some cake tomorrow."

"Good idea. Thank you." She hugged her arms around her body instead of reaching for Mitch's hand again.

Mitch shoved his own hands in his pockets and then

turned as Alex's radio buzzed to life at his hip. From his years as a military police officer, Mitch was attuned to the sound. Adrenaline suddenly zipped through his veins. He missed the sound of a call. Missed racing toward a scene.

"B and E at Dawanda's Fudge Shop on Main Street," someone reported through the radio.

Alex cursed softly. "I've got to go, you two. There's been another B and E. This is two in a week's time."

"I'm going with you," Mitch said.

Alex narrowed his eyes. "You're not SSPD."

"No, but you're short-staffed. I'm not letting you go into a B and E without backup."

"What about Kaitlyn?"

Mitch had almost forgotten about his date.

"Go. It's fine," Kaitlyn urged. "I'll stay a little longer and then get a cab ride home. Or maybe Paris can give me that ride after all."

Mitch's teeth ground together but he nodded anyway. "You sure?"

"Positive. Go help Dawanda. I'll see you later tonight."

CHAPTER FOURTEEN

*M*itch rode shotgun in Alex's police SUV, zipping down the familiar streets of Sweetwater toward Dawanda's Fudge Shop. As soon as Alex cut the engine, Mitch hopped out and followed him. As they stepped up on the curb, Mitch glanced in the shop window. No sign of anyone other than Dawanda sitting at one of the tables with her head in her hands. She looked up as a bell overhead announced their entrance.

"You okay?" Alex asked immediately, looking past her and around the store. "Anyone else here?"

"No. But the jackass left with everything in the register."

Mitch wasn't sure he'd ever seen Dawanda without a smile on her face. He didn't like it. "Did you recognize the intruder?"

Alex glanced over. "Let me ask the questions, okay?"

"Yeah. Sorry." Mitch ran a hand through his overgrown hair.

"Did you recognize the intruder?" Alex repeated, turning back to Dawanda.

"No. He had on a mask. I thought I recognized the voice but I don't know. It all happened so fast. He said if I didn't give him the money, I'd be sorry."

"Did he have a gun?" Mitch cut in, forgetting that he was supposed to stay quiet.

Alex shot him another dour look.

"No. Maybe. I'm not really sure. He kept his hands in his pockets the whole time."

"I see. Did he come in through the front of the store or the back?" Alex continued.

"The back, while I was making the fudge . . . Oh, darn it. I burned the fudge," Dawanda whined. "That makes me even madder!" She shot out of her chair and went to the kitchen.

As she did, Mitch headed to check the back door. It was unlocked and cracked open. He was careful not to touch anything as he glanced outside. No one in sight, which meant the thief wasn't a fool and didn't have a death wish, because Mitch had a mind to knock the guy's lights out if given a chance. Mitch wasn't part of the Sweetwater PD so he didn't have any rules to abide by.

"All clear," he said several minutes later as he returned to the front of the store.

Alex was leaning forward and getting a statement from Dawanda, who'd returned from the kitchen. "Any other details you can give us?" Alex asked her.

"I would if I could."

"Well, sometimes details come back after you've had a chance to relax. If you think of anything tonight or tomorrow, here's my cell phone number." Alex handed her a business card.

"Might want to keep the back door locked," Mitch added.

"I always do," she said.

Mitch furrowed his brow and turned to Alex. "There was no sign of forced entry. Looks like the perp just walked right in."

Alex looked at Dawanda. "Maybe you forgot to lock it this time."

"Would've been the first time that's ever happened." She rubbed her temple. "I think I'll just close up early tonight. There's no serving fudge after something like this. Or doing cappuccino readings." She winked at Mitch, even though her expression was still troubled. "Unless, of course, you're up for one, Chief Baker. I haven't had the pleasure of peeking into your future yet." Her face lit up just a bit as she looked at Alex hopefully.

Mitch did his best to contain a grin. "Yeah, buddy. It's your turn."

"Another day. Right now, I'm determined to catch our thief. This makes two in this area. I'm guessing another one of these stores will be hit next."

Dawanda's mouth dropped open. "I'll call the ladies and tell them to keep protection." Her eyes twinkled mischievously. "And by protection, I mean weapons."

Alex cleared his throat. If he was fazed by the comment, it didn't show. "I don't want a bunch of store owners packing guns down here, Dawanda. That can make things worse. I'll just have my officers patrol the area more frequently."

"Thought you were shorthanded at the station," she said.

Alex's gaze narrowed. "How'd you know that?"

"I know a lot of things, Chief Baker. People talk, especially when you offer them caffeine and sugar."

Mitch was already regretting what he was about to offer. "I'm in town through Christmas Eve. I can help." *What the hell am I doing?* Keeping a low profile at the bed and breakfast was one thing. Riding around the town as part of the SSPD was another.

Alex looked at him with interest. "Thought you were busy with the B and B."

"I have time, and you know I have the experience. Besides, I want to see this perp behind bars as badly as anyone. No one messes with Dawanda and gets away with it."

* * *

Gina Hargrove was right. Lights on the Lake was an event that should not be missed. The Angel Tree towered next to the lake like a beacon of hope to onlookers. Its light reflected perfectly in the pool of water. It was a sight to be seen. So was the cluster of bikers wearing Santa hats across the way.

Kaitlyn spotted Paris and waved. She didn't want to bother him for a ride though. He was in his element, and she wasn't ready to go back to the inn just yet. Coming from New York, she was used to getting lost in a crowd. In some way, being one of many was comforting. She headed toward a small park along the lake where a snow machine was set up for the kids and took a seat on one of the benches to watch them squeal with delight. The song "I'll Be Home for Christmas" filled the air around her.

She was home, she thought. She just wished the people she loved could be here with her for the holidays. Maybe Mitch was right. She should invite her parents to the inn to spend Christmas with her. There was a chance they'd say yes, although slim.

"Kaitlyn?" A woman stepped up to the bench and smiled brightly. She was dressed warmly in a coat and brightly colored knit hat that complemented her tanned complexion.

"Hi, Halona. I thought you would be working at the flower shop tonight."

Halona took a seat on the bench next to Kaitlyn and gestured toward Theo, who was playing in the snow with his uncle Tuck. "I closed early and headed over to join in the fun. I never miss Lights on the Lake. It's one of my favorite events of the season."

"I can see why. It's gorgeous," Kaitlyn said. Then she held up her laminated paper angel. "And for a good cause. I picked a six-year-old girl who wants a baby doll."

Halona held up a similar angel. "Nine-year-old boy who wants Nerf guns."

Kaitlyn laughed.

"Are you here all alone?" Halona asked.

"I was with Mitch but he left with Alex to go on a police call."

Halona furrowed her brow. "Oh my. I hope the eggnog wasn't spiked again. That stirred quite a ruckus last year."

"So I hear." Kaitlyn hugged her arms around her body for warmth as she watched Halona's son make snowballs, one after another, and pitch them at his uncle mercilessly.

"How's the bed and breakfast coming along?" Halona asked.

"Fine. Mitch and I have things running smoothly now, knock on wood." Kaitlyn knocked her fist along the wooden bench seat. "We've had several guests already, and reservations are booking up for next month. The article about the town in *Loving Life* magazine has helped."

"I've even seen an uptick in business at the flower shop," Halona told her, "which I have to say is nice because Theo's wish list gets more extensive each year."

The two women continued talking like old friends until

Theo came running over and stared at his mom with hopeful eyes. He didn't say a word though.

"Is it time for hot chocolate?" Halona asked as if reading some secret signal that Kaitlyn wasn't privy to. He nodded happily.

Halona turned to Kaitlyn. "Want to join us?"

Kaitlyn shook her head. "Thanks, but I better get back to the inn. Mitch's mom and aunt are watching the place tonight. I don't want to take advantage."

Halona stood. "That makes sense. Well, let me know if you ever need flower arrangements. I'll give you the friends-and-family discount."

Kaitlyn was touched. Her friends and family from New York might not be here with her for the holidays but she had one more person she could call a friend in Sweetwater. "Thanks. You guys have fun. Bye, Theo. Bye, Tuck."

"Keep Mitch in line, will you?" Tuck called back, taking his nephew's hand.

"That's easier said than done." Kaitlyn grinned as she watched them walk away, and then she stood and looked around. She still had the cab company's number programmed into her phone from her trip to the Tipsy Tavern. She decided to go ahead and start walking toward the parking lot before calling. Sometimes cabs parked there, waiting for customers.

Instead of seeing a cab when she got to the parking lot, Kaitlyn saw a dwindling collection of motorcycles. And one familiar-looking biker.

"Ho, ho, hooooooo. Where's Mitch?" Paris asked as she approached.

"He's playing cop," she said with a shrug.

Paris removed his helmet and extended it to her. "Hop on Santa's sleigh, then. I'll take you home."

She hesitated. Perhaps a cab ride was a better choice.

Only there didn't seem to be any in sight. Taking the helmet, she slipped it over her head. Paris moved the stuffed polar bear he had riding shotgun, and she straddled the bike behind him. Strangely enough, straddling a sexy guy like Paris did nothing for her. The only man she hoped to wrap her legs around tonight was Mitch.

The bike roared to life, and she hugged her arms around Paris's midsection. "I've never ridden on a motorcycle before," she warned.

He glanced over his shoulder with interest. "There's only one rule. Hold on tight," he said before zipping out of the parking lot and down the dim mountain roads.

* * *

Kaitlyn awoke just after midnight to someone entering her room. She recognized the shadow and the woodsy smell of pine.

"Hey," she whispered, rolling over to look at Mitch.

"I hope I'm not being presumptuous. I can always sleep on the couch," he said.

She reached for him, and he stepped toward her. "I was hoping you'd come to my bed." She yawned and propped her elbows up behind her, raising her upper body off the mattress. "How'd it go? Is Dawanda okay?" she asked, her thoughts circling back to earlier in the night.

"Yes. I'll fill you in at breakfast. There's no need to worry."

"Good. Now take those clothes off. Or am I being presumptuous?" she asked, nibbling her lower lip and biting back a mischievous grin.

"Not at all." He lifted his shirt over his head and tossed it to the floor.

Indeed, this was the only man who lit her up these days. Brighter than the Angel Tree at Silver Lake.

* * *

"Do I get an honorary badge?" Mitch asked Alex the next morning, as he walked into the Sweetwater Police Station. He already knew Alex would insist on a background check just for procedural reasons. Mitch was more than qualified to work here though. For a month. That was all he could offer. After that, he was moving on.

"We have the plastic kind we give to the kids when they come to visit," a uniformed woman said from behind the desk.

Mitch gave her a closer look and realized he recognized her. "Tammy?"

"The one and only. Hey there, stranger." The African American woman smiled back at him. She'd graduated from high school with Mitch, Alex, and Tuck. Tuck's sister, Halona, had been a year behind them all. It must've been ten years since he'd seen Tammy but she still looked the same. "You joining the force?" she asked.

Mitch gave a small nod. "Temporarily."

"Wonderful. Give the chief hell," Tammy said with a cheerful laugh.

"Will do."

"Hey," Alex said, looking somewhat intimidating, "I'm not above locking up any hell-raisers in the jail for a night or two. In fact," he said, turning to Mitch, "next time you need a place to crash, I've got a cell with your name on it." He lifted a hand and waved at Tammy. "See you after all the crime fighting."

"Don't forget to stop at Debbie's Donuts," Tammy teased.

"And bring me back one of the chocolate ones with rainbow sprinkles."

Alex rolled his eyes. "She thinks all I do is sip coffee and chat with the locals," he said, leading Mitch to an SUV with the SSPD logo in the parking lot. He clicked a button on his keychain, unlocking it, and then they both got inside. "Some days, she's right, but I'll never admit to it."

Mitch chuckled as Alex started the vehicle and pulled out of the parking lot. "I never would've expected Tammy to work at the station. She was quite the rule breaker in school."

"Yeah, well, life is full of surprises. For example, I'm surprised you offered to help out at the station. Don't get me wrong—I'm glad you did. We could use a good man right now. The holidays are a busy time around here."

"It's a win-win for us both, I guess. Another month locked away at the inn would be my undoing." And Kaitlyn might be his undoing in a completely different way. "After Christmas, I'm heading out as planned though. You might want to start interviewing officers now."

"Like it's that easy," Alex said with a head shake as he pulled up to a stoplight and waited for some pedestrians to cross. "I'll take as much help as you can offer." He glanced over. "I'll take having one of my best friends around as long as I can too. We've missed you, buddy."

The light turned green, and Alex refocused his attention on the road. Mitch was grateful because it gave him a second to swallow past his pesky emotion.

He cleared his throat. "So, tell me the truth. How is Tuck doing these days?"

Alex hesitated for a long moment. "I think he's doing okay. It was hard for him right after Renee died. He kept to himself a lot. Over the last six or so months though, he's started coming back out with me to the tavern. We've been hiking and climbing. He moved out of his old place with Renee. I think he's making a real effort to move on with his life."

"Where did he move to?" Mitch asked. He knew the town inside and out.

"A cottage on Blueberry Creek. It's oversized for just one man but you know how Tuck likes to commune with nature."

Mitch chuckled, remembering their friend's various selection of wildlife pets growing up. "Didn't he have a pet squirrel for a while?"

"That was better than the pet skunk that lasted a day." Both men started laughing like the kids they'd once been.

"We avoided him for a week after that fiasco," Mitch managed to choke out through shortened breaths of amusement.

Life hadn't been all bad here. It was easier to tell himself it was, but when he came home, the realization was like a sledgehammer to his system. Even though he and his mom had struggled financially after his father's death, life had been idyllic in this cozy mountain town. He never would've left if not for the accident.

"So, what's the deal between you and Kaitlyn?" Alex asked a moment later. "For a man who insists that he's not staying, you two were looking awfully cozy last night at Lights on the Lake."

They'd been awfully cozy last night in bed too, Mitch thought. And again this morning. "We have our own arrangement going."

"You know what they say about mixing business with pleasure."

Mitch turned to look at his friend and new boss. "She knows it's only temporary. Same as you."

"Doesn't mean I won't try to change your mind." Alex looked over briefly before returning his eyes to the road. "I'm guessing she's thinking the same."

* * *

Kaitlyn felt sentimental watching her first guests leave on Monday morning. She'd grown fond of all of them over the last few days. Even the Krespos, who'd spent most of yesterday in the bedroom. When they'd finally emerged, both had a glow and a smile on their faces. Then after breakfast, she'd helped them carry their belongings to their car.

"You might see us again," Mr. Krespo had said through his rolled-down window.

"You're welcome anytime." Kaitlyn meant it even though Mrs. Krespo hadn't been the easiest guest.

Now it was Chris and Nate's turn to depart.

"Thank you so much for staying at the inn," she told the couple.

"Thanks for having us. It's been an absolutely wonderful stay," Nate said. "And thank you for what you said to my mom."

Chris shook his head. "I still can't believe she called and invited us to come back for Christmas. And promised us a room together."

Kaitlyn's mouth fell open. "You're kidding."

"Nope." Nate chuckled softly. "She promised not to say a word about it too. She said we were grown men, and she wouldn't interfere. You got through to her, Kaitlyn."

"I only told her the truth. I'm so happy for you two but I'm a little sad this means you probably won't be needing a room here again."

Chris wrapped an arm around Nate. "I was thinking we could come back for our one-year anniversary. We certainly can't stay at your parents' for that occasion."

Nate grinned. "I love the idea."

"Me too." Kaitlyn watched them get into their car and waved as they drove away. She heaved a heavy sigh as she walked back inside the inn. She was expecting two more couples this afternoon. She needed to clean and prepare the now-empty rooms for whoever came next.

A little excitement buzzed through her. It was so much fun meeting new people and also unexpectedly fulfilling. She'd made a difference in the Trapps' life. She even felt like she'd helped the Krespos regain a little spark for one another.

Humming cheerfully, she headed to the laundry room to retrieve some cleaning supplies and then tromped upstairs to clean Mr. and Mrs. Krespo's room first. An hour later, she entered the room where Nate and Chris had stayed and paused at the small wrapped gift sitting on the edge of the bed.

"Oh no," she said, walking up to it and picking it up. She'd have to call and let them know they'd forgotten something. She paused when she saw her name on the tag.

To Kaitlyn

She sat on the bed's edge and peeled off the shiny Christmas paper slowly. Then she lifted the lid off a gift box. Inside were a beautiful ornament and a card. Kaitlyn removed the ornament first. It was in the shape of a house that could've been the inn. It appeared to be hand-carved and painted with great detail. She guessed they'd probably purchased it on Saturday night at one of the downtown shops. She couldn't wait to hang it on the tree downstairs. Next, she opened the card and read as tears welled in her eyes.

Thank you for being our home away from home. Love, the Trapps.

CHAPTER FIFTEEN

Over the next two weeks, Kaitlyn ate, breathed, and loved every second of her newfound life. Including the part where she shared a bed with a surly ex-marine.

Kaitlyn lay back on her bed now for just a moment. Her memory lapped over the sex she and Mitch had early this morning before he'd left to go to the station. It was the kind of sex where you wonder if you're still asleep. She'd been in the middle of a dream when he'd woken her. Her eyes had cracked open just enough to see him giving her that heart-melting smile of his. Then they closed again, and she'd writhed and moaned at all the things he'd done to her under those covers.

Even now, her face flushed. As much as she'd like to, she couldn't lie on her bed and think about him for the rest of the day though. There were things to be done, always, and people to catch up with.

She tapped the screen of her cell phone and pulled it to her ear, waiting for her best friend's voice to answer.

"Finally!" Josie said. "I was beginning to wonder if you'd fallen off one of those mountain cliffs and died."

Kaitlyn stared up at the ceiling fan above her. "More like died and gone to heaven. I love it here."

"So, it's booking up?" Josie asked.

Kaitlyn could hear the tapping of Josie's computer in the background. The woman could carry on a conversation and write her next article at the same time practically. "It hasn't slowed down for a second. I don't even know what day it is half the time because guests are coming and going continually."

"Rich people and retirees don't keep to weekend trips."

"I've noticed. But we've had couples celebrating their anniversaries too. And people staying here on business trips instead of getting a hotel room. I already have a waiting list started. It's reaching into the New Year."

"That's awesome. How long before you buy out the other guy and it's all yours?"

Kaitlyn's breath and excitement stilled in her chest. That was the plan, the goal, but she wasn't looking forward to saying goodbye. With the success of the B&B came the termination of her business relationship with Mitch. But what about the other relationship they were swept up in? "Um, well, I'm not sure. He says he's not in a hurry to be bought out, so..." Kaitlyn absently traced imaginary hearts on her quilt as she spoke. "We're making steady income now so I'm sure it's just a matter of time."

"And how long until you start sleeping with him?" Josie asked.

Kaitlyn choked on a gasp. It took her a moment before she could even answer. "No holds barred, huh?"

Josie laughed. "None. Last we spoke, you kissed him and liked it. Soooooo?"

"I'm pleading the Fifth."

Josie gasped on the other end of the line. "You slept with him already and didn't tell me? I thought we were best friends."

"We are." And Kaitlyn had always called Josie immediately after sleeping with a guy. Josie was her go-to person. Always. But sleeping with Mitch was different. If she told Josie, she knew she'd have to explore how she felt about him, because that's what they did. Only, Kaitlyn wasn't sure how she felt about Mitch.

Or she was and it was a little terrifying.

She pressed the heel of her palm to her forehead. "I'm in over my head this time, Jo."

"You really like him, don't you?"

Kaitlyn swallowed. "He's sexy. He can fix things and cook just about anything. He's a great listener and..." She shook her head. "He's a tough ex-marine who's secretly funny and sweet." And he could make her toes curl with pleasure. Josie didn't need that little detail though.

"Wow." It wasn't often that Josie was reduced to one word.

"So you can see my predicament."

"Yeah," Josie finally said. "This is why I bury myself in work. I'm too busy for my own drama. Let me know how this story ends. I'm rooting for him to fall madly in love with you."

"About as likely as you coming to Sweetwater Springs for a visit," Kaitlyn said hopefully.

Josie chuckled into the receiver. "I'm not planning a trip just yet. I have fires to put out here in New York. Speaking of which..." She grew quiet on the other end of the line.

"Yes?" Kaitlyn's stomach tightened the way it did when

she felt the subject turning in a direction she wasn't going to like. It was in Josie's tone of voice. The slight hesitation. The way her pitch lowered.

Goose bumps fleshed up on Kaitlyn's skin. She braced herself for impact. "What is it?"

"Well, there's a little buzz online that Bradley Foster got handsy with one of his leading actresses—that's all. She posted on social media yesterday but it was taken down quickly. I guess Bradley didn't like being outed publicly."

"Well, good for her. Someone needs to out that sleazeball."

"Agreed."

Kaitlyn sat up now, nausea rolling through her stomach. She hated to hear even the mention of Bradley Foster's name.

"One of these days, he's going to get what's coming to him," Josie said.

"I should've kneed him between the legs so hard he couldn't function to force himself on another woman again," Kaitlyn said, which made Josie laugh.

"Then you'd be in jail right now instead of at a beautiful B and B."

"True."

The bedroom door opened, and Mitch walked in. When he looked at her, concern etched itself in his features. Kaitlyn realized her eyes were stinging, not from tears but from anger. Bradley used his celebrity status and power to take advantage of people. To hurt people. She'd admired him, and he'd betrayed her trust by pushing himself on her and then lying about what really happened.

"Sorry," Mitch said. "I knocked but you weren't answering."

Kaitlyn shook her head. "It's okay. I guess I didn't hear you."

Josie cleared her throat on the other end of the line. "Listen, Kaye. Don't worry about that jerk. Just focus on Mitch and figure out how to keep him around a little longer. Anything that makes you smile is a good thing. You deserve happy—remember that. And Bradley and your old boss deserve a bad case of the crabs."

Kaitlyn burst into laughter. Josie was always good for that. "Thanks. I'll talk to you soon."

"You better."

They said their goodbyes and disconnected the call. Then Kaitlyn tossed her cell phone on the nightstand.

Mitch sat down on the bed next to her, the weight of his body tipping her toward him. Not that she planned on going anywhere else right now. Sharing space with him felt entirely too good, like a warm blanket on a cold, snowy night, which was a perfect analogy for her life right now. In some way, she felt like she'd been left out in the cold with the situation in New York. Then Mitch had come along and made her feel safe again. Wanted again.

"Everything okay?" he asked.

"In Sweetwater, yes. Meanwhile in New York, Bradley Foster is groping one of his leading ladies." She only hoped they kicked harder than she did. Or packed a mean punch. Maybe Mace too.

Mitch's body tensed beside hers. She had no doubt that, if she asked him to, he'd drive up the East Coast and make Bradley regret he ever met her.

He reached for her hand and gave it a gentle squeeze, his rough skin brushing against hers. Almost like magic, her worries fell away with just that touch. Mitch seemed to have that effect on her.

That was just one more reason she was glad he was around.

* * *

Since the Lights on the Lake event, there'd been three more robberies downtown. The robberies were small—chump change, really—and Mitch didn't quite get the point of the thefts. One incident had been the tip jar at the Sweetwater Café. A tip jar couldn't have held more than twenty bucks. It didn't make sense that someone would risk taking it and getting caught.

Mitch pulled his police cruiser to the curb in front of Dawanda's store and stepped out to go check on her. He also planned to nab a piece of her peanut butter fudge while he was at it.

Dawanda came barreling out from behind the counter as soon as he walked in, a smile on her face and her vibrant-colored hair poking into the air like an erupting volcano. "My favorite protector. Did you bring your friend?" she asked hopefully.

"Alex?" Mitch asked, remembering that she'd wanted to read his fortune in the cappuccino.

"No. Your lady friend. Kaitlyn."

Mitch shook his head. "No. Just me this time. Sorry to disappoint."

"You never disappoint." She had to reach up to pat his back and then pointed to a chair. "Sit. I'll get you some fudge and coffee to go. I know this street is much safer now that you're on the job."

"Temporarily," Mitch clarified. He didn't want anybody getting the idea that he was staying.

"Right. Right." She headed back behind the counter.

A few minutes later, she laid a white paper bag of fresh fudge and a foam cup of coffee on the table in front of him.

Mitch shifted to pull out his wallet. "How much do I owe you?"

"I don't charge knights in shining armor." She shoved her hands on her little hips like he'd insulted her.

"Well, I'm not taking this for free."

"Not free. In exchange, you keep me and my store safe and bring that girl of yours back sometime." She pushed the paper bag toward him in a not-so-subtle gesture.

"You are a stubborn woman, Dawanda." Which seemed to be a theme in his life right now.

"The best ones are." She winked and made a shooing motion as more customers entered the store. "Now, if you don't mind, I have paying customers to attend to," she teased.

"Thanks." He picked up the bag as he stood and then walked back to the cruiser on the curb.

"Officer! Officer!" someone called just as he reached his car door.

Mitch whirled to see a woman wearing a heavy jacket and knit scarf wrapped loosely around her neck. He knew exactly who she was the moment he saw her face, drawn tight with distress. She was apparently so upset that she had no idea who he was, however. "What's wrong?" he asked, bracing himself for her to recognize him at any second and start beating him with her purse.

"My nephew!" The woman's hands clasped the side of her face. "I can't believe I did that. I stepped out of my car just for a second to drop my Christmas cards in the post office collection box. I only stepped a foot away from the car."

Mitch's adrenaline dialed up. "What happened?"

The woman—Brian Everson's youngest sister—rubbed her temple and then pointed to a silver car a few spaces up. It was parked just shy of a large blue mail collection drop-off. "He's locked inside the car. I left my keys in the ignition...So stupid!" Tears started spilling down her cheeks.

Mitch touched her arm just briefly, then took off toward the car to assess the situation. Sure enough, there was a wide-eyed little boy, who couldn't have been older than three, sitting in a child's car seat in the back. Mitch futilely pulled on the passenger door's handle. His gaze darted to the locks on the driver's side. All secured.

He turned back to Brian's sister. What was her name again? He tried to remember. It started with a *p. Priscilla? Pamela?* She was the youngest of the five Everson children. Mitch thought she'd been in the same grade as Tuck's sister, Halona. "It's okay. Do you have a spare key hidden anywhere on the car?"

She shook her head. Then the toddler in the back seat, possibly seeing how upset his aunt was, decided to start wailing loudly.

Mitch gestured back to his police cruiser. "I need to get a tool. I'll be right back." A moment later, he returned with a three-foot-long rod called a BigEasy, used for just this purpose.

He turned back to the woman. *Penelope.* Yeah, that was her name. Penelope—Penny—Everson. No doubt she hated him as much as her parents did. "I'll be careful but there's a possibility this might damage your car," he warned.

She nodded hurriedly as the toddler screamed louder. "Please, I just want him to be safe."

"Okay." Mitch worked quickly, and a moment later, he opened the passenger side door. He pressed the automatic unlock button for the back seat, and Penny Everson whipped open the door and went to her nephew.

"I'm so sorry. I'm so, so, so sorry," he heard her tell the boy. She released him from his restraint and pulled him to her.

Mitch was about to turn and head quietly back to his

car—and get as far out of Dodge from any member of the Everson family as he could—until Penny called him.

"Officer?"

Mitch turned reluctantly.

She wiped a hand under her mascara-smudged eyes and offered a grateful smile. "Thank you so much. I don't know what I would have done if you weren't here." She patted the child's back as he calmed and melted into her shoulder. "I'm not usually so careless. It's just, the holidays and...It doesn't matter. There's no excuse. I made a mistake, and it could've been much worse if not for you." Tears sprung in her bright-green eyes.

"It happens," Mitch said. He knew all too well about making mistakes. "Just enjoy the rest of your afternoon. And your holiday."

She nodded as her eyes narrowed in. Her grateful smile was still set in place. "You look so familiar." Her gaze dropped to his name badge. "Hargrove."

He watched his last name register. That smile slipped, and confusion twisted her features. No doubt because Mitch wasn't supposed to be here. He'd made a promise to the Everson family that he would stay away, except for brief visits to see his mom, of course. But he wouldn't make his home here. That was the deal.

He was keeping his promise. He didn't plan on staying, even though wearing a police officer's uniform contradicted that.

Penny was still staring at him, gripping the boy now as if she were trying to keep him safe, possibly from Mitch instead of a locked car now. Or was that just Mitch's imagination?

The hero that Dawanda and even Penny made him out to be scattered like dandelion fluff in the wind.

What could Mitch say? *Don't worry. This isn't how it looks. I won't be here long.*

"Thank you again," she said, briskly this time. Then she turned from him and started loading the boy back into her vehicle.

Mitch turned as well and slunk back to his car, reminded once more why he couldn't get comfortable in his hometown.

* * *

Laundry had never been one of her favorite chores, and yet it was never done here. There were always linens to wash. Towels. Tablecloths. Not to mention her own clothes.

Kaitlyn leaned against the front of the washing machine that she'd just loaded with sheets from the guests who'd just checked out, hesitating a little to go back out into the main rooms where she'd have to socialize. Her phone sang "Carol of the Bells" behind her. Turning, she checked the screen, already knowing who it was. The ringtone was one she'd chosen for her parents, although it hadn't rung since she'd assigned it to their contact a few weeks earlier.

Taking a breath, she pulled the phone to her ear. "Mom. How are you?"

"Hello, sweetheart. All is well here. Your dad and I have been busy, busy with work. And you?" her mom asked in return, effectively bringing up the subject of work in one single breath.

Kaitlyn wasn't surprised. Work begot achievement, which begot success. And her success determined how much her mother had to boast about with her country club friends.

"Have you come to your senses yet? Ready to get back to work here in New York?"

Kaitlyn closed her eyes. So much for the laundry room being her "safe place" here in the inn. "Just the opposite, actually. Did you get the invitation I sent? For you and Dad to spend Christmas here at the Sweetwater Bed and Breakfast? Just say the word, and I'll reserve a room," Kaitlyn offered with forced cheer.

Her mom clucked her tongue into the receiver. "No, no. We have plans to go to the Bahamas this year, remember?"

Kaitlyn did remember but she'd thought maybe there was a chance they'd change their minds after receiving the invitation. She'd included a picture of the inn that she'd taken for the brochures. In the photograph, the mountains towered in the distance. Sunny beaches were nice, but during the holidays, snow and mountains were fitting. So was the idea of spending it with your family.

"Come to the Bahamas with us?" her mom urged. "I'm sure you can still get a ticket, although it might cost you an arm and a leg this late in the season. Or cost you the inn that you're so determined to revive."

Kaitlyn was literally seeing stars. "Mom, has it occurred to you that I'm actually happy here, doing something that wasn't your idea? I love hosting at this B and B."

"You used to say you loved your job in New York too."

There was a condescending tone in her mother's voice that made Kaitlyn clutch her cell phone even tighter.

"I'm sure if you spoke to your boss, he'd take you back, sweetheart. You might have to start at the bottom rung again and work your way back into their good graces, but..."

"Haven't you heard a word I've said? I'm not going back to my old job," Kaitlyn ground out with just a touch of irritation. Okay, more than a touch, in the same way that Bradley's moves on her had been more than an innocent sweep of his hand.

"I don't get it. You had a job that other designers would kill to have."

"Okay, Mom. If you really want to know," Kaitlyn snapped, "I didn't quit. I was fired."

Her mom sucked in an audible breath. "What? Why? What did you do?"

"Oh, I don't know. I was sexually harassed by America's favorite action hero, maybe." Kaitlyn's eyes suddenly stung.

"Are you talking about Bradley Foster?" Her mom had known that Kaitlyn was working for him. "Are you sure? Maybe you misunderstood?" she asked in quick succession. "He's married, isn't he?"

Kaitlyn blinked. "Yeah, because no married man ever tried to cheat on his wife," she said sarcastically. Hurt feelings blistered up. They'd been festering with every conversation she'd had with her mom since she left Beautiful Designs and the city.

"This must be some sort of mistake," her mom continued. "What were you wearing when this happened?"

Kaitlyn's mouth dropped open, and she pulled her cell phone back for a second to stare dumbfoundedly at it. "Clothes, Mom," she said when she finally brought it back to her ear. "I don't typically work naked, you know...Listen, I need to go."

"Kaitlyn, we're not done talking about this."

Oh, but Kaitlyn was. And if her mother questioned her one more time, she was going to toss her iPhone at the wall. Not wise, considering that it cost her a small fortune. "I have a guest who needs me," she lied. "Bye, Mom." She quickly disconnected the call and shoved her phone into her jeans pocket.

Well, that had gone well. *Not.*

The nerve of her mom questioning her. Why was it always the woman's fault if a man crossed a line? And of all the people who should believe a woman, it was her own mother.

Kaitlyn clutched the front of the washer, feeling it vibrate through her hands and up her arms. She gulped in a breath, then another, and another.

"Are you and the washing machine having a staredown?" Mitch asked.

She whirled to face him. "Just when I thought I'd gotten used to you sneaking up on me."

"Sorry. I tried to make noise as I approached but you were pretty absorbed in whatever you were thinking."

Kaitlyn looked down at her hands. "Yeah."

"Everything okay?"

He was always asking that. Always trying to fix her problems. She didn't want to weigh him down with any more of her baggage. "I'm fine," she lied. Then she looked back up and offered a smile, which wasn't hard when he was around. "Thought you'd be at the police station."

Now his expression turned crestfallen. "I was."

"Long day?" she asked, reading something in the lines of his face.

"Something like that." He shrugged. "Anyway, Alex forced me to leave. He won't let me work more than a normal shift."

"A bit of a workaholic, are you?" She'd already learned that about him. He always took care of whatever she needed. Never complained. She'd never seen him at rest, come to think of it. Well, except for after they were spent from making love.

"I like to stay busy," he said.

"Well, the B and B is running on autopilot at this point. I have nothing for you to do. Unless, of course, you want to mingle with the guests." She poked up a brow, knowing his answer.

"I don't." He leaned against the dryer beside her. "Not my thing."

"That's what you keep saying. But you looked like you were enjoying yourself the other night when I caught you playing cards with the new couple."

His mouth quirked to one side. "Putting me in charge of entertaining guests would be bad for business."

"You haven't scared people away yet." She winked. "Every room is booked, thanks to Josie's article."

"And you," he said. "People know a fraud when they see it. Guests are staying and enjoying themselves. That's because of you."

She leaned back on the washing machine. It was entering the spin cycle against her back, and with Mitch beside her, she might as well have been sitting on top of it. "And you. You helped. In the shadows."

It was his turn to lift a brow.

"Not *those* shadows," she said, thinking about their midnight trysts, which, yes, had been quite inspiring.

"So, what do you guys have on the agenda tonight?" he asked.

She turned to face him, her side vibrating off the machine. "A few of the guests are going to the Tipsy Tavern. The Nelsons are going out to dinner on their own. So, it's just us. Unless you're going to the tavern too."

His eyes darkened. "I was thinking about staying in. I prefer peace and quiet."

"Do you want me to leave you alone?" she asked, lifting her arm to trace a finger down his chest. She couldn't resist. The washing machine was going insane with its spin cycle, and her body was responding to it and the heat crackling between them. "There's a book I've been meaning to read anyway."

He pulled her to him and wrapped his arms around her waist. Her body complained against being torn away from the vibrating appliance but buzzed back to pure bliss in Mitch's embrace. "No. I like peace and quiet. And you. I like you most of all."

Her heart danced around like sugarplums in the beloved "Night Before Christmas" poem.

"The guests leave in twenty minutes. I was considering possibly climbing into the hot tub outside."

He leaned in and kissed her. His lips were warm. The friction of his beard scraped softly against the corners of her mouth. "That sounds perfect," he whispered. "I'm going to shower off while we wait. I worked up a sweat chasing a dog today."

Kaitlyn choked on a laugh as he pulled away, feeling loads better already. "Seriously?"

"Chasing dogs is evidently part of the job description. There's still a thief out there though, and I can't wait to bring him or her to justice."

"You're a good guy, Mitch Hargrove."

His gaze flicked down and out. He didn't believe her. She wished she could erase his past but she could no more do that than she could her own. Everyone had a past they wished were different. From what she'd seen, the town had already given him a clean slate. She wished he would give himself one too.

"Twenty minutes," he said as he walked out. "In the meantime, you can enjoy the rest of that spin cycle." With a wink, he left her on her own, which had been the only thing she'd wanted fifteen minutes ago when she'd walked in here. Now, being alone wasn't quite as appealing.

She glanced at her watch, wishing time away—even though lately she'd been wishing it to stop. So Mitch would never leave Sweetwater Springs.

* * *

Kaitlyn shivered as she stepped outside wearing a modest tankini bathing suit when a heavy winter coat probably would have been more appropriate.

Mitch stepped out behind her, two glasses of red wine in his hands. "I hope that Jacuzzi is warm," he said. "Wouldn't want you to catch a cold out here."

No chance of that, she thought, admiring his bare chest that narrowed to a pair of low-hanging swim trunks. She shivered again for an entirely different reason. Then she walked to the edge of the hot tub and dipped a toe in the water before stepping inside.

"Feel good?" he asked, handing her a wineglass once she was settled.

"Oh yeah," she moaned happily. "The temperature is just right."

He followed her in and took a seat next to her on the Jacuzzi's bench.

Sipping her wine, she looked up at the star-filled sky. "What an amazing view," she said in more than a little awe. "Romantic is an understatement for this place."

When Mitch didn't respond, she glanced over at him. He was staring at her with an unreadable look in his eyes. "I agree."

Butterflies chased around in her belly. After several weeks, they hadn't stopped. "Thought you weren't big on romance."

"Maybe you've sold me on the concept. Don't tell anyone though, okay? I have a reputation to maintain."

She giggled softly. "It'll be our little secret."

He set his glass down, and his hand disappeared under the water, finding her thigh.

She narrowed her gaze. "The guests could come back, you know? We'd be wise to keep our hands to ourselves just in case."

He grinned mischievously. "No one can see underneath these bubbles." His hand moved higher. "And I have an awfully hard time keeping my hands to myself when it comes to you. In case you haven't noticed."

"Oh, I've noticed." She put her glass down and leaned in to him.

He grinned. "I thought you were worried about the guests coming back."

"I'll take my chances." She crossed the rest of the distance and brushed her mouth to his. Both of their hands roamed under the thick layer of bubbles. She could feel Mitch's arousal as he pressed his body into her but they took their time, touching and teasing. No rush to do anything more. This was the ultimate foreplay until they retreated to the bedroom where they could be ensured privacy.

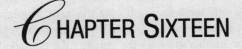

CHAPTER SIXTEEN

It was after six o'clock when Mitch finally left the police station the next day. His body was sore and achy from being folded up in a car half the day and walking the sidewalk outside the row of downtown stores the other half, keeping a watchful eye for suspicious activity. They still hadn't caught the thief who'd stolen from five stores now. They would though. Mitch was intent on that.

"Hey," Kaitlyn said, rounding the corner of the B&B's kitchen.

Mitch stopped to stare at her. Despite her smile, there'd been something bothering her since last night when he'd found her in the laundry room white-knuckling the front of the machine with tears burning her eyes. Whatever the problem, she obviously didn't want to talk about it.

Holiday music streamed down the hall. "What's going on?" he asked.

"Mr. Timsdale from Ohio is teaching a two-step in the ballroom," she said.

Mitch had been the one to check in Mr. Timsdale and his wife yesterday. They were on their way to visit family and had decided to stay in Sweetwater Springs for a couple of days.

"The guests seem to love it," Kaitlyn said. "I might have to hire someone to teach ballroom dancing in there regularly. It could be another draw for the inn after the holidays."

He nodded as he considered the prospect, not that he'd have any say in what happened here after the holidays. "That's not a bad idea."

Kaitlyn tilted her head. "I've been meaning to ask: Do you happen to know anything about the ballroom? What did my grandma and grandpa do with it?"

Mitch shrugged. "They danced. That was probably Mable and Henry's favorite room in the house. They always considered opening it up to the guests but it never happened. It was their special place, Mable used to say. I sneaked in there a time or two and watched. They were pretty good."

Kaitlyn shook her head, a smile lifting her cheeks. "So much I don't know about them."

"I'm happy to fill in the holes where I can," he offered.

"Thanks. Well, I hope my grandparents don't mind me opening up their special place for guests. I actually have another idea for the ballroom. I'm going to show a movie in there later. I found an old projector and several films in the shed. There were even a few Christmas flicks in the mix."

"Yeah?"

She nodded, her face lighting up as usual when she had one of her moments of inspiration. "What do you think? A little *Home Alone* or *How the Grinch Stole Christmas*?"

"I'll have you know I am not planning to steal Christmas this year," Mitch joked. "Although I have been compared to the Grinch many a time." His teasing worked to make her laugh, which was exactly what he'd intended.

"I have another surprise too." She gestured for him to follow her down the hall toward the kitchen, which seemed to be the heart of the Sweetwater B&B.

He could already smell the scent of cinnamon strudels as soon as he crossed the threshold. "You've been talking to my mom again, haven't you?" he accused, his mouth watering as she pulled the oven door open and allowed him a peek at what was inside. "She told you that cinnamon strudels were my favorite dessert?" he asked.

Kaitlyn shut the oven door and turned to face him. Her cheeks were suddenly flushed, and he wasn't sure if it was from the heat of the oven or from him standing so close. "I wanted to do something nice, to thank you for everything you've done. You didn't have to help or do as much as you've done for the inn. And for me."

She'd already thanked him a dozen times. "I would've been some kind of schmuck not to."

"True. But you didn't have to care." She folded her arms. "Anyway, Mr. Garrison called this afternoon. Since the time stipulation of the will is nearly up, he's coming by to check on things tomorrow morning. I invited him to breakfast."

Mitch nodded. "I'll cook and let Alex know I'll be in to the station a little later. He won't mind."

"Perfect," she said with an easy smile. It still didn't reach her eyes, and he decided to make it his personal mission to change that tonight. Whatever was bothering her, he wanted to erase it from her mind.

"So, how much longer until the strudels are ready?" he asked.

"One minute."

"I can do a lot of things in one minute. Starting with this."

He pulled her to him and planted a soft kiss on her lips. He stroked a finger along the side of her jaw as his thumb rested on the jumping pulse at her neck. After a moment, he pulled his mouth away and looked at her, long and deep. Those eyes worked as a flame, and he was their moth.

How the hell was he going to walk away from this woman in a couple of weeks?

The oven's timer beeped in the background.

Kaitlyn cast a glance over her shoulder. "Don't want those to burn."

"Just a second." He pulled her in again, needing one more little taste. Because she was the sweetest thing he knew. His love for cinnamon strudels had been before Kaitlyn Russo. Now *she* was his favorite dessert.

* * *

The next morning, Kaitlyn bumped her body against Mitch's as he taught her the art of making eggs Benedict in the kitchen. The well-rested guests would start stirring soon.

She, on the other hand, was tired. She had snuck off with Mitch midway through *Home Alone*. They'd hurried down the hall like a couple of horny teenagers. Like the college-aged couple who'd stayed at the B&B during Thanksgiving week. After posting the DO NOT DISTURB sign—a cute little trinket she'd picked up the other day—and locking the door they'd buried themselves under the covers but hadn't gone to sleep until well after midnight.

"I could get used to this," she said dreamily as they cooked.

"You could get used to what? Delicious breakfasts every morning or me?"

"Both." At her confession, a moment of panic streaked

through her at the thought that Mitch might think she was somehow implying she wanted him to stay. She wasn't. But she relaxed when she saw the easiness of his smile. Everything with him really was starting to be so easy. Yes, she could get used to the tasty dining, but also to him.

They carried the food into the dining room where one couple had already come down. Another lingered at the staircase. She quickly set the table, leaving an extra spot for Mr. Garrison, who was supposed to be arriving anytime now.

"Take a breath," Mitch advised as she straightened one of the centerpieces. "He's just checking that I haven't gone AWOL. He doesn't care if the bed and breakfast is in pristine condition. Which it is, by the way."

"I know." Kaitlyn glanced around at the guests filling the seats. "It's just that Mr. Garrison knew my grandparents. He knew this place. I want him to be impressed with what we've done here."

"It was mostly you." Mitch lowered his voice in that intimate way that lovers did when they were paying the other a compliment. It sent gooey warmness all through her. "And he will be impressed. He'd be crazy not to be. In just a short time, this place has been completely transformed. It's more than a B and B. It's an experience."

Kaitlyn narrowed her eyes. "Wow. I love that. More than a bed and breakfast—an experience." She clapped a hand over her chest. "I've been working with Paris on some graphic design ideas for pamphlets to advertise the B&B. Emma from the Sweetwater Café said she'd put some out for me. She said her restaurant is one of the first places tourists hit when they come to town."

"You're getting cozy with all the locals, aren't you?"

She shrugged. "Well, if this is going to be my home, I should make friends."

"I think putting pamphlets out is a great idea."

"And I can send some to Josie in New York. She'd send people here. I can put them everywhere to keep this place hopping all year long." Renewed excitement surged through her.

"Careful what you wish for," he warned teasingly.

"I love it when it's busy." She just wished, for the millionth and one time, that she could keep him on staff.

She busied herself filling the guests' coffee mugs and making small talk as she waited for Mr. Garrison to arrive.

"He should be here by now," she said, coming up to Mitch halfway through breakfast. Before he could respond, her cell phone buzzed in her pocket. She pulled it out and read a text.

Running late. Be there in fifteen minutes.

Kaitlyn frowned.

"What's wrong?"

"Mr. Garrison is running behind. He's going to miss breakfast with the guests, and his food will be cold."

"Again," Mitch said, talking calmly, "he's not here to shut you down."

To shut *you* down. "Right," she said, nodding. "You're right."

Mitch reached for his own cell phone now. It was his turn to look disappointed. "Alex wants me to call him. I'll help you with cleanup in just a minute."

"Sure." Kaitlyn stood there by herself for a moment, listening in on the conversations at each table. Mitch was right. This was much more than a bed and breakfast. It was an experience. She'd done more than the interior design here. She'd designed a place where guests were taken back to a time when electronics didn't run every second. Good old-fashioned fun happened at this inn.

A moment later, Mitch returned to the dining room, looking apologetic. "There's been another break-in. I have to go."

"Now?"

"I'm sorry."

"But Mr. Garrison..."

"He'll understand," Mitch promised.

Kaitlyn was shaking her head. "He'll be here any minute. What am I supposed to tell him?"

Mitch leaned in and kissed her cheek, which made her thoughts totally slam to a halt. He'd never shown any display of affection in front of the guests before. "Just tell him the truth. We're doing great. We make a good team. And I'm out making the streets of Sweetwater Springs a little safer these days."

With that, he hurried out the door, leaving Kaitlyn all alone to prove to Mr. Garrison that she and Mitch were fulfilling the conditions of the will.

* * *

Mitch moved through Julia Kent's bookstore downtown, looking at the upheaval of knickknacks and books. He knew from the past robberies that the thief was only interested in money. The burglar was likely an amateur who'd watched way too many *CSI* episodes. Why else would someone tear through the place but not actually take anything except for what was in the cash register? Another amateur move was robbing a bookstore. Everyone knew bookstores didn't have a lot of cash on hand.

"Hey, Julia." Mitch walked over to the store owner who

was seated behind the cash register, looking flustered. Her face was red and blotchy as she looked off into space, apparently attempting to gather her thoughts.

"I'm not sure what happened," she told Alex. "The robber was wearing a black ski mask, only it looked more like a black knit hat pulled over his head with holes cut out for his eyes and mouth." She laughed softly. "I know that sounds ridiculous."

Mitch was holding a small notebook in his hand. "Did he say anything?" Mitch asked.

She nodded. "He told me to sit in this chair and not get up. He also told me to close my eyes and not open them until I heard the back door shut."

Mitch jotted those facts down. "So he went out the back door?"

"Yes. At least I think he did. I heard the back door close. That's when I got up, grabbed my cell phone, and dialed 911."

Alex squeezed her shoulder gently, a comforting gesture that Julia seemed to appreciate.

Petty thief or not, this burglar was scaring people. "If you don't mind, I'm going to take one more look around," Mitch said.

Alex nodded. "Take your time. I've got a few more questions for Julia while you do."

Mitch took his time walking around the store a second time. He watched his feet, looking at the floor around the bookshelves. He'd enjoyed reading cozy mysteries as a kid growing up here in Sweetwater Springs. Maybe that was one of the things that appealed to him so much about law enforcement. He liked to solve puzzles. Liked to figure out whodunit.

His gaze caught on a small, white rectangular ID lying

just beneath one of the bookshelves. Mitch's steps quickened, and he bent to pick it up. It was a driver's license. *How idiotic can this perp be?* The ID read Kyle Martin and had the photo of a young seventeen-year-old pimply-faced boy with fair skin and red-toned hair. The ID said that Kyle was approximately five foot eleven, one hundred and forty pounds. All of the victims had described their burglar as being around six feet tall and very thin.

Bingo!

Mitch couldn't bring himself to be happy about it though. This was just a kid. Why the hell was someone so young, with so much future ahead of him, throwing his life away on something like this?

Alex looked up as Mitch approached the counter again.

"Found something," Mitch said.

Alex raised an eyebrow. "Oh yeah? What is it?"

"I don't think you're going to like it." He slapped the ID on the counter in front of Alex.

Alex picked it up and frowned. "I know this kid. He's a bit of a troublemaker around town. I've had to talk to him a few times. The kid doesn't have a father, and his mom is always working." With this information, Alex offered an apologetic look, as if maybe Mitch would take it personally. "He's angry, and he hangs out with the wrong crowd."

"Burglary is a felony." Mitch shook his head. "At his age, he'll probably be tried as an adult."

"It's possible." Alex poked his pen back into his front pocket. "I know where they live. Looks like we're making a house call."

"Do we need to call this in?" Mitch asked. "Backup?"

Alex shook his head. "No. Kyle won't put up a fight. His mom, maybe."

Alex turned to Julia and promised to call her later.

"Thank you both," she said, offering a wobbly smile. "I'm just glad it's all over. I might not sleep for a week."

"Trust me. Sweetwater Springs is still one of the safest towns I know," Alex promised, patting a hand on Mitch's back. "Especially with Mitch here on the job."

They headed out of the store and climbed into Alex's SUV. Mitch closed his eyes for just a moment. He'd been a stupid teen once too. It hadn't gotten him thrown in jail but it could have. He shouldn't have been on the road the night he ran into Brian Everson. It was a stupid mistake that he'd never be able to correct.

Alex waited for traffic to pass, did a U-turn in the road, and then drove toward Kyle Martin's home.

CHAPTER SEVENTEEN

"Wow, Kaitlyn. You've really given it your own spin," Mr. Garrison said.

They had toured the dining room, living area, sitting room, and ballroom, and were now walking down the upstairs hallway and peeking inside the guest rooms that were currently unoccupied.

"Each room has its own theme," Kaitlyn said. "My friend Josie helped me come up with that idea. Mitch helped me pull it off."

"It's wonderful," Mr. Garrison said.

"Mitch has really been a lifesaver," Kaitlyn continued, rambling nervously. "I don't think I could've done this without him."

Mr. Garrison turned to her at the end of the hall. "And what about when he leaves? The conditions are satisfied on Christmas Eve. That's not far away."

"Well, then I have Gina Hargrove down the street. She's been a huge help as well."

"Ah, yes, Gina always enjoyed helping out your grand-mother. It's convenient since she lives so close."

"Let me make you a cup of coffee."

"That sounds wonderful."

Kaitlyn led Mr. Garrison back downstairs where he sat on a metal stool at the kitchen island.

The brew was already in the pot. She grabbed two mugs and poured both three-quarters full. Then she grabbed cream and sugar and placed them at the center of the island before sitting down as well.

"Here you go." She pulled her own cup to her. It was her third cup this morning, which meant she was bubbling with energy and nerves, fidgeting almost uncontrollably, and talking at supersonic speed.

"You know, Mable was a matchmaker of sorts. I think that's part of what she was doing when she left the inn to you and Mitch."

Kaitlyn's eyes widened. "I thought she wanted us to run the B and B because of my creativity and Mitch's business mind."

"Sure, sure. That's what she said. But everyone who knew Mable knew she always had a hidden agenda. She set up a number of couples in this town, you know."

"No, I didn't know that."

"She's the person behind my first date with my wife."

"I had no idea my grandmother did that kind of thing."

Mr. Garrison chuckled. "Between Dawanda's cappuccino readings at the fudge shop and your grandmother, singles here have never had a chance. Have you met Dawanda?"

Kaitlyn giggled as she nodded. "Yes. She gave me a com-plimentary reading."

"And you didn't run from Sweetwater Springs scream-ing? Means you're one of us now."

Kaitlyn liked the sound of that. "It's part of the town's charm. So, you think my grandmother was trying to set me and Mitch up?"

"She never would've admitted to it, but..." Mr. Garrison shrugged. "I miss Mable's meddling ways."

"There's so much I didn't know about her. I wish we could've spent more time together."

"I'm guessing that's another reason she chose you. You can learn about her by living the life she lived. You're making it all your own, of course, but there's a certain lifestyle that comes with running a bed and breakfast. I'm assuming you want to continue on even when the conditions are met?"

Kaitlyn didn't hesitate. "Definitely."

"Because legally you and Mitch could sell this place. The way you have it running now, you'd probably make a pretty penny."

And she could go back to New York. Maybe reclaim her life and career there. "No. This is my home now."

Mr. Garrison seemed pleased by her declaration. "I sure do wish I could've talked to Mitch."

"I'm so sorry."

"Just good to know he's helping out. When Mable put him in the will, I had my doubts he'd even agree. It was a risky move, knowing Mitch's history here. Mable had faith he wouldn't leave you high and dry. That's just not the kind of man he is."

"He's also not the kind to stay once his promise is fulfilled." It was worded as a statement but Kaitlyn's tone of voice turned it into a question. She already knew the answer in her heart of hearts but some part of her needed confirmation from someone else. "I mean, he loves working at the police station. His mom is here. He seems happy. I know he has a past, but..."

Mr. Garrison frowned. "You and Mable are more alike than you know." With that, he stood. "I'll check in with Mitch later, before the condition of the will is officially up. We'll need to fill out some paperwork to turn this place completely over to you."

And that was his answer to her question.

Mr. Garrison shrugged. "Or not. Have a great day, Kaitlyn."

She followed him to the door. "Thank you. You too." Closing the door behind him, she blew out a breath. She wished Mitch had been here, but she thought she'd done well on her own. Hopefully, Mr. Garrison was convinced that she and Mitch were satisfying Grandma Mable's terms so far.

* * *

There were two cars in the Martins' driveway as Mitch and Alex pulled up to the curb. A clean, older model Honda Accord and a dirty, dented-up Toyota Corolla with missing rims. He guessed they belonged to Cassie and Kyle Martin, respectively.

"Let's have a chat with our burglar, shall we?" Alex said to Mitch, knocking on the front door.

A moment later the door opened, and a petite woman with bobbed black hair and a cautious expression peered back at them. Mitch glanced down at his uniform. He was willing to guess this wasn't the first time an officer had been to her door. He was also willing to guess she already knew this would be about her son.

"Hello, Cassie," Alex said with a friendly nod.

"Hi, Chief Baker." Her gaze moved to Mitch.

"This is Officer Mitch Hargrove," Alex told her. "He's new to the department."

"Good morning," Mitch offered, already feeling bad about what they had come to do. Although she was young, Mitch could see in Cassie's eyes that she'd endured a lot in her lifetime.

"I was wondering if we could speak to Kyle."

Her lips pressed together, and her eyes narrowed. "Is he in some kind of trouble?"

Alex offered a stiff smile. "For the moment, we just want to talk to him. Is he home?"

She nodded and gestured for them to follow her inside the house. "I'll go get him. You can wait on the couch."

Mitch and Alex sat on the edge of a faded couch with several tears patched up with duct tape. There were more than a few dings and holes in the walls too. They weren't a rich family, and this wasn't the best of neighborhoods. Being a single parent wasn't easy. He knew that from watching his own mom. Mitch had felt the pressure of making ends meet back then. Maybe Kyle was also feeling it.

A few minutes later, a tall, lanky kid—definitely not an adult yet, even though he was nearly eighteen—stepped out into the living room.

He cast a wary gaze between Mitch and Alex. "My mom said you wanted to talk to me," he said more to Alex than Mitch.

Alex nodded from the couch. "That's right. This is Officer Hargrove. We need to ask you a few questions."

"Yeah, whatever," the kid said with attitude.

"Why don't you sit down first?" Alex suggested.

Mitch remained quiet because the family was more familiar with Alex.

Kyle sighed and plopped into a worn recliner across from them. Mitch saw Ms. Martin lingering within earshot.

"I believe this is yours." Alex slapped Kyle's driver's license down on the coffee table between them.

Kyle's gaze swept over it. He shrugged, looking between them. "I lost it a couple weeks ago."

The kid was a bad liar. "I found it in the bookstore that was robbed downtown earlier today," Mitch told him.

Ms. Martin gasped in the background.

"Wasn't me. The thief who stole my license must like books too."

"He didn't steal books. Just cash." Alex kept his gaze trained on Kyle, who was doing his best to look uninterested.

"Thanks for finding it for me. No risk of getting a ticket for driving without one anymore." At this, the teen offered up a smile but his eyes were still dull and lifeless.

"Your fingerprints were at the bookstore too," Mitch lied. They hadn't had time to run fingerprints yet. Alex would probably have something to say about Mitch's white lie later.

Kyle shifted uncomfortably.

"There's more than a traffic ticket at stake," Alex continued, not correcting what Mitch had claimed.

"Kyle?" Cassie Martin stepped up to her son now. "Did you rob a bookstore? Is that where the money came from?" she asked.

Mitch looked at her. "How much money?"

He could tell she was hesitant to answer. Doing so would likely implicate Kyle. "My son is a good boy. If he did this, it's only because he was trying to help me. He's a good boy," she repeated.

Mitch's eyes flitted to meet Kyle's and then returned to her.

"I'm sick," Cassie confessed. "I have cancer, and the treatments will be expensive. I can't afford them, and even if I could, I wouldn't be able to work because the treatments would make me sicker. Not at first, at least. Kyle has been working long hours, doing side jobs, and raising money to help me get well." Her lips trembled. "He really is the best son a mom could ask for."

"Listen," Kyle spoke up, "I'll pay the money back, okay? All of it. I never meant to do anyone harm."

"Kyle!" Cassie's hands covered her mouth. "Why would you do such a thing?"

"Because I don't want you to die, all right?" Kyle shot back. "I need you. I would do anything to keep you well." He lowered his head into his hands. "I know it was stupid. Am I going to jail?" he asked in a small voice.

Mitch could hear his own teenaged self asking a couple of law enforcement officers that same question a decade earlier. He remembered the feeling of wondering if his next ten to twenty would be behind bars. Worse than that feeling was knowing that he was the reason that the rest of someone else's years would be in a wheelchair.

"You'll have to come down to the station, yes," Alex said.

"You're arresting him?" Cassie's dark eyes filled with thick tears. It reminded Mitch of when his own mom had arrived at the hospital after the accident. A couple of police officers came to talk to Mitch in his room. Once he was discharged, they wanted him to come down to the station for questioning. In Mitch's case, it had all been an unfortunate accident. But Kyle had purposely robbed several stores. Yeah, his reasons seemed almost noble if you looked at it from a teenager's viewpoint, but he'd still committed crimes.

"I'm afraid we have to," Alex said. "But considering the circumstances and Kyle's age, we might be able to work out a deal with Judge Ables. Can't make any promises about that though."

"It's okay, Mom. Don't worry about me." Kyle gave a

wobbly smile to Cassie, who had tears streaming down her cheeks now. If she couldn't afford medical treatment, she couldn't afford bail money either.

"He's right," Mitch told her. "We'll take care of Kyle. You need to save your strength for your own fight, and you won't be doing it alone. Sweetwater Springs takes care of its people."

"I don't like to ask for handouts," she said, lifting her chin. "It's not other people's responsibility to worry about me."

Mitch stood. "No, it's other people's privilege to help someone in a time of need. We'll figure it out. Together." The word *we* on his tongue surprised him. He hadn't been part of the Sweetwater community since he'd left town after high school. Ever since he'd returned here, he'd made a point of not including himself, especially when he referred to the bed and breakfast.

Alex nodded. "The police station and fire department have been known to join forces for fund-raisers. I'll arrange that side of things." He glanced over at Kyle. "Fund-raisers are legal, and I'm guessing we can rake in a lot more than can be taken from a bookstore register."

Kyle smiled weakly. "Thanks for helping her. She's all I have."

Mitch's stomach twisted. He knew that feeling of helplessness. Kyle didn't have to take on the burden of helping his mom alone though.

The three of them headed out to the police SUV and got in.

"Have I completely screwed up my life?" Kyle asked midway through the ride to the station.

"Everyone deserves a second chance. One mistake doesn't define you, son," Alex said, glancing at Mitch. "Unless you let it."

* * *

Kaitlyn's cell phone had rung four times since she'd started this new project. No doubt it was her mom—the last person she wanted to talk to right now. So she continued hanging fairy lights outside under the eaves of the covered porch. She'd seen something similar in a magazine recently, and it had looked so romantic. Perfect for the holidays too. The lights also reminded her of her first kiss with Mitch by Silver Lake under a blanket of stars. She'd never forget that moment, sweet and perfect.

The back door opened, and the man himself walked outside. Kaitlyn stared at him for a moment, trying to make sense of the picture in front of her. Mitch was dressed in his police uniform and holding a bouquet of flowers. The image did not make sense in her mind.

"What are you doing?" she asked.

He held out the assortment of brightly colored daisies. "For you. I stopped at Halona's flower shop on the way."

"They're beautiful." She stepped off her ladder and walked to him. "What did I do to deserve this?"

"Oh, I don't know. Put up with the likes of me."

She laughed, taking the flowers and sweeping them under her nose. "You're not so hard to put up with."

"I'm sorry I wasn't here this morning. I know it was important to you. How'd it go with Mr. Garrison?"

She looked up at Mitch, remembering how Mr. Garrison had told her about Mable's matchmaking ways. Was this her grandmother's grand finale of matchmaking? "It went fine. He was sorry you weren't here, of course, but he understood. So do I."

Mitch's wooden posture softened. "So I can skip the groveling part?"

She laughed again. "Yes, please skip over that part. You don't strike me as someone who'd get down on your knees anyway. I did figure out a way you can make it up to me though."

He raised one brow, and if she wasn't mistaken, he looked a little worried. "Yeah?"

Kaitlyn held her bouquet under her chin, the soft scent still lingering in the air. "It was your mom's idea actually."

Yep, that was definite concern lining his forehead. "You've been talking to my mom? Now I'm worried."

Kaitlyn laughed. "She came over earlier to watch the place while I went grocery shopping. And before you ask, yes, she looked fine. You can see for yourself when she gets here in a minute."

Mitch folded his arms in front of him. "Why is my mom coming here?"

Kaitlyn suppressed the small quiver of guilt in her belly. Since she and Mitch had inherited this B&B, he hadn't watched it for her on his own once. Yeah, he'd done a lot of repairs and handled any of the maintenance that the inn needed but Mitch hadn't played host. "The downtown stores are staying open late tonight for last-minute shoppers. Your mom and aunt Nettie invited me to go with them, and I would really like to."

Color drained from Mitch's cheeks. "So who will be watching the inn tonight?"

She lifted her brows, waiting for him to come to the natural conclusion. "It'll only be for a few hours. I've set aside a movie to play in the ballroom for entertainment. And hot chocolate."

"I don't entertain."

"So you've said." Kaitlyn smiled softly. Gina had warned her that Mitch would try to get out of this but she'd told

Kaitlyn to stand her ground. He was capable, and it was just as much his responsibility as hers, at least until Christmas Eve. "I'm sure you'll do fine."

The doorbell rang before he could continue to argue.

"That's them now. Do you mind getting the door while I put these flowers in a vase? Thank you, Mitch," she said, walking past him. Not that he'd agreed. She'd let his mom do the final persuasion. He didn't seem to be able to tell Gina no.

Once Kaitlyn returned from the kitchen, the other two women were waiting excitedly by the door for her. Mitch, on the other hand, looked like a pound puppy, frightened and caged. Gina tugged Kaitlyn's hand through the door, tossed a wave over her shoulder at her son, and then they made their way through the biting cold of the night.

"Don't feel bad for a moment," Gina said, patting her arm. They all climbed into Gina's sedan in the driveway. "It's good for him."

"And shopping is good for us," Nettie said, climbing into the front passenger side.

Kaitlyn took the back seat. "I do have Christmas shopping to finish up, including gifts for the angel I selected off the tree during Lights on the Lake."

"The downtown stores will have everything you need. I'm certain of it," Gina said.

Ten minutes later, they parked in the overflow lot for the row of stores and made their way through shop after shop. Kaitlyn picked out a hand-knitted scarf for Josie and a second one for her mom, even though she probably wouldn't see them over the holidays. She found a baby doll that cried and peed for the little girl she'd pulled off the Angel Tree, along with extra outfits and a toy stroller. Her dad was getting a new tie per usual.

At Dawanda's fudge shop, Kaitlyn got some dark chocolate fudge for Paris, who had been not only her first guest at the inn but also one of her first friends here in Sweetwater Springs.

There was only one person left on her list to buy for. Mitch. Gina had gotten him several shirts and a mug featuring a picture of a thermometer indicating an improved mood at the bottom of the cup after he'd drunk all his coffee. But Kaitlyn had no idea what to get him. Hopefully it would come to her before the big day.

Arms full of bags, the three women finally made their way back to the car and drove back to the inn.

"How do you think Mitchy fared on his own?" Nettie asked Kaitlyn, angling her body to talk to her in the back seat.

"Honestly, he's a better host than he thinks. I'm sure he did just fine."

"And how hard is it to turn on a movie and serve some drinks?" Gina said on a laugh. "Maybe he'll realize he has a knack for it after all and decide to stay."

Kaitlyn's heart sank as she watched the lighted homes blur by while they drove. Some little part of her had hoped the same thing when she'd left Mitch to watch the inn tonight. It was the season of hope after all—even if she thought that one particular Christmas wish was hopeless.

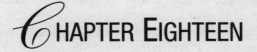

CHAPTER EIGHTEEN

$\mathcal{M}$itch checked his watch. Then his phone. Where were they?

He'd started the movie and served the cocoa. He'd even smiled and asked a few of the guests if they needed anything. There were only two couples downstairs tonight because the Nelsons had also gone shopping and the Amabiles had gone to dinner. Even with only four people to entertain, he was counting down the seconds until the real innkeeper returned.

He heard the front door open and took off down the hall toward the women's laughter.

"Oh, hi, Mitch." Kaitlyn removed her coat and hung it on the rack beside the door. "Everything okay?"

Her brow wrinkled with concern as she looked at him. He supposed if he looked in a mirror right now he'd have a strained look on his face. Put him in charge of a few hardened criminals and he'd be A-okay. Leave him with two bubbly, chatty couples who expected him to mirror their enthusiasm, and he felt like he was going to come out of his skin.

"Of course," he said, feeling relief wash over him at just the sight of her. "Looks like you guys had a good time."

Kaitlyn looked down at the assorted bags in her hand. "I might've gotten a little carried away," she admitted.

"Nonsense," his mom said, waving a hand. Then she stepped up to kiss Mitch's cheek before removing her coat as well.

"Staying?" he asked.

"Nettie and I thought we'd watch the last of the movie, if you don't mind."

"And Kaitlyn promised us that you'd make hot chocolate," his aunt Nettie said, also removing her coat. "Plus, I thought I'd catch you in action as a B and B host." She winked at him playfully. Then his three favorite women headed to the ballroom together, taking the couch that lined the back wall.

A little jealousy flared up inside him as he leaned in the doorway, where he'd stood most of the night. Kaitlyn was his, not theirs.

"Cheer up, lad," one of the guests said, stepping up beside him. Mr. Peters was in his midfifties and had come here for an anniversary retreat with his wife. "You're supposed to be happy that your girlfriend is getting along with your family. Trust me—it's rare," he said in passing and headed back to his seat beside his wife.

Mitch had wanted to tell Mr. Peters, *She's not my girlfriend*, but couldn't. Because by all definitions, that's exactly what Kaitlyn had become. They were long past a fling and very much exclusive. He even felt possessive of her with his own family members. And the fact that she was sitting beside his mom and aunt and having such a good time was kind of attractive in its own odd way.

Ever since this morning when he and Alex had talked to Kyle, something had been niggling around in the corner of his mind. This community supported each other. That's what he'd told Ms. Martin. People deserved second chances. That's what Alex had told Kyle. So why couldn't that be true for him too? Despite his best efforts not to, he loved this community. Everyone here had supported him after the accident. Well, except for the Everson family, but who could blame them? They loved Brian.

Mitch had been thinking about his own past since he'd left Kyle at the juvenile detention center. He'd never apologized to Brian in person. There'd been a civil lawsuit against Mitch at the time, and his lawyer had advised him to stay as far away from the Everson family as possible. Mitch had won the case because it was just an unfortunate accident. The facts supported him. But he'd never gone to face Brian like a man afterward. He should have. He'd never apologized for what had happened and the part he'd played in it. Maybe if Mitch's father had been alive, he'd have told him to man up and do just that.

Mitch swallowed thickly. It was finally time to pay Brian a visit. It wouldn't be easy but it was the right thing to do. He was tired of running from his past. Tired of being ashamed for something that happened a long time ago. He'd been just a kid, like Kyle, and he was ready to make things right.

The sound of Kaitlyn's laughter drew him in. Glancing over, he saw the three women looking at him. It was obvious whatever they thought was funny pertained to him. He straightened from where he leaned in the doorway and headed to the couch. "Okay, I give up. What's the joke?"

His mother had a hand to her chest, and he thought she

looked happier than he'd seen her in a long time. Family, friends, and laughter were a salve to the body and soul. "I was telling Kaitlyn about the girl across the street when you were growing up."

Mitch groaned. "Mom."

"You had such a huge crush on her, even though she was two years older than you."

Mitch rubbed his forehead. "All the guys on our street had a crush on Alison Winters."

"Aw, how sweet," Kaitlyn said. "You still remember her name."

"Oh, it was sweet. He would even leave little notes and special trinkets on her doorstep," his mother continued, much to his chagrin.

Mitch groaned again. "That's it. I'm supervising the rest of your conversations tonight."

"But I was just about to tell Kaitlyn about the time you ran away from home."

"She doesn't need to know that story, Mom. Let's just say I was seven years old and I didn't make it very far."

That time, he thought. When he'd run away from home at the age of eighteen and joined the marines, he'd gone across the world. And the things he was running from had come along with him every step of the way.

Tomorrow, he decided. He'd stop running from his ghosts tomorrow.

After the guests had gone back upstairs and his mom and aunt Nettie had gone home, Mitch joined Kaitlyn in the kitchen. He watched as she loaded the hot chocolate mugs into the dishwasher. "I think my mom really likes you."

She turned to face him. "Well, I really like your mom. She reminds me a lot of my friend Josie back home."

"So Josie is a fifty-year-old woman who is a workaholic and likes to cook and tell embarrassing stories about her son?"

Kaitlyn closed the dishwasher door and pressed the On button. The motor groaned in the background as she straightened and stepped over to him. "Not exactly. They're both feisty though. And they make me laugh. Your aunt Nettie is pretty awesome too."

"Well, I love to see you laugh," he said. "Even if it's at my expense."

Tilting her head to the side, her eyes hooded sexily. And he knew exactly what she was in the mood for. *He* was in the mood for the exact same thing.

Her cell phone rang on the counter, which made her smile fall away.

"What's wrong?"

She shook her head. "I'm sure that's yet another call from my mom."

"You can't avoid her forever."

"I know. I'll talk to her later. All that shopping wore me out."

As if on cue, she yawned, and the hooded look in her eyes was gone. She *really* did look tired now.

"You go on to bed," he said. "I'll finish cleaning up the kitchen."

"Really?" Her eyes widened a little bit.

"Yeah. I'm still partial owner here, at least until next week."

That was supposed to make her smile but instead her frown deepened. Did she wish he would stay as much as he was starting to wish the same?

That was crazy though. Impossible.

"Good night," he said, urging her to bed. "I'll see you in

the morning." If he could manage to keep his hands off of her until then.

* * *

Kaitlyn had told Mitch she was tired, and that was true, but she didn't feel like sleeping. Her mind was on overdrive suddenly. Her cell phone dinged with an incoming text. She reached for it, read the screen, and considered throwing the phone against the wall, not for the first time today.

> Kaitlyn, you're acting like a child. Call me back and let's discuss the situation.

"The situation?" Kaitlyn said on a scoff, fury funneling in her belly. She stared at her mother's words in disbelief.

Another two points go to Bradley Foster. He'd groped her, cost her a job, and now he might cost her the relationship with her own mother.

Kaitlyn plopped back on the bed and stared at the ceiling. There was a time when her mom had been her best friend. She would take Kaitlyn to the park every weekend, and her mom would make a huge deal over finding the perfect picnic spot to lay their huge, red-checked blanket. Then they'd eat, talk, and laugh so hard that Kaitlyn sometimes wondered if her food would come bubbling back up. Once they were done eating, her mom always loved to lie back and stare up at the clouds.

It was Kaitlyn's favorite game back then as well. "That's a dinosaur," she'd chirp, pointing at a puff of cloud.

"I see an elephant over there."

Kaitlyn blinked up at the high wood-paneled ceiling of

her room now, considering the memory. In the markings of the wood, she could almost make out designs in the same way she had with the clouds as a little girl. She wasn't a child anymore though. That was the point and the thing that her mom didn't quite get. Kaitlyn could make her own decisions and live her own life.

And she knew when a man crossed the line with her.

The bedroom door opened, and Mitch stepped in, his eyes trained on her. "Thought you were going to sleep."

Kaitlyn sat up in bed. She was still dressed and held her cell phone in her hand. "I guess I'm not tired after all."

He nodded, not moving for a moment.

"Thank you, by the way." Her anger was starting to fade now that he was here. Her breathing smoothed out just a little bit. "For the flowers and tonight, for washing the dishes and cleaning up the kitchen. And for being here."

"It was nothing, really," he said.

She'd seen his panicked look when she'd asked him to host the guests for movie night. He could have refused. There was no way she could make a strong man like him stay downstairs and play nice. He'd done it of his own volition because she'd asked him to. At his core, he was one of the good guys just as he'd claimed several weeks ago as they'd fought in the front room.

He hooked a thumb behind him. "Want me to give you some space? I can sleep on the couch or—"

"No. I only need space from the world right now, not you. *You* can stay." In fact, Mitch had a way of making the entire world fall away once that door was closed. "Why don't you hang the DO NOT DISTURB sign?" she suggested.

His left brow lifted just slightly, and she found herself

smiling. He was wrong. He was good with people. Good with her. "Yeah?" he asked.

She lifted her hands and started to unbutton her top. It wasn't fury funneling in her belly anymore. No, it was desire, and it threatened—*promised*—to sweep them both up in its cyclone. "Better turn that lock," she said, as her fingers popped the third button down.

He did as she asked and then flipped off the lights. The night-light came on automatically, filling the room with just enough light so they could find each other. Even without the light's help, she'd have tracked down the woodsy, highly sensual scent of him. In just a few short weeks, her body knew this man. Craved him.

His arms locked around her, and then they made love like it was the most natural thing in the world. When he held her, it felt like a promise that everything was going to be all right, and she believed it. She believed what she saw when his eyes bore into hers, even though she wasn't quite sure what they said. Something wonderful though.

At some point in the night, she fell asleep in Mitch's embrace. Her eyes flickered open to read the clock on the nightstand. One a.m. The inn was quiet, and Mitch's breathing was steady on her shoulder as he hugged the back of her.

Smiling softly, she returned to sleep.

When her eyes fluttered open again at five a.m., the weight of his arm was gone. She turned to find his side of the bed empty except for a note on the pillow. She rolled forward and grabbed it.

You're beautiful when you sleep. See you tonight.

Mitch

It wasn't the warmest or the fuzziest, but even so, her insides buzzed happily. She could get used to this, she thought again, shuffling across the room toward the bathroom.

Except no, she couldn't.

* * *

There was a piano sitting on Mitch's chest.

At least that's what it had felt like since he'd walked into the Everson Printing Company and asked to speak to Brian more than thirty minutes ago. Brian wasn't there yet because Mitch had arrived as soon as the store had opened this morning. The young employee behind the counter said he expected Mr. Everson to arrive anytime.

Mitch's gaze flicked to the door that led to the back room. He'd hid like a coward when Brian had come into Dawanda's Fudge Shop on his night downtown with Kaitlyn. He was ashamed of that behavior. For one, he was a marine, a cop, and he wasn't supposed to duck or hide from anything. He was supposed to face his challenges head-on. That's exactly what he planned to do today. And whether Brian accepted his apology or not, this was a step in the right direction.

Brian had always been a nice guy in high school. Mitch had looked up to him and his three brothers. Everyone had, it seemed. Brian Everson was the star athlete of the Everson clan. By all predictions, he was going to bring a gold medal home for long-distance running in the Olympics the following year after he graduated. But no one had predicted the accident on that icy mountain road.

Mitch pulled out his phone and texted Alex.

I'm coming in late today. I have an errand.

Alex's response was quick.

I told you to take the day off. People are going to
think I'm taking advantage of my newest officer if
you don't.

Mitch frowned. What was he supposed to do with a day
off? And he was a new officer at SSPD but also temporary.
Alex should work him while he could.

Before Mitch could argue, the door to the back room finally opened, and a female clerk came out. She spoke briefly
to the younger male clerk whom Mitch had talked to earlier. Then their gazes flitted over, and Mitch knew they were
talking about him. The male clerk nodded and headed in his
direction.

"I'm sorry, sir," he said, looking apologetic and not meeting Mitch's eyes directly. "Mr. Everson is really busy this
morning and is unable to meet with you."

That piano on Mitch's chest turned into a baby grand.
"Did you tell him who I was? That Mitch Hargrove wants to
speak to him?"

"Yes, sir," the clerk said.

"I see." With a sigh, Mitch stood. "I'd like to leave my
phone number and where I'm staying, in case he wants to
get in touch later." Mitch knew Brian wasn't too busy to talk
to him right now. There weren't even any customers yet. Part
of Mitch wanted to go behind that counter, open the door to
the back room, and find Brian anyway. Brian needed to hear
his apology. And Mitch had things he needed to get off his
chest, like this baby grand piano, for one.

Mitch left his contact information with the clerk and
walked out into the parking lot. Now what? Alex had insisted he take today off, and Mitch suspected if he ignored

that order and showed up anyway, Alex might just shove him in one of those jail cells in the back.

Sliding behind the steering wheel, Mitch stared out at the open road. The mountains could be seen clearly today, almost purple in the bending sunlight. The first thing that came to mind for how to spend the day was being with Kaitlyn. But he needed to collect his thoughts when it came to her. He'd known there was a possibility that Brian wouldn't forgive him but he hadn't considered that Brian might not even talk to him.

He could go to the juvenile detention center to visit Kyle Martin. The court was trying to figure out what to do next in that situation but Cassie was pleading to have her son home for the holidays.

Kyle probably needed some time with his jumbled thoughts too. Not some older know-it-all who thought he had any good advice to give. Obviously, looking at the way Mitch had twisted up his own life, he didn't.

So instead, Mitch drove his truck to Evergreen Park. He was dressed in a T-shirt and loose-fit jeans along with a pair of sneakers. Just right to go for a short hike up the foothills to see the springs. Hopefully Brian would contact him later, once he'd had time to think. Something told Mitch that wasn't going to happen though.

It'd been wishful thinking that had brought him to the Everson's Printing Company this morning. Now it was back to reality.

CHAPTER NINETEEN

$\mathcal{B}$reakfast was served. The kitchen was cleaned. The guests were all off doing various things and seemingly happy.

The bell above the B&B door sang out, and in walked Paris in his usual black jeans. Instead of a black shirt, today he wore a festive red-and-black checked, button-down flannel. The transformation from biker to mountain man had begun.

"Hey," he said.

Kaitlyn smiled. "Hey. How's it going at Ms. Hamilton's?"

Paris frowned as he placed his laptop on the coffee table in the living room. "Let's just say I miss you and this inn. And I mean that in a completely platonic kind of way. I don't want to get on Mitch's wrong side again."

Kaitlyn laughed as she scooted over for him to take a seat beside her. "You were never on his wrong side."

Paris grunted and sat down. "He didn't like me when I first got here. I get it. He saw me as a threat on his territory."

"I doubt that. If Mitch had it his way, this inn never would've been his territory."

"I wasn't talking about the B and B." Paris gave her a sidelong wink and then pulled the laptop to him. "So, I think I have a handle on what you want. I put this together late last night. If you don't like it, be honest."

"I will." She nodded, bubbling with anticipation. She'd hired Paris to help with some promotional materials for the bed and breakfast early last week. She would have reached out to him regardless, but after looking at his website, she'd fallen in love with his work. Who knew her first guest had been such a graphics whiz?

He tapped a few keys and pulled up a design he'd prepared for the B&B with the name written in a fancy yellow script. Purple-toned mountains rose behind the words. It was simple, tasteful, and she didn't want to blink.

"It's perfect." She stared at the image until it blurred. Even then, it was gorgeous. "I mean it," she said, finally looking over. "I love everything about it."

He smiled gratefully. "I can tweak it if there's something you want to play up or down."

"Paris, this is even better than I had envisioned. It'll look amazing on the front of a brochure. You are very talented. Thank you so much." She leaned in and gave him a huge hug.

"It was nothing. Really. And I'm serious," he teased, pulling away. "I don't want to be on the other side of Mitch's fist if he walks in on us."

Kaitlyn swatted Paris's shoulder. "Don't be silly. How much do I owe you?" Whatever it was, it was worth every penny.

Paris shook his head. "Merry Christmas, Kaitlyn. I may have been your first guest here, but you were my first friend."

Her mouth dropped open, and emotion gripped her, strong and fierce. "I can't accept something so nice."

"You can, and you will. Didn't anyone ever teach you it's rude to turn down a gift?"

Kaitlyn drew a hand to her chest, so touched by his gesture. "Well, I got you something as well. Nothing nearly as generous as your graphic design, but I did want to give you a gift." She hurried over to the Christmas tree in the corner, where Paris's present was wrapped in shiny silver paper with a large red bow. "Merry Christmas, Paris," she said, handing it over.

He took his time opening it, and it occurred to her that maybe Paris didn't receive too many presents. He'd grown up in the foster care system. He didn't have family, and he was new in town. This might be the only present he got this year.

"It's not much," she explained, once Dawanda's fudge was revealed.

"Are you kidding? Dawanda's fudge is the stuff that wish lists are made of." He grinned and stood. "Thanks."

"You're welcome. And Paris, if you don't have any plans, please feel free to come over here for Christmas breakfast. I haven't decided on the final menu yet but it'll be festive and you're always welcome here."

"Sounds good. I'll even wear my Santa hat," he promised as he started to pack up his computer. "I'll send you the final graphic tonight."

"Great."

Kaitlyn walked him to the door and then turned as the phone began to ring.

"Uh-oh," Paris said. "Looks like more guests are calling to book their stay."

"I hope so. We're full over Christmas already. But there's

always room for one more for breakfast. Don't forget," she told him.

"I won't."

Kaitlyn closed the front door behind him and then ran to catch the phone. "Sweetwater Bed and Breakfast. Can I help you?"

"Yes. Is this Kaitlyn Russo? Mable Russo's grand-daughter?" a woman asked on the other end.

"Yes, it is."

"Hi there. This is Summer Rivera. We met at your grand-mother's funeral a few months ago. Do you remember? I heard you took over the B and B. How is it going?" she asked in one long string of words.

"Fine, thank you." Kaitlyn struggled to recall meeting anyone by the name of Summer Rivera. There'd been so many people at Mable's funeral though. It'd been a whirl-wind day, and she'd shaken a hundred different hands. Then she'd immediately flown back to New York, never dreaming that she'd be dropping everything and moving here only a month later.

"Well, I was calling to officially welcome you to town and to see if you would be carrying on your grandmother's generous tradition of donating cakes to the Hope for the Hol-idays Auction."

Kaitlyn twirled her finger in the cord of the phone. "Oh. I'm afraid I don't know anything about that."

"The Hope for the Holidays Auction is something the town•puts on every year. We choose a family in need and auction off all kinds of things, including your grandmother's homemade cakes. They were always very popular at the auc-tions."

"Oh." Kaitlyn leaned back against the wall. "Well, I can guarantee I'm nowhere near as good a baker as my grandmother, but I'll certainly agree to making a couple cakes for the cause."

"Terrific!" Summer cheered. "This year we're supporting a single mother with cancer. Mable usually made at least ten."

"Ten?" Kaitlyn repeated, wondering if she'd heard correctly.

"At least, but often more than that because they brought in so much money for charity. And her gingerbread cheesecake was the most popular. If you could make a few of those, that would be spectacular."

Gingerbread cheesecake? "Well, I'm...well..." Protests stuck in Kaitlyn's throat. How could she possibly refuse to donate to a charity her grandmother had supported? "Okay," she finally said. "I'm sure I can make that happen."

"Oh splendid. You are a dear, just like Mable always said. The auction is next Wednesday. I'll be in touch."

* * *

The movies Mitch liked the best were the ones with a ticking time clock. Time ticked down and the hero, Daniel Craig, Jason Statham, or any one of those action stars—to exclude Bradley Foster, whom he'd never liked—had to race to some sort of finish line to save the world.

Mitch had his own ticking time clock, and it was nowhere near as exciting. It'd been over twenty-four hours, and Brian hadn't called him. He didn't want Mitch here, and Mitch respected that. Mitch couldn't deny that he had feelings for Kaitlyn though. Deeper feelings than he'd ever had for any woman before. Was he just supposed to walk away?

He pulled into the parking lot of the Sweetwater PD and waved at Tammy as he walked inside.

"Hold on. Alex wants to speak to you," she said.

"What about?"

"Dunno. It's never good when the boss summons you though."

Mitch slapped a hand on her desk playfully. "Unless the boss also happens to be your best friend." He headed down the hall to Alex's office and offered a courtesy rap on the door before pushing it open. "You summoned?" he said dryly.

"Yeah. Hey, Mitch." Alex leaned back in his chair. As usual, he was dressed in a nice button-down shirt and a pair of faded jeans. Chiefs didn't have to wear the uniform if they didn't want to. Mitch was jealous of that. After all his years in the marine corps, he didn't much like uniforms. Even so, he supposed he'd be wearing one at his security job next month too.

"I'm still here for another week." Mitch plopped in the chair in front of Alex's desk. "If you tell me you don't need me anymore just because the Sweetwater Springs thief has been caught, you and I are going to have words."

Alex stared at him. "I'm not letting you go. In fact, I'm trying to keep you. Jackson Curtis resigned this morning."

"What? Why would he do a thing like that?"

Alex shrugged. "Well, between you and me, Jackson is going to ask his girlfriend to marry him. And she doesn't like the idea of marrying a man in this line of work."

Mitch laughed out loud. "Really? It would be different if we were in a big city but this is Sweetwater. Our most sought-after criminal is a seventeen-year-old boy trying to save his mom from cancer. I'd hardly call this a dangerous job." At least not compared to what he'd been up against as an MPO.

Alex leaned back in his chair. "I've been shot at," he said.

"I've had a knife pulled on me. I mean, yeah, it was a ninety-year-old woman wielding the knife but she could've done some serious damage." Alex cracked a grin. "This life isn't for everyone. I always knew I wanted to grow up and be in law enforcement just like my dad."

Mitch nodded, remembering well how Alex had wanted nothing more than to play a good game of cops and robbers growing up. Mitch had played right alongside him. Mable had always joked that they'd been cut from the same cloth.

"And I always knew for me that would mean not getting involved with someone."

"That doesn't even make sense, man," Mitch argued, sitting across from Alex.

"I watched how my dad's long hours here at the station affected my mom. I promised myself, when I decided this was the career I wanted, I would leave relationships to everyone else. That's just me. Most of the other employees here are happily married, and I'm happy for them."

Mitch shook his head. "I give up. Why are you telling me all this?"

"Because I want to offer you a job. Probably not as exciting as the security contract you have lined up in Virginia, but I know you and Kaitlyn have something good going. Thought you might consider staying awhile longer. We could use a guy like you. Especially now."

Mitch didn't say anything for a long moment.

The thought had already been niggling around in the back of his mind. He'd tried to ignore it because of the promise he'd made to the Eversons.

"Just say you'll consider it," Alex pressed.

Mitch gave a small nod. "I'll consider it."

"Great. That's halfway to a yes."

"Or halfway to a no, depending on how you look at it."

Alex pointed a finger. "I'm an optimist when it suits me. Now, get to work, Officer Hargrove. Sweetwater needs you. And if you see a ninety-year-old woman with a knife, heed my warning and take her seriously."

Mitch chuckled as he stood up. "Will do, Chief."

* * *

"Don't worry about the cakes," Gina told Kaitlyn a couple days later as they sat across the table from each other. "I'll come over on Wednesday morning and help you. I have Mable's gingerbread cheesecake recipe too."

Kaitlyn slid a cup of peppermint tea in front of Mitch's mother, who'd stopped by after cleaning one of the neighbor's homes. "Really? I won't turn down the help, if you're offering."

Gina chuckled. "I know your grandmother has big shoes to fill but Mable didn't do all of these things on her own, you know. She had help. Mine and Mitch's. Townspeople stopped in to give her a hand too after Henry died."

Kaitlyn grabbed a cookie off a plate that she'd set out for the guests. "Thank you. For everything. I'm not sure what I would've done without you and Mitch these last couple of months."

"Well, I'm sticking around so don't worry about that."

Mitch, on the other hand, wasn't sticking around, and they both seemed to know it. Even if Kaitlyn was still a tad bit in denial over that fact.

"What's that over there?" Gina asked, gesturing toward a wooden pallet that Kaitlyn had picked up outside the grocery store the other day. She'd covered it with chalkboard paint and hung it on the wall.

"I made that to display movie choices for the guests.

Movie nights in the ballroom are popular lately. Not everyone comes down but some do. Mable and Henry had quite
the collection of films too. I thought I'd let the guests start
voting between a couple of choices."

"Well, you are as smart as you are creative. I love the
idea."

"Thanks." Kaitlyn smiled to herself, taking another bite
of cookie. At Beautiful Designs, her ideas had always been
shot down by her boss. Here, there was no one to tell her
what she could or couldn't do. With her newfound freedom,
her ideas seemed to be flowing faster than she could jot them
down in her little notebook.

Gina pushed back from the table. "Thanks for the tea,
dear, but I better head back to the house and see what Nettie
is up to."

"How long is your sister-in-law in town for?"

"Oh, at least through Christmas," Gina said, grabbing one
more cookie. "Honestly, it's been nice having her around.
I've resorted to talking to myself over the years, which I
guess could be considered a little crazy. Now I still talk to
myself but there's someone else in the room. Makes me feel
a little less off my rocker."

Kaitlyn laughed as she followed Gina to the door. "I've
always heard talking to yourself is a sign of intelligence."

"Really?" Gina looked intrigued. "Well, I'll see you
bright and early on Wednesday. We'll make a day of it. It'll
be fun."

"Sounds perfect." Kaitlyn hugged Gina and then watched
her head down the steps. There was a marked chill in the air
from earlier. The forecast was calling for snow in the next
week. Just in time for Christmas. And who knows? Maybe
if it snowed hard enough, Mitch would have to stay a tad bit
longer.

With a *brrrrr*, Kaitlyn closed the door, barring out the chill. She started toward the fireplace to stoke the flames but stopped short when she heard a crash upstairs. It'd come from the *Anne of Green Gables* room.

Another crash jolted Kaitlyn where she stood. Then she took off running. Even from the bottom step, she could hear the raised voices.

"It's okay," Kaitlyn assured one of the other guests, who was peeking outside her door at the commotion. She wasn't sure if that was the truth or not. Her steps quickened as she heard a choice word puncture the air. "Ladies! What's going on?" Kaitlyn asked as she entered the room.

Doris Manchester, an older woman who wore a visible hearing aid, pointed a shaky finger across the room at Sally Huddleston, the guest whom Kaitlyn had checked into the *Gone With the Wind* room yesterday morning. "I told that woman her guitar playing was bothering me."

"Well, I paid for a room just like you," Ms. Huddleston said. Ms. Huddleston was probably in her early fifties. If Kaitlyn remembered correctly, she was a music teacher at a private school in Ohio. "That means I get to play my instrument anytime I want."

"But I paid for a room and I came here for some peace and quiet."

"Then turn your hearing aid off!" Ms. Huddleston shot back.

Ms. Manchester's mouth fell open. Then both women turned to look at Kaitlyn as if waiting for her to make things right.

Kaitlyn looked between them, her mouth gaping open too. She had no idea how to fix the situation.

"If she plays her guitar one more time, I'm going to march into her room and break the damn thing," Ms. Manchester threatened.

Ms. Huddleston gasped as if the other woman had tossed a toad in her direction.

Kaitlyn held up her hands. "Hold on, ladies. I'm sure we can work this out."

"I want another room away from this woman," Ms. Manchester demanded.

"Fine by me," Ms. Huddleston said. "And if you touch my guitar, I'm going to call the police."

"You wouldn't."

"I certainly would," Ms. Huddleston promised.

At that very moment, a Sweetwater Springs police officer just happened to walk into the room.

* * *

"I heard the voices from the front door," Mitch said. He'd taken the steps two at a time when he'd walked in and heard the commotion. "Is everything okay?"

Kaitlyn blew out a long breath. "Oh, you know, just a little disagreement," she said, even though her voice sounded tight.

"No." Ms. Manchester turned to Mitch and jabbed a finger in the air at Ms. Huddleston. "That woman threatened me. Lock her up!"

"I did no such thing," Ms. Huddleston huffed. "She said she was going to break my guitar!"

Mitch tossed a sideward glance at Kaitlyn. "Do we have any rooms that we could move one of these nice ladies to?"

"We're full," Kaitlyn said, looking completely flustered.

"I see." He poked his tongue at the side of his cheek as he tried to think. There was no good solution, which was sometimes the case. These two women either had to stick it out in neighboring rooms or one of them had to leave. "Well, if either of you are unsatisfied with your stay here, you can feel free to leave and your stay so far will be at no cost." They'd both already stayed one night so this seemed like a deal to Mitch.

"I'm not leaving," Ms. Huddleston said.

"Neither am I," Ms. Manchester added. "I read about this B and B in a magazine. This is a romantic holiday experience, and I'm old. I could die at any moment. I need romance."

Kaitlyn stifled a laugh.

Mitch frowned at her. Laughing at an angry old lady was never wise. He remembered Alex's warning about avoiding old ladies with sharp knives. He quickly assessed whether Ms. Manchester had one.

"Do you think that you could play your guitar in another room?" Kaitlyn asked. Her question was hesitant as if she was concerned the women were going to turn on her at any moment.

Ms. Huddleston cocked her head to the side. "And where would that be?"

"Well, the ballroom is empty during the day. You can feel free to play guitar in there. There's even a nice couch set up along the wall."

"I suppose I would be agreeable to that."

"Great," Mitch said, grasping on to her agreement. He was, after all, a man, and men liked to find solutions to problems. "Would you like me to carry your instrument down for you?"

Ms. Huddleston's eyes widened. "No one touches my instrument except me."

Mitch took a step backward. "No problem." He was just happy the standoff had been mediated. As he walked back through the populated hall, he spoke to the guests. "Everything is fine. Please go back to relaxing and enjoying your stay here."

"Wow." Kaitlyn grinned at him. "That sounds like something an actual bed-and-breakfast host would say."

"I'm nowhere near a B and B host but I did get offered a job today."

Kaitlyn was matching his every step down the stairs. She paused at the landing. "Alex?"

"Yep."

"I'm not surprised."

Excitement swam through him. Then the memory of Brian Everson sending him away snubbed out that feeling. "I'm not sure I can accept the offer."

Kaitlyn's expression turned crestfallen. "But you love working there. And you and Alex are friends. It would be a dream come true if I could work with my best friend, Josie, every day."

"I don't know. Seeing Alex daily might drive me crazy." He was only teasing, of course, and deflecting from the real issue. Alex was a great guy, a true friend, and he'd be a good boss too. "I told him I'd think about it."

Kaitlyn's face brightened just a touch. "I hope you do."

He and Kaitlyn had never discussed him staying before, and she'd never let on that she wanted him to stay. But right now, seeing the hope shine through her eyes, he thought maybe she did.

"Did you cast your vote yet?" Kaitlyn asked then.

"Vote?"

"It's movie night. I hung a chalkboard in the dining room this morning with some options for movies to watch tonight. I asked the guests to cast their votes."

"You are full of ideas, aren't you?" He lifted a finger to slide a hair away from her cheek, locking it behind her ear.

Just that simple touch made his fingers itch for more. He wasn't sure he would ever get enough of the woman standing in front of him.

"Just feeling inspired these days," she said, almost shyly. "There's something about this town and the people. It's impossible not to fall in love with it all." Her gaze hung on his.

She was talking about the town and the people. Not him. But she was looking at him with those bedroom eyes that inspired the hell out of him. He'd taken this thing between Kaitlyn and him too far, half of him thought. The other half protested that he hadn't taken it far enough. Not yet.

The silence of his phone in his pocket was deafening. *Come on, Brian. Call!* he silently pleaded as he looked at Kaitlyn. *Please call.*

CHAPTER TWENTY

Kaitlyn was in a daze as she set out the breakfast she'd prepared for the guests in the dining room. When she'd awoken this morning, Mitch was gone. There'd been a note on the kitchen counter telling her he'd gone to the station early to work on a case. He hadn't mentioned any new case lately though. She couldn't help wondering if he was already distancing himself in preparation to leave next week. She hoped not. They had so little time left together, and she wanted to savor it, moment by moment.

Her phone rang in her pocket, jolting her from her stupor. She pulled it out and glanced at the caller ID, still not ready to speak to her mom. Instead of her mom's picture, it was Josie's that filled her screen.

Kaitlyn stepped out of the dining room for privacy and put the phone to her ear with a smile. "Hi!"

"I hope I didn't wake you," Josie said.

Kaitlyn laughed. "I was already up. I'm surprised you're awake at this hour though."

"Are you kidding? I haven't gone to sleep yet," Josie admitted.

That statement didn't surprise Kaitlyn one bit. Even with Josie's night owl ways, she always seemed to be so put together. She never had dark circles under her eyes or a single hair out of place. Josie was a machine, and Kaitlyn admired the heck out of her friend.

"I've been meaning to call and catch up," Josie said. "How are things going down there?"

"Busy."

"Glad to hear it. And what's going on between you and Mitch?"

"His job here is done on Christmas Eve, and he's still planning to leave."

"Oh." Josie sounded surprised. "It sounded like you really liked this one. After all you've been through these last few months, I was wishing you a little happiness in the love arena."

"Me too." Kaitlyn pulled in a breath. "But life keeps going. I don't need a man to make me happy."

Josie snorted. "Now you sound like me."

Kaitlyn couldn't remember the last time Josie had been in a serious relationship. Maybe never. Josie sometimes went out "for drinks" with a guy but it never amounted to more than a casual date. Josie had never been one to give her heart to anyone, which Kaitlyn had always found strange. Josie was one of the most caring, generous people she knew. She had a lot to offer in a relationship if she were interested in having one.

"Mitch is starting a new job in January," Kaitlyn added. "I don't really have any choice but to accept that he's leaving and to move on."

"I'm sorry. Maybe you should give online dating a try,"

Josie suggested, the keys of her laptop still clicking in the background. "We just ran an article in *Loving Life* on couples who've found love that way. Did you know that one-third of marriages start with online dating?"

"As I said, I don't need a man right now." Or she did, but only a certain man would do. "I do, however, need more contact with my best friend."

"Agreed. I'll put a reminder in my phone so we can chat at least weekly."

This made Kaitlyn roll her eyes, although she was still smiling. "Sounds good."

She and Josie talked a little while longer, and then Kaitlyn disconnected and went into the dining area to make sure everyone was okay. There was a lively discussion going on about the movie they'd watched last night.

Ms. Manchester was against happily ever afters even though she'd been married to her husband for forty-six years. "No one said we were happy," she said gruffly to the group.

Mr. Manchester just wrapped his arm around his wife's shoulders and squeezed gently. "We're more than happy," he declared, soliciting an *aw* from the other guests. "I'm over the moon that this woman has stayed with me for so long."

Ms. Manchester melted into his side, and when she turned to face him, her expression softened. "I still prefer the movies without happily ever afters. It's more realistic."

Kaitlyn could agree. Her feelings for Mitch were the closest she'd ever had to being in love, and the thought of him leaving physically hurt. It would be hard to watch him go and say nothing. But what could she say? She understood his reasons. She'd been a fool to let herself feel as much as she did, and it would take a while to recover. Love wasn't something she wanted to participate in again for a very long time.

So, no, she wouldn't be dipping her toe into online dating, as Josie had suggested.

Kaitlyn glanced around at her guests. Instead, she'd live vicariously through the couples who booked rooms here at the inn, and maybe that would be enough.

* * *

Mitch was having a bad case of déjà vu. Once again, he was sitting in the Everson Printing Store and waiting to see Brian. In the middle of the night, he'd awoken to a recurring nightmare about the accident. Only this time, Brian was dead and so was Mitch's mom. Life was ruined, and as usual it was all his fault.

Mitch hadn't been able to go back to sleep after that. Instead, he'd gone for an early morning jog, showered, and had driven back here. He wouldn't give up so easily this time. After all these years, Brian deserved his apology. And Mitch deserved closure.

The young clerk with pimpled skin kept casting awkward glances toward Mitch in the waiting area. Then the backroom door opened, and the female clerk came out just like last time. Instead of turning to the younger male, however, she walked directly to Mitch and smiled warmly.

"Good morning, sir. Mr. Everson is ready to see you in his office now," she said.

Relief poured through Mitch. He was going to at least have a chance to tell Brian how sorry he was about the events that had taken place that fateful night when one lie had cost so many so much. This was something he should've done a long, long time ago. "Thanks."

Mitch stood and followed her through the storeroom door and down a well-lit hallway to the last office on the left. A nameplate on the door read EVERSON in big block letters.

The clerk offered a courtesy knock before turning the knob and opening the door for Mitch to enter. As he stepped into the office, he expected to see Brian in his wheelchair. Instead, a graying man behind a large oak desk stood and shoved his hands on his narrow hips.

"Hello, Mitch," Frank Everson said. Just like when Frank had come to see him at his mom's house when he was seventeen years old, there was no smile or offer to shake hands.

"I came to see Brian." Mitch stepped farther inside the room but didn't sit. And he didn't plan on sitting. Frank was not the man he came to talk to.

"I thought you and I had an agreement, son," Frank said.

"I'm not your son," Mitch bit out.

"Right. My son is in a wheelchair, thanks to you."

Guilt and anger warred within Mitch. One emotion begged him to back down, walk away. The other prompted him to stand rooted in that office. "With all due respect, sir, it was an accident. I never meant to hurt Brian, and you know that. All I want is to talk to him, man to man."

Frank frowned, his eyes hard. "You were careless, irresponsible, and foolish back then. And you made a promise to my family, which it looks like you're not man enough to keep."

Mitch folded his arms in front of him. Frank was right. He had been foolish and irresponsible. But what Alex had said for Kyle Martin was true for him too. One mistake didn't define a person. Mitch was tired of letting his past hold all the power. The accident was the reason his mom had taken on so much work. The reason he'd left town and joined the military instead of staying and going to the police academy with Alex. The accident had dictated every choice Mitch had made since he was seventeen years old. It had to stop now. "I want to tell Brian that I'm sorry."

"Why? To ease your guilty conscience? No, you don't get to do that." Frank walked to the office door and held it open—Mitch's cue to get the hell out. "The Everson family still has a lot of power in this town, Mitch. Your mom lost her job but there's more to be lost unless you honor your promise and leave Sweetwater Springs."

Mitch clenched his teeth so hard that pain shot up his jaw. "Is that a threat, sir?"

"Take it any way you like. I'd take it as a promise."

Mitch didn't offer a goodbye as he stormed down the hall and out of the building.

* * *

Ten cakes to donate to the Hope for the Holidays Auction. Piece of cake.

By Wednesday at noon, the entire kitchen looked like it'd exploded. There was cake batter, flour, and every color of frosting smeared across Kaitlyn's apron. It was likely also on her face and in her hair.

"We are a sight," Gina said on a laugh as she slipped the last Bundt pan into the oven. "I'll help you clean up this mess while it bakes," she offered, pulling back and straightening as she shut the oven door.

"No. You've already helped more than enough. I can get all this." Kaitlyn spanned her arms out to encompass the full kitchen because not one spot had been neglected in their mess. "Really. Go home and relax."

Gina narrowed her eyes. "Now you're starting to sound like my son." She pointed a finger in Kaitlyn's direction.

"Speaking of which, you keep an eye on him and make sure he doesn't tear into one of these cakes."

Kaitlyn grinned. "Maybe I'll make one more cake just for him. He deserves it after all he's done here."

Gina chuckled, flour dusting the air as she did. "Mitch will always do what he thinks is right. Following Mable's wishes and helping you fix up this B and B was the right thing to do, no doubt about that. Mitch wouldn't have been able to live with himself if he'd left."

"He's gone above and beyond what Mable asked of him though."

"Yep. That's Mitch's way too." Gina lifted her apron from around her head.

"I suspect he gets all those wonderful traits from you," Kaitlyn said, smiling warmly at the woman. "Thanks again for coming by today."

"I was glad to do it, dear. Call me anytime. But right now, since you insist on sending me away, I'm heading home to shower."

Kaitlyn followed her down the hall and through the front room.

When Gina opened the door to leave, Mitch was standing on the other side.

He looked between Kaitlyn and his mom. "What's going on here?"

His mom went in for a hug. "Now that's no way to greet the woman who suffered fourteen hours in labor with you."

Kaitlyn's grin fell short at Mitch's grim expression.

"You've been cooking?" he asked his mom in an accusatory voice.

Gina pulled back. "Kaitlyn was nice enough to allow me to help with the Hope for the Holidays cakes. I offered, and she did me a huge favor by accepting. I hope you're not prepared to lecture me on cake baking, because I'm not yours to order around."

His eyes narrowed on Gina. "Not my orders. Doctor's orders. It's supposed to be your day off."

"Doctor, schmoctor. I told you that Dr. Jacobs cleared me to return to my normal activities. A low iron level isn't going to kill me, Mitch, and I've been taking my supplements dutifully. Now stop your fussing. I'm going home to make sure Nettie is behaving herself."

"You're the one who needs to behave," he said in a less-than-teasing tone.

Gina hugged Mitch one more time, leaving a thick film of flour on his shirt. Then she waved and headed down the steps.

Kaitlyn felt an *uh-oh* tremor through her because Mitch still didn't look happy for some reason, and she didn't think it was due to his mom cooking with her for the last few hours. "Your mom really loves being here. She offered to come over and help me bake," Kaitlyn explained. "I couldn't tell her no."

"Yes, you could have. She's supposed to be slowing down, not taking on more work."

Kaitlyn stepped past him and closed the front door in case Gina was still within earshot. "I made sure she didn't do too much. Cooking is not exactly strenuous activity, Mitch." Even though cooking ten cakes had turned the kitchen into a sauna, and Kaitlyn's arms were already sore from all the batter stirring. "We had a nice time. I love your mom's company. The guests seem to enjoy her too."

He shook his head. "Did you also have her scrub the floors and toilets while she was here?"

Kaitlyn pulled back. "What?"

"She's not going to be your hired help after I'm gone," he bit out. "Do you understand?"

Kaitlyn didn't understand. Not at all. The Mitch she'd gone to bed with last night had been sweet and gentle. The one she was looking at right now reminded her of the burly guy she'd sat down and argued with in this very room a couple of months ago. "I think your mom is old enough to take care of herself. She's survived just fine without you all these years."

Kaitlyn didn't mean that to come out so harshly but Mitch tensed like she'd tossed a bucket of ice water on his head. "I'm sorry. I know you had your reasons for leaving town before. All I meant was—"

He held up his hand. "I know what you meant. And I'll be gone this time next week. I just need to know that Mom will be okay. Not accepting every job offer that comes along. She doesn't need the money. I'm making sure of that."

"I didn't pay her," Kaitlyn said. Although she wasn't sure having Mitch's mom work for free was any better in his mind. "She did it for charity." Kaitlyn swallowed back her hurt feelings. "Maybe it's not about the money. Have you ever considered that? Maybe she likes to work. I know it's hard to understand for someone like you but maybe your mom enjoys being with people."

"Someone like me? You mean heartless? Cold?" he asked.

Who is this man? She didn't recognize him. Had something happened this morning? "That's who you pretend to be, at least. But I've seen a different side of you," she said, softening her voice. She didn't want to fight, even if it was obvious that was exactly what he was looking for. He was picking a fight with a sledgehammer right now. "Your mom doesn't want your money, Mitch. She wants you to stay." As much as Kaitlyn wanted the same. "You can, you know."

His dark eyes narrowed. "Can what?"

"Stay. I know we haven't discussed it," she began, suddenly spurting out what she'd been hoping to bring up tonight over dinner. Definitely not in a moment where Mitch was upset and worried. But her words came anyway, almost without her permission. "I can still buy you out of your half of this place. You can pay off your mom's house. But you can also stay. You don't have to leave Sweetwater Springs." She fidgeted nervously with her hands. "I mean, I know the security job is offering a lot more money, but..."

"Staying was never part of the plan, Kaitlyn."

This was not how she was supposed to be bringing up this conversation. They were supposed to be flirting over a delicious dinner and maybe on their second glass of wine. Then she would broach the subject that, in her fantasies, he'd only been waiting for her to bring up. Because staying was what he wanted too. He'd vow to make amends with the ghosts of his past, for his sake and hers. Then, knowing they wanted the same thing, he'd walk around the table, kiss her, and tug her down the hall to the bedroom. That was what was supposed to happen.

"But plans were meant to be broken," she said weakly. It sounded like a plea even to her own ears.

Mitch kept his gaze steady. The warmth she'd seen so many times was gone. He really did look cold and heartless right now. "Not these plans."

CHAPTER TWENTY-ONE

$\mathcal{R}$eason one for why Mitch couldn't stay: He had a high-paying job that would set his mom up for life.

Reason two: The town may have forgiven him but Brian Everson hadn't.

Reason three: If Frank Everson's threat had any credibility, Mitch had to leave. He'd never forgive himself if he was the reason Kaitlyn lost the Sweetwater B&B. Wasn't that the reason he'd agreed to the will's stipulations to begin with? To save this place for a woman he didn't even know at the time? Now that he knew her, he was willing to do whatever it took to preserve her family's business.

Like a fool, he'd gotten too close. He'd allowed himself to have feelings for Kaitlyn. To hope that maybe what she was proposing could be true. But it couldn't. He knew that, and she needed to know it, and believe it too.

"This was never meant to be a real thing," he said, already seeing the shine of her eyes. If she started to cry, that would be his undoing. *Please don't cry*, he mentally pleaded. Ending things would be hard enough as it was. But necessary. "We had a good time but we always knew it would end. Time's up."

There is that damn ticking time clock.

She didn't respond at first. Her tears stayed at bay as she blinked back at him, a flurry of emotion storming in her irises. "I see," she finally whispered. "This was a business partnership, and you and I were having a good time on the side."

Mitch nodded, feeling like the world's biggest jerk. "That's right."

"I know that. I was just saying that if you wanted to stay for your mom's sake, you could. But like I said, she's a grown woman. She doesn't need you." Kaitlyn lifted her chin, and he suspected she was speaking for herself as well. And judging by the coolness of her eyes now, she also didn't want him anymore.

"I see. It might be best if I go ahead and pack up my things. I can stay at Alex's place until the conditions in the will are met."

"That's probably best," she agreed, refusing to meet his eyes now.

"Just let me know when Mr. Garrison plans to stop back by, and I'll be here."

She gave another curt nod. "Okay."

He started to turn and walk away but then hesitated and looked at her. "Kaitlyn, for what it's worth..."

She held up a hand. "Don't. It's fine. Obviously, it wasn't worth very much."

* * *

Mitch was walking away from the best thing that had ever happened to him, and he knew it. Kaitlyn was the first person to make him feel whole since the accident. She'd filled this huge crater in his soul. How the hell was he supposed to turn away from that and never look back?

He got into his truck and drove to Alex's house. Tuck's Jeep was parked beside Alex's police SUV in the driveway. Between the two of them, Mitch was sure he could find a place to stay tonight. His mom didn't have room and he didn't feel like fielding questions from her or Aunt Nettie about what had happened between him and Kaitlyn anyway.

Mitch walked right inside, not bothering to knock on the front door. "I would think a police chief would know to lock his front door," he called as he cut through the living room.

Alex turned to look at him with surprise from the kitchen. "I would think anyone stupid enough to break and enter would know not to do so at a police chief's house."

"Hey, Mitch," Tuck said before biting into a sandwich at the table.

"Hey, man," Mitch replied.

"Want a PB&J?"

"No, thanks." Mitch pulled out a chair and sat down, feeling fifteen years older suddenly. Like he'd been served his own jail sentence. "Do you think one of you could put me up for the next couple of nights?"

"Uh-oh. Did you and Kaitlyn get in another fight?" Alex asked.

"I wouldn't say fight. I just broke up with her."

Both Alex and Tuck looked at him as if he were crazy.

"I thought you were smarter than that, buddy," Alex said. "I never would've offered you the job at the police station had I thought you were that dense."

Mitch lifted his gaze. "And I'm not taking the position with the SSPD."

Alex cast a grim expression. "Why is that?"

"I have my reasons."

"I doubt any of them are good ones," Alex said.

Mitch was so tired of defending himself. He wasn't even sure if he believed his own reasons anymore. "All I know is I can't stay. So, back to my question. Which one of you is going to let me stay with them tonight?"

"We're going out," Tuck told him, wiping a smear of purple jelly from the corner of his mouth. "Why don't you come with us? And whoever doesn't get lucky is the one that gets to bring your sorry butt home."

Mitch looked between his friends. Alex didn't mind dating but like he'd told Mitch when he'd offered him the job at SSPD, he wasn't ever going to get serious with anyone. His career was too important to him. Tuck talked a good game, but whenever they went to the bar, he typically just drank his beer and watched everyone else. He didn't hit on the ladies, even though Mitch was sure Tuck could have anyone he wanted. Perhaps, once you've experienced a love like Tuck and Renee's, your heart stalled. Is that how it would be for Mitch? Now that he'd been with Kaitlyn, no one else would ever compare?

"Fine," Mitch said. "I'll go out." A night of drinking sounded like a good idea right about now anyway. And between his two friends, it was a good bet he would have his pick of where he wanted to stay tonight.

* * *

Kaitlyn listened for the front door to close. The guests were all gone. Some had gone to dinner, others to the Hope for the Holidays Auction, where Kaitlyn had planned to be herself. Claiming she was sick, she'd asked Gina and Nettie to go in her place. Gina had sounded undone with excitement.

Tears slipped out of the corners of Kaitlyn's eyes as she lay back on the couch. For the last two months, she'd wanted nothing more than a full inn but tonight she was glad she was all alone here. It would be unbecoming of a host to bawl her eyes out in front of the guests. Grandma Mable would surely agree with that.

Kaitlyn felt like she'd been discarded along with the table scraps. Her own fault. Mitch had always been up-front about his intentions. At least with his words. His actions had offered her a glimmer of hope that she'd recklessly grabbed on to though. She'd allowed herself to fantasize about something more between them, and in her wildest fantasies, she and Mitch had created the ultimate partnership.

She grabbed a box of Kleenex along with a large bag of chocolates because if you were going to have a pity party, you needed to do it right.

Twenty minutes later, once all her tears were dry and the box of Kleenex and bag of chocolates were empty, Kaitlyn showered and headed into the kitchen to pour herself a healthy glass of red wine—just what the doctor ordered for a broken heart. Climbing onto the couch in the living area, she turned on the TV. She was hoping to find a Hallmark movie and live vicariously through the actors and actresses on-screen. Their problems could be fixed in a two-hour time slot on television. Hers couldn't.

Halfway into a lighthearted tale of two fated lovers, the doorbell rang. Kaitlyn froze. The guests weren't expected back anytime soon and they were free to walk in.

A new guest?

She did have one vacancy in the *Pride and Prejudice* room.

Thank God, she'd showered after her crying episode. The mascara streaks were washed away and hopefully some of the puffiness of her eyes had gone down too. She didn't want to scare off any potential guests.

The doorbell rang again, and she realized she was taking too long to answer. Jumping up from the couch, she ran over to the door, opened it, and froze. "Mom? Dad? What are you doing here?"

Her parents stood on the porch with luggage in hand.

"We needed to see if you were okay," her mom said. She was dressed in a bright-red parka, black leggings, and boots all the way to her knees. Even so, her slight frame trembled in the cold.

"You could've just called," Kaitlyn said.

"I did. You didn't answer." Her mom gave a sheepish smile.

"You didn't have to come all the way down from New York. What about your Bahamas cruise?"

"It's Christmas, darling. This is where we should be this year." Her mom stepped over the threshold and wrapped Kaitlyn in a tight hug. Then her father let go of his luggage and wrapped them both in his wide, encompassing arms. It was surprising, and it felt really good. So good that Kaitlyn almost dissolved into tears for a second time tonight.

"Come in, you two," she finally said, sniffling. A second box of tissues was in order.

Her parents retrieved their luggage off the porch and brought it inside.

"Wow, sweetheart. This place is amazing." Her mom stared in awe at the front room, her gaze falling on the large Christmas tree, sparkling magically in the sitting area. "Did you do all this by yourself?" she asked, turning back to Kaitlyn.

"Um, no. I had help." Kaitlyn didn't want to get into the details of her last two months. Not tonight.

"Your decorating skills really shine in this place," her father agreed.

A compliment from him was akin to gold. From her mother, platinum. "Thanks."

Both of her parents looked at her with serious faces.

"I'm sorry I questioned you," her mom said quietly. "You would never invite such negative attention—I know that. Are you all right? Did that man hurt you?"

Kaitlyn swallowed. "Yes. No. I'm fine."

"We can threaten your former employer with a lawsuit," her father said, looking for a solution as usual. "You were sexually harassed by a client, and Beautiful Designs wrongfully terminated you. That's unjust."

Her mother nodded in agreement, her entire expression pulled down by the gravity of her sadness. "We'll pay for a lawyer, dear. We'll fight this. Bradley Foster can't do this to you or your career. You've worked too hard to be knocked down like this."

Kaitlyn had only worried about defending a lawsuit against herself. She'd never considered filing one against Bradley or her former employer. She didn't want to get wrapped up in legal battles though. And she certainly didn't want her old job back. "I don't want a career in New York. This is where I want to be now."

She waited for her parents to argue and rattle off what was best for her the way they always had. When she'd chosen electives in high school, they'd always vetoed the ones she wanted most and strongly advised the ones they said "would take her further in life." When she'd chosen a small college off the grid, they'd told her in no uncertain terms that she'd be attending the top college in New York state for interior design. One of the best in the country.

Instead of challenging her now though, her mom wrapped

her arms around her and hugged her tightly once more. "I think this is the perfect place for you." She pulled back and looked at Kaitlyn with shiny eyes that caught the twinkle of all the Christmas lights in the room. "And I can't wait to see the rest of the inn."

"Your grandma would've been so proud, honey," her father added. "Your mom and I are proud too."

Kaitlyn hadn't thought she had any tears left to cry but several streamed down her face suddenly. "Thank you."

He cleared his throat. "Now the big question is, Do you have a room available for us tonight?"

Kaitlyn laughed as she wiped her cheek. "You're in luck."

* * *

Going to the Tipsy Tavern with the guys last night had been a welcome distraction, so Mitch was back again tonight, drinking soda this time.

A waitress came up to his table and laid a beer down in front of him. Lucky for him, Nadine was off tonight. That was one thing Mitch could be thankful for. Another was two friends willing to put up with his scrooge-erific demeanor.

"What's this?" he asked. "I didn't order alcohol."

"Courtesy of the woman at the corner table," the waitress told him.

Mitch's gaze followed the direction that she was pointing and saw three women staring back at him. They all appeared to be in their midfifties and waved as he looked over.

"What do you want me to tell them?" the waitress asked.

Mitch didn't want to hurt the women's feelings by sending the drink back, and something told him they weren't flirting. "Nothing. I'll walk over and talk to them myself."

"Suit yourself," the waitress said with a half shrug and then turned and continued to the next table.

Tuck raised an eyebrow. "Seriously? You dump Kaitlyn, and now you're going to go seduce a bunch of fifty-year-olds? No offense—they're beautiful fifty-year-olds but they're pretty much your mom's age. That's a little weird."

"I'm not seducing anyone." Mitch pushed back from the table. "I'm just going to thank them for the drink." Working at the bed and breakfast and at the police station these last several weeks had softened his antisocial tendencies. He had to admit he kind of liked meeting new people now, even if he wasn't in the best mood tonight.

Without another word to Tuck or Alex, he grabbed the beer and walked over to the women's table. "Hi, ladies. Just wanted to say thanks for the gift."

The woman on the left nodded. She had overstyled white-blond hair that made a helmet around her round face. "You don't remember me, do you?"

Mitch zeroed in on her in the darkened tavern. Something about her eyes was familiar but he couldn't put his finger on where or how he knew her. "I'm sorry," he said, shaking his head.

"It's okay. I was your language arts teacher in high school."

"Mrs. Lambert. Right," Mitch said, remembering her immediately with the hint.

"You were more interested in the girls than my lessons back then." She shared a glance at the other two women.

Mitch gave them a closer look too. Both had also worked at Sweetwater High, although he didn't think he'd ever been in either of their classes. "I paid more attention than you know," he said. "I rather enjoyed reading *Moby Dick*." And it was weird saying the word *dick* in front of his old high school teacher.

All three women laughed.

"So, you're back in town?" Mrs. Lambert asked.

"No, actually, I'm leaving in a couple of days."

A frown settled on her lips. "Oh, what a shame. You know, I always worried about you after what happened. I worried about Brian for a while too, but I stopped being concerned for his well-being a long time ago."

That statement struck Mitch as odd. The tavern was crowded so maybe he misunderstood. If there was anyone to worry about, it was Brian. He was the one whose entire life had veered off course. He was the one who was supposed to be an Olympic gold medalist by now. The one in a wheelchair for life. "What do you mean?"

"Well, Brian took something terrible that happened to him and found his purpose in life. If he had become an Olympian like he had planned, he might not be where he is today."

Mitch's brows knit more closely together. Fifty years wasn't old but he was beginning to wonder about Mrs. Lambert's mental status. "You mean the printing store?"

Mrs. Lambert nodded. "Yes, among the other businesses he owns."

"You mean his family owns," Mitch corrected.

"No, *Brian*. He's quite the businessman," Mrs. Lambert told him. "Of course, owning your own business is nice but it's his work with the Special Olympics that I'm most impressed with. The way he coaches those children is so inspiring. The newspaper has done several write-ups on him over the years."

The other two women nodded in unison.

"Brian coaches for the Special Olympics?" Mitch asked.

"I didn't know that." How would he though? He'd closed himself off from knowing anything when it came to the Everson family.

"Yes," the third woman at the table said. She had a librarian look about her, with thick glasses and shoulder-length, pin-straight hair. Mitch thought maybe she actually was his school librarian once upon a time. "His wife too. She has a physical disability as well, you know."

"No." Mitch hadn't known that either.

"She doesn't use a wheelchair too often but sometimes when her multiple sclerosis flares up, she does."

"Oh, Brian seems to adore Jessica," Mrs. Lambert said, beaming under the dim lights of the bar. "I've never been a fan of Brian's father, Frank, but those two couldn't be more different. I mean, even though Brian doesn't get along with his father, he still lets him run the printing store."

Mitch pulled out a chair and sat down at the table with the women now. His body was suddenly too heavy to hold up. "Brian and his father don't get along?" he asked.

"Well, no," Mrs. Lambert said. "Not for some time now. His father was always so sports oriented. Even after the accident, he pushed Brian to enter the Olympics. It was never Brian's dream to be an Olympian though. He wrote a narrative paper in my class once telling me so. He asked me not to share it so I didn't." Mrs. Lambert shook her head. "I guess the cat's out of the bag now so it's okay."

Mitch was trying to wrap his head around this new information. Even though he hadn't planned on drinking tonight, the beer in his hand looked appealing right about now. He pulled it to his mouth and took a long pull. When he set it back down, he asked, "So Brian doesn't work at the printing store with his father?" Because that little tidbit stood out.

"Well, I'm sure he drops by there from time to time but he

has so many businesses. He practically owns all the downtown shops," Mrs. Lambert continued.

Mitch leaned forward. He'd been policing the stores on Main Street for weeks. He'd seen Brian at Dawanda's Fudge Shop once but that was as a customer. He'd seen Brian's sister Penny too.

"All those store owners would have lost their life's work if Brian hadn't swooped in and bought it all. Some bigwig commercial businessman wanted to snap up all that realty, and he would've too."

"That would've ruined some of Sweetwater's charm," the woman on the right said, shaking her head with a cluck of her tongue.

Mrs. Lambert nodded in agreement. "Brian was a real hero to save it all. And you," she said, pointing her finger. "We hear you're a hero these days as well. You caught the thief who was wreaking havoc down here."

Mitch shook his head. "He wasn't much of a thief, if you ask me." Just a scared kid who reminded Mitch a whole lot of his younger self.

Mitch wrapped his fingers around his beer as his mind raced. It was Frank Everson who'd turned him away both times Mitch had tried to see Brian. Did Brian even know Mitch wanted to talk to him?

Mitch stayed and chatted with the ladies just a few minutes more, and then he got up and returned to the table with Alex and Tuck.

"Thought you weren't drinking tonight," Tuck said, lowering his gaze to the beer in Mitch's hand.

Mitch set it down in front of him. "Brian Everson owns the downtown shops we've been patrolling," he said, looking at Alex.

Alex stared at him for a moment and then gave a slow

nod. "On paper, but the shop owners still have complete control. They all had substantial flooding after the last year's winter storm. The costs to repair were steep and a commercial realtor wanted to buy it at a steal. The store owners couldn't possibly have afforded to turn him down, if not for Brian."

"Why didn't you tell me?"

"A lot of people around here don't know. Besides, you've always insisted you didn't want to hear about the Everson family," Alex told him. "I respected that."

Mitch nodded. He'd shut down every conversation pertaining to Brian over the years. It was too painful. His philosophy had been that what he didn't know couldn't hurt him. "I want to know now. Where can I find him?"

Alex pulled out his cell phone and tapped the screen. "The man is everywhere. Sometimes I go long stretches without seeing him, and sometimes I run into him several times a day."

Tuck agreed. "The wheelchair doesn't slow Brian down one bit. He's even been climbing with me a time or two."

Mitch raised a brow. The image he'd carried in his mind along with all the guilt wasn't accurate. Mitch was more paralyzed than Brian, it seemed.

"I have his contact information in my phone," Alex said. "You want his number?"

Mitch hesitated and then nodded. He'd already been shot down twice in his efforts to talk to Brian. Maybe the third time would be the charm.

CHAPTER TWENTY-TWO

Kaitlyn awoke the next morning with mixed emotions. Mitch was no longer in the space beside her like he'd been for the last few weeks. Along with the empty space in her bed was a void in her heart. She'd never been in love before so she guessed she'd also never felt the full extent of a broken heart.

It hurt. A lot.

After dragging herself out of bed, she went to the bathroom and then retrieved fresh clothes from her chest of drawers. A few minutes later, she walked into the kitchen to get started on breakfast: a sunrise frittata. She wanted to start off her parents' day with the full bed-and-breakfast experience. After that, she planned on giving them a tour of the inn. She hadn't gone into detail last night about what had happened with Bradley but she suspected they'd have questions. They told her they believed her story though, and would stand beside her no matter what she decided to do.

Honestly, she just wanted to let the past go. It was a mess

but everyone had messes. Some weren't as easily forgotten, like Mitch's. She understood that. What she couldn't come to grips with was the way he'd treated her when he'd ended things the other day. She wanted to believe he thought he was doing her a favor by being such a brute but maybe that was just the real him, the Mitch she'd first met two months ago, standing in the front room and adamantly stating that he wouldn't be agreeing to the stipulations of Mable's will.

But he'd changed his mind. And after a while, he'd changed. She'd watched the transformation. He'd become happy here. At home here.

Unwilling to waste a moment more dwelling on something she couldn't change, Kaitlyn carried the breakfast plates to the table and greeted everyone, playing the part of the happy hostess. Since she'd arrived, she hadn't had to pretend that was true. Today, however, it took effort.

"Good morning, dear." Her mom beamed from the table, sitting beside her father. As usual, her mom was perfectly put together. Her hair was already styled and her makeup applied tastefully.

"How did you sleep last night?" Kaitlyn asked, joining her parents after all the guests had been served a plate.

"Like a baby," her father said with an appreciative nod.

"Oh, the bed was so soft. And it's amazing how quiet it is here. You'd think being in a house full of people would be dreadfully loud but it wasn't."

"Well, you're used to being in a home smack-dab in a city full of millions, Mom. Sweetwater Springs is a small community."

"It is. And it's a nice change of pace." Her mom forked a piece of her frittata into her mouth and closed her eyes. "Oh, George. You must try this food our daughter has prepared. It's so good."

He dutifully took a bite, and Kaitlyn couldn't help the satisfaction mounting inside her at impressing her parents. "Delicious," he affirmed. "She definitely didn't get her cooking talents from you, Marjorie," he told Kaitlyn's mom, whose mouth popped open before laughing.

"No, I'll admit that's true," her mom said.

After breakfast, Kaitlyn took them through each room of the inn while her mother oohed and aahed at all the furnishings.

"You always did have so much imagination," her mom commented.

Kaitlyn ended the tour of the house in the ballroom and told them about the movie nights they'd had here and her plans to possibly hire someone to teach ballroom dance lessons in the future. "It really has been so magical seeing this place come alive. I know exactly why Grandma Mable loved this B and B so much."

"Your grandparents didn't buy this place until after I left for college," Kaitlyn's father said. "I never spent enough time here to really fall in love with it."

Kaitlyn's mom placed a hand on her shoulder. "I might not have supported you coming to stay here at first but I was wrong, honey. If this place makes you happy, then your father and I will just have to plan on coming down here every couple of months to see you. An added bonus is we can stay in a different themed room every time we visit."

Kaitlyn's father chuckled. "You've been saying we need to have more romantic getaways. I hear this is one of the most romantic towns in the country."

"For the holidays, at least." Kaitlyn grinned. "Sweetwater is planning their annual Sweetwater Festival this spring. I hear it's an amazing time. You two should come down for that."

"Maybe we will," her mom said, casting a glance at Kaitlyn's dad.

Kaitlyn hoped they would as she led them toward the back door. "Do you want me to show you outside?"

"Sure," both her parents said with what sounded like sincere excitement.

"We'll have to get our coats," Kaitlyn said. "It's freezing out there. But I've started making plans for the landscaping once it warms up." She'd be carrying out those plans on her own, however. From here on out, she and this inn were on their own.

* * *

Mitch nearly missed the turn into his mom's driveway. With his cloud of thoughts hanging heavily on his mind, he was on autopilot, driving toward the B&B and Kaitlyn. But he'd broken up with her. It was for the best, he kept telling himself, even if he couldn't seem to convince his heart. It felt like someone had used that vital organ inside his chest as a punching bag over the last four days.

After parking, he walked up the driveway carrying a treat for the two women inside.

His mom and aunt Nettie were sitting at the dining room table playing a game of Rook when he walked in.

His mother immediately lifted her head and sniffed the air. "Dawanda's fudge," she said, her eyes rounding like a five-year-old child's.

"And you're excited to see me too, right?" he asked, dipping to kiss her temple. As he did, he scrutinized the color of her complexion and the skin under her eyes. She really was doing better these days. The symptoms she'd had when he'd first come to town had been alleviated with rest and supplements. That would make leaving for his security job so much easier.

"Of course, I'm excited to see you," she said. Mitch turned to his aunt. "Hey, Aunt Nettie. Is Mom behaving?"

"What do *you* think?" Nettie asked.

"I think I'd be worried if you said yes."

Nettie emptied the bag of fudge onto a paper plate at the center of the table. "You were always my favorite nephew. And if you keep supplying us with this stuff, you always will be."

"You plan on staying awhile?" he asked, pulling out a chair and sitting down across from them.

Nettie looked up at him and then flicked her gaze to his mom.

This tripped his gut's radar. "What?" he asked, looking between them.

"I haven't told him yet," his mom said, looking a shade guilty.

"Told me what?" He sat up straighter, suddenly going through the worst-case scenarios of what she would say. Maybe he'd let his guard down too soon. Maybe she wasn't doing better after all.

His mom frowned. "Stop your worrying," she ordered. "It's written all over your face. What I have to say is no big deal. Nettie is just moving in with me, that's all."

He raised an eyebrow as his thoughts caught up to speed. "Why? I thought the doctor said you were just exhausted. You just need to slow down, which means *not* taking on more jobs," he said, reminded that his mom had been helping Kaitlyn at the Sweetwater B&B a lot these days.

His mom raised a hand. "The doctor says I'm fine, yes. But my small health scare got me thinking that I'm tired of being alone. What if you hadn't shown up when I collapsed?" She shook her head. "Not only that, with you here, I realized that I'm lonely in this house all by myself."

"And I've been lonely living in my RV," Aunt Nettie added.

"We're not getting any younger," his mom explained. "People need someone to grow old with, and, well, we've decided we want to be that for one another."

"Sure beats waiting on another loser to break my heart." Aunt Nettie laughed as she licked remnants of a piece of fudge off her fingertips. Mitch's aunt had never married. Growing up, he'd watched her get close a time or two but it had never worked out. "An added bonus is that I get to see my nephew from time to time." She winked. "If you come around," she added, and then took another bite out of her fudge square.

"He will. Mitch has a girl here," his mom shared.

His mom and aunt really were like two best friends when they got together. Mitch almost felt like a third wheel in this conversation.

"Actually, Kaitlyn and I have decided it's best if we end things. I've been staying with Alex for the last couple of days."

"What?" His mom was visibly upset.

"Don't worry. I'll be back to visit you and Aunt Nettie." And Alex, Tuck, and Dawanda. He had family here. Friends. This was his hometown. "I'm happy for you two," he told his mom and aunt. "I think this is a good thing."

"It is," his mom agreed as he reached for a piece of fudge himself. Both his mom and Nettie swatted at his hand.

"I thought you brought this for us," Nettie complained.

"Word of wisdom," his mom offered. "Never come between a woman and her chocolate."

Mitch chuckled. "Noted."

"Another word of wisdom. Whatever noble reasons you think you have for cutting things off with Kaitlyn, forget them. Those are in your head. You need to listen to your heart."

"Mom, I'm going to Northern Virginia. I have a job lined up. One that will pay enough to let you stop working for good."

His mom put her fudge down—the first clue that he was in trouble—and narrowed her eyes. "Mitchell Douglas Hargrove, I never said I wanted to stop working. I love working. Go to Virginia if you must but I'm going to continue exactly what I'm doing. I'll slow down, maybe. Nettie is going to help me clean houses. We're going to be a team, right, Net?"

Aunt Nettie licked the sticky fudge residue off her index finger with a loud smack. "That's right."

"And stop sending me money. I don't need it. I never have," she said, reaching a hand out to rest over his. "The only thing I need is for you to be happy."

That's all he'd ever wanted for her as well. "Ditto," he said, unable to say anything more for a moment.

"Seeing you happy is what makes me happy, son," his mom said, offering his hand a little squeeze before reaching for another piece of fudge.

Mitch swallowed past the melon-sized lump in his throat.

"Fine," Aunt Nettie said, lightening up the sudden heaviness in the room. "I'll share a piece of my fudge with you." She broke a piece off and handed it to him. "But just this one time."

"Thanks."

Nettie shrugged a shoulder. "I just want you to be happy too."

After leaving his mom's house, he climbed into his truck

and leaned back against the headrest. Without Kaitlyn, he wasn't sure if he'd ever feel true happiness again.

His cell phone dinged in the center console, and Kaitlyn's name lit up the screen and everything inside him for a moment. "Hello?"

"Hi," she said in a flat voice.

"Hi." He wanted to tell her that he missed her. That he was sorry. He was a fool. Nothing had changed between them though. Even though he had Brian's contact information in his phone, he hadn't called. And there was nothing to indicate that Brian would welcome talking to him any more than Frank Everson had.

"I need you," Kaitlyn said, igniting hope in a spring he'd thought had dried up. His heart responded with a hard kick. He didn't deserve to be needed by her but it felt good. Like air at peak elevation.

"Mr. Garrison called. He's stopping by for breakfast one last time tomorrow. He wants to make sure we've met our end of the deal. You weren't there last time," she pointed out.

"I'll be there tomorrow."

"Good." With that, she hung up on him.

* * *

Kaitlyn had set up Mr. Garrison's spot at the table beside her. She'd intended for Mitch to sit on Mr. Garrison's other side but somehow he'd moved to sitting across from them.

She kept her gaze down on the food in front of them.

"This is delicious. Who made it?" Mr. Garrison asked, looking between them. "Kaitlyn or you, Mitch?"

Mitch had only walked in the door five minutes before Mr. Garrison arrived. And in those five minutes, Kaitlyn had successfully avoided looking at or talking to him.

She hated him.

She *loved* him.

She hated that she was in love with him. So in love that she couldn't taste the food she was chewing because it hurt to be near Mitch. Hurt to be around him after he'd broken her heart into a million little pieces that she feared would never reassemble.

"Kaitlyn cooked this morning," Mitch said. Then he rattled off several stories about their time together here at the inn. How he'd helped her master Grandma Mable's made-from-scratch biscuits. The repairs he'd done. The tree they'd put up right after Thanksgiving.

Kaitlyn didn't say a word. She was barely listening because she didn't want to revisit the time they'd spent here together. Whoever said it was better to have loved and lost than to have never loved at all was wrong. Shakespeare? She guessed he would've liked this story because the ending wasn't a happy one.

"Sounds like Mable was right. You two have been a good team," Mr. Garrison said.

From her peripheral vision, Kaitlyn saw Mitch nod. She didn't move. They had been a good team. They really had.

"Tomorrow is Christmas Eve. I know you had a plan to sell your half of the B and B to Kaitlyn at the end of the timeline, Mitch." Mr. Garrison reached for his cup of coffee. "Is that still what you'd like to do?"

Kaitlyn swallowed painfully, waiting for Mitch to respond, but it seemed to be taking forever. Finally, she looked up. "Yes, that's what we both want," she blurted out.

Mr. Garrison looked up from his coffee. Then he turned to Mitch. Kaitlyn finally looked at Mitch too. It was hard to hate him when she met his eyes. There was so much to find there: pain, sincerity, warmth.

Not love for her though. They were business partners, and even that relationship was ending tomorrow.

"Yes. I'm not cut out for running a bed and breakfast. This is what Kaitlyn was born to do. She takes after Mable in that way. She can make anyone feel at home. She's smart, creative, and tireless in the work here." His gaze slid to hers and stuck. "She's pretty amazing."

Fresh pain poured through her. How could he be so nice after the way he'd walked out the other day? After the way he'd turned off the feelings they'd shared so easily?

Mr. Garrison took one more sip of his coffee and scooted back from the dining room table. "Okay, then. I'll need each of you to stop by my office anytime tomorrow or thereafter. You'll both have papers to sign."

"Do we have to come together?" Kaitlyn asked, standing from the table as well.

Mr. Garrison frowned. "No. I know you'll have your hands full here at the inn, and Mitch has obligations elsewhere with his new job. Just anytime you're free. I can even swing by here with the paperwork if that'd be easier for you, Kaitlyn."

"Thank you." She walked Mr. Garrison to the door.

"I know I've already said it but your grandparents would be proud. They're probably smiling down on this inn right now."

Kaitlyn hoped that wasn't true. They'd done well with the inn, yes. But Kaitlyn wouldn't wish for Mable to see what a mess her attempted matchmaking had made.

Mr. Garrison shook Kaitlyn's hand and then reached for Mitch's, who was standing right behind her now. So close she could smell his familiar pine smell, like a freshly cut Christmas tree. Kaitlyn squashed all the attraction that buzzed to life inside her.

After Mr. Garrison descended the porch steps, she closed the door and addressed Mitch, keeping her back to him. "Your job here is done. You can go."

He didn't move.

She turned and walked past him, back into the dining room to clean up the dishes.

"I meant what I said. You're in your element here. And you are amazing," Mitch said, following her.

Her jaw tightened. "So amazing that you can hardly wait to leave." Her eyes darted to his. "So, get on with it. Leave."

CHAPTER TWENTY-THREE

*M*itch glanced around the restaurant. It was relatively quiet for the moment. The lunch crowd wouldn't hit for another half hour. When he'd mentioned that he was meeting Brian Everson, the hostess had seated Mitch along the window, where there was more space and handicap accessibility.

Mitch interlocked his hands in front of him on the table and blew out a pent-up, nervous-as-hell breath. He was a little shocked that Brian had even agreed to meet with him when he'd called earlier. Mitch just needed to say his piece. He wanted to look Brian in the eyes and tell him how sorry he was about everything that happened on that cold, icy night that changed so many lives.

Friendly voices filled the air as the restaurant's entrance opened and Brian rolled in with his wheelchair. Mitch kept his head down and listened to the greetings.

After a moment, the hostess headed back down the aisle, leading Brian toward Mitch.

Mitch took a breath and looked up, meeting his former

classmate's youthful face. It was almost as if nothing had changed in the last decade. But appearances could be misleading. For instance, looking at Mitch, one might not be able to tell that he was terrified right now. But he was. Sitting across from Brian was scarier than any scene he'd ever walked in on as an MPO. Mitch had learned to hide his emotions well over the years, starting after the time his dad passed away.

Brian extended his hand first. "Hey, Mitch. Looks like you beat me here," he said in a friendly voice.

Mitch smiled stiffly. "Hey, Brian. I've only been here a few minutes." Lunch had been Brian's suggestion but maybe meeting for drinks would've been a better idea. Then Mitch wouldn't be facing at least an hour of what promised to be an awkward conversation. "Thanks for agreeing to meet with me."

"Of course." With ease, Brian positioned himself at the table across from him.

"What can I get you to drink?" the waitress asked.

Brian tapped a finger to his mouth thoughtfully. "I think I'll have a sweet tea, if you don't mind."

"Of course, Mr. Everson," the waitress said with a bright smile that told Mitch Brian came often and tipped well.

"I'll have the same." Mitch willed his heart to slow down as the waitress scribbled on her notepad.

"You got it. I'll be right back with those," she promised in a cheery voice before walking away.

When she was gone, Mitch looked Brian in the eye for the first time since the accident. Ten years seemed to evaporate before him. "I'm sorry," Mitch said.

Those two words broke out of him and threatened to shatter his very existence. His heart hammered despite his efforts to stay calm, cool, and relaxed.

Brian smiled back at him. It wasn't a fake gesture. Brian's smile radiated from more than his lips. It poured through his twinkling eyes and beamed from the glow of his skin. "Me too."

Mitch sat there a second, trying to process that response. He would have understood a *go to hell* more readily. "What?"

"I should've reached out to you. I know it wasn't easy dealing with the aftermath of the accident. I also know my family fired your mom. My dad threatened you and asked you to leave the only home you ever knew. I'm sorry for that, Mitch. No one should ever feel run off from their hometown."

"But I'm the one who ran into you. I'm the reason you're in that chair," Mitch said, working hard to control his emotion.

Brian laughed softly. "Well, if it's true, then maybe I ought to thank you as well."

"You are confusing the hell out of me right now, man," Mitch said. He could feel the corners of his mouth pulling up in a tiny smile though.

"Come on, Mitch. Life doesn't just happen."

"It doesn't?" Because that's exactly how life seemed to go. Things just happened, and sometimes they sucked.

"I don't think so, at least," Brian said, sounding a lot like Dawanda. "If that accident had never happened, who knows where I'd be."

Mitch stared across the table at the man he barely knew. If the accident had never happened, Brian would have walked into this restaurant. He might have two or three gold medals on display in his home.

"Sure, I was angry when I first found out I was paralyzed. It wasn't fair. I spent my entire life up to that point training for something that I couldn't do anymore. But because of my accident and my training before that, I'm able to help hundreds of kids now."

"So I hear," Mitch said.

The waitress sat the drinks down in front of them. They both thanked her and waited to continue talking until she had walked away.

"I've spent the last decade trying to pay penance for your injuries. Now you're telling me it's okay."

Brian took a sip of his sweet tea. There was a thoughtful look on his face. "Yeah, it's okay. Honestly, I snuck out of my parents' house that night. I shouldn't have been on that road either." He shook his head. "It was all just one big mistake. Or it was orchestrated by some higher power for a reason we'll never begin to understand."

Mitch had been feeling sorry for Brian all this time but now some part of him was jealous. Brian was happy. Mitch could see it on his face. It wasn't an act. It was real.

For the next hour, they talked like old friends over burgers and fries.

"I'm not sure if you're planning to stay in Sweetwater Springs for any amount of time," Brian said, "but I can guarantee my family won't stand in your way. This is just as much your home as it is ours. And my dad is all talk, little action."

"From what I hear, you hold all the power around here now," Mitch said.

Brian gave his head a shake. "I don't know about that. I own a lot of property, yeah. I might even run for mayor next year."

Mitch's brows rose. He wouldn't hesitate to vote for the guy in front of him if he was a citizen in this town.

"What my dad never understood is that power doesn't

come from threatening people. It comes from serving them."

When the bill came, Brian insisted on paying for Mitch's meal.

"I can't let you do that," Mitch argued.

"You can pay for mine next time. I enjoyed catching up with you. Let's do this again, man," Brian said. He laid enough cash down to more than cover the charge and they left the restaurant.

Mitch hit the unlock button on his truck. "Honestly, I'm supposed to be leaving in the next couple of days. I'm not sure when I'll be back."

"Supposed to be?" Brian asked. "You don't sound so sure about that."

Mitch shrugged. "Either way, next time I'm in town, I'll call you. We'll definitely grab a bite. Seeing that you bought my lunch today, I owe you."

Brian shook his head. "You don't owe me a thing." And that statement held more meaning than just who had paid for lunch.

Mitch watched Brian get into his vehicle and load his wheelchair effortlessly. He was doing okay. More than okay.

When Mitch got back into his truck, he expelled a heavy breath. A weight had been lifted off his chest and shoulders. Brian didn't blame him for what happened. Mitch didn't need to steer clear from him, and the Everson family was no threat to the Sweetwater Bed and Breakfast. Frank's threat had been as empty as the current gas tank of Mitch's truck.

He'd fuel up first. Then he'd work on figuring out his life. There was no reason he had to leave unless that was truly what he wanted. If he were creating his own wish list for Santa, what he truly wanted was Kaitlyn.

Could she ever forgive him though? He'd cut her off like

a loose end. The hurt in her eyes was something he'd been revisiting in his head for the last couple of days. He'd never meant to hurt her but it'd seemed like the right thing to do at the time. A sacrifice for the greater good. He couldn't just walk back into the inn now and say, "Just kidding. I want to stay."

Can I?

* * *

Bah humbug.

It was the day before Christmas, and that's what Kaitlyn was really thinking as she smiled across the breakfast table at her guests, including her parents. Festive music jingled in the air along with the delicious aroma of cinnamon and butter from the pastries she'd served this morning. There was lively conversation going on at the table about what the guests had done last night.

"We were thinking we'd go out tonight," Kaitlyn's mother said. "What do you suggest we do, Kaitlyn?"

Kaitlyn blinked them all back into focus. "You could go downtown to Dawanda's Fudge Shop. It's world-class."

Numbness radiated through her, from her cheeks, still puffed up from smiling, to her toes.

"And ask for a cappuccino," Gina said, walking into the room with a pot of coffee. She'd shown up this morning, bright and early, to help with breakfast. Kaitlyn was more than capable of doing this on her own but she'd been grateful anyway. Gina said Mitch wasn't staying with her but didn't elaborate. Maybe he'd called Alex or Tuck. Or maybe he'd gone home with that waitress from the Tipsy Tavern for another baggage-free one-night stand. What she and Mitch had was supposed to be baggage-free as well.

It would all be over soon though. Mitch would go to Mr. Garrison's office to sign the necessary paperwork to sell his portion of the inn to her. She could wait until after Christmas to do her part. They wouldn't even have to see each other again. The idea of that made her breakfast sit unsettled in the pit of her stomach. She'd fallen in love with him, despite her head knowing that it was a bad idea. Her heart had overridden that truth.

"A cappuccino would hit the spot," her father said at the table, pulling her attention back to the here and now.

"It's too bad you missed the Hope for the Holidays Auction the other night," Gina continued, making easy chitchat. "We raised over ten thousand dollars for one of our families in need. One of Kaitlyn's gingerbread cheesecakes brought in over three hundred dollars itself!"

Kaitlyn's smile was sincere for the first time this morning. "Really?" she asked. She hadn't heard that detail yet.

"Oh yes. Our ten cakes alone brought in a thousand dollars combined."

"That's wonderful!" her mom said. "Was it Mable's recipe?"

Kaitlyn nodded. "The money from the auction is helping Cassie Martin, a single mother from town who's battling cancer."

"That's right." Gina sat at the dining room table with her own cup of coffee. "My son has been helping out at the police department these last few weeks. Cassie's son got in a little bit of trouble with the law, trying to acquire money for his mom's cancer treatments. Once Sweetwater Springs found out she was sick, well, the whole community rallied around to help. That's just how townsfolk here are. Your mother was one of the finest for that," Gina told Kaitlyn's dad.

"Her heart was always in the right place," he agreed.

"Sweetwater Springs sounds like a great community," her mom said, eyes suspiciously shining. "Is Ms. Martin's son still in trouble?"

Gina shook her head. "Since he's a minor, Judge Ables let him off with a stern warning and a whole lot of community service."

"Really?" Kaitlyn asked. "I didn't know that either."

Gina nodded. "It's amazing how things work out."

"Three hundred dollars is a lot to pay for a cake," Kaitlyn's dad said, "but I'd pay as much to taste Mom's recipe one more time. It really was the best."

"Who knows?" Kaitlyn said, swallowing past a tight throat. "Maybe Santa will bring you one this year."

"Speaking of Santa, we need to finish up our shopping," her mom said. "What do you want this year, Kaitlyn?"

Nothing that her parents could buy in downtown Sweetwater Springs. Kaitlyn either wanted Mitch or a shiny, brand-new heart. "Just having you two here with me this holiday is enough."

* * *

The doorbell rang later that afternoon while Kaitlyn sat reading a book. With her parents occupying the last room, the inn was full. The sign out front indicated as much. Hopefully, Kaitlyn wasn't going to have to disappoint a prospective customer and turn them away.

When she opened the door though, Kaitlyn was greeted by two familiar faces. "Halona and Theo, what a lovely surprise!"

Halona held out a large poinsettia plant. "Here you go.

This is from my flower shop. I always brought Mable one this time of year."

"That's so nice of you. Please, come in." Kaitlyn led them through the front room, noticing that young Theo stuck close to his mother's side. Kaitlyn hadn't asked but she didn't think there was a father in the picture. She'd run into Halona several times over the last month and she'd always been alone or with her brother, Tuck. "Would you like some tea and cookies?"

Theo's eyes widened but he didn't make a sound.

"I'll take that as a yes," Kaitlyn said with a grin. "If it's okay with your mom." She looked at Halona.

"Of course. Cookies are his favorite. He'll love you forever," she promised.

Kaitlyn took them to the dining room and placed the poinsettia at the center of one of the tables. "You two have a seat. I'll grab the refreshments." She walked to the serving table that she kept stocked for the guests during the day and made two cups of hot tea. She grabbed the plate of cookies and turned back to her visitors.

"It looks great in here," Halona commented.

"Thanks. It's been a lot of work, but totally worth it." Kaitlyn slid the plate of cookies beside the poinsettia and then placed Halona's cup of tea in front of her. "Do you bring gifts to a lot of townspeople?" Kaitlyn asked, sitting across from them with her own cup.

Halona nodded. "We like to thank the business owners who support the flower shop. Mable always sent her guests my way for special occasions. She didn't really have a choice, I guess. I'm the only florist in town."

Kaitlyn laughed. "Well, I'm sure she would've sent guests to you anyway."

Theo chomped happily on his treat as they chatted.

"I grew up with Mitch, you know," Halona said after a lull in the conversation. "I always hoped he'd find peace after the accident." She looked down at her hands and then to her son. "We lost Theo's father in an accident last year. He and I weren't married but Theo has taken the loss hard. I wonder if there are some things that people just don't ever recover from."

Kaitlyn's heart pinched hard for the child sitting in front of her. "I'm so sorry to hear that."

Halona broke off a piece of her cookie. "Thanks. Mitch seems different these days than he has during his past visits home. I was wondering if it had anything to do with you."

Kaitlyn shook her head. "I don't think so. We aren't really talking anymore."

"Oh." Halona's beautiful features twisted. She looked sincerely disappointed. "Well, seeing his difference gave me hope that people can let go of the things that haunt them."

Kaitlyn wanted to believe that too. Even if Mitch was leaving, even if he'd broken her heart beyond repair, she did hope he found peace one day. She wanted him to be happy wherever he was.

She looked at little Theo. She wished him peace too. It couldn't be easy for him losing a parent so young. Finishing off his last bite, he stared at the plate of cookies.

Kaitlyn lifted one and offered it to him. "Here you go, sweetheart. One more won't hurt. But after that, I have to save the rest for Santa. He's coming tonight, you know."

Theo's eyes rounded.

Halona ruffled the hair on top of her son's head. "Oh, we know. We have cookies at home for him too."

By the time Kaitlyn opened the door to say goodbye to her visitors, the temperature had notably dropped outside.

Santa was coming, and according to the local meteorologist, so was a snowstorm.

Mitch, on the other hand, was likely packing his bags to leave at this very moment.

* * *

In addition to being Christmas Eve, today was Mitch's last day on the job with SSPD. Since he was still in town, he'd told Alex he'd work so that the officers with family could be home.

The day had been uneventful so far. Everyone in Sweetwater Springs seemed to be celebrating quietly with the ones they loved. Mitch had spoken to his mom earlier. She'd gone to the inn to help Kaitlyn and was planning on spending the afternoon with Nettie. Two peas in a pod, they were. He really didn't have to worry about her anymore. She was taking care of herself, splitting her workload with Mitch's aunt, and was living a good life.

Mitch pulled the SSPD cruiser he'd been driving for the last month up to Cassie Martin's house. Kyle was on the front porch stringing festive multicolored lights.

Mitch put the car in park and headed up the driveway. Hearing him approach, Kyle glanced back, his gaze turning wary when he saw Mitch dressed in uniform.

"Whatever it is, I didn't do it this time," the teen called out, continuing with his task.

Mitch laughed softly under his breath. "I'm not here for the department, although I hear you're doing a good job keeping up with your community service sentence."

Kyle shrugged. "Beats serving time in juvie."

"Decorating the day before Christmas, huh?" Mitch asked, taking the end of the string of lights and holding them up to the banister for Kyle to attach.

"Better late than never, my mom always says. Plus, some women brought a bunch of decorations over for us. They offered to help put them up too, but my mom volunteered me to do the work. The women said the decorations would be good for my mom's spirits. If that's true, then I'll do it."

Mitch nodded. He understood exactly how the kid felt. Ever since his dad had died, Mitch had felt the same way about his own mother. Whatever it took to make her smile. To keep her safe. Secure. He'd failed at that task often enough but it had always been his not-so-secret mission in life.

"Your mom is lucky to have you," he told Kyle.

"Yeah, well, I'm lucky to have her too. She's all I got."

Mitch understood that as well. At least, that's how he used to feel. All this time, he'd had more than he realized though. He'd had Mable and Henry. Aunt Nettie. Dawanda. Alex and Tuck. Even Halona. There was a whole town full of people here that had readily welcomed him back these last two months, even though he'd abandoned them in some ways.

"Just don't forget to be a kid, okay?" Mitch said.

Kyle's gaze slid over to him. "I'm not a kid."

"Right. Don't forget to enjoy your youth a little, then. Do things for yourself while looking out for your mom. Live your life and be happy, because that's what she really wants for you." Maybe it was the holiday making him sappy but his throat tightened as he gave Kyle his best advice.

Kyle didn't look all that impressed. "What are you? One of the wise men?"

"Kyle Martin!" Cassie said, waving a finger as she stepped out the screen door and onto the porch. "That is no way to talk to Officer Hargrove." Mitch was glad to see the single mom in good spirits. Hopefully, this time next year, she'd be cancer-free.

"Mom, you're supposed to be resting."

Mitch closed his eyes as he listened. If the similarities between his family and this one got any stronger, he'd wonder if God was pulling his chain. Or Mable in heaven with her meddling ways.

"And it's cold out here. You're supposed to stay warm inside," the teenager nagged.

Cassie tsked, ignoring him. "Merry Christmas, Officer Hargrove," she said.

"Please, call me Mitch. Merry Christmas to you too. How are you doing?"

"Good, thanks to you and the community. I have high hopes for the new year too." She smiled brightly. "I have pie in the house if you'd like a slice."

"Afraid I can't stay," he said. "I'm on the job. Just thought I'd play the role of one of the wise men while passing through."

Kyle cracked a smile.

And since Mitch was still feeling wise and sappy, he pointed a finger at the teen. "Also, don't do drugs and stay in school."

With a wave, he started to walk away until a little yellow furball darted out of the bushes. Once it stopped moving, he saw that it was a golden retriever mix.

"That's the stray that's been coming around here all week," Cassie called from the porch. "He doesn't seem to belong to any of my neighbors so I wish I could take him inside, but my immune system is low right now. Do you want a puppy, Mitch?" she asked with a hopeful lift in her voice.

"I'm afraid I'm not in the market for a dog," he said, turning back to Cassie.

She hugged her arms around herself. "I'd hate for the poor thing to be out here when it snows tonight."

Mitch's gaze dropped to the pup, who repeatedly propped his paws on Mitch's leg and then returned to all fours. It woofed softly. "I can take it back to the station and see if someone there wants him."

"That would be great," Cassie said. "Thank you so much, for everything."

Mitch stooped and collected the soft little wiggler into his arms and double-checked that it was indeed a boy. Then he returned to his cruiser and set the puppy in his passenger seat. Apparently tired from his surge of energy outside, the puppy lay down and put his head on his front paws.

"Good boy," Mitch said. He started the car and continued through the streets, all welcoming and festive with lights and wreaths. *Loving Life*'s article hadn't fudged anything. Sweetwater Springs truly was a great place to spend the holidays. He'd forgotten that. Or he'd pushed it out of his mind because it hadn't seemed like an option for him. It was romantic too. His thoughts took a stroll through the memories of his time here with Kaitlyn. The cappuccino reading at the fudge shop. Their trip to Merry Mountain Farms to get a tree. Even though it'd been cut short, Lights on the Lake had been festive and romantic too. He regretted that every Christmas season couldn't be spent here, with Kaitlyn, doing the same.

A short drive later, he walked into the station with the puppy under his arm.

"Who's this?" Alex asked, looking up from the paperwork on his desk as Mitch entered his office.

"Your new pet," Mitch said.

Alex was already shaking his head. "Nice try, but no. I don't have time for a dog right now. Especially a puppy. He's cute though. You should keep him."

Mitch didn't have time either. He set the puppy on the floor to run around for a moment and then placed his gun and badge on Alex's desk.

Alex nodded. "Still scared shitless, huh?"

Mitch shoved his hands on his waist. Once upon a time, those would've been fighting words but they were true. "Yeah," he admitted. "I messed up with her, and there's nothing to say I won't do it again." He couldn't use his mom or even the Eversons as an excuse for leaving town this time. This was all on him. He was sick of feeling like the bad guy no matter how much good he did.

"If you could have seen the look on Kaitlyn's face." Mitch shook his head, hating himself for causing her more pain. She'd been through enough over the last few months with Mable's passing, getting fired, and giving up the life she was accustomed to in New York to come to the mountains of North Carolina. "It doesn't matter my reasons; I handled it all wrong. I should have told her that I...I..." He stumbled over his words. There was only one word that completed that sentence.

Love.

He swallowed thickly. "I should've told her that I loved her," he said quietly, more to himself than Alex.

Alex didn't look surprised when Mitch blinked and looked up at him.

Had Mitch really been that thick skulled? He knew he cared about Kaitlyn. Admired the heck out of her. Knew he was wildly attracted to the woman and could possibly never get enough of her, if given the opportunity. But the way he felt for Kaitlyn Russo went beyond all of that. Over the last two months, he'd fallen in love with her.

Alex leaned forward on his elbows. "Great. So why don't you go tell her that right now?"

Mitch didn't move. He felt like he'd just been hit over the head with a large block of ice.

"Listen, I don't need one of Dawanda's cappuccinos to

predict you'll screw up and hurt her plenty more times," Alex said. "You will. But if you leave town tomorrow, you'll hurt her even more. You deserve to have this, buddy. You are a good man and a good officer." Alex slid the badge back in Mitch's direction and looked up.

So much for Mitch's wise man act. He was the biggest fool of all. Picking up the badge, he nodded at Alex. "Looks like I'll be reporting for duty tomorrow."

"Tomorrow's Christmas, buddy. Spend it with the people you love. And maybe that puppy over there."

That was good advice and Mitch planned to do just that. He hadn't known what, if anything, to say to Kaitlyn to fix how he'd behaved. There'd been no fixing it in his mind. Now he knew the answer though. All he had to do was tell Kaitlyn the truth. He loved her. That he was an idiot. And then he planned on begging for a second chance. He wasn't going to run away from his mistakes this time. He was going to face them head-on.

Mitch stepped over to his little friend, who was spinning in circles while chasing his own tail. He could relate. Scooping him up, he headed down the hall away from Alex's office and past the reception desk.

"Merry Christmas, Mitch," Tammy called after him.

"You too, Tammy. I'll see you in a couple of days."

"Glad to hear it!"

The cold air surrounded him as he stepped onto the sidewalk. The sun had dipped below the mountain peaks now, making another ten-degree drop at least. He needed to hurry before daylight dwindled completely and he missed his chance to make things right today. He had one more important person he had to go see before Kaitlyn though.

CHAPTER TWENTY-FOUR

$\mathcal{K}$aitlyn sat in front of the Christmas tree, watching the lights wink at her. The inn had only three couples tonight. All of them had joined Kaitlyn and her parents earlier this evening for the Christmas Eve service at the community church. At this hour, the guests had retreated to their rooms, leaving her to enjoy a private nightcap. She was grateful for the solitude because tomorrow she needed to wake early and make a breakfast worthy of Christmas Day. Gina and Nettie were coming to help, of course. Paris would be there too. It was going to be a full, wonderful day. She wouldn't even have time to think about Mitch.

Hopefully.

A mournful sigh burrowed in her chest, close to her heart. This time next year she probably wouldn't even remember what he looked like. How he smelled. The way his voice took on a deep timbre in the bedroom when he curled in behind her, wrapping her in his arms and making her feel like there was no safer place in the world.

Kaitlyn lifted her glass of red wine and took a healthy gulp. Appropriate for her current mood, it tasted bittersweet on her tongue. She tried to steer her thoughts to something happy, and the name of the child she'd chosen off the Angel Tree at Silver Lake came to mind. Kaitlyn imagined the little girl joyfully opening her new doll and all the accessories she'd picked out. The Angel Tree was a tradition Kaitlyn wanted to participate in every year. Giving to someone else was the very heart of Christmas.

She finished off the last sip of her wine and decided one more glass might be nice. After that, she'd turn in.

As she headed toward the kitchen, Kaitlyn grabbed a fire poker and moved the logs around to keep the flames burning in the fireplace. It'd begun to snow a few hours ago. When she awoke tomorrow, the ground would be a soft blanket of white. It would be a magical white Christmas. Her first in Sweetwater Springs, but not her last.

Something scratched at the front door. Kaitlyn whirled, nearly dropping her wineglass. It was just the winter storm, she decided. Then the scratching sound came again. She stuck her wineglass on the mantel and tightened her hold on the fire poker. Her heart thrummed like a drummer boy nestled inside her chest. She was being silly. She wasn't alone at the B&B. No one would be foolish enough to break in.

The doorknob turned.

Kaitlyn swallowed. Potential guests would knock. The only person who wouldn't knock wouldn't be coming back.

The door opened, and Kaitlyn gasped as a pale-colored puppy with a large red bow around its neck barreled through the entryway toward her. She immediately put the fire poker down and dropped to her knees to pet its soft fur. "Aren't you the cutest thing?" she said, laughing as it climbed onto her lap and proceeded to lick her cheek. "Where did you come from?"

As if on cue, she heard the front door close and Mitch entered the room.

"What are you doing here?" she asked.

He was dressed in a heavy coat dusted with fresh snow. His beard was also dusted and sparkling with soft white flakes. "This little guy has nowhere to go," he said, gesturing to the squirming puppy in her arms. "He was hoping you'd have room for him at the inn."

Kaitlyn's mouth dropped open. She hadn't even considered getting a pet.

"His name is Mr. Darcy," Mitch added.

"Well, how can I say no to that? That's perfect." She looked up and connected eyes with Mitch. Big mistake.

"Merry Christmas, Kaitlyn," he said quietly.

Tears threatened at the base of her throat. She held Mr. Darcy tightly against her suddenly aching chest and stood to face him. "Thank you. If that's all, I was just about to head to bed. Tomorrow will be a busy day here." Busier with Mr. Darcy running around, but she didn't mind that. What she did mind was Mitch standing there and looking at her that way.

"I have something else for you." He held out a thick orange manila envelope.

She placed Mr. Darcy on the floor and took the envelope with shaky hands. She knew exactly what this was.

"I stopped by Mr. Garrison's after my shift," he said.

"Great." She swallowed thickly. "Thank you. I'll go to the bank after Christmas and start the process of taking out a loan to pay you."

"No need for that. I'm not selling my half of the bed and breakfast to you anymore."

Kaitlyn whipped her head up. "What?"

"I know." He held up a hand to fend off any arguments

she was about to fire back at him. "We had an agreement but I'm backing out of it."

"You want to keep the B and B?" Her mouth fell open.

"No. I'm not keeping my half either. I'm giving it to someone. It's a Christmas gift of sorts."

"A Christmas gift?" she repeated. This had all come down to Mitch giving his half of the inn away as a present?

Kaitlyn opened the envelope hurriedly. She didn't want another partner. If it wasn't going to be Mitch, she'd rather go into debt and buy him out. She yanked the documents out and read, her eyes tearing up when she saw the name printed on the bold line. "I can't believe this."

Somehow Mitch was standing even closer to her now. "I hope you're not disappointed."

She shook her head. "This is ..." Kaitlyn was desperately trying not to cry.

Don't cry. Don't cry.

"I am doing my very best to hate you right now, and you're making it nearly impossible." She blinked back her tears and looked at the name of her new business partner again. Gina Hargrove. "She's going to be so happy, Mitch. You are a really good son."

A good man too, she thought. The kind of man she wished she could have as her own. He was strong, hardworking, thoughtful, and one of the most giving people she'd ever met. He'd give the clothes off his back to someone in the middle of that mounting winter storm outside if it was asked of him.

The only thing he wouldn't give fully, unconditionally, was his heart to her. Maybe that's why he'd brought her a puppy tonight. It was her consolation prize for falling in love with him.

He took a step toward her. "There is one stipulation in that contract."

Kaitlyn couldn't even see the fine print anymore. Her eyes were so blurred with tears. "There's always a stipulation," she said on a small, humorless laugh.

"Now that I don't own the inn anymore, I kind of don't have a place to stay either."

She hugged the manila envelope against her chest, pressing it against her rapidly beating heart. "Well, I'm sure you'll find something when you get to Virginia."

"That's the thing. I'm not going to Virginia anymore. I thought I'd stay and help Alex keep the streets of Sweetwater Springs safe from women wielding fire pokers."

"Really? That's great, Mitch." For him and Gina, and the town. But what about her? Could she really see him and not be with him? Would she be able to move on from what they'd had together if she were constantly running into him at the grocery store or coffee shop?

A million thoughts were swirling around in her head like wind-battered snowflakes on their downward spiral toward the ground.

"I also thought I'd stay on the small chance that you ever forgave me for being such a fool."

She cocked her head to the side. "Christmas *is* a time for miracles, I guess."

He grinned. "And love. It's also a time for love."

Everything inside her froze. Every muscle, every breath.

"I love you, Kaitlyn," he said in a low, gruff voice. "I'm in love with you."

Tears swam in her eyes now, too many to hold back. They streamed off her cheeks faster than she could wipe them away with her shaking hands. "I love you back."

"Well, *that* is a miracle." He reached inside his coat pocket and pulled out a piece of mistletoe.

"From the Merry Mountain Farms," she said, looking up into his eyes. She loved those eyes. Loved this man.

"I wanted to use this on you so badly that night it made my head spin."

She lifted his arm to hold the sprig over her head. "So kiss me now."

Dutifully, as always, he bent and brushed his lips to hers as Mr. Darcy circled them and woofed excitedly at their feet. Pulling away, she met Mitch's gaze, and her heart answered with love. *He* was her home. And there was no place she'd rather be than with him for the holidays.

EPILOGUE

Two months later

The grand reopening celebration for the Sweetwater Bed and Breakfast was going well so far. Over the last couple of weeks, Kaitlyn had sent out flyers to everyone in town for the all-day open house event. She had Mable's famous homemade cookies and tea available, and several towns-people were huddled in one corner of the room enjoying themselves while admiring the designer touches that Kaitlyn had made. Other guests were exploring the newly opened walking trails behind the inn.

"This is a wonderful turnout, don't you think?" Gina asked, coming up beside her.

"It really is." Kaitlyn adored having Gina as her part-ner in this business. She was hardworking, and she genuinely loved doing for others. She made the guests feel at home, and she was full of stories about Mable and Henry's days at the inn. Kaitlyn felt like she was getting to know her grandparents a little more by spending time with Gina.

"My two favorite women," Mitch said, stepping up beside them with Mr. Darcy, considerably bigger now, at his side. He leaned in and gave Kaitlyn a soft kiss on the cheek. "Hey, beautiful," he whispered in her ear and then lifted his head to look at Gina. "Hey, Mom. Where's Aunt Nettie?"

"Oh, she's showing one of the women from our book club the garden outside. It's such a pretty place this time of year."

The garden had been Nettie's idea. It was a masterpiece of vibrant colors that attracted birds and butterflies and guests.

"Mom, do you think you can manage the event on your own for a little bit?" he asked then. "I need to borrow Kaitlyn."

Gina put a hand on her waist. "What kind of silly question is that? Of course I can. You two go on ahead. Mr. Darcy and I will handle things in here."

Kaitlyn laughed softly as he tugged her down the hall and toward the bedroom. "Can't this wait, Mitch?"

He stopped in front of the closed door. She'd closed it to make sure today's visitors didn't wander. The entire inn was available for the open house with the exception of their private quarters.

"I've waited long enough," he told her. "I can't wait any longer."

* * *

Mitch was still pinching himself over how much his fortune had changed in the last couple of months. He'd gone from a jaded loner who was lost in the world to working at the Sweetwater Springs PD during the day and coming home at night to the most caring, gorgeous, intelligent woman he'd ever met.

Dawanda had been right. He'd fallen quick and hard, and he was staying in Sweetwater Springs forever. Well, minus the romantic escapades he planned to take Kaitlyn on, starting with their honeymoon.

If she said yes.

He reached for the doorknob of their room now. This morning, while Kaitlyn and his mom had been busy preparing the final touches in the B&B to welcome the entire town, he'd holed up in their bedroom. He wasn't an interior designer by any means but he was proud of what he'd pulled off in a small amount of time.

"Okay. Close your eyes," he told her.

"What? Why?" Kaitlyn looked at him with uncertainty.

"I thought you trusted me."

Her dark hair fell over her cheek as she cocked her head to one side. "I do."

"Then close your eyes," he said again, smiling back at her. She was gorgeous, inside and out. He loved her more than he knew he could love anyone. And the feeling only kept growing, expanding inside him, threatening to crack his entire chest wide open.

Kaitlyn closed her eyes, and Mitch waved a hand in front of her face to make sure she wasn't peeking.

"No cheating," he instructed and then opened the bedroom door and led her inside. For a moment, he was nervous, wondering if it was enough. Kaitlyn's rooms were expertly designed down to the smallest detail.

But no. This was perfect.

"Open your eyes," he said after angling her body to face the bed.

Her eyes fluttered open and bounced from the bed to the

wall and the ceiling above it. Her lips parted slightly as she looked around. "You did all this?" she finally asked.

"Our room needed a theme, don't you think?"

The bedspread was still one of Mable's quilts. Mable had been integral to their relationship. Sneaky even after death, she was the one who'd brought them together. Above the bed, Mitch had strung just a few strands of twinkling lights. They reminded Mitch of their first kiss under a blanket of stars by Silver Lake. He'd tried so hard to ignore his attraction to Kaitlyn that night, which seemed so long ago now, but he hadn't stood a chance.

He watched as she took in every detail.

"Is that the picnic basket we used at Evergreen Park the other day?" she asked.

He nodded. "Yeah." He'd used the basket to hold books under the nightstand.

Her gaze swept around the room where he'd hung various pictures of random moments together and the places they'd been in town. There was a picture of Dawanda's storefront. One of Silver Lake. Kaitlyn's gaze kept going back to the large eleven-by-eighteen picture above the bed. The one Mitch had taken on his phone and had blown up at the Everson printing shop with Brian's help.

"Kaitlyn and Mitch Forever," she read.

He'd carved it in a tree outside, right below the words he'd found while hiking the newly established walking trails out back: *Mable and Henry Forever.*

"In case you haven't realized yet, that's the theme of our room. I know we're not famous, but..."

"It's perfect," she whispered, turning to him, her eyes glistening with happy tears. He didn't mind making her cry if it was because she was happy. She deserved happiness, and so did he, he'd realized. Making Kaitlyn smile did that for him. Serving her, supporting her, loving her made him happy.

Taking both of Kaitlyn's hands in his, he continued forward on his mission. "I have traveled the world looking for a place where I could feel whole again. Never in a million years did I think that would be right back where I started." He slowly dropped to one knee in front of her.

Kaitlyn sucked in an audible breath, and he was fairly certain she could guess what was coming next, given how many of those romantic movies and books she enjoyed. He just hoped he lived up to her expectations. He wasn't perfect. He was human after all. Flawed. Those flaws didn't make him unworthy though. He understood that now.

"You are my world, Kaitlyn. I love you, and I want to spend the rest of my life showing you just how much. I want to grow old with you here, just like your grandparents did."

Reaching into the front pocket of his shirt, he pulled out a simple round diamond. Old-fashioned but timeless.

Kaitlyn gasped once more. "How did you get my grandmother's ring?"

"She left it with Mr. Garrison. He had instructions to give me the ring if things worked out between us. If they didn't, this ring was to go to you anyway."

"Sneaky woman," Kaitlyn said on a tearful laugh.

Mitch looked at the ring and then held it up to her. "Marry me, Kaitlyn, and I'll try to be the man you deserve."

She lifted a hand to touch his cheek. "You are the best man I know, Mitch Hargrove. *Our* love story is my favorite. All of those other couples I named the inn's rooms after have nothing on us."

He glanced at the ring and back to her, swallowing hard. "Still waiting here. Do I, uh, need to give this back to Mr. Garrison?"

"Don't you dare." She held out her left hand. "This is where it belongs."

"And you are where I belong," he said as he slid it onto her finger. Then he rose back to his feet. "I love you, Kaitlyn Russo soon-to-be-Hargrove," he whispered.

"I love you back, and I can't wait to be your wife."

He smiled back at her. "I was thinking a Christmas wedding might be nice."

She gasped with excitement. "With lights and poinsettias. We can get Halona to help with that. And we'll need a huge Christmas tree. The biggest on the Merry Mountain Farms' lot."

Mitch laughed out loud. "If you're there, I'm there. Tux and all."

She went up on tiptoes and pressed her lips to his in a soft kiss that evolved to something deeper. "I can't wait," she whispered, finally pulling away.

"Me neither." He gave a longing glance at the bed. There'd be plenty of time for private celebration later. Right now, they had a house full of people who cared for them and wanted to share in their good news.

Taking her hand, they went back down the hall to their home filled with family, friends, laughter, and love.

Grandma Mable's Gingerbread Cheesecake

The quickest way to Santa's heart is a slice of my ginger-bread cheesecake. Your home will always be the first on his list if you set aside a piece of this delicious dish!

*Yields 12–14 slices and a whole lot of yumminess

Ingredients

Crust:

- 2 cups of ground gingerbread cookies (homemade is best, but store-bought gingersnaps are fine in a pinch)
- ¼ cup butter, melted

Cheesecake filling:

- 3 packages (8 ounces each) of cream cheese, room temperature
- 1 cup brown sugar
- 2 teaspoons vanilla
- 3 eggs
- ¼ cup unsulfured molasses
- ¼ teaspoon salt
- 2 teaspoons ground ginger
- 2 teaspoons ground cinnamon
- 1 teaspoon ground nutmeg
- ½ teaspoon ground cloves
- ½ teaspoon finely grated lemon zest (optional)
- A heaping helping of Christmas cheer!

Cranberry topping:

- 1 cup granulated sugar
- ½ cup orange juice
- 1 package (12 ounces) fresh or frozen cranberries
- Whipped cream, powdered sugar, or molasses (optional)

Instructions

1. Preheat the oven to 350 degrees. Line a 9-inch spring-form pan with parchment paper and grease the sides.

2. Double wrap the outside of your springform pan with aluminum foil for a water bath.

3. In a small bowl, add your crushed gingerbread cookies and stir in melted butter while naming Santa's reindeer (or for 15–20 seconds).

4. Press the mixture evenly onto the bottom of your springform pan and then 1/3 of the way up the sides. Make sure no one sees you licking the spoon afterward. That'll put you on the naughty list!

5. Bake until the cookie crust is set (the time it takes to write out two Christmas cards, or about 10 minutes).

6. Transfer the pan to a wire rack to cool completely.

7. Reduce oven temperature to 325 degrees.

8. In a stand mixer, add the cream cheese and beat until fluffy.

9. Add in the brown sugar and beat until fully combined, then add in the vanilla and the eggs one at a time. Make sure you scrape the sides of the bowl so that everything is evenly blended.

10. While humming "We Wish You a Merry Christmas," add the molasses, salt, ginger, cinnamon, nutmeg, cloves,

and zest (optional) and mix on medium speed until fully combined.

11. Pour the mixture into the springform pan. Then place the pan into a larger pan and fill the outer pan with an inch of hot water (to prevent your filling from cracking).

12. Bake at 325 degrees in the water bath for 60 minutes.

13. While the cheesecake bakes, it's the perfect time to prepare the topping. In a saucepan over medium heat, stir the sugar and orange juice until the sugar dissolves. Add the cranberries and cook until the skins pop. Let the cranberries cool to room temperature and then chill. (Or this is a great way to get rid of any leftover cranberry sauce that you may have from a holiday dinner. I won't tattle on you.)

14. After baking the cheesecake, place on a wire rack to cool for 1–2 hours at room temperature. Optional: while waiting for the cake to cool, settle onto the couch to watch your favorite holiday movie.

15. Transfer the cake to the fridge for at least 8 hours. If you've got an event that just won't wait (aka Hope for the Holidays), place the cake in the freezer for 1–2 hours.

16. Decorate your cake with the cranberry topping. For extra *mmm*s from your guests, serve with swirls of whipped cream blended with powdered sugar or molasses.

Warning: May cause spontaneous moaning, eye rolling, and possibly a marriage proposal if served to your significant other!

Enjoy,
Mable

Come back for a visit to Sweetwater Springs as ambitious, successful magazine editor Josie Kellum falls head over heels... and ends up in physical therapy.

Please turn the page for a preview of *Springtime at Hope Cottage*.

Available Spring 2019

CHAPTER ONE

Definitely not in Kansas anymore.

Or, in Josie Kellum's case, New York City. She'd barely stepped off the ramp and into the airport before she'd realized she was in for a culture shock. And that was saying a lot, considering her home state was a proud blend of people from around the world. All cultures and people except perhaps the sort that lived deep in the mountains of North Carolina.

Readjusting the carry-on bag on her shoulder, Josie weaved her way toward Baggage Claim. Just looking around, she could guess who the locals were, arriving back home from their travels. They didn't seem to be in a rush to go anywhere unlike her city counterparts, who were few and far between. Even now Josie was rushing, though her flight had landed early, and for the first time in ages, she wasn't chasing a deadline.

She slowed at Baggage Claim and retrieved her brightly colored luggage.

Understandably, her best friend, Kaitlyn Russo, couldn't meet her here today. Kaitlyn ran a successful bed and breakfast, which demanded someone always be there to play hostess. When Josie had assured Kaitlyn she could grab a cab to Sweetwater Springs, Kaitlyn had only laughed.

"A forty-five-minute drive will cost you those red-soled shoes you love so much."

"Christian Louboutins," Josie corrected. "And they're more than shoes. So I'll just rent a car, then."

"When was the last time you actually drove a car, Jo?"

Kaitlyn raised a good point. Josie took public transportation everywhere she went. She didn't own a car, and she'd never driven one down the side of a mountain.

"Don't worry," Kaitlyn told her. "I'll find someone to pick you up. Mitch has a friend that drives that way all the time. Maybe he can swing by and drive you in."

Mitch's friend. That was the extent of Josie's knowledge on who she was looking for right now as she scanned the surrounding area. There were a few people holding signs as they stood against the wall near Baggage Claim. An older woman with white hair. An African American man in a uniform of some sort. Maybe Josie should've thought to make a sign that read MITCH'S FRIEND to hold up.

As Josie was pondering what to do next, someone tapped her left shoulder. She whirled around, catching one heel of her Christian Louboutins on the wheel of her rolling luggage. She tried to steady herself with the handle but it retracted with her quick movement.

Was she being mugged? Because that would be the ultimate irony. All these years, she'd lived in the city where she was most likely to get mugged, and a small-town airport was where it was going to happen.

Two arms latched on to either side of her, breaking her

fall. How nice of her attacker to keep her from hitting the floor. Looking up, she met two darker-than-night eyes cast in a tanned, angular face.

"You can take everything except my computer. And my phone," she said as she tried to get her feet back under her.

"Excuse me?"

"Not that I think you want a luggage full of women's clothing but there's a little money in there." She pulled away from him and then secured her cross-body purse. Opening it quickly, she snatched a small can of Mace.

"Whoa!" The man took several steps back and held up his hands. "What are you doing?"

"Defending myself. You grabbed me from behind."

The man's dark brows dove toward his nose. He could be a model. He didn't need to attack innocent women if he was struggling financially. This guy was far better looking than some of the models in *Loving Life*, the popular magazine that she worked for.

"I didn't grab you from behind. I tapped your shoulder. Are you Kaitlyn's friend?"

Josie swallowed hard. "Are you…Mitch's friend?"

He gave a small nod before glancing back down at her can of Mace still primed at his face.

"Don't you know you're not supposed to touch people you don't know?" she asked, shoving her can back into her purse. "That'll get you killed in some places."

"And evidently blinded here," he muttered. "No good deed goes unpunished."

Josie cringed. "Listen, I'm sorry. I just…I was expecting you to be holding a sign and standing over there." She gestured toward the small group of sign holders.

The man followed her gaze and nodded. "Okay. Any

other expectations I should know about? Because I happen to like my eyes. I prefer to keep them."

She laughed nervously. She kind of liked his eyes too. And his face. His skin was a perfect bronze color that made her suspect he was American Indian. "Um, no. Well, yes. I guess we should make introductions since we'll be spending the next forty-five minutes in your vehicle together." She held out her hand. "I'm Josie Kellum. Aka Kaitlyn's friend." He took her hand, and a shock wave of warm tingles slid up her fingers and down her spine.

"Tuck Locklear. Mitch's friend." He looked down at her bags. "I'd like to help you with your bags—the ones with women's clothing and a little money—if that's okay."

"Um, yes. Thank you."

Way to go, Josie. She tended to get a little high strung after pulling several late-nighters in a row. It was a combination of not enough sleep, too much caffeine, and too little human interaction. She'd needed to finish her upcoming articles before this trip though. That way she could relax and let her hair down, so to speak.

Tuck led her to a Jeep in the parking lot and loaded her luggage into the back while she climbed into the passenger seat. A large chocolate Lab lifted its head from the floor of the back seat as she settled in.

"Oh, hi there. And who are you?" she asked on a laugh.

Tuck climbed into the driver's seat and petted the Lab's head. "This is Shadow," he told her before addressing the dog. "She's a friend, Shadow. Lie down."

The Lab looked at Josie once more and then did as Tuck asked.

Josie noticed the dog's harness read THERAPY DOG in large block letters. She wondered why Tuck needed one, but considering they'd only just met and she'd already tried to single-handedly blind him, it was best not to pry. "Thank you again for picking me up."

"It's not a problem."

She waited for him to say more. When he didn't, she filled the silence with the next obvious question. "So, what do you do?"

"Do?" He glanced over.

"For a living. I'm the executive editor for the lifestyle section of *Loving Life* magazine. Not that you asked."

Work was always her crutch in social situations. Other people tended to tell tales of their latest vacation. Or they whipped out pictures of their significant other or their pair of angelic-looking kids. Some even had cute, far-too-spoiled dogs that they showed off proudly on their cell phones. Everyone had someone, even Lisa Loner, the woman who'd been dubbed the office's wallflower. Just last week, Josie had been cornered by Lisa in the hall while going for her third cup of coffee. In a rare show of personality, Lisa had been bubbling with excitement to show off her new engagement ring and tell the dramatic story of how the guy she'd just met had proposed.

Even though Josie was skeptical of such a short relationship, she also found herself feeling small in some way. She didn't have a guy or dog to love her unconditionally. She lived alone in a tiny apartment on the Upper East Side. The closest she'd come to any sort of vacation in the last year was happening now, sitting shotgun in a Jeep with a man who likely regretted agreeing to this favor.

"I'm a physical therapist," he said.

"Oh." Josie looked over, trying to fit Tuck into the mold of all the physical therapists she'd met before. Most of them were clean-cut ex-jocks wearing khakis and polo shirts. Although handsome, Tuck had long hair and his muscles were lean rather than bulky. He wore a relaxed pair of jeans and a T-shirt. "Kaitlyn said you come this way often. Do you work at a hospital nearby?"

"There you go with those expectations again." A smile lifted his cheeks. "No, I see patients in the wild, meaning at their homes, out in public, and sometimes literally in the woods. It's more natural than using exercise machines in an air-conditioned building with a TV mounted on the wall."

"Sounds interesting," she said, keeping to herself the fact that, if she were a patient, she'd prefer the machines and daytime television.

"Shadow is my therapy dog. She works alongside me."

Hearing her name, the Lab lifted her head once more.

Josie was about to pet her but then pulled her hand away. She'd written an article on therapy dogs once. There were rules about socializing with them.

"It's okay," Tuck said. "Shadow isn't working right now."

"Oh. Good." Josie moved her hand and petted the top of Shadow's head. She was soft and leaned into Josie's touch. "What a good girl you are." Even though the dog wasn't working now, Josie felt herself immediately relax.

Then her cell phone dinged loudly from her purse. Josie faced forward and pulled it out to check the caller ID, and her stress level jumped right back up—both because of the endless fires to put out at her workplace and because she'd taken that moment to look out her window at the steep drop of the mountainside.

Turning away from the window only led her eyes to her driver, which spiked her blood pressure for a whole separate reason.

* * *

Tuck knew the type. Work obsessed, self-absorbed, and, judging by her luggage and fancy leather purse, materialistic.

Not his type.

He listened as Josie talked on the phone, suddenly sounding firm and a tad bossy. His own phone vibrated in the middle console. He shifted his gaze for just a second as he navigated down the mountain. Sweetwater Springs was only another ten miles away, and he couldn't get his passenger to her destination soon enough.

Tuck recognized the number on his caller ID as the same one that had called earlier. A Beverly Sanders had left a message asking him to call her back. He hadn't yet. He wondered if the woman was a prospective patient. If so, she should've called his office number. He had a secretary that he shared with the local home-health occupational and speech therapists in Sweetwater Springs. Only current patients got his cell number, and only to use during emergencies.

After a moment, his phone dinged with another voicemail. He'd check it later. Right now, his passenger was still talking on her own phone.

"All right, Dana. Yeah. I'll take care of it...I know I'm on vacation but this can't wait...Uh-huh. Bye." Josie tapped a button on her phone and placed it in her lap.

From the corner of his eye, Tuck caught his passenger looking at him. She opened her mouth to speak. *Can't we just ride in silence the rest of the way?*

"So, Kaitlyn and Mitch are happy, huh?" she finally said.

Tuck gave a small nod. "Mitch is happier than I've seen him in a long time." And Mitch deserved it after all his years running from the ghosts of his past. Tuck, on the other hand, was faced with his late wife's ghost every day. Even now, after moving to a new home on Blueberry Creek, Renee seemed to be everywhere.

His fingers gripped the steering wheel tightly as he refocused on Josie.

"Kaitlyn seems happy too," she said. "I miss her back home in New York. We used to have lunch together at least once a week."

Tuck guessed that Josie had to schedule those lunch dates in her calendar. She probably scheduled her showers too.

And he shouldn't be thinking about her in the shower. While her personality wasn't the most attractive in his opinion, he could admit that her looks were. She had long, naturally blond hair that was pulled back in a tight ponytail. Her skin was smooth and creamy. By all appearances, she looked like she hadn't seen the sun in years. When she'd captured his attention with a can of Mace primed at his face, he'd stared at her long enough to see that her eyes were almost a turquoise blue.

Josie's phone made a ridiculous, high-pitched meow from her lap.

Shadow stood at attention in the back seat and gave a soft bark.

"Sorry. That's just a text message alert," she told Shadow. "I don't have any cats stowed away with me—I promise." She read the text and started laughing to herself.

In contrast to the meow, this was a pleasant sound. Tuck smiled for a moment.

Then her phone meowed again. And again. It continued to meow while her fingers tapped against the screen in response until he pulled his truck onto Mistletoe Lane where the Sweetwater Bed and Breakfast was located.

He pulled into the driveway of the two-story Victorian

house that his friend Mitch and his fiancée, Kaitlyn, had inherited last November and parked. "This is it."

"Wow." Josie stared out his windshield at the inn.

Tuck pulled his gaze away to keep from staring at her. "I'll, uh, get your luggage and help you in." He hopped out and opened his back hatch to retrieve her belongings.

Josie was standing beside him before he knew it with her laptop bag thrown over her shoulder along with that expensive-looking purse. "I got it," she said. "Thanks again for the ride." Without waiting for him to respond, she grabbed the handle of her luggage from his hand and smiled at him.

"You sure?"

She nodded. "Positive." She held out her other hand.

"What's that?" he asked, looking at the folded cash.

"For your troubles."

He lifted his gaze to those turquoise eyes. "I'm not a cab driver, and it wasn't any trouble."

She cocked her head. "I know but you didn't have to go out of your way for me."

If he couldn't tell by looking at her, this would have given away the fact that she wasn't from around here. People in Sweetwater Springs didn't mind helping each other out. It was one thing he appreciated about his hometown. He'd seen the stark contrast of other communities when he'd gone to college, first for his bachelor's degree and then for his master's. As far as he knew, there was no other town quite like this one, which is why he was never leaving again.

"Josie, you made it!" Kaitlyn called out as she headed down the steps of the house.

Josie turned her attention to the innkeeper, and both women squealed with delight. Tuck imagined that Shadow was standing at alert again in the back seat. His cue to get back in the Jeep and leave.

"Thank you, Tuck!" Kaitlyn shouted.

"No problem." He waved and shut the door. He was running late for dinner with his friend Alex Baker, the police chief in Sweetwater Springs. Before going to the Tipsy Tavern, however, he needed to drop Shadow off at home.

Tuck was almost to the cottage he'd recently purchased on Blueberry Creek when his phone started to ring. The caller ID showed the same number that had called before. That woman was bent on talking to him tonight. He started to reach for the phone to find out why but stopped short when he heard a high-pitched meowing from the passenger seat. It meowed a second time, and Tuck couldn't help grinning. Josie Kellum was undoubtedly losing her mind right about now.

He parked in his driveway and commanded Shadow to follow him to the backyard. Then he returned to his Jeep and wavered only momentarily on which direction to drive. Back to the inn to return Josie's cell phone or to his dinner destination? He couldn't keep the chief of Sweetwater Springs police waiting, now, could he?

Besides, maybe it would do the beautiful Josie Kellum good to disconnect from her busy city life for just a while longer.

About the Author

Annie Rains is a *USA Today* bestselling contemporary romance author who writes small-town love stories set in fictional places in her home state of North Carolina. When Annie isn't writing, she's living out her own happily ever after with her husband and three children.

Annie loves to hear from her readers. Please visit her at:

http://www.annierains.com/
@AnnieRains_
http://facebook.com/annierainsbooks

Local florist Teri Summers has her hands full of mistletoe in preparation for the holiday, yet finding someone to kiss is her last priority. But when the gorgeous new doctor makes a connection with her special needs son, Aiden, Teri finds herself wondering if she's finally found happiness in this season of joy.

For a bonus holiday story from another author that you may love, please turn the page to read "A Midnight Clear" by Hope Ramsay.

Author's Note

This story started out as a nebulous idea about a child who didn't like Christmas. That idea took me to the Internet, and that led me to many, many resources about autism and Asperger's syndrome.

I wasn't so sure I wanted to tackle that issue, but I emailed my good friend Caroline Bradley, who is the mother of a wonderful son who is on the spectrum. She had a lot to say about Asperger's kids: what it means to be the mother of a child with special needs and the difficulties of negotiating the holidays.

So I would like to give Caroline my deepest and most heartfelt thanks for her willingness to share with me, for her encouragement, and for being the incredible mother that she is. I could not have written this story without her help.

CHAPTER ONE

Teri Summers tore through the doorway of the Last Chance urgent care clinic, skidded over the polished floor, and sagged against the reception desk. Dana Foster looked up from her paperwork, a tiny angel pin glittering from her red cashmere sweater. The angel winked at Teri.

Or maybe Teri was hallucinating because of hypoxia. She had just run all the way from Last Chance Bloomers—a distance of at least a mile. "Is Aiden all right?" She wheezed like a broken accordion.

Dana gave her a benign smile and said, "It's like I told you on the phone, Teri. It's a minor injury. He's in with Doc Crawford right now. Through the doors, the cubicle on the right."

Teri took one step toward the double doors before Dana's words registered. She stopped. Turned. "Doc Crawford?"

"The new doctor. He's from *Boston*." Dana pronounced the name of the city with a broad "a" sound and rolled her eyes in a way that didn't inspire confidence.

"Where's Doc Cooper?"

"He's gone off to Florida to look for retirement property. He'll be back after Christmas, but he's retiring in February."

Teri had just begun processing this news when an altogether familiar howl pierced the quiet of the waiting room. Oh boy. Disaster had struck, just as she'd feared. Aiden's injury might be minor, but her son didn't do well with doctors.

She followed the screams to Aiden's examination cubicle, where a big guy in a white coat blocked her way.

Judy Cabello, Aiden's after-school caregiver, stood facing the doctor explaining things while she wrung her hands the way the guilty do. When she said "Asperger's spectrum," she whispered the words as if Aiden carried the plague or something.

Teri stifled the urge to join Aiden in a primal scream. Instead, she swallowed back her anger. It burned down her parched throat. "What happened?"

The doctor turned, and Judy said, "Oh, hi, Teri. I'm so sorry."

"What happened?" she repeated.

"Uh, well, we were outside searching for some pinecones to make a Christmas wreath. I turned away for just one minute, and Aiden went off climbing the woodpile. He was talking to his angel when he fell. He's got a gigantic splinter in his thigh. He freaked out, and I didn't know what else to do."

You could have called me at the store instead of bringing him here and letting Dana scare me to death. But Teri didn't say that out loud. Judy had tons of experience with special needs kids, just not kids like Aiden. Bringing Aiden to the doctor to have a splinter removed had to rate right up there with overreactions of the century. Aiden didn't do doctor's visits well.

Teri turned toward the guy blocking the path to her son. He looked like he'd come directly from central casting for some medical TV show.

"Excuse me," she said as she stepped around him and finally saw Aiden's injury. The word *splinter* didn't give the three-inch shard of wood sticking out of Aiden's thigh the respect it deserved. The calm facade she'd been trying to maintain melted. She wanted to fly to Aiden's side and gather him up in the biggest mommy-hug ever. But Aiden didn't like mommy-hugs.

Aiden needed his angel.

"Where's Raphael?" Teri asked Judy.

"I don't know," Judy replied. "It's probably at home, or maybe lost in the woodpile. I didn't take the time to look for it. I just brought him right here."

Teri resisted the urge to criticize. Judy should have known not to leave Raphael at home. The resin figurine stood five inches high. Miriam Randall, a member of the Christ Church Ladies' Auxiliary, had given it to Aiden two years ago, right after they had moved to Last Chance. The old lady had told her that Raphael was the angel of healing.

Teri didn't believe Aiden needed "healing." He was the way he was and she loved him for himself. But the figurine had somehow become Aiden's main comfort object. Without Raphael, she and Aiden were up a creek without a paddle, as the saying goes.

"The injury isn't as serious as it looks," Dr. Crawford said, his voice deep and mellow as Tennessee whiskey, even if it did have a definite Yankee bite to it. "But I need him to stay still for a few minutes. If you can't calm him down, we'll have to sedate him."

Not good. She hated sedating Aiden. He'd be groggy and

out of sorts for days afterward. She had to do something to regain control. So she climbed up on the examining table beside Aiden, careful not to touch him. She bent over him and started singing "It Came Upon a Midnight Clear." For once, the song was in season.

She sang the carol a half dozen times while Aiden's screams morphed into moans and then a definite hum, followed, finally, by his high, clear, boy soprano voice.

Thank you, Lord.

They sang the carol three or four more times, until Dr. Crawford cleared his throat and said, "We really need to deal with the splinter. Do you think white noise would help?" He took the stethoscope from around his neck, held it up, and gestured toward his ears.

Bless him. He'd shown remarkable patience for the last five minutes. Doc Cooper would have given up a long time ago and gone looking for a hypodermic needle and a sedative.

The new doc met her gaze, his brown eyes steady and reassuring. Oh boy, the new doc from "Bah-sten" was a class-A dreamboat. She gave the meddling church ladies of Last Chance a week before they started trying to find him his soul mate.

She nodded in his direction and then got right up in Aiden's face. "Aiden, Doctor Crawford needs to fix your hurt leg. Would you like to try his stethoscope?"

The doctor moved slowly so as not to startle Aiden. He dangled the apparatus where Aiden could see it. The boy didn't make eye contact but he nodded, all the while humming his comfort song.

The doc spoke again. "Okay, I'm going to put it in your ears. If you don't like it, I'll stop." He gently put the ear pieces in Aiden's ears and pressed the end of the stethoscope to his chest. Aiden finally went still. But he continued to hum his song.

"This is about as good as it's going to get," Teri said. "But you'll need to treat this like the most delicate surgery. Aiden hates being touched."

The doctor nodded and went to work, moving slowly to cut away the jeans and extract the splinter without ever once touching Aiden with anything other than the cold, hard steel of his instruments. And yet, Dr. Crawford's hands were gentle and competent and skilled. He made short work of it, and after he confirmed that Aiden was up-to-date on his tetanus shots, they were done with the scary stuff.

She needed to get her son home as quickly as possible, so she gently took the stethoscope from Aiden's ears.

Big mistake.

Aiden grabbed it back and started to howl and flail again.

Damn.

She did the unthinkable. She pried his fingers from the stethoscope and handed it back to the doctor. "Thanks, Doc. Sorry to rush, but I need to get him home, where we can gain some control. If you could just leave some instructions with Dana, I'll call back for them."

Time to leave Dodge in the dust. And since she'd already touched Aiden, she figured she might as well haul his butt out of the clinic. Judy had the car here so they could make a hasty departure.

She lifted Aiden from the examining table. He'd weighed almost sixty pounds at his last checkup. Teri could still lift him, but when he arched his back and kicked her hard in the shin, she let him go. He didn't hit the floor hard enough to hurt anything, but that didn't matter. He immediately threw himself on his back and started banging his head on the floor.

Damn. Damn. Damn. How could this be happening? Again.

Teri had fallen in love with Aiden the moment they'd put him in her arms eight years ago. But when he howled like a torture victim, when he slammed his head against the floor like he wanted to break his brain, when he kicked and spat and lashed out at anyone and everyone, it still felt like a big, fat rejection.

All of her efforts to calm him, to love him, to protect him were inevitably rebuffed. She didn't know if she could keep this up for much longer. But then again, what else could she do? She couldn't just fall out of love with her son.

So she steeled herself like a Southern magnolia. Her son might be a disaster, but she loved him more than life. And she always had her good manners to cling to. She looked up at the doctor. "I'm so sorry he's behaving like this. It's not you. Trust me. Maybe we can stay here for a moment until he calms down?"

"It's fine. Take whatever time you need. I'll write out instructions for the care of the wound and leave them with Dana." The kindness in Dr. Crawford's eyes undid her.

But Aiden ruined the moment. He stopped howling, sat up, and glared at the new doctor before finally using his words. "You're stupid," he said.

The doc recoiled and departed so fast that Teri didn't even have a chance to apologize a second time. Aiden had learned that word at school and had been repeating it to everyone he met. No doubt the other kids called him stupid all the time.

But he wasn't stupid.

He was different.

* * *

He ignored her outburst. "What seems to be
today?"

She pouted. Evidently she expected him
was a patient man. He waited.

A minute passed in charged silen
you don't have any medical issue
the next patient." He started to t

"No, wait. There's no nee
Bray said. "That may be th
down here we value ma

He ground his ba
smile. What the he

After anoth
arthritis. It's

He che
kind of
sure
sh

a portion of
two-year commitment to the people of
it wasn't just the money that had brought him here. Dr.
Massey, his mentor, had insisted that a two-year stint in the
Corps would make him a better doctor.

Dr. Massey would tell him to suck up his frustration. The
NHSC made a point of sending guys from Boston to rural
towns in the South. That was part of the experience.

He cleared his throat and shoved aside the privacy curtain
for the next examination area. Before he could even introduce himself, a large woman with gray-blue hair greeted him
with, "Who in blue blazes are you?"

"I'm Doctor Crawford. I'll be taking over for Doctor
Cooper." Tom was so tired of saying this.

"You will not."

the problem

to leave. But he

before he said, "If
, I guess I'll move on to
rn away.

to be rude, young man," Mrs.
e way folks up north behave. But
nners."

ck teeth and gave her his best bedside
ck had happened to Southern hospitality?
long silence, Mrs. Bray said, "It's my
cting up again."

ked her file and found nothing that indicated any
arthritis. She had high cholesterol and blood pres-
Her BMI was unhealthy. He wouldn't be surprised if
e had some arthritis at her age, but she'd never seen Dr.
Cooper about it. At least not according to the records.

"I just need some pills," she said.

"What kind of pills?"

"You know, the pills that Doc Cooper gives me."

He immediately went on guard. "What pills are those?"

"You know, the little white ones. He gets them from his special cupboard in his office. I'm sure you'll find the information in my file. I've had rheumatoid arthritis in my hands for years."

What was going on here? He didn't like this one bit. But he tried to mask his concern from the patient. Instead he asked the woman a series of questions and made an examination of her hands, where she said she felt the most pain. He found no evidence of joint damage or trauma.

Was Mrs. Bray one of those attention-seeking patients?

Or was the beloved Doc Cooper handing out painkillers to bored little old ladies?

He sat on the stool and made eye contact. "Mrs. Bray, I can't give you pills because Doc Cooper didn't put any information in your file about what kind of medicine he was giving you. I can prescribe some extra-strength ibuprofen. But since I also don't see any indication in your file that you've been evaluated by a rheumatologist, I think it might a good idea for you to see a specialist. I can—"

The old lady's eyes bugged out as she interrupted. "I don't have time to run up to Columbia to see specialists. That's why you're here, young man. Now, I'd like my pills."

"I'm very sorry, but I don't dispense pills. And I don't know what Doctor Cooper was giving you. He's made no notation in the files. So if you're having problems with your hands, I think we need to send you to a specialist. I can have Dana see about getting you transportation up to Columbia or the nearest regional center. But if you're having pain in your legs or knees, that could definitely be because of your weight. I think we—"

"I didn't come here to talk about my weight." Mrs. Bray climbed down from the examining table and picked up her purse. "I'm leaving." She put her nose in the air and marched from the examining room out to the reception area, where she told Dana, in a voice loud enough for Tom to hear, exactly what she thought of "that Yankee doctor."

It didn't make Tom feel any better to hear Dana agreeing with every word the old lady said.

AIDEN SPEAKS

There are nine choirs of angels: Seraphim, Cherubim, Thrones, Dominions, Virtues, Powers, Principalities, Archangels, and Angels. Some angels don't look like people. Like Thrones. They are just wagon wheels with eyes and wings. I think it would be cool to see a wheel with eyes. But only if it's an angel wheel.

I don't like looking at people's eyes.

I don't like mashed potatoes.

I don't like candles. Watching the fire makes my head feel funny.

Raphael is an archangel whose name isn't in the Bible. But he's mentioned in the Talmud. He's supposed to fix people. I don't know what that means.

Mom found Raphael in the woodpile where I dropped him. Raphael has a blue cloak, and it says "Made in China" on the bottom of his feet.

I practiced Bach's Prelude and Fugue No. 1 in C Major while Mom made dinner. The music is nice because it's just lots and lots of scales, and I can pretend that there is nothing but the notes. And I like thinking that there are only notes and nothing else. Especially no people.

Then I went to bed. And when I woke up, I had Cheerios for breakfast but not with bananas. I don't like bananas in milk. I ate my banana without the milk. And then Mom said, since it was Sunday, we could visit the angels.

I sang "It Came Upon a Midnight Clear" twenty-seven times while Mom drove.

CHAPTER TWO

Practically everyone in Last Chance, South Carolina, went to church on Sunday morning. Teri would have gone too, but she couldn't keep Aiden from making inappropriate and unkind remarks about the quality of the choir's singing.

He didn't do well in Sunday school either. He just wanted to talk about angel verses to the exclusion of all other parts of the Bible. This frustrated the volunteer Sunday school teachers.

So about six months ago, Teri had started bringing Aiden here, to Golfing for God, to worship. Golfing for God was a Bible-themed putt-putt place. Holes one through nine depicted Old Testament stories, like Jonah and the whale. Holes ten through eighteen depicted stories from the New Testament, like the miracle of the loaves and fishes. And finally, the new section of the golf course, opened just last year, was dedicated entirely to angels. Teri had to hand it to Elbert Rhodes, the owner of the golf course. He had created a masterpiece, complete with larger-than-life fiberglass angels that Aiden adored.

And now, even in December, with the course closed for the winter, Elbert had given her permission to bring Aiden to visit the angels any time he liked. Of course, when Elbert talked about angels, he might mean the nine fiberglass angels gracing the new section of his mini-golf emporium. Or he could just as well be talking about real-deal angels.

Golfing for God was notorious for its angel sightings. Teri didn't really believe any of the stories about the miniature golf place, but Aiden took them for gospel truth. He believed that if he sat quietly for long enough, he'd get to meet a real angel one day. Aiden had a capacity to sit quietly for unnaturally long periods of time.

Teri usually had Golfing for God to herself on Sunday mornings. But this morning a black Volkswagen SUV with Massachusetts plates was sitting in the parking lot when she arrived.

Her suspicions were soon confirmed when she found Dr. Crawford inspecting the hole dedicated to Luke 2:10, where a heavenly host of angels hovered on wires over three poor shepherds and their flock. The putting green required a golfer to navigate through the legs of several fiberglass sheep to the hole in the center of the town of Bethlehem. Elbert had hung some red metallic garland around the perimeter of the town's buildings. It was festive, but kind of tacky.

Aiden didn't bother to greet the doctor, but made his way to the hole celebrating Psalm 91. The angel there wore a blue gown and had a beatific expression on his face. He sat down on the bench and got very still. Too still for a typical eight-year-old.

"Hello," Teri said as she strolled toward the new doctor in

town. "I didn't expect anyone else to be wandering through a mini-golf place on a cool December morning."

"To be honest, I overslept and I didn't want to walk into mass late, especially since it's my first time at St. Mary's. I didn't want to make a bad impression on Father Weiss. So I decided to come here instead. I've been told this place can be a religious experience."

She sat down on the bench near Bethlehem. "I know the feeling. We come here on Sundays instead of church. Aiden has perfect pitch, and he complains when the choir sings out of key. That gets him into trouble with Lillian Bray, the chairwoman of the Episcopal Ladies' Auxiliary."

This elicited a chuckle.

"Have you met Lillian Bray?" she asked.

"I have. I'm sure she doesn't care for being corrected by a precocious eight-year-old."

Precocious? Jeez. No one ever used that word to describe Aiden.

Dr. Crawford sat beside her. Her core heated. Was it his physical presence or the words he'd just spoken?

"Thank you for saying that," Teri said. "It's kind of you, especially after the way he behaved yesterday. There was nothing precocious about yesterday's meltdown."

"He was in pain yesterday. People say and do a lot of things when they're in pain."

She turned toward him. Dr. Crawford was movie-star handsome, with dark hair that spilled over his forehead. He had laugh lines around his mouth and his warm, compassionate brown eyes. It looked as if he smiled a lot. All that smiling had given his face character.

"Thanks for being so patient with him yesterday. And please, don't take what he said to heart. He's in a phase where he says ugly things to everyone. He's picked up a bunch of new words in school. And normally when Aiden picks up new words, I'm thrilled. He didn't start talking until he was four, and then only so he could sing his favorite songs. Now I wish he'd never learned the words *stupid* and *idiot* and *dummy*."

"And that makes you like most other mothers. My own ma used to wash my mouth with soap every time I used the word *stupid*. Old-fashioned but effective." He paused for a moment. "Not that I would recommend that approach."

His words assaulted the shell Teri kept around her emotions. No one had ever suggested that she was an ordinary mother. Mothering Aiden took all she had to give sometimes. Her son was not ordinary.

The doctor leaned back on the bench, a picture of male grace. A question formed in his deep, dark eyes as he gazed toward Aiden.

"He's waiting for an angel," Teri said in answer to the doctor's unspoken words. "There are stories about angels appearing here at Golfing for God. Aiden believes them with his whole heart."

"My sister has a kid. His name is Jimmy. He's a little younger than Aiden. It's a fun age. He believes in angels too. Along with the Easter Bunny, the Tooth Fairy, and, most of all, Santa. I'm going to miss my nephew this Christmas, but Ma is coming to visit around New Year's. She insisted. She wasn't all that thrilled when I decided to sign up for the National Health Corps. The truth is, I haven't spent much time away from Massachusetts."

Oh, the poor man. He was homesick. Her heart melted a little for him. She couldn't imagine being away from her large family at Christmas. Especially since her nieces and nephews were like little Jimmy. She got her dose of childlike wonder from them. Aiden might believe in angels, but he didn't believe in anything else.

She let go of a big sigh.

"That sounded sad, Mrs. Summers," the doc said.

"Not sad. Just wistful, I guess. You see, Aiden isn't like your nephew. He doesn't believe in the Tooth Fairy or Santa. In fact, he actively dislikes Santa. He always has. To start with, he doesn't like the color red. Don't ask me why, it's just the way it is. And no matter how many times I tell Aiden that Santa isn't a real person, he still doesn't get it. He sees all those Salvation Army Santas and to him they're all the same person. He thinks Santa is an army of evil clones or something. It scares him silly. But angels—well, that's a whole different story. He believes they are real."

"Aren't they?"

She turned toward him. He was so handsome it almost hurt to look at him. And he was gazing right back at her with such an earnest look in his eyes that she knew right then he wasn't trying to be clever or funny.

"Mrs. Summers," he said after a long, charged moment, "anyone who's spent any time at all in a hospital knows that angels are for real."

* * *

Teri Summers was pretty in a girl-next-door kind of way, with a dusting of faint freckles across her nose, and eyes that seemed to change color depending on the light. Today her eyes were gray. She didn't wear a wedding ring, so Tom assumed that she was managing Aiden all on her own.

She was doing a pretty good job of it. Like his sister, she was brave and determined.

And alone.

He was alone too. And away from his family for the first Christmas ever.

"So what's Christmas like in Last Chance?" he asked.

"We have a big get-together at the park near city hall to light the town tree. I get pretty frantic this time of year. I'm a florist. I own Last Chance Bloomers, and the holidays are my busiest time of year—even busier than Mother's Day or Easter. I oversee the decoration of the town tree. And I decorate most of the downtown merchants' spaces. I run around a lot this time of year." She kept her eyes focused on Aiden as she talked.

"I'll bet you do. Does Aiden help?"

She shook her head. "No, I use a babysitter a lot during the holidays." She looked down at her hands, her guilt palpable.

"The tree lighting sounds like fun," he said, just to make conversation.

She nodded. "We do other fun things. The Episcopal choir puts on an annual concert on Christmas Eve, which is worth attending. And of course every one of the churches in town puts on a children's Christmas play. You know, Doc Cooper and his wife organized the play at Christ Episcopal for years and years. I just heard that Lillian Bray has volunteered to organize it this year. But a lot of the parents aren't very happy about that. You wouldn't, by any chance, have experience in that department, would you?"

He cleared his throat. "Uh, no. And besides, I'm Catholic and I'll be on call Christmas Eve."

"Doc Cooper was on call too. Of course, his wife was there to back him up."

Clever. Was she flirting, or just trying to figure out his marital status? "I don't have a wife."

That brought a giggle. "I figured as much. And"—she

turned and faced him, her eyes smiling in the pale winter sunlight—"I ought to warn you. Every church woman in the county of any denomination is going to consider it her God-given duty to match you up with someone."

No, not flirting after all. "Me? I'm a Yankee from Boston. I got the feeling everyone in town thinks I'm a liberal carpet-bagger and I should go back home, which, of course, I'll likely do when my commitment to the National Health Service Corps is fulfilled. It's usually a two-year commitment." He played up his accent as he spoke.

"Give people time. They'll come around. And I'm telling you that you are not immune, just because you come from up north and aren't planning on staying for more than two years. The matchmakers of Last Chance target newcomers. They have this idea that if they can match you up with someone, you'll stay longer. It's their way of keeping young people from moving away to the city. So I'm warning you. Watch out for Miriam Randall and her niece, Savannah. People say that they have a knack for matching people up, but I think they're just a couple of meddling busybodies."

"I take it that you've been a victim of their meddling?"

She frowned. "Well, no. Of course not. I mean, I'm divorced."

"Oh. Divorced people are immune, then?"

"Uh, well, no. But, you know, I'm not going to find a soul mate. I mean, there's Aiden."

"And?"

She blinked at him. "You know, Doctor Crawford, I do appreciate that you think Aiden is precocious, and that I'm just like any other single mom. But the truth is the truth. Aiden is a special needs child. What man in his right mind would want to marry into something like that?"

* * *

On Sunday night, Teri collapsed in front of the TV with a glass of red wine. Aiden was down for the night, and she planned to indulge herself by watching the TNT movie version of *A Christmas Carol*. The one with Patrick Stewart. She hoped it would put her in the holiday spirit.

She loved Christmas. But her business added so much stress that work could ruin the mood. And, of course, Christmas wasn't exactly Aiden's favorite time of year. Sometimes, for example, Teri fervently wished that every Salvation Army bell would miraculously go silent, just to spare Aiden. He hated the sound of bells.

She had just put her feet up when her cell phone rang. She muted the TV and answered. Her sister Meredith was on the line. "Hey, Merry, what's up?"

There was an awkward beat of silence before Merry spoke. "Momma asked me to call you."

"Oh?"

More hesitation. "Uh, well, you see Brad, Julie, Laura, Momma, and me, we all had a talk, and we think it might be best if you and Aiden didn't come home for Christmas this year."

Teri sat there for at least half a minute, saying nothing, while her body went hot and then ice cold. Surely she must have misunderstood her sister.

"Did you hear me?" Merry said.

"I heard." Teri's voice sounded thin and far, far away inside her own head.

"I'm sorry, Teri. We love you. And we love Aiden, but the truth is he upsets the other children. Becky, Travis, and Ella are all at that magical age when they believe in Santa, you know? And the older kids play along. But Aiden's incapable of doing that. Honestly, I don't want him spoiling it for the little ones. And I figure it might be easier for you. Remember how he pitched a fit at the dinner table last year when Momma wanted him to eat his mashed potatoes? You can't even take him to midnight services. I really hate to do this but . . ." Her voice trailed off.

Teri sat there watching the scene where Scrooge blows off his nephew's invitation for Christmas Eve. How ironic. Scrooge's family wanted to include him, even though he was an unpleasant miser. While in real life, her own family wanted to exclude her, even though she knew how to "keep Christmas," as well as anyone.

She didn't know whether to cry or scream. It wouldn't be Christmas without going home to Momma's. Teri had four siblings and eight nieces and nephews. With all those kids and spouses and aunts and uncles dropping in, it was like a family reunion every year.

Of course there were the rituals—the midnight services at the church she'd attended as a child, hanging the stockings, getting the kids to bed, putting together toys. And Christmas morning was always so much fun—all that noise and chaos and joy.

Joy for her.

But Aiden hated it all. He would stay up in the guest room, watching videos on an iPad, utterly disinterested in the presents and the decorations and the rest of the family. All that chaos and the pressure to eat Momma's cooking would inevitably lead to a meltdown.

Poor kid.

She thought back to her conversation this morning with Dr. Crawford. She'd as much as admitted the truth to him. Christmas was supposed to be magical for children. But for Aiden it was nothing but painful.

"You okay with this?" Merry asked.

"Would it matter?" Teri managed to say around the knot in her throat.

"Honey, please. We know you'll miss us. But we were thinking about Aiden as much as the little ones. It would be better for you to visit when there isn't a holiday. We really do care about him. But you know..." She couldn't finish the sentence.

We know you'll miss us? Really? Would *they* miss *her* or *Aiden*? She wanted to dive right through the phone line and strangle her older sister. Did she even know how selfish she sounded?

The muscles along Teri's neck clamped into a spasm that sent pain radiating down her spine and up into her head. Right now, she wanted to throw herself on the floor and have her own gigantic meltdown.

But she didn't. She swallowed down all those raging thoughts and feelings and said, "Uh, yeah, I'm okay."

And then she hung up the phone.

CHAPTER THREE

The Society of American Florists estimated that pink poinsettias accounted for only 6 percent of all the poinsettias sold during the holidays. Teri figured Ruby Rhodes, the proprietor of the Cut 'n Curl, was a major contributor to this statistic. Ruby had purchased no fewer than a dozen large pink poinsettias, along with two magnolia wreaths and several yards of matching garland, for both the inside and outside of the beauty shop.

Teri lugged the plants and greenery into the Cut 'n Curl early on a rainy Monday morning. The weather matched her mood. She was still reeling from Merry's bombshell. Teri had never been alone at Christmastime. What was she going to do?

Of course, she wasn't exactly going to be alone. Aiden would be there. But celebrating Christmas with Aiden was like being with someone from another culture or religion. Aiden didn't see Christmas as a special day. To him, it was just a day like any other, except that the people around him made him do things he hated and feared—like eating mashed potatoes at a table with candles burning on it.

Well, she'd need to do *something* for Christmas. It might be an interesting challenge to figure out which parts of Christmas Aiden actually liked. The thought lifted her spirits. She could name one thing right off the bat. He liked the angels who visited the shepherds. So maybe they'd put up angel ornaments or something.

Teri busied herself putting together a faux tree in the Cut 'n Curl's reception area while Ruby and her daughter-in-law Jane took care of the morning customers—Thelma Hanks and Millie Polk. Thelma and Millie were BFFs who considered gossip to be their main occupation.

The ladies were going at it hot and heavy today. The subject was Arlene Whitaker, the owner of Lovette's Hardware and Ruby's sister-in-law. Arlene had become the favorite topic of the moment because Savannah Randall had told everyone that Arlene would be finding a new love—a man with a boat.

So naturally the folks in town were certain that Arlene, a widow, was having a late-life fling with Roy Burdett, a recent divorcé.

"If you want my opinion," Thelma said, "Arlene is too old to be looking for a soul mate." Thelma was sitting at Ruby's workstation, where the beautician was applying dye to her roots.

"She's not that old," Millie said. Millie, her own roots already loaded with dye, sat at the manicure table with Jane leaning over her hands. "I'd like to think that, as long as there's life, there's hope of finding love. Don't you, Ruby? I mean, I know Arlene was married to your brother, but Pete's gone now, and she deserves happiness."

"Uh-huh," Ruby said.

"Well, I'm just saying that Arlene already got her soul mate in Pete," Thelma said.

Jane looked up at Thelma. "Everyone said the same thing about Stone. And look at him now, happily married for the second time."

"Well," Thelma said, "I just can't imagine Arlene taking up with Roy Burdett. I mean, he's *divorced.*"

Teri cringed at the way Thelma said the word. Of course divorced people deserved happiness. Why should divorced people be excluded from happiness just because their first marriages crashed and burned?

Good question, especially since Teri had doubts about this herself. Sometimes she wondered if she was worthy of love.

"And besides," Thelma continued, "Roy spends most of his time at Dot's Spot."

"Not anymore," Ruby said. "He spent a month at one of those places where they dry you out. Dottie told me he hasn't been in the bar in at least a month."

"Well, I just think it's wrong for Savannah to be handing out marital advice to middle-aged divorcés and widows instead of young people." Thelma turned and gave Teri a meaningful look.

Teri held Thelma's gaze. "I'm *divorced* too," she said and then looked away.

"Oh," Thelma said. "Uh, honey, I didn't mean—"

"Yes you did," Ruby said. "Teri, honey, don't you listen to Thelma. I think Millie has it right, where there's life there's always the hope of finding true love."

Teri gave Ruby a smile, but her heart wasn't in it. How could she find true love when even her own family had banished her for Christmas?

She went back to decorating the tree. She tried to tune out

the gossip, but her ears pricked when Millie said, "Oh, girls, you won't believe what I heard about Lillian."

"Try me," Ruby said under her breath.

"I saw her at choir practice yesterday, and she was fit to be tied because that new Yankee doctor refused to prescribe her arthritis pills. He wanted her to see a specialist. Can you imagine?"

"You'd think he'd let her keep taking her pills while she scheduled an appointment," Thelma said. "Doesn't he care that she's in pain?"

"Apparently not. I don't think I'll be going there anymore," Millie said.

"And where would you go?" Ruby asked. "It's not like there are any other doctors in Last Chance. That's why the government sent down a Yankee. He's one of those Health Corps docs."

"Well, I'm sure not going to see that Yankee. He sounds insensitive."

"I met him, and he didn't come off that way at all." The words left Teri's mouth before she could think about it. She found herself staring into the surprised gazes of everyone in the shop. "He was kind to Aiden. Really, really patient with him, and Aiden was having a very bad day."

Ruby smiled. "Well, that's nice to know." She turned and glared at Thelma and Millie. "And since when have y'all ever let Lillian Bray color your opinions about folks in this town?" She turned back to her work.

"Maybe she really does need to see a specialist," Teri said.

"That's exactly what I think," Ruby said.

But Ruby's attempted intervention would probably have little effect on Millie and Thelma. By the end of the day, Teri figured everyone in town would have an entirely wrong impression of Tom Crawford.

Teri finished placing the pink poinsettias. Maybe she should call Tom—Dr. Crawford—and warn him.

No, that would be foolish. Tom Crawford was handsome, and kind, and thinking about him made her insides warm up. Calling him was out of the question. Besides, a phone call wouldn't stop the gossip.

That would require a miracle.

* * *

On Wednesday, Tom left his room at the Jonquil House B&B and headed downstairs into a Christmas tornado. Boxes cluttered every space. More than a dozen red poinsettias lined the hallway like redcoats on parade. A big pile of greenery sat on a drop cloth before the fireplace, perfuming the air with the clean, woodsy smell of fresh-cut pine.

Teri Summers stood right in the eye of the storm.

Her hair was pulled back in a no-nonsense ponytail. Her face looked fresh and clean. Her outfit today consisted of faded blue jeans and a big, hand-knit snowflake sweater that made her look like the spirit of Christmas decor.

She was the epitome of cute, with a nice shape and eyes that sparkled with Christmas merriment.

Tom had been thinking a lot about her since they'd run into each other at Golfing for God. He wondered how she might react if he asked her out for a dinner date. Quite probably she'd shoot him down. But he'd never know if he didn't try.

He checked his watch. He still had a few minutes before he needed to leave for the short commute to the clinic. He strolled into the inn's living room. "Good morning."

She looked up from the box of tree ornaments she had just opened. "Oh!" She startled and jumped back a foot.

An adorable frown lowered her brow. "What are you doing here?"

"I'm staying at the inn while I look for a permanent home. Housing in Last Chance is wicked hard to come by. What are *you* doing here, besides making a mess?"

"Oh, sorry." She blushed holly-berry red. "Um, I'm here to decorate. I promise I'll have everything in order by the time you get back from the clinic." Her eyes looked more brown than gray today.

Jolts of energy zinged through him, leaving him in a decidedly merry mood. It looked as if she planned to trim out every square inch of the inn. He couldn't wait to see what she accomplished. He was a sucker for pine roping. Not to mention mistletoe. "I'm looking forward to seeing the finished product."

"Um, Doctor . . . Tom. I heard something yesterday and I've been trying to decide whether or not to tell you about it."

"What?"

"Just some gossip. Honestly, the town runs on gossip. I'm sure you've figured that out by now. But anyway, Lillian Bray is running her mouth about how you . . ." She stopped speaking and the holly-berry blush reappeared. "Don't get the wrong idea," she rushed on, "I'm not prying or casting any doubt on your abilities as a doctor. But Lillian is doing that. And people listen to Lillian. Which is a mystery, really, but they do."

His merriment vanished. He'd heard the gossip. He'd even made a quick call to Jeff Cooper. It turned out that, in Jeff's opinion, Mrs. Bray was just looking for attention. So Jeff had been giving her sugar pills to keep her happy. That wasn't exactly practicing medicine by the book, but it certainly kept the old busybody from making trouble.

Tom wasn't about to tell anyone Jeff's little secret. He also wasn't planning on adopting the old doc's method of handling Lillian Bray. Handing out placebos to troublesome patients wasn't good medicine. It might ultimately compromise Mrs. Bray's health.

He'd have to weather Mrs. Bray's public disapproval. But it might not be so hard knowing that someone like Teri Summers cared about what people in town said about him.

He chose his response carefully. "I know Mrs. Bray isn't pleased with me," he said. "But if she has RA, she needs to see a rheumatologist so we can get her on the best meds to slow the joint damage and manage her pain." His voice had dropped into that professional tone he'd learned as an intern at Boston Medical Center.

"Oh, well, I just thought you'd like to know." She gave him the tiniest smile and then turned away toward the naked Douglas fir the inn's owners had set up late last night.

"So, what are you doing this evening?" Tom asked.

She turned to look over her shoulder. "Doctor Crawford, are you asking me out on a *date*?"

He couldn't tell if she was shocked or surprised, so he gave her a nonchalant shrug. Maybe he could fool her into thinking he wouldn't be disappointed if she declined. "I am. I was wondering if you would introduce me to the barbecue in this town. I've heard it's excellent."

"It is excellent. Much better than anything you've got in Boston." She turned all the way around to face him. "But I'm afraid I'm busy tonight."

"Oh, all right. Some other time then." He backpedaled, and his prosthesis almost tripped him up. He stifled the urge to massage his knee. He was just proud enough not to want Teri to know about his missing leg.

He'd lost it as a result of bone cancer at the age of seven.

His "peg leg," as Jimmy liked to call it, had been with him for a long, long time, and he was mostly steady on his feet. In truth, his scars from that time were far less visible.

He took another step back, steadier on his one foot. Luckily, Teri hadn't noticed his awkwardness. Good.

"I'm putting up my own Christmas tree tonight," Teri said in a rush, as if she was trying to explain her rejection. "Well, anyway, I'm going to try. But you know Aiden might not like it, so I was just going to, you know, put up something small and maybe put some angels on it or something. So I . . ." Her voice trailed off. Her face got redder.

"I see," he said.

"Uh, well, Aiden and I are going to be on our own this Christmas, you know. And I need to put up a tree. I haven't done that in a long, long time. I'm not sure how Aiden will react."

"Want some help?"

She stood silent for the longest moment, either trying to compose herself or weighing the pros and cons. "You'd do that?" she finally asked.

He opted to play this scene straight. No need to give her a speech about his past. The less said about that the better. "I'm pretty good at putting up Christmas trees. Although"—he looked around at the mess—"I might not be up to your professional standards."

Her mouth quirked as if she were trying to keep it from trembling. "My professional standards mean nothing. Aiden has definite likes and dislikes, and this year I thought I'd try to tailor Christmas to *his* standards, instead of forcing him to celebrate the holiday by everyone else's." She bit her lower lip.

"Sounds like a good plan to me." Man, she had one kissable mouth. Too bad he hadn't caught her under the mistletoe that she was clearly planning to hang before the day was out.

"Yeah," she said with a little nod, "it does sound like a good plan, doesn't it? I have no idea where this is going to lead though."

Neither do I. "I'm adventurous."

"I think that's true. You came all the way from Boston to the middle of nowhere to do battle with Lillian Bray and the rest of the busybodies in this town. That takes courage."

He was surprised. Ma had told him that joining the NHSC had been an act of supreme stupidity. "So, what time?" he asked.

"Uh, well, I guess about six."

"Six it is, then." He turned and made the quickest of getaways before she realized that he'd just sort of invited himself over.

CHAPTER FOUR

Had she actually invited Doc Crawford for dinner? She parsed through their conversation. She didn't remember issuing any invitation. But she did distinctly remember that he was planning to show up at about six o'clock.

They hadn't exchanged emails or addresses or anything. So maybe the idea of a dinner date with Dr. Crawford was a figment of her imagination. Some "undigested bit of beef" as Scrooge would say.

Yeah, beefcake. Tom Crawford was like some unholy combination of TV's Dr. Derek Shepherd and Dr. Doug Ross.

So why on earth was he coming to dinner tonight? He couldn't possibly be interested in her. Maybe he was just lonely and she was the only person in town who had a nice thing to say about him. Lillian Bray sure had poisoned the well.

Well, she sure wasn't going to do anything stupid or special for him. Not that she would have done anything special if she had purposefully invited Tom for dinner. Aiden was a food tyrant.

So she popped a frozen chicken lasagna with alfredo sauce into the oven and headed out to the storage shed to find her Christmas decorations.

She'd boxed up those decorations when she'd moved from Columbia five years ago, right after the divorce. She hadn't laid eyes on them since. Most of them would stay in the box, but her white twinkle lights should be okay. And the small, artificial tree that had once decorated her dorm room at college would be perfect for the low-key Christmas she would have this year.

Her throat knotted at the thought.

She wanted a real tree. She wanted swags and garland and a zillion candles all aflame. But what she wanted conflicted with what Aiden needed. So she'd settle. It would be fine. It would be good. Aiden might actually have a Christmas to remember.

Besides, it was silly to spend the money on a real tree, since Aiden hated anything to do with Christmas.

She prayed that white lights would be okay. And she'd dig out her collection of angel ornaments—at least the ones without red on them. She might also try to put out her German Christmas nativity carousel. It had angels by the dozens. Of course, she wouldn't be able to light any of the candles in Aiden's presence, but maybe if she set it up without the candles, he'd enjoy it. Or maybe not. He was very particular about his angels.

She had just pulled the artificial tree from its box when the doorbell rang. Teri glanced at her watch—6:00 p.m. on the dot.

Damn. He was punctual. Was that a Yankee trait?

Well, he would soon discover that she hadn't put on the

dog for him. Which was fine, because she wasn't interested in any romance. And relationships were out of the question.

In spite of these realities, her heart pounded when she opened the front door and found Dr. Crawford standing there with a bottle of wine in hand.

He extended the bottle. "I hope you like Soave. I'm partial to Italian wines, and I know that Aiden has issues with the color red. So I brought white."

A flush climbed up her body from her toes to the top of her head. He was the picture of male beauty, wearing an Irish fisherman's sweater and a pair of jeans. For goodness sake, the curl in the middle of his forehead looked Superman-esque. How the heck did he manage that? It was perfect.

And perfect guys were scary.

"Uh, come in," she said. "I was just putting the tree together."

He strolled into her living room and stopped to watch Aiden at the spinet piano. Her son was in his music trance, playing one of the exercises from the *Well-Tempered Clavier*. Teri didn't know which one or in what key. They all sounded more or less like scales to her. She wasn't a big fan of classical music, and Bach least of all.

Tom turned toward her. "That's Bach, isn't it? Is he playing without music?"

"It is Bach. He can memorize the music with just one glance. He thinks in music, instead of words. But here's the thing, I've taken him up to Columbia to play for experts. They say he has potential, but that to be a virtuoso, he needs to learn how to play with more emotion. I'm not sure that's possible for him. But he's young yet. When he gets a little older, I'll need to figure out how to get him lessons with a master piano instructor. Right now, we're just working on our verbal and life skills."

She was babbling. He couldn't possibly be interested in all the details of Aiden's profound gift for music. It was a gift that came with a huge price tag.

So she shut her mouth abruptly and turned toward the kitchen, needing to put distance between herself and Dr. Dreamy.

"We're just having frozen chicken lasagna with white sauce and a green salad. And when I say green, I mean green. We don't eat tomatoes or red peppers or anything like that. We can only have other green things in the salad, so there will be some green peppers and green onions. No white ones. Food has to be one color."

Damn. She was *still* babbling. Well, maybe it was a good thing to give Tom a full accounting of Aiden's rules about food, so he'd understand what he was getting into. And so he wouldn't even think about getting too close.

He followed her into the kitchen. "The wine's already cold. Where's your corkscrew?"

She handed him the bottle opener and pulled down a couple of glasses. He made short work of opening and pouring the wine; his long-fingered hands were as beautiful as his face.

Boy, she really had been living in her own little cloister for too long.

"I'm surprised a florist puts up an artificial tree," he said.

"I don't want to spend the money for a real one. At least not until I know that trees are one of the things Aiden likes."

He handed her a glass. "You don't know?"

She took the wine, practically strangling the stem in her grip. "No. Most Christmas trees have something red on them. Red is evil in Aiden's world. And to be honest, I haven't put up a tree for myself in five years."

He lifted his glass. "Well, then, this is a green-letter

day. Here's to discovering Aiden's Christmas likes and dislikes."

The wine was super dry and almost astringent. It made her mouth pucker. She wondered where he'd gotten it. Surely not anywhere in Last Chance. It wasn't the kind of wine people bought in this little town. It was the kind of wine a Yankee might have brought down from Boston. Was he trying to impress her with his northern ways?

Well, she was more of a beer drinker. Most folks in town were beer drinkers first. Tom would learn that eventually.

And then in two years he'd go back to where he came from.

"Brace yourself," she said. "We're likely to discover that Aiden likes absolutely nothing about Christmas."

* * *

Teri Summers was putting up one barrier after another, and using Aiden to deflect Tom's advances. He understood why.

He'd seen his own mother do the very same thing. After Pop died, Ma made a point of telling every man who walked through their front door that Tom was a cancer survivor. She'd get long-winded about the yearly tests, the uncertainty, the long days in the hospital when he was younger.

And she fiercely protected him long after he needed her protection. He loved Ma, but sometimes she was a little bit too fierce. He could see that in Teri, too. She was a terrific mom, but she needed more in her life, just like Ma did.

After dinner, they adjourned to the living room—a long space with a big bay window at one end. Teri resumed the job of assembling a small artificial tree and tried to engage Aiden. The kid was completely uninterested.

Tom could hardly blame him. The tree was lame.

It looked exactly like a plastic version of Charlie Brown's Christmas tree. All the more so because the gigantic bay window dwarfed it. Teri made the situation worse with her bright and shiny conversation about how much fun it was going to be to put lights on the dreadful thing and hang angel ornaments all over it.

Tom didn't know whether she was trying to convince Aiden of this lie or herself. Either way, it wasn't working.

Instead of engaging, the kid pulled out a plastic storage box filled with Matchbox cars and dumped them on the floor. Jimmy had cars like that, and Tom's nephew would make engine sounds and stage spectacular crashes with his cars.

But Aiden's play was entirely different. Aiden began to sort the cars by color.

Tom decided that the way into Teri's good graces was through Aiden. Besides, sorting Matchbox cars seemed like way more fun than decorating a plastic tree that was kind of lopsided. So he got down on the floor, somewhat awkwardly because of his prosthesis, and started helping Aiden.

"You're doing it all wrong," Aiden said without looking at him. "You're an idiot."

Good thing Teri had just left the room in search of an extension cord and therefore didn't hear her son's judgment on his sorting skills. Tom took the criticism in stride. "Oh?" he said. "What am I doing wrong?"

"You hafta sort them by color, and then the Hot Wheels come before the Matchbox ones, and then you have to put them in the right order. Coupes first, four-doors second, then vans and trucks and hot rods."

"Oh. Okay. I got it." He was about to ask about cars with racing stripes until he noticed that none of Aiden's cars were red or had racing stripes. The kid was a color purist.

When they had the cars all sorted according to Aiden's rules, Tom said, "So you don't like Christmas, huh?"

Aiden cocked his head but didn't make eye contact. "Santa is a bad, mean man."

"Okay, but Christmas is about more than Santa, right?"

Aiden didn't respond.

"Your mom says you know your Bible verses. So I'm sure you remember the story in the Gospel of Luke about the time when Jesus was born."

Aiden made brief but significant eye contact. There was a bright gleam in his pale blue eyes. Then he spoke in a rapid fire manner: *"Et pastores erant in regione eadem vigilantes et custodientes vigilias noctis supra gregem suum et ecce angelus Domini stetit iuxta illos et claritas Dei circumfulsit illos et timuerunt timore magno…"*

Wow. It had been a while since Tom had studied Latin, so he couldn't say exactly what the words meant, except that he caught the word *angelus* so he knew the kid was reciting something about angels.

But Aiden quickly clarified the issue by providing an English translation. "And there were in the same country shepherds watching and keeping the night watches over their flock. And behold an angel of the Lord stood by them and the brightness of God shone round about them: and they feared with a great fear…"

Once he'd finished the complete translation, Aiden said, "The King James version is different though." He proceeded to recite that translation as well. He punctuated his recitation by saying, "I can't read Greek yet."

Tom looked up at Teri. She'd given up on the tree and stood there holding a strand of twinkle lights in her hands, a sheen of tears in her eyes and a small half-smile on her kiss-able lips. "He memorizes the Latin, but he can't really speak or translate it." Any mother ought to be proud of these accomplishments, but Teri's voice sounded brittle.

Tom held her gaze for a fraction too long as electricity hummed along his internal circuits. He looked away before his body shorted out.

"Well," he said to Aiden when he'd regained control, "I guess you do know all about the story of the first Christmas. It has nothing to do with Santa."

"Or Christmas trees either." Aiden didn't make eye contact with either Tom or Teri as he unloaded this zinger.

"No, but we always put angels on top of the tree."

"Not always. Last year, there was a star on top of the town tree. And Grandma had a star too."

"For the Star of Bethlehem," Tom said.

Aiden shrugged and started picking up his cars and putting them back in their storage box.

"Would you like to have a big tree with an angel on the top?" he asked.

He got no answer. Which was better than a flat-out no.

"Okay, so would you mind if your mom and I put up a big tree in the bay window with an angel on the top?"

"No red stuff on it. Red is evil."

"No red. Would gold be okay?"

He got no response.

"Okay, so we're going to get a real tree. Would you like to take a walk with me and your mom up to the Jaycees lot by the Methodist church? They've got trees there. You could pick the one you liked best."

"Are we going to see the angels?"

"Well, it's dark, and I'm sure Golf—"

"We can go see the angels," Teri interrupted.

Tom turned his gaze on Teri. The sheen of tears was gone. In its place was a tiny smile that revealed a dimple in her left cheek that he hadn't noticed before. Her smile was as good as hot chocolate for warming up his insides. "Golfing for God is kind of a long walk, don't you think?" he asked.

"Yes it is, but we're not going to Golfing for God. We're going to make a tour of nativity scenes. Every churchyard in town has one on display, and they all have angels. It might take a little while before we get to the Methodist Church and the Jaycees lot. But I warn you, we know only one Christmas carol and you might be sick and tired of hearing 'It Came Upon a Midnight Clear' before we're done."

AIDEN SPEAKS

There are four angels in town. One at the AME church. One at Christ Church. And two at the Methodist church.

There was only one angel at the Methodist church the last time Mom and I took a walk.

None of the churches has a heavenly host. Only Golfing for God. But the heavenly host at Golfing for God has only twelve small angels. The Methodist angel is ten feet tall.

I can't figure out if the second angel is a boy or a girl. It kinda hurts to look at that angel. It's bright and makes my head feel kinda funny. It's like looking at a candle, only not as scary because it's an angel.

It told me that Raphael was bringing me a present on Christmas Eve.

I don't like presents wrapped in red paper.

I don't like surprises. The new Methodist angel is a surprise. I don't know if I like it.

I told Mom about the angel and the present.

She said she didn't see the second angel. But that's not a

surprise. I see lots of things that other people don't see. Like how Dr. Tom didn't notice the difference between Matchbox cars and Hot Wheels cars until I showed him.

Dr. Tom bought a Christmas tree called a Douglas fir. It's five feet three and a half inches tall. Dr. Tom carried it back home on his shoulder. It made the house smell funny. Mom put a lot of gold stuff on it.

I played Bach's Prelude and Fugue No. 1 in C Major seven times in a row without making any mistakes before Mom told me it was bedtime.

CHAPTER FIVE

So far it had been an okay evening, maybe even a good one. Teri had to take her blessings in small doses. Counting them too soon could make them evaporate.

But Aiden undeniably enjoyed the tour of the nativity scenes in town. And Dr. Tom, as her son called him, said he had enjoyed the walk too.

Aiden also hadn't objected to the tree. He might not have put a single ornament on the branches, but sometimes his indifference was the best Teri could hope for. He even went off to bed without a struggle.

Best of all, her son more than tolerated Dr. Tom, and that was a positive, if slightly terrifying, sign.

A woman knows when a man is interested. Teri wasn't imagining things. But she refused to lead with her heart. Her heart was bruised and battered and busted. She ought to hang a sign on her chest that said "Fragile, Extremely Breakable."

So, when Tom didn't leave right after the tree was finished, she escaped into the kitchen, where she brewed a pot of coffee and thought about her next moves. She needed distance.

And what better way to accomplish this than to push him back into the doctor box where he wouldn't pose a threat to her equilibrium.

She poured the coffee into two blue mugs with happy snowmen on them. Then she headed back to the living room, where she started speaking before she could even hand Tom his cup.

"So, what's your professional opinion?" she asked. "About Aiden, I mean. He notices small details that most of us ignore. But this business about an invisible angel in the Methodist churchyard isn't a small detail, is it? Do you think, as a doctor, that it's possible for a kid like Aiden to imagine an angel? To be honest, I didn't think he was capable of something like that. He's always been so utterly literal up to this point in his development."

She handed Tom his mug. He sat on her battered couch, looking comfortable. Of course he was at ease. He practically oozed self-assurance. And why not? He probably had a zillion girlfriends up north. She imagined women threw themselves at him all the time.

He took a slow sip from his coffee. For a Yankee, Tom sure could take his time about some things. He didn't fit the stereotype, except for his accent.

Which he chose to employ. "Sit down, Teri, you've been on your feet all day." He patted the couch next to him.

Damn. She wanted to sit down. She also wanted to run into the kitchen and hide in the broom closet.

He seemed to understand her dilemma. He didn't force the issue, thank goodness. Instead, he just assumed the doctor role, as she had hoped he would. "Maybe you're underestimating Aiden," he said. "Children have vivid imaginations.

I don't see why a kid on the spectrum can't imagine things. Look at Temple Grandin. She imagined a better way to manage cattle, and she's autistic."

"Yes, but there's a difference between imagining a new way to manage livestock headed for the slaughter and just imagining a conversation with an angel."

"Teri, I wouldn't worry about this. Isn't it a good thing that he's imagined an angel who's going to give him a present? He's just projected the whole Santa thing onto his friend Raphael. I don't see that it's something to worry about."

"Okay. But what happens when Raphael lets him down?"

"And you're so sure that Raphael will do that?" His eyes reflected the tree's lights like a holiday beacon. "Sit down, Teri. It's been a long, hard day for you."

She sat, but not right next to him. It seemed wise to leave a little distance.

He put his coffee down and massaged his left knee.

"I hope you didn't do something to your knee carrying the tree back for us," she said. "We could have gotten someone to deliver it for us tomorrow."

"What, and miss the fun?" He inhaled through his nose. "It finally smells like Christmas in here. There's nothing quite like a Douglas fir for the scent, is there?"

"Thank you. Really. The tree is wonderful. But you've been massaging that knee ever since we got back."

"I didn't hurt my knee carrying the tree, Teri. It's an old injury."

"Football?"

He chuckled. "I'm getting the feeling that football is a religion down here."

"That's because it is. Especially college ball."

"I hate to disappoint you, but I never played football." He

bent over and pulled up the left cuff of his blue jeans. Instead of a sock-clad ankle, a mechanical foot was shoved into his Nike and a shiny metal post came out of the shoe's collar.

"Oh!" It was all she could manage. She hadn't even noticed a limp, except when he'd carried the tree back from the lot. "Uh, were you wounded in Iraq or Afghanistan?" she asked.

He shook his head. "It's amazing how many people ask me that. It tells you something about the kinds of injuries our soldiers are sustaining these days. But no. When I was just a little younger than Aiden, I was diagnosed with bone cancer. I lost the leg when I was seven. Luckily they caught the cancer early. The docs saved the knee and my life."

"Well, thank goodness for that." Teri suddenly didn't know where to look or what to do with her hands. So she clasped her coffee cup and hid behind it.

"It was a long, scary few years. Ma and Pop had to sacrifice a lot for me, to pay the doctor bills and to see me through all that radiation and chemotherapy. I lost my hair, and all the other kids in my class got scared of me. So you see, I know something about what parents go through when they have kids with challenges. I'm not equating myself or my problems with Aiden's. I'm just saying that I understand."

She finally found the courage to put her mug down and turn toward him. Damn. He was handsome. Too handsome. He shouldn't be interested in someone like her. Yearning for him was dangerous. She'd get hurt.

But there he sat with a truly intense look in his eyes that put flutters in her gut. And how could she not desire him? Somehow he'd brought the holiday spirit right into her home. She hadn't thought it was even possible for that to happen this year. Not after her family had abandoned her.

Tom scooted toward her.

She knew what was coming. He even hesitated for a moment, as if to give her time to pull back if she wanted to. But she didn't pull back. She didn't even want to anymore. She let him move in.

His mouth was warm and firm as it closed over hers, his tongue soft when it connected with hers. The kiss unleashed a torrent of carnal thoughts and urges that Terri had dammed up years ago, when her marriage had failed. For a moment, she lost her mind. She ran her fingers up through his hair. He did the same to her. She was about to suggest something ridiculous when he pulled back.

"I've had a very nice time, Teri," he said. "Can I come for dinner tomorrow?"

He stood up.

He was leaving?

Uh, probably a good idea. She walked him to the door. They kissed again, and it was harder the second time not to suggest something that would really have the gossips working overtime.

Wow. Poets wrote sonnets about kisses like the one she and Tom had just shared. The kind of kisses that come right before the happily-ever-after. The kind that awaken true love. Teri had waited all her life for a storybook kiss.

But as she watched Tom stroll away from her door she reminded herself that fairy tales were about as real as the angel Aiden thought he'd seen in the Methodist churchyard.

* * *

Somehow Tom Crawford managed not only to invite himself for dinner and kisses on Tuesday, but he showed up to be fed, take Aiden to see the angels at the Methodist churchyard, and dispense a few more killer kisses on Wednesday. Thursday he disappeared without explanation.

This turn of events confirmed that Teri had inadvertently developed an unrequited crush on the new doc in town.

And then Friday morning he called, surprising the heck out of her. She was at her workbench in the shop assembling yet another magnolia leaf wreath. She put down her tools and punched the Talk button. "Tom," she said in her huskiest come-hither voice.

"Morning," he said, his voice deep enough for any woman to fall right into it. There ensued an adolescent moment of silence in which Teri's pulse climbed and her insides melted. That, alone, should have cautioned her. This crush on Tom was foolish. She should say goodbye right now.

But she didn't.

"Last night I signed a sublease on a furnished condo at Edisto Pines," he said into the silence. "I didn't have much to move in so I'm officially out of the Jonquil House B and B. I'd like to invite you and Aiden for dinner tonight."

Dinner? At some place other than home? Not a good idea. But somehow Teri couldn't quite say that out loud. No man had ever offered to cook her dinner before. Certainly not her ex, who expected her to be a wife, mother, florist, chauffeur, maid, cook, laundress, and bottle washer. Having a man cook for her was...Well, it turned her on.

But then, she'd been living like a nun the last few years so that shouldn't have surprised her.

When the silence stretched into awkwardness, Tom took an audible breath and said, "Look, Teri, I get it. Aiden can be funny about food. But I think I can manage it. And besides, he needs to get out more. And so do you."

He was right, of course. "What are you planning to serve?"

"Well, I've got a pot of Boston baked beans in the slow cooker. Usually I eat the beans with bratwurst. These foods are both sort of brown. Aiden doesn't have any issues with brown food, does he?"

"No. But I don't think he's ever eaten baked beans or bratwurst, which means he'll probably turn up his nose."

"I could make mac and cheese for him. I make a mean mac and cheese." Tom's voice sounded warm and smiley.

"Mac and cheese is his favorite food."

"Of course it is. It's every kid's favorite food."

"I thought doctors frowned on mac and cheese."

"It's like everything in life. Mac and cheese in moderation won't kill you."

"Thank the Lord, because sometimes it's the only thing that gets me through dinnertime."

He laughed. "So, six thirty?"

She paused, a flock of excuses circling her mind. This was going so fast. Maybe she should put on the brakes.

Or maybe she should just say yes.

* * *

Tom was looking forward to hosting Teri and Aiden for dinner, even if he wasn't the world's greatest cook. Ma and Martha had both told him that his baked beans were quite tasty, and that meant something, because his mother and sister were both terrific cooks.

And who could screw up brats? Plus, his condo came with a gas grill out back and the locals definitely believed in year-round grilling. But that was easy when the average daytime December temperature was sixty degrees.

So he had the menu, simple as it was, covered.

Still, he wanted to make the evening special. So he'd gotten a no-iron white tablecloth and some votive candles at Walmart. A bouquet of orange lilies from the BI-LO completed his dinner table.

So, when the doorbell rang at six thirty, the table was set, the food was ready, and the candles were lit.

He hurried to his door and let his guests into the small vestibule entrance. Teri had her hair down. She wore a gold Christmas tree pin on her moss green cable-knit sweater. Her changeable eyes picked up the color of her cardigan as well as the pin's sparkle.

Aiden stood right in front of her, wearing a blue jacket and his school uniform, which consisted of blue chinos and a white golf shirt. He was clutching his angel figurine—Raphael, the angel of healing.

Tom caught Teri's gaze for a long, intimate moment before she held out a Tupperware container. "I brought Rice Crispies treats for dessert. They're Aiden's favorite." Their hands brushed as she handed over the cookies. Reaction zigzagged through him like a bolt of lightning.

Tom backed away from the door, anticipation rising in his chest. He couldn't wait for Teri to see the table, set with candles and flowers. He had a feeling that no one had made an effort for Teri in a very long time. And he wanted her to know that, even though his cooking skills were limited, he viewed this dinner as special.

She took two or three steps into the apartment—just far enough to see into the dining room. The look on her face went from merry to horrified. Her eyes widened, she gasped, and then she said, "Oh, shit, candles."

He'd never heard her use an expletive before. So he turned, expecting to find his dinner table on fire or something. But there was nothing wrong with the candles. The table looked perfect.

Teri rushed into the dining room just as Aiden began to howl.

Tom had heard this scream once before, on the day Aiden had come to the clinic. The boy shrieked as if the candles had branded him, or scalded him, or flayed the skin from his body. Even though the candles were in the next room. The sound raised Tom's hackles.

His healer instincts took over. He raced to Aiden's side. But as he reached for the boy, he remembered the rules. He held back while confusion and helplessness assailed him. He was a doctor. He was supposed to help people in pain, but this was beyond him.

He got down on his knees, even though his prosthesis made that difficult. "What is it, Aiden?" he asked, balling his hands into fists to stop himself from touching the child. Every instinct screamed that the boy needed to be hugged, touched, protected.

"It's the candles," Teri said from behind him. "He's terrified of them."

Tom looked over his shoulder. Teri had blown out the votives. Smoke curled up from the wicks, perfuming the air with an acrid scent.

"I'm so sorry. I didn't know," he said. All his great plans had come apart at the seams.

"It's okay. I didn't think you'd put candles on the table," she replied. "It was a sweet gesture, really." She sounded tired and maybe even a little embarrassed.

What an utter disaster.

Just then, Aiden turned and ran back toward the front door. He threw himself into the corner where the wall met the door frame. He started rocking, banging his head against the wall with each forward motion. Then he began to sing "It Came Upon a Midnight Clear" in a breathless, terrified way.

Tom pushed himself up from the floor with some difficulty and hurried to Aiden's side, aching to touch him, to comfort him, to stop him from banging his head against the wall. But he held back. It was the hardest thing he'd ever done. He needed to do something. And then he remembered what Teri had done in the clinic. So he began to sing the Christmas carol, consciously slowing the song's rhythm so Aiden would slow down too.

A moment later, Teri came to stand beside him. She began to sing in a clear alto that complemented Tom's bass and Aiden's soprano. After a few times through, the music transformed itself from frantic to uplifting. Tom had been too busy to do much singing in the last few years, although he'd been in his high school chorus.

He'd forgotten how singing could sometimes feel precisely like praying.

AIDEN SPEAKS

I don't like surprises. I don't like candles. Candles make my head feel funny.

Dr. Tom surprised me with the candles. I sang "It Came Upon a Midnight Clear" thirty-seven times before my head felt better.

Then we ate dinner. I ate mac and cheese. I like mac and cheese.

Then me and Mom and Dr. Tom took a walk to see the angels. The big Methodist angel told me I should go to the tree lighting.

I told Mom about the Methodist angel. She said, "We'll see."

And then Dr. Tom said, "I can take him, if you're going to be busy."

And Mom said, "We'll see."

We went home at ten o'clock. Mom said it was too late to play piano.

I was mad at Mom. I went to my room.

She came in twenty-three minutes later and read me the story of "The Emperor's New Clothes" from the book *Andersen's Fairy Tales*. She said the story had an important lesson in it about telling the truth.

The people in the story were all liars. I don't like liars. I don't ever lie.

I told Mom I wanted to go to the Christmas tree lighting.

And she looked at me for thirty seconds before she said, "We'll see."

She turned out the light.

I went to sleep.

CHAPTER SIX

Teri had been responsible for decorating the town tree for the last four years. On the night of the lighting, she was crazy busy. But for the first time, she was also nervous. In fact, the butterflies in Teri's stomach had gone militant.

She was worried about the lights because she'd switched out the multicolored ones for plain white. And she'd done that because Tom was bringing Aiden to the lighting ceremony. She couldn't risk having any red lights on the tree this year.

Aiden had never wanted to come to the tree lighting before, and Teri had been happy to continue that tradition. But this year Aiden had changed his mind. He wanted to come. He was insistent. And Tom had taken Aiden's side, which she most definitely resented.

But then again, how could she resent Tom? For the first time in eons—maybe ever—a man had actually lit candles for her. Every time she thought about Aiden's reaction, she inwardly cringed.

Of course, Tom had rolled right along with the punches. There had been a moment when they were singing together when she'd almost felt as if they were a family.

Which was another reason for the queasiness in the pit of her stomach.

Tom had upset her equilibrium. She felt as if she were trying to balance while simultaneously walking about three feet off the ground. Tragically, she'd never been any good at gymnastics. A heart-breaking spill inevitably loomed in her future. Not to mention the fact that the members of the Christ Church Ladies' Auxiliary and the Methodist Altar Guild were sure to notice sooner or later. And since Lillian had stirred up a lot of dislike for Tom, that would be bad for her.

Oh, good Lord, what was she going to do? Falling for Tom Crawford was easy. He was like an answer to her prayers. No one should be so perfect.

And yet his kisses *were* perfect. The way he'd responded to last night's disaster had been perfect. And then he'd called this morning and offered to take Aiden to McDonald's for dinner and then bring him to the lighting ceremony later. And that was the perfect solution for managing Aiden.

Even worse, Aiden wanted to spend the evening with Dr. Tom. Although the allure might have had more to do with McDonald's fish sandwiches than Tom Crawford himself.

How could she say no? Aiden's father had never once offered to take Aiden anywhere. And besides, this year was supposed to be about tailoring Christmas to suit Aiden.

So she'd instructed Judy to hand Aiden off to Tom this afternoon.

Still, having Aiden attend the tree lighting was fraught with danger. The Davis High a cappella choir would be singing several secular holiday songs, none of which had any lyrics about angels. Aiden was likely to pipe up at any moment, singing "It Came Upon a Midnight Clear." Or, worse yet, he might get upset because someone sang out of key.

Thank goodness Santa wasn't making a guest appearance. If Santa had been on tonight's program, she would have insisted that Aiden stay home.

As the hour of the lighting approached, her heart and stomach decided to instigate an internal riot. She refused to faint or hurl. That would be so unprofessional.

She took her place on the steps of city hall right next to Mayor Abernathy and County Executive LaFlore and tried to breathe deeply. Panic would not help. She still had to make sure the tree blazed into glorious light when the time came.

A group of almost a hundred people had gathered in the town square. Tom and Aiden stood in the front row, each of them wearing goofy, green-and-white-striped stocking hats. How on earth had Tom gotten her son to wear stripes?

She didn't know. But they looked like a couple of Santa's helpers. Not that she'd ever tell Aiden that. Her neck spasmed the moment Mayor Abernathy kicked the ceremonies off by introducing the Davis High choir.

Here it came. Aiden would misbehave. He would say something terrible.

The choir launched into a rousing rendition of "Jingle Bells" in four-part harmony.

She kept her gaze trained on Aiden, ready to jump into the fray the moment things unraveled. But nothing happened.

Aiden made no objection to the singing. In fact, he didn't seem to be paying any attention at all.

He stood as still as one of Elbert Rhodes's fiberglass angels, looking up at the twenty-foot blue spruce that had come all the way from Colorado. Teri glanced up but didn't see anything amiss. Except, of course, that a star topped the tree instead of an angel. Oh, boy. *Please, God, don't let him object to the tree-topper.*

The choir finished their song, and Mayor Abernathy stepped to the mic. He welcomed everyone and then introduced Reverend Timothy Lake, who said a short prayer. And then the public school kindergarten class came up to the podium, where a dummy button had been set up.

The mayor and the kids counted down. "Three, two, one…" The kids pushed the dummy button, and Clay Rhodes, well hidden behind the tree, plugged in the power.

Thousands of white twinkle lights came on and illuminated swags of gold tinsel. The crowd applauded…for the most part. Teri heard a few voices of dissent.

The mayor leaned toward Teri. "I don't remember approving a budget for new lights."

"You didn't. I paid for them myself."

The mayor gave her the stink eye.

"I'm not charging the city for them, so don't worry."

The mayor still looked perturbed, and it occurred to Teri that she'd probably lost this job for the foreseeable future. But it was worth it if Aiden could come to a tree lighting and not misbehave. She looked down at her son. He wasn't really paying much attention to the tree. He was still looking up. And Tom was smiling one of those I-told-you-so smiles as he gazed right into Teri's eyes.

For some reason, the look on his face annoyed her.

* * *

"The angel says I need to be here at midnight on Christmas Eve," Aiden said.

Tom pulled his gaze away from Teri. "What?"

"It says I have to be here at midnight. You know, like in the song."

"Is the angel up there?" Tom glanced up at the top of the tree. No angel, just a star.

"It was there. Didn't you see it? It was the Methodist angel."

Tom hunkered down, feeling the pressure on his knee. He tried to look Aiden in the eye, but the boy didn't like making eye contact. From what he'd read, that was pretty common for kids on the spectrum. Seeing things that weren't there wasn't common though. Kids on the spectrum tended to be literal.

A tiny part of Tom wanted to believe that an angel would appear in the little town of Last Chance at midnight on Christmas Eve, even though believing something like that was insane. He was a doctor and a scientist. That side of him immediately began to wonder whether there was a medical reason for the boy's visions.

But Tom, the man, was more than a doctor and scientist. Once he'd been a little boy too. And that little boy, with his strong Catholic faith, had been willing to tell anyone who would listen that his guardian angel had been with him in the darkest days of his illness. He'd never actually seen the angel though. But seeing was not necessary for believing. He'd *known* the angel was with him.

"Well," he said to Aiden, "I guess we'll have to come back here at midnight on Christmas Eve."

Aiden nodded but didn't make eye contact. "I have to come. The angel said it was important."

"What angel?" Teri asked as she joined them.

Tom stood up and faced her.

"What's this about midnight on Christmas Eve?" she asked.

"The angel," Aiden said, "it told me I needed to be here at midnight. Like in the song. You think the angels will sing for me?"

"Maybe," Tom said, even though Teri was giving him a deeply worried look that edged on annoyance. He'd definitely overstepped a boundary here. But what else could he say? He wasn't going to disabuse Aiden's faith in angels. He doubted he would succeed even if he tried.

* * *

Good grief, Tom was *encouraging* Aiden's angel fantasy. And as much as she was overjoyed that Aiden had behaved, she couldn't let this go on any longer.

"Aiden, there is no angel," she said.

Her son looked at her. "You're a liar," he said. "I don't like liars. I want to go home now." He turned and headed down Chancelor Street toward home.

"Aiden, stop," she said, chasing after him. She got a few steps before Tom grabbed her by the arm.

"Teri, why on earth did you say that?"

"What?"

"About the angel."

"Because the angel isn't real. If he comes out here at midnight, he's going to be disappointed. It's not like with Santa. I mean, I can buy presents and fill stockings. But how can I possibly make an angel appear at midnight?"

"You can't. You just have to have faith."

Teri had no answer for this. So she pulled her arm out of his grasp and followed Aiden.

Tom followed her.

When they got home, Teri unlocked the door for Aiden, but then turned to face Tom.

Her emotions reeled. She was so angry with him that her hands shook.

"You don't know me or my son," she said.

"Look, Teri, I—"

"No, Tom, you've had dinner with us a couple of times. You bribed Aiden with McDonald's. But you don't live with him day to day. So you don't understand. If he goes to the town square at midnight he's going to be disappointed. Honestly—" Her voice broke. "It's hard enough with my family banishing me. I just need to have a reasonably calm and peaceful holiday. That's all I want. A calm holiday that Aiden can enjoy on some level. Going on a wild goose chase after angels doesn't sound like a calm and peaceful holiday to me."

"I'm sorry. I didn't mean to—"

"Look, Tom, things are happening way too fast. I think we need to back off a little bit, you know? And I'm just not sure that encouraging Aiden about this angel is healthy."

"Okay. I understand about you and me. It is happening fast. But the truth is, I'm deeply attracted to you."

Teri's face heated. She was attracted to him. The wild, crazy, lonely woman inside wanted to throw open her door and let the man in. But she couldn't. She was Aiden's mother first. She had to protect her boy. "I'm sorry, Tom, really I am. Good night." She tried to close the door on him, but he leaned in, blocking the jamb.

"Teri, I understand why you need some time and space. I do. And I know you don't think I have the right to give you advice about Aiden. But I want you to think about letting Aiden go to the village green at midnight on Christmas Eve. It could be like the way you take him to Golfing for God instead of church on Sunday. Going to the green could be a substitute for midnight mass."

"And what if nothing happens? What if the angel abandons him?"

"That's generally not what angels do."

"And what, you're an angel expert?"

"No, but—"

"Good night, Tom." She closed the door firmly in his face.

CHAPTER SEVEN

Tom had plenty to occupy his time over the next week. He worked overtime at the clinic on digitizing the medical records. It was a thankless job, especially since Dana, his assistant and the woman who worked with the records, was angry with him. Lillian Bray had definitely done some damage to his reputation.

Tom also introduced himself to Father Weiss at Saint Mary's Catholic Church, bought some items for his new apartment, finished his Christmas shopping, and mailed off a package of gifts to his mother, sister, and nephew in Framingham.

But being busy hadn't done one thing to drive Teri Summers from the back of his brain. She'd settled in there, like the snow on the Berkshires in late November. She wasn't going anywhere for a long, long time.

If she hadn't been a florist, he might have bought her a big bouquet of roses with an apology or something, not that he felt the need to apologize for anything. But giving flowers to a florist seemed kind of dumb. And as much as he wanted to bypass mass tomorrow and run into Teri at Golfing for God, that would be just a bit too much like stalking her or something.

No. He needed another excuse to bump into her. So he started buying lunch at the Kountry Kitchen. The café sat right in the middle of downtown Last Chance, across the street and one block north of Last Chance Bloomers. Flo, the waitress at the Kitchen, gave him less than friendly service, but he kept coming back every day, just so he could walk past Teri's shop every noontime.

She was in there. He knew this because he always stopped and looked in the window. He'd done that six days in a row. And she was still letting his calls go to voice mail.

This daily routine felt distinctly adolescent. Noontime was, without question, the best time of the day because he'd catch a glimpse of her. But he was getting nowhere fast.

A week after the tree lighting, he was sitting in the Kountry Kitchen picking at his barbecue sandwich when a woman with blond hair, brown eyes, and a voluptuous build slipped into the booth's facing bench. "Hey," she said, "I'm Savannah Randall. I need to have a word with you."

Tom tensed. Here it came, someone else who wanted to bawl him out about Mrs. Bray or explain to him how things worked in this town. The whole Lillian Bray situation, overlaid with his frustration over Teri, had left him feeling like a failure. He'd come here to serve these people. But they didn't want him here.

He forced a phony bedside smile. "What can I do for you, Mrs. Randall?"

"Not one blessed thing, Doc. It's what I can do for you." She turned over her shoulder and called to the waitress. "Flo, can I have a Diet Coke?"

Flo gave Savannah a hard look and turned away, ignoring Mrs. Randall the way she frequently ignored Tom.

Mrs. Randall tossed her blond hair back over her shoulder. "Florreta, you hear me. Don't you ignore me. And don't you give me that look. Lillian went up to see a doctor in Columbia yesterday. And you know what? She's got arthritis in her knees and the doc's put her on some pills that actually work. Everyone in this town knows Doc Cooper gave her sugar pills. How on earth were sugar pills supposed to help her?"

Savannah turned back toward Tom with a grin. "Don't you worry, hon, folks will come around. In fact, I heard that Lillian's husband is grateful to you for insisting that she go see a specialist."

A moment later, Flo came back with Savannah's Diet Coke. "Is what you said true?"

"It is. And y'all should quit talking trash about the new doc. I heard he graduated at the top of his medical class and could have been a surgeon but decided on family medicine instead."

Flo gave Tom a small smile. "Really?"

He nodded. "I didn't have the heart for surgery," he said. Another strike against him as far as Ma was concerned.

"You want some more sweet tea?" Flo asked.

"No, thanks, I'm fine," he said.

Flo eyed Savannah again. "You here to give him advice?"

Savannah blushed to her hairline. "I'm just visiting with the new doc, Flo."

"Uh-huh, I can see that." She turned and walked away.

"Well," Savannah said on a rush of air, "I guess the rest of the town is going to know that I dropped in to say hey."

"Uh, yeah, I guess so. Thanks for making an announcement about Mrs. Bray. I'm happy to hear that she's getting the medical attention she needs."

"Me too. But to be honest, that's not the only reason I dropped by. Honey, you need help."

"I do?"

"Yes, you do. And I'm going to give you some. You see, the truth is, walking by Last Chance Bloomers and looking in the window every day is not going to get you what you want."

So people had noticed his ineffective courtship of the town florist. That was slightly humiliating. "Okay, what should I do? I can't exactly send her flowers, can I?"

"Why not?"

"Because she's—"

"Buy them at the FTD florist in Allenberg and send them to her with something romantic on the card. Write the card yourself too. The note's the important thing. Teri needs more than a little shove to jump into the pool again. She's convinced herself that no one could ever be interested in her."

"So I gather."

She gave him a warm smile and reached across the table to pat his hand. "Everyone here loved Doc Cooper. And it's hard for folks to change. But I want you to know that I approve of you sending Lillian to see a specialist, and I approve of you telling Arlo Boyd he needs to go on a diet. And also, I'm bringing my aunt in next week for her annual checkup. She's getting real old. I'm worried about her."

"Everyone gets old, Mrs. Randall."

"Oh, for goodness sake, call me Savannah. And, really, Tom, when it comes to courting a woman, you just need to be persistent. Teri has built a wall around her heart and then dug a moat just to be sure. I can see you've already shaken the foundations of that wall. You just need to keep up the siege." She leaned in again and spoke in a near-whisper. "And it's perfectly okay to play dirty."

"Play dirty?"

"Go for her most vulnerable spot. The one thing she's foolishly trying to protect."

"Aiden?"

Her smile lit up her face like a dozen flaming candles. "You are a very smart man. I'm a mother, Doc. I've learned the hard way that being a mother means letting go of your baby from the very moment he comes into your arms. If you do your job right, you have to let him take falls and experience disappointments and, well, help him grow up. That's hard for any mother. But a mother with a sick or special child—well, it's nearly impossible. And I have a strong feeling that you understand exactly what I mean."

"You're talking about my childhood, aren't you? But how could you possibly know..."

Savannah pushed up from the table. "Don't ask me how I know things, Doc. I don't even understand it myself. But I have a strong feeling that your childhood will give you all the answers you need. God bless you, Doc, for seeing the truth about Teri. And Lillian.

"And welcome to Last Chance."

* * *

Teri's front doorbell rang just as she was putting away groceries. It was 6:00 p.m. on the Saturday before Christmas. She was dog, dead tired. Everyone and their brother wanted their Christmas flower arrangements. She was sick to death of red roses, red carnations, and red poinsettias. In fact, she was starting to see red when she closed her eyes.

So it was kind of surprising, and maybe a little bit like falling into the Twilight Zone, when she opened her front door to find Jasper Wilkins, the delivery guy for her competition, standing on her porch holding a vase with a dozen white roses in it.

No red roses, red carnations, red holly berries. Just white roses.

"Hey, Teri," Jasper said with a big, slightly toothless grin. "These are for you. Looks like you've got yourself a not-so-secret admirer—the new doc in town." He handed her the vase. "Looks like you're in for a very merry Christmas." He winked before he turned and headed back to his panel van.

Oh boy, everyone in town was going to know that the new doc had sent the local florist a dozen white roses. White, for goodness sake. Hell, she only ever used white roses in bridal bouquets.

Although she had to admit that a dozen white roses in a simple vase made a real statement. She put the flowers on her dining room table not knowing precisely what to think. No one had ever sent her flowers. Ever. Not even her ex-husband. Not on Mother's Day, or Valentine's Day, or their anniversary.

She hadn't ever expected flowers from anyone. She had the flower situation covered. She brought flowers home from the store. She grew flowers in her perennial border. She was the treasurer of the Last Chance Flower and Garden Club. Flowers were her thing. Guys knew this and stayed away.

But Doc Crawford was not like other guys. He wasn't staying away, was he? She stood there absolutely gob-smacked. Until this moment, she hadn't even realized what she was missing. All these years making arrangements for other people. Writing out romantic cards. Hell, helping clue-less guys come up with romantic cards. And she'd never, ever been on the receiving end.

She plucked the small card from its plastic holder and opened it. The handwriting was bold, masculine, and just a tiny bit illegible. Betsy Ashworth, the owner of the FTD florist shop in Allenberg, hadn't written this card. Tom had written it himself.

Her pulse went erratic, just like it did every noontime when the man strolled down Palmetto Avenue and stopped to glance through the windows of her shop. He'd been doing this for a solid week, and as much as she didn't want to ad-mit it, that daily moment when Tom walked by Last Chance Bloomers was the best moment of her day.

She read the card.

> *White roses to remind you of angel wings. Meet me at the village green at midnight on Christmas Eve.*
>
> *Love,*
> *Tom*

Love? Goodness, he'd signed the card with the L-word, and it made her heart pirouette in her chest and her mouth go dry.

Village green? No one in town referred to the town square as the village green. No one except Tom, the Yankee from Boston.

What was she going to do about this? She wasn't ready to fall in love with anyone. In her experience, romantic love was highly overrated. Not only had her ex been an idiot, but the guys who bought flowers from her were just as likely to send a dozen red roses to their mistresses as their wives. In fact, more so.

More important, she wasn't ready to meet him for an angelic experience. Chances were, a meeting like that would turn into one of Aiden's epic meltdowns. Not on Christmas Eve in the middle of town. Let Aiden have his annual Christmas meltdown in private this year. Isn't that what her family had wanted when they uninvited her?

No, she wasn't ready for Tom or the angels or the town square at midnight.

She picked up the flowers, ready to toss them in the trash. But she couldn't throw them away. They were so beautiful. So utterly thoughtful. And the man who sent them was kind and patient and knew how to kiss.

"Damn," she muttered as she set them back down. What was she going to do now?

* * *

Teri did nothing about the roses, except maybe enjoy them in a clandestine way. And she might have enjoyed them even more if Tom had continued to stroll by the store. But on the following Monday, four days before Christmas, Tom didn't make his daily noontime trek to the Kountry Kitchen. And he didn't do it on Tuesday either. And he didn't call. Or show up unexpectedly. Or anything.

It was as if he'd disappeared.

Of course, she didn't call him to thank him for the flowers. She'd consciously decided not to do anything about them. And by doing nothing, she'd sent her own message to him.

She wondered if he was still planning to show up at the town square on Christmas Eve, like one of the characters out of that Nora Ephron movie, *Sleepless in Seattle*, where the hero and heroine agree to meet at the Empire State Building on Valentine's Day.

Unfortunately life was not like the movies.

But someone forgot to tell the members of the Christ Church Ladies' Auxiliary this fact. Those ladies seemed to think that life—especially when it came to romance—was exactly like the movies. And when Betsy Ashworth, the owner of Allenberg Flowers, mentioned the roses and the contents of the card (which she'd read, contrary to ethical business practices) to Millie Polk, it was inevitable that every busybody in town would know about Tom and Teri's clandestine meeting at midnight.

Now every customer who came through the doors of Last Chance Bloomers wanted to know if she was planning to meet "that Yankee doctor" at the town square tonight.

The majority of her customers thought it would be oh-so-romantic, even if he was from up north and talked funny. People's attitudes toward Tom were beginning to thaw, especially since that specialist up in Columbia had found something wrong with Lillian and put her on medicine that was actually helping her.

Of course the town might be warming to the new doc, but Lillian had lost a lot of face, so she wasn't all that keen on any of Last Chance's single ladies taking up with that new doctor. She didn't mince words when she bustled into the shop on Christmas Eve morning to pick up her centerpiece. "Teri, you cannot go meet that man at midnight. He's a Yankee, and you know he's going to leave in two years."

"I have no idea what you're talking about." This was Teri's standard reply to the question she had to answer at least ten times every day. She pulled Lillian's centerpiece out of the refrigerator.

"Piffle, of course you know what I'm talking about." Lillian appraised the flowers. "Goodness, Teri, you've outdone yourself." The centerpiece consisted of a swag of Douglas fir interspersed with sprigs of variegated holly and red glass balls. A wide, wired red velveteen ribbon looped on either side of a three-inch red-cinnamon scented candle. She'd made about ten of these centerpieces over the last few days. They were quite popular this year.

"Thanks, Lillian. I'm glad you like it."

"I do." The large church lady looked up. "But I don't want you getting involved with that man. It's not as if Miriam—" Lillian bit off the end of her warning when the old-fashioned bell above the shop's door jingled. Good thing, because Teri really didn't much like it when Lillian started pointing and waving her finger. It was a sure-fire indication that the woman was about to go righteous. And it was mildly uncomfortable to find herself agreeing with Lillian Bray about the wisdom of going out to the town square tonight at midnight.

"Oh, good gracious, it's you, Savannah," Lillian said interrupting her own tirade.

Savannah Randall gave Lillian a wide smile that didn't quite reach her eyes. "Hey, Lillian, I just came to get my centerpiece."

"It's ready," Teri said, escaping to the back room. Savannah's centerpiece was nothing like Lillian's. In fact, Savannah's centerpiece had been a labor of love. Not many folks in Last Chance were looking for something different when it came to Christmas. But she could always count on Savannah.

Savannah had just finished redoing the old Victorian house that had belonged to her family for generations. She wanted something that evoked an earlier time. Teri had created a centerpiece entirely out of natural materials. A swag of magnolia leaves provided the arrangement's backbone. She'd wired orange and clove pomanders to the swag to provide the bulk of the color and a wonderful scent. Tucked around the oranges were sprigs of juniper, pheasant feathers, bundles of cinnamon, and orange pyracantha berries. Aiden would have liked this arrangement. It had not a smidgen of red anywhere in sight.

"Oh my word," Lillian said in an avaricious voice the moment she saw Savannah's centerpiece. "That's just gorgeous. Teri, why on earth didn't you advertise this one?"

"Because it's one of a kind. Savannah commissioned it specifically."

"Oh." Lillian's nose went right in the air. Typical.

She picked up her flowers and gave Teri the evil eye. "You remember what I said, now, you hear? You stay away from that man." She turned and left the store.

"I'm assuming she was talking about Doc Crawford?" Savannah asked, apparently in no hurry to get home and do whatever still needed to be done for tomorrow's holiday.

Teri rolled her eyes. It was rude, she knew, but really. "It would be terrific if the people in this town would just mind their own business."

"It would be. But it's not going to happen." Savannah smiled. "So Lillian thinks you should stay away from the town square, huh? That's kind of sad, really. She can't even be grateful to the doctor who paid attention to her."

"I guess that is kind of sad," Teri said.

"And what about you? How do you feel about the new doc?"

Teri gave Savannah a sober stare. Savannah and her aunt Miriam had a reputation for handing out infallible romantic advice. So there was no way she was going to spill her heart.

Savannah's smile warmed and reached all the way to her eyes this time. "I know this is scary for you, Teri. But, honey, I'm going to give you just a little bit of advice. You should examine your heart and do what it tells you to do. And besides, you have to admit that it's kind of exciting to have a man like Doc Crawford send you flowers."

Teri let go of a completely pathetic sigh. "You won't believe this, but I've never gotten flowers before."

"Of course you haven't. Who sends flowers to a florist?"

"Right. And his note was—well, he kind of hit me right where my doubts are."

"Of course he did. He strikes me as a smart and kind man. I suppose he became a doctor because of what happened to him as a kid. In my opinion, he's got a terrific bedside manner."

"You mean his cancer?"

"Oh, is that what it was? I didn't know. I just knew that he'd been sick as a child."

"He lost his leg."

"You're kidding me? Really? He doesn't even limp."

"He's got a prosthesis. Below the knee."

"Well, I reckon if he's setting up clandestine midnight meetings with you, then you must know him better than a lot of folks in this town." There was a mischievous glimmer in Savannah Randall's eye.

"Savannah, quit. It's embarrassing. Every darn person who's come through the door today has wanted to know what I'm going to do."

"What *are* you going to do?"

"Stay home." She said it clearly and succinctly. She hadn't even known that the decision was made. But that amused sparkle in Savannah's eye had turned the tide. Everyone in town wanted her to risk her heart on a guy who was practically a stranger. A guy who wanted her to allow her son to make a fool of himself in front of the whole town. The more people who expressed interest in her decision, the easier her decision became. She had to keep Aiden away. The angels weren't going to visit the little town of Last Chance. She had to protect him from that disappointment or he'd pitch one of his fits. She wasn't going to let that happen just because she had the hots for Tom Crawford.

That old adage about "nothing ventured, nothing gained" could be turned around on its ear. Nothing ventured, nothing lost was equally as true. And she was not about to lose her head over Aiden's angel fantasies. As for her heart—well, she didn't want to lose that either.

AIDEN SPEAKS

I played the Prelude and Fugue in F from Book II of J. S. Bach's *Well-Tempered Clavier* three times before dinner and four times after dinner. Mom made roasted chicken, which is white. We had white potatoes, but they weren't mashed. Mom took all the brown stuff off them. We had cauliflower, which is white.

I hung up a stocking with a snowman on it. Mom will put stuff in it tonight and then pretend that someone else did it. That's a lie. I don't like it when Mom lies.

At nine forty-seven, Mom said, "It's time for bed."

I said, "It's still one hundred and thirty-three minutes before midnight."

Mom said, "It's your bedtime."

I said, "But we need to be at the town square at midnight."

Mom didn't say anything for about thirty seconds. Then she said, "We are not going to the town square."

This made my chest feel funny. My head felt funny too. I

went upstairs and found Raphael and sang "It Came Upon a Midnight Clear" ten times.

At ten thirteen, Mom came in my room and said, "Put on your pajamas. I don't want any trouble from you."

I don't make trouble. I don't lie. I decided to put on my pajamas just to make her go away. I like being alone. I turned out the light. I stayed in my bed and counted seconds and minutes.

Mom opened the door fifty-seven minutes later but she didn't say anything. I pretended to be asleep.

At eleven twenty, I got out of bed and put on my blue pants and my white shirt. The hall was dark. I went downstairs. The lights on the tree were still burning, and there was stuff in the stocking.

I got my coat and mittens and opened the door.

It was pretty warm outside so I put my mittens in my pocket. Mom doesn't like it when I lose my mittens. I heard a siren, which made my head feel funny. I don't like sirens. I don't like ambulances, especially if they are red.

I walked to the town square.

I waited.

CHAPTER EIGHT

Tom Crawford had a quiet Christmas Eve at home in his new one-bedroom condo. He nuked a chicken pot pie and settled in with a good book. It was lonely, but that was okay. He had an important appointment at midnight.

And not at church either. It would be odd, not going to midnight mass, but Tom had this feeling, down in his gut, that he was supposed to be at the village green at midnight. It was as if fate was pushing him in that direction. He had no doubt that Teri would be there waiting for him, even if she hadn't called or communicated with him since he'd sent the flowers. And he truly believed that an angel might make an appearance, and who would want to miss that?

It was absurd to have such unshakable faith. But you couldn't argue with a determined heart.

Maybe it was what folks in town said about Savannah Randall and her matchmaking advice. Maybe it was hubris, plain and simple. Maybe it was knowing that guardian angels truly did exist for some children, especially sick children and the ones with big challenges. He didn't care. He wasn't into analyzing this. Down where it really mattered, he just *knew* that Teri and Aiden would be waiting for him at midnight.

And then, at precisely eleven twenty-five, just as he was getting ready to stroll down to the village green, reality burst his bubble. His pager buzzed with the emergency code that required him to check in immediately or head to the clinic with all due haste. When this code appeared, it meant someone was battling for his or her life. Emergencies didn't give a crap about a midnight rendezvous or potential angel encounters.

He swallowed his disappointment and checked in. The dispatcher said it was a motorcycle accident with multiple injuries to the lower extremities and potential head trauma. The EMTs were bringing the patient to the clinic to be stabilized and triaged. If the injuries were severe enough, he would be sent via LifeNet helicopter to the Level 1 trauma center in Columbia. Otherwise, the patient would be sent on to the regional medical center in Orangeburg.

Tom met the EMTs at the door of the clinic five minutes later.

"I'm Doctor Crawford. What do we have?" he asked them.

The lead EMT said, "It's Elbert. He's been in a motorcycle accident."

"Elbert? Elbert Rhodes?"

"You know him?"

"Not personally. What do we have?"

"Male patient, mid-sixties. He's got a compound fracture of the right tibia with a lot of debris in the wound. I think it's probably a Grade III fracture. Possible concussion. Road rash on the right upper quadrant. His BP is sixty over ninety and falling. There may be internal injuries. We started a saline drip. He's conscious, but confused."

Annie Jasper, the on-call RN, came running through the doors and spoke with the EMT. "Matt, oh my God, I heard that Elbert got in an accident," she said.

"I'm afraid it's true. He was making a run to the 7-Eleven for something. A pickup ran the red light down on Route 78 and hit him. Knocked Elbert sideways. The pickup driver's from over in Bamberg. Damian said he registered point one three percent BAC. He definitely had one too many eggnogs."

"Have Elbert's next of kin been notified?" Tom asked.

"Yeah. Elbert's oldest son is the county sheriff. He's on his way. The rest of the family is probably in church right now. Elbert isn't much on going to church."

The EMTs parked the gurney in the emergency triage area. Tom assessed Elbert's injuries while Annie seamlessly took over the job of monitoring and reporting on the patient's vital signs. His blood pressure was low and falling. His pulse was thready.

The fracture was a mess, filled with debris.

"We better call the helo from Orangeburg," Tom said.

"Done," said the EMT.

Tom leaned over and got right in the patient's face. "Elbert, can you hear me?"

Elbert Rhodes opened a pair of gray eyes. His pupils looked normal and reactive. So maybe the helmet had saved him from the worst of it. Head trauma was the single most common cause of death in motorcycle accidents. The lower extremity injuries and road rash were common. But the falling BP was the most serious thing. He needed surgical help, stat.

"We're going to get you on some pain meds and clean

up and splint your leg," he said to Elbert slowly. "And then we're going to fly you up to Columbia. You understand?"

Elbert blinked once, and then his gaze shifted away. He seemed to be staring at something on the ceiling. Tom followed his gaze, but there was nothing to see.

"She's here," Elbert said.

"Who's here, Elbert?" Annie asked.

"So pretty. Angel." And then he lost consciousness. Annie reported another precipitous drop in his BP.

Tom went into automatic emergency mode—his medical training and several rotations in the ER kicking in. He pulled out all the stops. When the LifeNet helo took off for the trauma center in Columbia, Elbert Rhodes was still alive, and his condition, while critical, was stable. Tom believed his patient was going to make it.

* * *

Teri had checked on Aiden a little after eleven. He had been fast asleep, thank the Lord. She had expected Aiden to have a full-out meltdown over the angel issue. She was glad he'd accepted her decision not to go traipsing off to the town square on a fool's errand.

It was better this way.

For both of them.

Now it was just before midnight and she didn't quite know what to do with herself, besides sitting here in her bedroom feeling lonely.

Right now everyone in her family, except the youngest of children, would be at midnight services. And after church there would still be stockings to fill and toys to assemble. She'd never gone to bed before midnight on Christmas, except when she was very little.

But here she was pulling her PJs out of the drawer.

She wondered what Tom was doing right now. She imagined him waiting for them in front of the town tree, with the lights twinkling in his eyes and sparking in his hair. She wondered how long he might linger there. Would he be disappointed? Would he call tomorrow?

Damn. She was being stupid. She didn't need a man in her life—not if he intended to encourage Aiden's angel fantasies.

Although she had to admit that Tom wasn't a bit like her ex. Her ex had walked out on her because he couldn't deal with Aiden. Tom, on the other hand, had gotten on the floor to play with her boy. The night of the candle debacle, he'd stood there singing with Aiden for a good twenty minutes—until all of them were hoarse. He'd gotten Aiden to wear stripes. He'd walked with him to the Methodist churchyard three times in a week.

And then there was all the other stuff. The candles on his dinner table. The flowers. The kisses. And the way he'd patiently pursued her despite Aiden's horrid behavior. Tom seemed entirely unconcerned about Aiden's challenges.

She sat on the edge of her bed, thinking these things through. Thinking about her conversation that afternoon with Savannah Randall.

Holy God. She was an idiot.

The town matchmaker—from a line of infallible matchmakers—had stood in her flower shop this afternoon talking about Tom's childhood like she knew all about it. But she didn't really know about it, did she? What had Savannah said?

Something about Tom being kind because of his childhood experiences.

Yeah, kind and wise.

Tom's childhood. Of course.

She checked her watch. Oh crap, she'd been sitting here for almost an hour debating with herself instead of seizing the opportunity that was right in front of her face. It was five minutes to midnight.

They could make it. Aiden might have to go in his PJs. She rushed into Aiden's room.

"Wake up, kiddo, we're going to the—"

The bed was empty. Aiden, it would appear, was way smarter than his mother. He'd left without her.

AIDEN SPEAKS

I waited for the angel for exactly twenty-three minutes. When it arrived, it scared me. Just like in the Bible verse from Luke.

A white light shone around it that was so bright I couldn't look at it without making my eyes feel funny. I couldn't really see because it was so bright. Looking at the angel was like looking into the sun, but I couldn't close my eyes.

"Be not afraid," it sang in the key of D, like a hundred voices all together in perfect harmony.

I wanted to sing too. But my head felt funny and I couldn't remember the words to my favorite song. All I could remember were the verses from the Book of Revelation where it says that the angels fought against a dragon and slayed it. An angel this big could probably break a dragon in half. This angel was bigger than the Methodist angel. It was twenty feet tall—as tall as the town Christmas tree.

Real angels were a lot bigger than Raphael.

The angel laughed, and it was as if it were singing a chord

in the key of C. "I *am* Raphael, little one," he sang. Then he bent toward me, reaching out.

I couldn't step back. I wanted to, but my feet didn't work. I don't like being touched, not even by an angel.

I couldn't even move when he put his hand on my head. I waited to feel the weight of it. I waited to feel the creepy, crawly feeling that always happens when someone touches me. But Raphael's touch didn't feel heavy or creepy. It was like his light got all inside my head and made it feel really, really weird. But it wasn't scary or anything like the funny feeling I get sometimes when people touch me.

And then the angel was gone.

I looked up and I looked left and I looked right, and then I looked behind me. I finally looked down.

One of Mom's candle holders was there right in front of me. There was a white candle in it. The candle was burning.

I got ready to run away because I don't like candles. They get inside my head and scare me. Sort of like the angel did.

Only when I looked at the candle, it was different this time.

The candle was pretty. The flame moved around, and somehow the light reminded me of the big angel. The real Raphael.

I picked up the candle. I turned around because there was a sound coming from down the street. People in the Methodist church were singing.

They were singing "It Came Upon a Midnight Clear."

And I sang with them.

CHAPTER NINE

Teri heard Aiden's voice before she found him. His high, clear boy soprano sounded angelic in the cool, clear night. The words of the old Christmas carol were like a beacon leading her in the darkness.

> *It came upon a midnight clear,*
> *That glorious song of old,*
> *From angels bending near the earth,*
> *To touch their harps of gold:*
> *"Peace on the earth, goodwill to men*
> *From heaven's all gracious King!"*
> *The world in solemn stillness lay*
> *To hear the angels sing.*

This time, though, Aiden was singing it loud and clear as if he was performing the song, instead of using it to comfort himself. She turned the corner and saw him, standing in front of the town tree holding a candle in his hand.

A candle.

Burning in the brass candle stick that she'd bought the Christmas of her senior year at college. Aiden must have taken the candlestick from the sideboard, where she'd put it out as a Christmas decoration.

This made no sense. Why would Aiden even touch that candle? Every time he passed it, he would remind her that he didn't like candles. And how did the candle end up lighted? Did Aiden even know how to use matches or a lighter?

She wasn't the only one heading toward the town square. At least two dozen people who had just come from midnight services were strolling up Palmetto Avenue, drawn by the beautiful, innocent sound of Aiden's singing. And he just kept it up, in a joyful kind of way. Standing there wearing his school uniform, and his gray coat, and the striped, green-and-white elf hat that Tom had given him. And he just kept singing his favorite carol over and over again—every blessed verse.

He looked like an angel himself. Or maybe a fashion-challenged elf. Either way, he had those people smiling and nodding and thinking about the meaning of the season.

Tears sprang to Teri's eyes. Of course she was relieved to have found him safe and sound. But she'd never doubted where she would find him. She should never have tried to keep him away from the town square.

Her tears went so much deeper. He was here, singing a carol, on Christmas. He was holding a light—a symbol of the holiday. He'd connected with Christmas. Finally.

She covered the last few yards in a jog. Her heart light. The weight on her shoulders suddenly lifted. Now she just needed to find Tom. He probably had something to do with this.

But Tom wasn't there. Miriam, Savannah, Todd, and Dash

Randall were there. Jenny and Gabe Raintree were there. Mike and Charlene Taggert were there. So were Ross and Sabina Gardiner, along with Eugene and Thelma Hanks and Nita and Zeph Gibbs. And a half dozen more. They were all watching Aiden and smiling.

A tsunami of disappointment smacked Teri sideways. Tom's absence sucked a lot of the joy out of this moment. Had he been playing with her? Had he lost interest when she didn't call him after he'd given her the flowers? Was he as unreliable as her ex? She tried to push all those negative thoughts back behind a steel door in her mind. They had no business being here on this night.

Of all nights.

The important thing was that Aiden had made miraculous progress tonight. He was celebrating Christmas in a meaningful way. Watching him hold a candle and sing like an angel was nothing short of an answered prayer.

* * *

Tom watched the helicopter rise and then noted the time. Midnight.

His night was not yet over. The Sheriff Department's cruiser sat in the parking lot. He still had to brief the next of kin. And that took a lot of time.

When he'd finished, it was almost one o'clock on Christmas morning. He'd missed his romantic rendezvous.

He drove straight home, but sat in his car for a good twenty minutes feeling drained and slightly depressed. It wasn't easy to deal with an accident like Elbert's on Christmas. Talking to the family about the grave nature of Elbert's injuries was a complete downer. For the Rhodes family, and for him too.

That was the thing about being a family practitioner. You got to know the people you cared for. He could have avoided this. He could have become a surgeon. But he'd known that surgery wasn't his calling.

Dr. Massey, his mentor at Boston Medical Center, had been the one who gave him permission to follow a different course. Dr. Massey had told him that his gift lay in making connections with people.

Maybe that was true. He'd felt connected to the people here tonight. And helping Elbert this evening made him feel better about his choices. Savannah Randall was right too. People were coming around. Mr. Bray had even called him to thank him for insisting that Lillian see a specialist.

So maybe this assignment would work out. But he still felt empty and kind of homesick. He wanted to talk to someone.

Well, not just any someone. He wanted to talk to Teri. He also wouldn't have minded making out with her. He was in sore need of some love tonight.

He also wanted to know what had happened at the village green. Had Teri and Aiden shown up? Had the angel put in an appearance?

He hoped so. For a moment he'd felt as if the angels were there with Elbert, looking over him.

He didn't feel like sleeping, so he fired up the engine and headed back into town. He parked a block away from the green and strolled down to the Christmas tree. The little town of Last Chance was deserted at this time of the morning, even on Christmas. The one stop light in town cycled from red to green without a car in sight.

It was practically balmy—much too warm to be Christmas, as far as Tom was concerned. He didn't have to button up his coat as he stood at the base of the tree, basking in the glow of its lights. He hadn't put up a tree in his condo. He stood there regretting that decision.

He'd never outgrown his childhood love of evergreens, tinsel, and twinkling lights. The tree lifted his heart a little bit. He looked up.

Something wasn't right. Something had changed. There should have been a lighted star on the top of the town tree. But where once there had been a star, now there sat a brass angel with a silver halo and a harp of gold.

Had Teri swapped out the tree topper? Had she played Santa for Aiden?

Oh, he hoped so.

His heavy heart lightened. If Teri had played Santa for Aiden, then maybe she'd changed her mind about him. Maybe that angel up there was sending him a message.

He turned away from the tree. The walk to Teri's house wasn't long. In less than five minutes, he stood in her front yard. The lights in one of the upstairs rooms were still on. He thought about throwing a pebble at the window and having a Romeo moment, but decided that ringing the bell was probably a better idea.

He waited for a long time. He'd probably awakened her. He was feeling like a teenager, unsure and kind of confused, but determined nevertheless.

The door finally opened, and Teri stood there on the threshold wearing a red plaid robe over her pajamas. She had sheepskin slippers on her feet.

"I know it's late," he said.

A tiny frown rumpled her brow. "I missed you at the town square."

"You came? Really? Are you the one who swapped out the angel for the star?"

"What?"

"The angel. On the top of the tree."

"What angel?"

"You didn't swap out the star?"

"No."

"Teri, there's an angel on the top of the town tree. I just saw it. It's made of brass. It has a silver-colored halo and a golden harp."

"Like in the carol?"

"What carol?"

" 'It Came Upon a Midnight Clear'—there's a lyric about the angels bending toward the earth to touch their harps of gold."

"Oh, yeah. What happened at midnight?" he asked, a shiver working its way over his shoulders.

"I don't know. I was late. I got there about five minutes after midnight. Aiden was holding my little brass candle stick, with a lighted candle, and singing like—" She broke off for a moment, her voice wobbling. "Well, to be honest, he was singing like an angel, Tom. Honestly, I think there was an angel in our town tonight. It was Aiden. He was *holding* a candle. I just don't understand how or why that happened."

He moved forward and took her by the shoulders. "I'm sorry I missed it. I was called to the clinic."

"Oh," she said on a long breath. "I should have realized."

"You missed me?" He couldn't help but smile. Maybe the mysterious angel had been put there just for him. Just to make him take a chance.

She nodded and then brushed away a tear. "Who was sick?" she asked.

"Not sick. Hurt. Elbert Rhodes. He was in a bad motor-cycle accident. We had to fly him up to the trauma center in Columbia."

"Oh, my goodness, is he going to be okay?"

"He should live, but he's got a long road to recovery. He's in surgery right now. You know, it was funny. He was conscious for a short time when he got to the clinic. And he was talking about angels. I guess that's not anything remarkable when it comes to Elbert Rhodes."

They stood there for what seemed like an eternity before Tom screwed up his courage. "Teri, can I come inside?"

A tiny smile tilted her lips. "Yes. And I'll tell you a secret."

"What's that?"

"Savannah Randall as much as told me today that you and I belong together."

He chuckled. "Teri, the flowers were *her* idea."

"And the note?"

"Well, I wrote the note and, no, she didn't tell me what to say. I'm really, really sorry I couldn't meet you for a romantic Christmas rendezvous."

She threw her arms around his neck. "Now that I know the reason, I'm glad you were there for Elbert and not with me. Tom, I've been an idiot. Tonight I just feel as if somehow God has blessed us in some way. I think the angels did visit the little town of Last Chance tonight."

"Me too."

And then he kissed her under the mistletoe that hung in the door's threshold.

And it was a fairy-tale kind of kiss. The kind of kiss that makes a woman believe in angels and happily ever after.

About the Author

Hope Ramsay is a *USA Today* bestselling author of heart-warming contemporary romances. Her books have won critical acclaim and publishing awards. She is married to a good ol' Georgia boy who resembles every single one of her Southern heroes. She has two grown children and a couple of demanding lap cats. She lives in Virginia where, when she's not writing, she's knitting or playing her forty-year-old Martin guitar.

You can learn more at:

HopeRamsay.com
Twitter, @HopeRamsay
Facebook.com/Hope.Ramsay